THE

SOJOURNERS

J. WILLIAM HAUCK

The Sojourners

Copyright © 2014 by J. William Hauck

eBook ISBN: 978-0-9904348-2-5
Paperback ISBN: 978-0-9904348-3-2

White Ladder Books

ALSO BY J. WILLIAM HAUCK

Chronicles of the Watchers Series

Elijah's Awakening

Elijah's Quest

The Sojourner Series

The Sojourners

The Soul Seekers

The Searchers

The Sheep Rancher's Series

The Sheep Rancher's Daughter

The House by the River

To those who risk their lives fighting the dark forces of evil.
May their sacrifices make this world a better place.

FOREWORD

The Balkan Peninsula has known strife and conflict for more than two thousand years. Conquered by the Greeks and Romans, and occupied by the Turks and Communists, its people have never known lasting peace and freedom. In 1990, with the fall of the Soviet Union, the ethnic Albanians of Kosovo began their quest for liberty and independence from Serbia and its strong-armed president, Slobodan Milošević. The Serbs, a people separated from the Albanians by culture and religion, tried to stop it.

CHAPTER
ONE

Livoc, Kosovo - 27 April 1999

JUSUF HASANI GAZED UNEASILY out the old, distorted window of his grandmother's home. His dark eyebrows and short beard were visible in the reflection of the glass, but his eyes, heavy with worry and lack of sleep, faded into the shadows of his face.

It was spring. The snow was melting in the mountains, and the lilies were pushing through the ground around Livoc. An early morning rain caused the roads and tile roofs to glisten as the sun broke through the clouds. It should have been a beautiful day in South-eastern Kosovo, but the news that the Serbian soldiers and Special Police had moved into their town had cast an ominous pall.

Jusuf had heard the stories that at first were too terrible to believe. Serbia had been tightening the noose on his country for years, but the stories of marauding Serbs in the north brutally attacking Albanians caused many to flee their homes. Some called those who left cowards, but others said they were the smart ones.

Before the snow fell, many had fled south into Macedonia. It was spring now, and with tensions increasing, there were more willing to take their chances on the roads south. Some said the roads weren't safe and went into the hills.

Jusuf had considered leaving, but he couldn't go without his family, and he knew a trek through the snow-covered hills would kill his grandmother before any Serb would. And even if they were to leave, where would they go? Where was safety, he wondered? Where could they go to escape the insanity of ethnic hatred? To the hills? To live like fugitives? Like animals? Jusuf had spoken of leaving many times with his grandmother, his *gjyshe*, but to her, the thought of leaving her home, even in the face of death, was out of the question.

It was a popular sentiment, believing there was safety in numbers. Some said those who spoke of the murdering and looting Serbs from the north were only frightening good Albanians. They reasoned if everyone stayed in their homes, as a unified people, they could stand up to the invaders, the robbers of freedom and country. But that reasoning melted like the late spring snows once Albanian blood ran.

The massacre of fifty ethnic Albanians in Račak, three months earlier, was the tipping point. The Kosovo Liberation Army vowed to retaliate, but that provided little comfort to the locals who knew such acts would only bring harsher reprisals from the north.

The attacks moved further south. Tensions increased in Livoc when an elderly farmer, just ten miles from town, was found burned with a bullet hole in the back of his head. More attacks followed. More than Jusuf cared to remember. With each, the hatred in the hearts of the local Serbs swelled. That which was before tolerated became intolerable. Those who were before neighbors became enemies.

Thoughts of the hatred and killing disturbed Jusuf, and he spent much of his time in escape. His vehicle of freedom was the silver screen. Jusuf loved movies and worked at a local cinema. To him, being paid to run a projector and watch movies was the ideal job. He loved Westerns the most. Clint Eastwood was his idol, and he had seen every movie he had made many times. His favorite was *Pale Rider*, and he had it on video cassette along with dozens of other Eastwood movies he had memorized. That was how Jusuf learned English.

Jusuf's English language skills proved helpful. He often entertained his Serbian boss Dejan Deletic with cowboy impersonations or famous movie quotes. Deletic even had him personally translate movies that weren't subtitled. While Jusuf's understanding of the English language was limited, his imagination was enough to fill in the blanks.

While the Serbs were the clear minority in Kosovo, they had the best jobs. They were the business owners, the bankers, and the doctors. Some Serbs were kind. Some were not. Jusuf's employer had always treated him well. Before the unrest, Deletic gave Jusuf free passes, which Jusuf used as gifts for family and friends. Those were simple and peaceful times, but times had changed. Those Serbs who were before kind had become less so, and those who were never kind had become hateful.

Jusuf had seen the change with many but never imagined it would have affected his employer and friend. But with each house the Serbs burned in Kosovo, Deletic's kindness waned. The free passes were the first to go, and then he stopped paying Jusuf and the other Albanian workers. Jusuf at first thought nothing of it as he had worked once for two weeks without pay when one of Deletic's investments went bad. Jusuf loved his job and trusted his employer would once again take care of him, but after two weeks, Deletic told him there would be no more pay. Two days later, Deletic told Jusuf to leave and not come back. Jusuf was devastated. Not only had he lost the job he loved, but he had also lost a friend.

Over the next month, Jusuf watched things go from bad to worse. The division between peoples became more apparent and couldn't be stopped. Hatred was in the air, and like a toxic gas, it had spread and was choking everyone.

Jusuf sat up when his neighbors across the street emptied out of their old row house. Mentor Kelmendi, the graying father, was the last to leave and locked his front door as if a lock and bolt could stop the storm of terror that was coming.

Jusuf felt a tug in his chest as he saw Lirie, Mentor's fourth daughter, scurry next to her father with a bundle of clothes under her arm. His eyes followed her flowing brown hair that hung to her waist, and he wished she would turn so he could see her lovely face one last time. Lirie had been a neighbor for as long as Jusuf could remember, and he had feelings for her for just as long.

Jusuf thought of the first time he had watched Lirie dance. It had been nine years, but he could still remember her graceful, flowing motion. It was on that day she first told Jusuf of her fondness for him. He remembered the warmth of her touch, softness of her hands, and sweetness of her fragrance. Jusuf and Lirie wanted nothing more than to be together, but her family was staunch in the Muslim traditions, and like her older sisters, her marriage would be arranged. It broke Jusuf's heart to know Lirie would never be his, but their tradition was stronger than either of them.

Jusuf was there the day Lirie married a man she didn't know or love. After six years, the couple had borne no children, and in unjust tradition, Lirie was blamed and labeled barren. When Lirie's husband became disenchanted with her, the heartbroken and ashamed woman returned to her father's home in disgrace.

Lirie's homecoming was a bittersweet time for Jusuf. He was pleased she was home and knew it would be only a matter of time before her husband divorced her, making it possible for them to be together. But the stigma of a barren woman wasn't an easy thing to overcome, and though Jusuf still loved her, tradition once again kept them apart.

Jusuf's heart ached as he watched Lirie walk with her father down the uneven pavers, pulling their belongings in a small rusty wagon. He felt a surge within him as she looked toward his window. Jusuf wanted to run out and stop her, to bring her home with him, but he couldn't. He sadly watched her continue down the street, wondering if he would ever see her again.

It was some time after the Kelmendi family had left that Jusuf turned from the window. He eyed his grandmother warming her feet by the fire as she knitted with boney fingers that defied her eighty-two years. "*Gjyshe*, the Kelmendi family just left. They took clothes and food and left their home."

Jusuf's mother looked up nervously from her book and watched as the matriarch slowly shook her head.

"*Gjyshe*," Jusuf persisted, "my friend Dren said the militia and Special Police are not far from here. They're burning houses. There are even rumors of them killing people and taking women."

The old woman glared at her grandson before returning to her work, her fingers furiously twisting the yarn. "This is our home. It is *my* home. I will not leave it to *them*."

Jusuf turned to his father in protest. Father Hasani's unkempt gray hair swirled atop his head, and his gray beard was thick with only a week's growth. While Jusuf considered his father wise because of his years, he had passed little knowledge down. His father was a man of few words, and Jusuf couldn't remember him saying more than a handful at a time, especially in public. Father Hasani was a worker, like all in the Hasani family. While he provided for the family, they lived in his mother-in-law's home, and he respected her wishes.

Father Hasani's face was unchanged as he listened to the grandmother's declaration. His indifference frustrated Jusuf. While not a man of action, Jusuf thought of himself as a fighter at heart, a trait he had inherited from his mother. Knowing his friends and neighbors were leaving and he couldn't, angered him. "What will we do if the police or soldiers come? This is just a house! It is not worth dying for!" Jusuf pleaded.

His grandmother's eyes didn't move from her work. "It is *our* home. It is what we are. It is *our* land. It is *our* beliefs. It is *our* life. They will not chase us off like frightened sheep."

"Then we will die here like *fatted* sheep," Jusuf sighed.

"Go. You are free to leave," the grandmother said with a dismissing wave.

Jusuf gulped. He would be going nowhere.

The grandmother's gaze rose from her work, and she studied the twenty-eight-year-old dreamer. The wrinkles on her aged face gave away her years, as did her thin white hair hidden beneath her head-scarf, but her eyes were young and alive with ideas and hope of freedom and liberty. They were ideas and dreams she feared would never be again.

————

CHAPTER
TWO

SALI NOLI WAS A TALL, solidly built man with deep-set eyes and a thick, dark mustache. A father of five, he was a peaceful man. He would have much rather been home with his family or working on a car than doing what he knew he must.

With a worn canvas pack hung over his leather jacket, Sali pushed his bicycle along the dirt road into the clearing, his breath visible in the morning air. Rubbing an oil-stained hand over his mustache, he nervously approached the large group of men standing near the road. He had heard stories about the newly formed army, of how they had already stood up to the invading Serbs and chased them out of villages, but as he looked over the men gathered, he saw ill at ease farmers and uncertain laborers. Some were too old to fight; others were too young to know what they were fighting for. Although most stood barehanded, some had brought weapons. A few carried rifles passed down from the First Great War; others had knives or swords strapped to their sides. One man had a pitchfork, another an ax. All appeared anxious as they restlessly milled about, waiting to receive some type of training, along with bullets and weapons.

As Sali looked closer at the men gathered in the clearing encircled by tall pines and freshly sprigged maples, he noticed a few moving about in mismatched camouflage uniforms. These men had looks of defiance and anger that made Sali glance away when they came near. These men were from the Kosovo Liberation Army, he decided.

Leaning his bike against a tree, Sali noticed two old trucks parked off the road. To the rear of one truck, two farmers unloaded wooden crates. With the top of one crate removed, Sali saw the dulled, black metal and brown wooden stocks of the Kalashnikov rifles stacked inside. He swallowed as he thought of himself holding and firing such a weapon. Sali felt a tightening in his chest as he looked about the crowd of fifty men. There was no reason to be afraid, he told himself. They were his people, his brothers. Like him, they had come to protect their homeland and join the army that would liberate Kosovo.

As Sali anxiously skirted the group's edge, he recognized a man called Kuq, or Red, for his bright red beard. While Sali had known Kuq since their youth, he couldn't remember his name from before he had the beard. Walking toward Kuq, Sali nodded when they made eye contact.

"Sali, it's been a long time," Kuq said with an uneasy smile.

"Yes, it has."

"You will fight then?" Kuq asked with probing eyes.

Sali sighed. While he wanted to protect his home and fend off the Serbs, he wondered if the men before him could do so. "Yes...yes, I will fight. And you?"

Kuq shrugged. "I don't know. I think I'm more curious than anything. I wanted to see who was here."

Sali nodded as he looked over the other men gathered. There were familiar faces, but many he didn't know.

"Your family? Have you moved them to safety?" Kuq asked as he tore off a piece of dried mutton and offered it to his new friend.

Sali took the meat and shrugged. "Where is safe?"

"Across the border. There are many going there."

"I told my wife that if things got bad not to wait for me, but to go. You know how wives are," Sali said, chewing the mutton.

Kuq nodded vaguely. He didn't know how wives were.

"It is hard to travel. Our little one is only two. I hope they can stay there. We'll protect the villages around Vitina, yes?" Sali asked, biting off another piece of jerky.

"I don't know what the plan is. They don't look too organized, if you ask me."

"Fellow countrymen, listen to me!"

Sali looked over the heads of the crowd and saw a uniformed man standing on a box.

"I'm not an inspirational speaker...I'm a soldier. I have but one duty, and that is to kill the Serbian rats that have infested our land."

Sali looked around to gauge the crowd's reaction; it was weak and uncertain with only a few echoing agreement.

"We have weapons here for those who will use them. Guns and bullets have come from our people all over the world. There are many who fight with us—our brother Albanians. In America, many of our brothers are sending us money. They are also fighting against the enemy. Now it is time for us to do our part!"

There were a few scattered cheers from the group.

"Our people need help. The West—NATO—has given us no guns to defend ourselves; instead, they drop bombs on our enemies. Like kicking a hornet's nest, they cause the stinging to be worse. Now, we must do with what we have. We must *kill* and *kill* and *kill* until there are no more Serbs in our land!"

The cheers and nodding heads were more exuberant this time. Sali's deep-set eyes shifted about in uncertainty. Not wanting to be left out, he also nodded.

As the soldier spoke of the Serbs' plundering and murder, the men around Sali became increasingly vocal and agitated. The farmers and laborers, who were before anxious and tentative, were now shaking their fists and spitting bravado-filled words of hate. Sali felt the bitter anger build within him. Like the rising steam of a teakettle, it moved up his neck and into his head until he too was spouting words of anger. He had put up with the cruel and wrongful ways of the Serbs for too long, and it was time for a change, he told himself. But he had no sooner done so than he thought of his family. *Who will care for my wife and children while I'm away?* Then came the coldest thought of all. *Who will care for them if I'm killed?* Taking a step back, Sali looked at the incensed would-be soldiers. He felt the heat leave his head and the pounding in his chest lessen. He wasn't ready yet. His family needed him.

Sali thought of his lovely wife Gentiana. When they married, they had great dreams, but like everyone else he knew, they had settled for the ordinary. The opportunities went to the Serbs; that was the way of things, and Sali and his wife learned to be happy living in want.

Sali lived a simple life. Every day he rose before the sun to do chores with his two oldest sons. He then rode his bicycle the two miles to the shop where he worked on old, failing automobiles, trying to keep them running for those wealthy enough to own them. He was a good mechanic, but even a great mechanic often had trouble keeping decade old Yugos and Trabants in working order.

Sali thought of his wife, of her soft fair skin and thick brown hair. Though he had not been gone long, he already missed her and his children. He loved them all, but was especially close to his two oldest boys. They often played soccer together on the rutted dirt road before their home, and he was proud of the men they were becoming.

Sali drew in an anxious breath as the speaker and two soldiers approach.

"What's your name?" asked the heavy-browed leader.

"Sali Noli," he replied, standing a little taller.

"What was your work?" asked the leader as he studied Sali.

"Mechanic."

"*Hmm*. Were you any good?"

"The best," Kuq interjected.

The leader turned to the red-bearded man, who had a large belly that hung over his belt, and asked, "And what did you do?"

Kuq shrugged. "I did many things, I—"

"You had no job," the leader grunted.

Kuq didn't respond.

"We can use a good mechanic—*if* you'll fight." Sali was a tall man with wide shoulders and thick arms; the leader liked what he saw. "Do you know how to shoot a rifle?"

"Yes...I shot one once as a boy," Sali shrugged.

"Good...it's not too difficult. You point at what you want to kill and pull the trigger."

Sali grinned at the simplicity of the comment.

"Do you have a family?"

"Yes, sir."

"You're here to protect them, then?"

Sali considered the question, then nodded.

"That's good, but it's not only your family but his and his," the leader said, pointing to Kuq and another man. "It is for all of our families and our land too."

"Yes, sir," Sali said with a serious nod.

The heavy-browed leader looked Sali in the eyes, and then with a grin said, "You will make a good soldier. I can see it in your eyes. You will kill many Serbs and…I think you will like it."

Sali half-smiled as the leader motioned to a soldier standing beside him, who thrust a worn AK-47 into his arms. Sali looked down at the cold weapon and felt its lifelessness. The charismatic leader gave an encouraging nod before moving to the next man.

Sali was about to offer his thanks when another soldier stacked three bullet-filled magazines on top of the rifle. When the magazines started to slide, Sali grabbed them. He watched the leader speak to the next man, then glanced at Kuq, who was holding his own rifle.

Sali eyed the instrument of death in his arms and wondered if things would ever be the same. The luster of the brass casing at the mouth of the magazines reminded him of his home's doorknob. While Sali wanted to help defend the land, a part of him wished he was a home opening that door.

CHAPTER
THREE

THE HARD SLAP spun the woman to the floor of the humble dwelling. Her fearful eyes shot back at the intruder, a red welt marking the man's hand on her cheek.

"Don't talk to me like that, you Albanian witch!" the mash-nosed soldier growled as he leered down at the trembling woman.

"Please, this is my home. These are my children," the woman pleaded as blood trickled from her nose down her satin cheek.

The soldier standing above her saw her five frightened children and hesitated.

The oldest child, an eleven-year-old boy with short brown hair, watched the Serb militiamen with wide eyes as the younger children huddled beside him.

Another Serb, dressed in matching camouflage fatigues, moved closer. He had a shaved head and a brown beard. His proximity gave the mash-nosed soldier new resolve, and he snarled, "This is *not* your land...it's *ours*! Leave now, with the rest of your Muslim dogs!"

The mother pulled her torn dress closed with one hand and wiped away the blood with another, smearing it across her cheek. Not yet thirty years old, Gentiana Noli was attractive, and while she was afraid of what the two hateful Serbs might do to her, she was more frightened for her children. "Where?" she cried, her body trembling, tears rolling down her cheeks. "Please, where do we go?"

The boy's eyes filled with tears. The terrible stories of the Serbian Special Police killing people—the stories some said were myths—felt very real to him now.

"What's this?" snarled the bald soldier as he reached for a silver heart necklace around the mother's neck.

"No, you can't have it!" The frightened mother yanked the necklace from her neck and threw it across the room.

"Don't worry, we'll find it later," growled the bald Serb. "Where is your man? Is he a KLA terrorist?"

"No, he's a mechanic. He's just gone to work," Gentiana lied. "He'll be back soon. Then we'll go."

"If he's Albanian, he's a *coward*," sneered the mash-nosed soldier. "He's run to hide like a scared little lamb." Both men laughed. The bald Serb handed his rifle to the other, and with a lustful gleam, moved closer to the frightened mother. After kneeling beside her, he ran his hand up her trembling leg. "You're alone then. You're lonely."

"No," Gentiana breathed, looking anywhere but the man's eyes.

"Mama!" cried one of the children.

"Get them out of here!" snapped the bald Serb.

Gentiana could smell his breath. It stunk of liquor. "Lek," she sobbed, turning to her oldest son, "don't let the children see."

The eleven-year-old Lek tearfully gathered his siblings in tight around him. He wanted to take them out of the house, away from the danger, but he couldn't leave his mother.

The mash-nosed soldier turned to the crying children. "What should I do with them?"

"Get them out of here!" snarled the bald Serb as his hands climbed Gentiana's dress.

"*Please, don't,*" Gentiana gasped.

The front door burst open, bounced off the wall, and caused the two militiamen to turn in surprise. The horrified Gentiana brought her legs together and slid away from the Serb.

A large man with dark hair and a thick goatee filled the doorway. Dressed in matching camouflage pants, it was his brown leather coat, cowboy hat, and snakeskin boots that set him apart from the others. He saw the attractive woman with the torn dress, pushed up the front brim of his cowboy hat, and smirked. "Misha, you might want to take her outside for your fun. This house is on fire."

Lek's eyes widened when another Serb entered, drizzling gasoline from a can along the floor into the back bedroom. When the Serb emerged, a trail of fire followed him.

"No! My house!" cried Gentiana.

The Cowboy's grin, framed by his black and gray goatee, widened as Gentiana jumped to her feet and frantically gathered her choicest belongings. She yelled for the children to help, but they stared as if hypnotized as the flames climbed the walls.

With smoke filling the room, the Cowboy slung his AK-47 over his shoulder and did a quick search for valuables. Finding none, he left the burning home.

"Get out!" yelled the bald Serb as he yanked Gentiana toward the door, causing the few items she had gathered, including a photograph of her husband, to fly across the room.

"Let go of her!" cried the scrawny Lek, jumping to his feet.

"Go ahead," growled the mash-nosed Serb, his hatred recharged. "You'll end up dead—like your *coward father.*"

Lek's jaw slackened at the terrible thought. "Mother!" Lek gasped, as the men dragged his screaming mother out the door. He wanted to protect her, to chase the cruel men from their home, but his trembling arms and legs were immovable. Even his voice was gone. Lek felt his eyes shrink inside his head as he watched, as if from a faraway place, the men drag his sobbing mother from the house, her hands reaching for her children. The last man out looked back at the children with a pale, ghostlike face, then closed the door, leaving them inside the burning house.

Lek stared at the door, frozen in fear. It wasn't the choking smoke or the cries of the children that jolted him from his trance, but his eight-year-old brother Haxhi's urgent tug.

Lek looked on in horror as flames crawled along the ceiling above them. A flower wall-hanging near the front door burst into flames and dropped fiery fragments that started another fire.

Lek fanned away the smoke as he moved toward the door, which now had flames dancing above it. With his frightened siblings huddled behind him, he reached for the brass doorknob but cowered as the fire surged behind them. Overhead, the ceiling seemed alive as hungry flames chased out of the bedroom and dark, billowing smoke made it harder to see and breathe.

Choking from the smoke, Lek pulled open the door. The cool rush of air intensified the flames behind them. Lek looked for the soldiers through teary eyes as he stumbled out of the burning house. When he realized he was alone, Lek turned back to the fiery doorway and yelled, "Hurry, get out!" He spotted his baby sister standing inside screaming, and darted back into the house and scooped her up.

The fire was growing faster now, and a wall of heat pushed the small children through the burning entry. Two-year-old Jrfete held tight to Lek's neck as they hurried through the doorway. She screamed as flames jumped at her and singed her brown, frizzy hair.

Once they were a safe distance from their home, Lek, with eyes and lungs burning, searched for the soldiers. They were nowhere in sight, but neither was their mother.

Feeling the heat behind him, Lek turned back to the flames climbing from the roof of his house. The thick black smoke swirling above it gave the afternoon sky a strange orange hue. A loud cry caused Lek to look back to the doorway where he saw his four-year-old brother, Rexhe, still standing inside.

"Rexhe! Get out of there!" cried Lek, but the frightened four-year-old, obscured by the smoke, didn't move.

Lek's eyes widened as flames swirled around the doorjamb, causing its yellow paint to curl and brown. After setting down his protesting sister, Lek dashed past the licking flames, grabbed Rexhe, and ducked back through the fiery entry. Feeling his shirt was on fire, Lek spun, but his skin quickly cooled in the spring air.

"Why did you stay in there?" cried Lek as he set the coughing and sputtering Rexhe down. "You could have died!"

The four-year-old Rexhe, who had elf-like ears and pouty eyes, held up their mother's silver heart-shaped necklace.

"You're a brave little man. Give it to me. I'll keep it for Mama."

The still coughing, Rexhe handed Lek the necklace which he placed in his pocket.

Feeling the growing heat of the fire, Lek gathered up his crying baby sister Jrfete and tried to calm her as he had seen his mother do. Fearing the soldiers might return, Lek looked for a hiding place. He started for the old stone barn, but when he noticed its door ajar and heard men laughing inside, he pointed to the tall leaning pine down and across the road. "Let's get under the tree," he said, making sure each of his siblings, Haxhi, Arta, and Rexhe were with him.

Haxhi, who had short black hair and dark rings around dark eyes, held Arta with one hand and the still-coughing Rexhe with the other as they hurried under the old tree. With its broad base and full branches forming a protective canopy three feet off the ground, it was a favorite play spot for the children.

Lek was trying to quiet Jrfete, whose yellow hand-me-down dress was blackened and singed on one side, when the other children crawled under the tree beside him. With heart pounding and eyes wide, Lek searched for the soldiers. Down the road, other houses were ablaze. Lek's gaze moved across the placid fields and tranquil hills that lined their once peaceful village. His eyes were drawn to a car parked in the weeds. It was on fire, with black smoke billowing from its tires. Lek followed the rolling blackness. The sky was brown and thick from fires across the valley.

Lek turned back to Haxhi. He knew his brother was frightened, although he tried to hide it. His six-year-old sister Arta didn't hide her fear as she looked on with large, weepy eyes. But the elfish-eared Rexhe seemed more curious.

"How long do we have to stay under here?" whimpered Arta.

"Not long," Lek replied. "We need to wait for Mama."

The bed of needles on which they sat insulated them from the damp, cold ground beneath. But as the minutes slowly passed and the heat from their burning home lessened, Arta began to shiver. Lek looked sadly at Arta as she slid beside him and watched their house burn; her large eyes red, her fleshy cheeks trembling. She seemed unaware of the dirt and pine needles in her long, shiny hair her mother had washed just that morning. "I'm cold," she whispered. "Can we go somewhere else?"

"No," Lek said, holding Jrfete tight and rubbing her back to quiet her fussing. "We need to stay here. We're safe here."

"From the bad men?" asked Rexhe.

"Yes. Now stay quiet, or they'll hear us."

"Why did they burn our house?" Arta asked, wiping away tears.

"Because they're bad men," shrugged Haxhi. Normally a sober child, Haxhi was even more so now, his mouth tight, his dark eyes alert and searching.

"Will-will they hurt Mama?" fretted Arta.

"*Shh.* Don't talk or they'll come with their guns," Lek warned.

"They'll come and *kill* us," Haxhi grimly added.

"*Shhh!*" Lek glared at Haxhi, who turned away. The elfish Rexhe seemed the calmest of all and looked as though they were playing a game.

The sound of voices and laughter caused Lek to turn to the stone barn. His eyes widened when four soldiers emerged. Lek waited for flames or smoke to follow, but they didn't.

"The soldiers are coming," Haxhi gasped.

"*Shh,*" Lek warned as he put a stifling hand over his infant sister's mouth, but she bristled and screeched. After removing his hand, Lek bounced her, hoping she wouldn't give them away.

Lek held his breath as the boots drew closer. He glanced at Haxhi, who was frozen with fear, and jumped when an empty vodka bottle landed in the nearby weeds. As the soldiers passed, not twenty feet away, Lek gave the others a warning glance and quietly bounced the fussing Jrfete. But her whimpering caused one of the Serbs to pause. Lek's body tightened when the soldier turned and started back toward their hiding place.

With his rifle in hand, the soldier approached the tree and bent down. Lek pulled back as he met eyes with the mashed-nosed soldier. He held his breath as the kneeling Serb, just feet away, turned his rifle on them. Lek pulled the trembling Arta close as he looked down the barrel into the Serb's glazed eyes. The soldier's vacant expression didn't change when he pulled his rifle away and pushed himself to his feet.

The children watched breathlessly as the Serb caught up to the others walking down the rutted road away from the burning houses. Lek's fearful gaze turned back to the barn as two more soldiers emerged. He wondered if his mother was inside. Lek followed the soldiers until they disappeared from view.

After releasing a stressful sigh, Lek turned to Haxhi. Their eyes met in a kind of drained blankness. It was the growing cry of Jrfete, hungry for their mother's milk, which broke Lek's stare.

Lek considered getting out from under the tree to find their mother. But fear that the soldiers might return kept them huddled under it.

A half hour passed. With the elfish Rexhe asleep on the pine needles and Jrfete content with her thumb, all was still as Lek listened for the familiar call of their mother.

Lek looked up the rutted road past the apple trees and stone barn to the still burning homes. He didn't notice the peaceful hills beyond the valley. He didn't hear the gentle breeze moving through the trees, nor the cooing of the doves on the barn. Lek heard only the popping and cracking of their burning home; the only home they had ever known. His face emptied when its roof succumbed to the flames and collapsed, sending a plume of ash into the dirty gray sky.

The children watched the flakes of ash float down like falling snow. With wide eyes, Arta said, "Look, it's snowing."

Lek shook his head sadly. "No, it's not snow."

———

CHAPTER
FOUR

AFTER AN HOUR, their home was a glowing heap of cinders, ash, and debris inside a once white stucco shell. The fireplace that had warmed them through the cold winter nights stood alone, jutting above the crumbling remains.

The sun, though hidden behind the clouds and smoke, was low in the sky, and Lek recognized it would soon be dark. His mother had still not returned, and he ached for her. Lek worried about his father too. He had left three days earlier to join the people's army and protect their village from the invading Serbs. *Why didn't he come with the Army? What if something happened to him? What if he's...* Lek's eyes filled with tears. He knew he had to be strong, but didn't know how. *They'll come back.*

Four-year-old Rexhe raised his head and whined, "I'm hungry."

"When is Mama coming back?" asked a worried Arta.

Lek was picking the pine needles from Arta's hair when Haxhi, who had tried to be as strong as his brother, said, "I'm hungry too. Can we go find Mama now?"

Lek sighed, his chest heavy from the responsibility. "Okay, but we must go quietly. There might be more soldiers."

Haxhi put an arm around Rexhe and nodded.

Lek crawled out from under the pine tree and looked up and down the road. The sun was below the western hills now, and the air was brisk. While there were fires still burning, those houses were heaps of glowing cinders and thinning plumes of smoke. But a few houses stood unharmed. There was the stone barn the neighbors shared and, beyond that, the Lushi home. On looking closer, Lek thought he spotted smoke rising from its chimney into the darkening sky. *Maybe the Lushis are cooking dinner. Maybe Mama's with them.* "Come on. Let's find Mama before it gets dark."

Tired and whimpering, Jrfete reached up to be held. Her brown, frizzy hair, which was shoulder length on one side but singed shorter by the flames on the other, framed her pouty face. Hoisting her in his arms, Lek waited for the others to emerge, then started up the road toward the stone barn.

"I'm hungry," whined Rexhe.

"I know. Maybe the Lushis will feed us," Lek said, pointing to the home some distance off.

As they approached the old stone barn, four chickens ran out, as if to greet them, then scattered and ran away. Lek noticed Rexhe, who loved to chase the chickens, didn't seem to care.

As they passed the barn, Lek remembered the laughing, drinking soldiers who had come out of it. He slowed and strained to see inside through the open door. Just visible in the shadows was an overturned barrel of grain and clumps of scattered hay. He was about to continue walking when he spotted movement in the shadows. His first thought was to run, fearing there might be soldiers still inside, but he realized it could also be his mother.

Tilting his head to look inside the barn, Lek watched and waited.

"What-what's wrong?" Haxhi fretted.

Lek didn't respond, his gaze fixed, his heart pounding.

"I'm hungry," moaned Rexhe, tugging on Lek's arm.

Lek was about to pull his eyes from the barn when the neighbor's mangy dog emerged from the shadows. Lek jumped, and his startle caused Arta to cry and Haxhi to step back. "It's okay, it's just the Lushi's dog," Lek sighed. But his eyes narrowed when the agitated dog turned in circles and went back into the barn.

Sensing something wrong inside the barn, Lek studied its entrance, his chest rising and falling. He knew what he must do. Lek gulped, handed Jrfete to Haxhi, and muttered, "I'll be right back."

"No. Where are you going?" fretted Arta.

"To look in the barn," Lek breathed.

"What if the soldiers come?" Haxhi asked.

Lek looked up and down the empty road. "I won't be long. Stay here." About to enter the barn, Lek looked back to be sure they weren't following. He saw their frightened faces and gave a reassuring nod before continuing.

As Lek inched toward the shadowy barn's entrance, his view inside expanded. He paused when he spotted the distressed dog pacing near a pile of hay. A terrible sense of dread filled Lek as he continued into the shadows. A part of him wanted to turn back, but he knew he couldn't. He had to see what was inside.

Lek continued through the barn's sliding door and gasped. Lying in the hay, not twelve paces from him, was the sprawled body of a woman. Lek's heart stopped. Fearing it was his mother, he stretched to see the woman's turned face. Still unable, he took a careful step. When Lek noticed her torn-open dress, he breathed again. It wasn't his mother's dress.

Unsure if she was dead or alive, Lek inched closer. He gulped when he realized it was his sixteen-year-old neighbor, Desanka Lushi, staring across the barn. "Desanka," Lek whispered. Grimacing, he waited for her to blink. She didn't. Lek saw no blood, only her torn, crumpled dress and lifeless stare. His legs began to wobble.

Lek turned to Haxhi and the anxiously waiting children. With morbid curiosity, he looked back at the brutalized body. He had seen the lovely Desanka working in the garden just yesterday and wondered how this could happen to anyone so full of life.

Numb and with a sickening pain in the pit of his stomach, Lek turned from his dead neighbor to her dog, lying calmly on the hay just feet away, its head resting on its front paws.

Uncertain of what to do, Lek started for the door. He had only taken a step when he noticed something else in the shadows to his left. He stopped mid-stride, his jaw slack, his eyes wide. It was another body. Lek forced a swallow down his dry throat as he strained to discern the shape of the second woman lying in the hay. She too had a gathered and torn dress; only this was a dress he recognized. It was his mother's dress.

Trembling and not wanting to believe his eyes, Lek edged closer. The familiar dress was ripped and hanging from the pale woman's body. His eyes were afloat in tears as he drew closer and saw his mother staring back at him.

"Mama!" cried Jrfete, who had crept into the barn beside him.

Lek jumped and swept the infant up in his arms to shield her from the terrible sight. Uncertain of what to do, his heart pounding, his mind numb, Lek hurried from the barn. Jrfete arched her back and screamed in protest as she reached back for their dead mother.

Lek gulped in the outside air as Jrfete cried and fought against him. Through teary eyes, he saw Haxhi and Arta nervously watching while a grumbling Rexhe lay on the dirt road. Lek wanted to cry. He wanted to scream in anguish, but he couldn't. He thought of his mother's life-less stare and questioned what he had seen. *It was dark. Maybe that wasn't her,* he told himself, knowing it was. *Jrfete recognized her too.*

Lek ached inside as he struggled with what to do. More than anything, he wanted someone to hold him, to make this terrible, unspeakable moment go away, but there was no one. He glanced numbly back into the barn and then continued to the other children.

"What's wrong? What's in there?" Haxhi asked, seeing his broth-er's anguish.

Lek's lips moved, but no words came out. He forced a swallow. "There-there's someone...someone *dead* in there," he finally managed, before stumbling off toward the Lushi home.

"Who? Who is it?" Haxhi gasped, his eyes locked on the barn.

Lek shook his head, unable to speak.

"Can we eat now?" Rexhe groaned, holding his stomach.

Lek looked at the young boy with a sickened face. Food was the last thing on his mind. "No! You don't always have to eat!"

"But...I'm hungry," Rexhe whimpered, the corners of his mouth curled down.

Lek looked from Rexhe to the others. He wanted to run away, but he knew he couldn't. They needed him.

"Please…I'm hungry," Rexhe cried.

Lek considered telling his brother no. They had mush for breakfast and several slices of bread and squash for their midday meal, but that was five hours earlier, before the Serbs had come, and Lek knew they were hungry. His mind numb, Lek nodded and said, "Let's go to the Lushi's house."

"When will Mama come?" Arta asked with a worrisome look.

Lek's eyes welled up, and his voice cracked as he tried to speak. The tears he had wished for earlier were all too willing to come now. He pushed them away and muttered, "I don't know."

When they reached the half-opened door of the Lushi home, Lek paused, then handed Jrfete to Haxhi. "Let me go in first to make sure it's safe."

Haxhi took Jrfete, then grabbed the six-year-old Arta when she tried to follow. "Wait out here."

Arta, whose large brown eyes were full of concern, stepped back without a fuss.

When Lek pushed the door open, he felt resistance from the other side. He listened for the sound of life, of talking or even crying, but heard nothing. With eyes wide, he entered the humble three-room home which had housed five, including the dead Desanka.

The air inside the dark house was thick with the scent of scorched wood and melted paint. As Lek's eyes adjusted to the failing light, he saw a room in disarray, with clothes scattered and furniture overturned. Across the room was a wall charred by an extinguished fire; at its base a blackened rug, damp with water, and an overturned bucket. Lek noticed a shirt on the floor and jumped when he realized it was still on a man's back. Lek cocked his head and grimaced. It was Fan Lushi, father to the girl in the barn.

Lek stared at the lifeless body sprawled next to the fireplace in a pool of red-tinged water. A red stain on the man's back, along with a bloodied left hand and missing ring finger, caused Lek's stomach to turn. Upon realizing there might be someone still in the house, Lek spun around. The room appeared vacant, but he stretched his head this way and that as he checked each shadow and nook for a murdering

Serb. Convinced there was no one else in the room, Lek turned to the hallway, which led to the rest of the house.

After gathering his courage, his mouth dry, his eyes searching, Lek started for the hallway. As he passed the kitchen table, he noticed a pan of cooked rice spilled on the floor. With one eye on the darkened hallway, he kneeled down, waved away the flies, and pushed the spilled rice into the pan. After setting the pot on the table, he continued his search.

Passing the bathroom, Lek gasped when he spotted someone looking back at him. With his heart pounding, he stared at the boy, looking back at him. When Lek realized he was looking into a mirror, he breathed again. Lek's chest was heaving as he inched forward to the first of two bedrooms. The ransacked room had two small beds and a toppled armoire. The second bedroom was much the same.

Satisfied the home was empty, Lek returned to the kitchen, opened the small refrigerator, and found leftover mutton and a half-full bottle of milk. He found a partial loaf of bread and a wedge of cheese and placed them on the small table near a broken window. Lek pulled the draperies closed and righted a toppled chair. He considered turning on the overhead light but remembered the soldiers. After spotting a small candle and matches near the stove, Lek lit the candle and moved it to the table. He recoiled when its light revealed a red-stained knife on the table. Beside it was a bloody handprint. Lek used the knife to scrape the broken glass off the table, then moved the knife to the sink. After wetting a rag, he wiped off the table as he had seen his mother do. The bloody handprint took longer, but soon disappeared. Lek glanced back at his dead neighbor, gathered up some of the scattered clothes, and covered his head and bloodied back. He then went back to the door and quietly called in the waiting children.

Haxhi's eyes were wide and searching as he entered with Jrfete still in his arms. But Rexhe and Arta were concerned more with food and moved to the flickering light of the table. They quickly helped themselves to the pot of rice, bread, and cheese while Lek searched for a bottle for Jrfete. Finding only ordinary tin cups, he poured milk into one and watched Jrfete slurp it down, spilling some on her dress.

"Is that Mister Lushi?" Haxhi whispered, upon seeing the poorly hidden body.

"Yes," Lek nodded. "Will you help me take him out after we put them to bed?"

"We're sleeping here?" Haxhi asked with a raised brow as he eyed their dead neighbor.

"It's better than under the tree. There are beds and blankets."

Haxhi sighed. He looked through the crack in the drapes out the broken window. It was now dark outside. "Should we light a fire?"

"No, not tonight. There might be more soldiers."

"Who was in the barn?" Haxhi asked, eyeing Lek.

"Desanka," Lek whispered.

"Was she…*dead*?"

Lek nodded sadly.

Haxhi sighed. "I liked her. She was nice."

"Me too."

"When is Mama coming home?" Arta asked as she picked spilled rice from her dress.

Lek could feel Haxhi's eyes on him and struggled with the words. "Maybe in the morning."

"Aren't you going to eat?" Haxhi asked.

Lek shook his head.

"Why did those men hurt Mama and burn our house?" Arta asked as she pulled the burned crust from her bread.

"Because…they're Serbs," Lek muttered, his gaze distant.

"Oh," was Arta's response. Then, after some thought, she asked, "Why don't the Serbs like us?"

"I don't know," Lek breathed.

After tidying up a bedroom, Lek coaxed Arta, Rexhe, and Jrfete onto one of the small beds and placed a heavy blanket over them. When he returned to the front room, Haxhi was staring at the body.

Lek lifted the dead man's right arm. It was heavy and stiff. "Help me pull him outside."

Haxhi reached down for the left arm, then stopped when he noticed the severed finger. "Why did they cut his finger off?"

Lek shrugged. "I don't know. To take his ring?"

Haxhi grimaced. "*You* take this arm."

Lek dropped the arm and climbed over to the other.

It took fifteen minutes of pulling and tugging to get the body through the doorway and into the weeds beside the house.

"Can we leave him here? I'm tired," groaned Haxhi, his breath visible in the cool night air.

"Yes." Lek released the rigor mortised arm and watched it sink into the weeds.

Haxhi looked across the moonlit valley to the faint glow of dying fires in a half-dozen burned-out homes. "Where do you think they took Mama?"

"I don't know," Lek replied, his eyes avoiding the barn. He considered telling his brother the truth, but couldn't. Lek felt a lump in his throat as he thought of his mother lying in the cold barn. He thought of the neighbor's dog and others like him and wondered what they would do to her? Lek didn't know what to do. He wanted his mother back. He wanted to hold her again, but she was gone forever. Lek began to cry.

"Do you really think they'll bring Mama back in the morning?"

Lek turned away and wiped his eyes. In a trembling voice, he said, "Yes, I think she'll come back then."

———

CHAPTER
FIVE

CAPTAIN JONATHON "JACK" Richards, USMC, sat quietly in the operations room of the USS *Kearsarge* with fifty other officers as he waited for the nightly Kosovo briefing. Five weeks had passed since he had said goodbye to his wife and son. Richards often thought of that dreary North Carolina day when wives, girlfriends, and Marines stood on the hard, gray concrete, choked back tears, put on brave faces, and said their goodbyes. He could still hear the soft whimpering of teary-eyed children fighting off the worry their daddies might never come home. His son, Andrew, was only four years old. He didn't yet understand his father was going and might not return. In a way, he was used to it as Jack Richards had been away for half of his life. Andrew, or Drew as they called him, had his mother, and to him, that was enough. The idea he was a redundant part of his son's life caused Richards some heartache and feelings of guilt as he thought of his family, an ocean away.

Jack Richards swallowed as he pictured his wife Carolyn with her lovely blue-green eyes and long, honey blonde hair. He could still see her on the tarmac, with Andrew standing beside her, his hand in hers. He remembered his son's uncertain gaze up to his stoic mother, sensing something was wrong but not knowing what. Richards knew his wife was strong. Marine wives had to be, or they didn't stay wives long.

Richards knew she didn't think he could see her once he boarded the bus and it started off, but he could. He saw her lower her waving arm and turn away with hunched and trembling shoulders as the anguish of another six months of loneliness and worry overcame her. He saw her kneel and embrace their son as she sought comfort. All Richards could do was turn away.

Five more months. That's not so long, he told himself. He would miss Andrew's birthday but would be there for Halloween and the Holidays. *It could be worse.* He forced down the lump in his throat and looked at the officers seated with him. Some were quietly visiting, a few were in thought, considering their lives and families half a world away. Richards looked at the front of the room where a major was readying notes and saw his murky reflection in a dark television monitor.

Richards was barely thirty-five years old, but he looked older. His brown hair, shaved on the sides and back, "high and tight" in Marine lingo, showed a hint of curl on top. His high cheekbones and persistent tan gave him an almost American Indian appearance, although there was none in his bloodline. A fine scar in the fold of his chin was a reminder of his childhood when his brother pushed him off the top bunk. His dark brown eyes stood out from his face and gave him a piercing, commanding quality.

Richards was an Arizona boy, all too familiar with the sun. But his tan had faded, as it usually did once a cruise began and he became a 'bottom dweller' with the other Marines on board. At just over six feet, he wasn't especially tall, but he was solid and broad-shouldered and walked with the gait of a confident athlete.

Richards was the captain of Delta Company, part of the United States Marine Corps' Twenty-Sixth Marine Expeditionary Unit. Besides his company of 130 Marines, there were five thousand other Navy and Marine Corps personnel, all part of Operation Joint Guardian, impatiently waiting 150 miles offshore in the Adriatic Sea. Charged with working with NATO to stop the ethnic cleansing and bring to justice the Serbian leader, Slobodan Milosevic, Richards and the others had grown frustrated. Despite the persistent NATO bombings, night after night they heard reports of ongoing Serbian aggression against the people of Kosovo. While President Clinton had told the country there would be no land assault, every man and woman in the operation knew there would be. It was just a matter of time.

Richards and the other officers got to their feet when Colonel Ramsay, a tall and sturdy Marine with buzzed hair and a prominent chin, entered the room and barked, "Take your seats!" Sitting back down, Richards looked at another captain pretending to be already asleep.

After clearing his throat, Ramsay, who was dressed in the standard black and green camo fatigues, started in his monotone voice, "Marines, this is a special intel briefing. Now, I know what you're saying. They're *all* special."

Polite laughter rolled through the room.

"This is Mister Gani Musovac," Ramsay said, pointing to a short, thin, olive-skinned man with thick, slicked-back hair. "Mister Musovac is an analyst for the CIA. He's an expert in the military security situation inside Kosovo. And gentlemen, he has some very interesting information." Ramsay moved aside to allow the analyst to position his notes on the podium.

"Thank you, Colonel Ramsay," Musovac said with a subtle Croatian accent. "Some of what I tell you today you may already know—and I apologize in advance—but much of what I have is new. And in the event ground forces are put into Kosovo...it may prove very valuable to you."

The Marines straightened up in their chairs, Richards included.

"I am sure you have gotten the latest troop estimates in Kosovo, so I will—"

"Excuse me, Mister Musovac," Ramsay said, leaning forward. "Why don't you update us?"

"Yes, Colonel. In Kosovo, there were approximately 16,000 VJ troops when the bombing started on March twenty-fourth. Now there are just over 20,000."

"I thought the bombing was supposed to chase them *out*," scoffed a major next to Richards.

Musovac ignored the comment. "Colonel Ramsay asked me to touch on the force structure of both the Serbian and the KLA units. I will do so briefly. The *Vojska Jugoslavije* or VJ is the Yugoslav Army. They are divided into 'regulars' and 'reservists.' The VJ has 85,000 to 114,000 regular personnel with another 200,000 reservists—that is inside Serbia. Before the expulsion of the OSCE compliance verifiers from Kosovo, there were 197 tanks, 178 armored personnel carriers of assorted types, 358 artillery pieces, thirty-seven MiG-21s, and an array of small arms, anti-tank, and anti-air weapons. We know that number has also gone up considerably since the NATO bombing started."

The analyst continued to describe the various factions of growing Serbian forces, ranging from Serbian regulars to special police and even a militia, all with the goal of claiming as much territory, spreading as much terror, and killing as many ethnic Albanians as possible as long as possible. The report illustrated what everyone already knew: an air assault by itself wasn't effective.

"Currently, the Yugoslav forces are coping with two tasks," the analyst continued. "Number one: Defeating the KLA, and two: Preparing for a NATO ground attack. As I already mentioned, they have widened the security zones to ten kilometers. They are also building their positions south of Gnjilane and entering villages in what before were deemed 'quiet districts.' In short, the VJ and MUP are working overtime to clear out what they can in Kosovo and get ready for war."

Richards listened closely to the analyst and his seemingly endless flow of information. He set down his pen and sat back as Musovac started into Serbian maneuvers and battle tactics. Much of it he had heard before, but it sounded fresher, more current from this man. He hoped he would never have to draw on the data, but it was valuable nonetheless. After twenty minutes, Musovac changed gears and started on the KLA.

"There are many unconfirmed reports of atrocities—terrible things. Unfortunately, in several cases, it appears reprisals were carried out in retaliation for either KLA activities or NATO bombings."

"So, what you're saying," an officer interrupted, "is the bad guys are beating up the good guys, and it's time for the cavalry to roll in."

"Not yet," Colonel Ramsay grinned.

A captain raised his hand and asked, "What's all this about, anyway? Why do the Serbs have it in for the Kosovo people?"

"Yeah, can't we all just get along?" a black officer quipped.

Everyone laughed.

"It's a matter of history. It's always about history," shrugged the analyst. "Until ten years ago, the communists controlled the region. They suppressed both groups—the Christian Serbs and the Albanian Muslims—both physically and culturally. When the communists left, the Serbians filled the power vacuum."

"That still doesn't explain the fighting," said another captain.

"Both countries were suppressed for decades by the communists and became very secular. Now that they have their freedom, they are trying to reclaim their culture. The ethnic Albanians, for example, are only thirty percent observant. They don't follow Islam like we see in the Middle East. They have lost their religion and are trying to get it back. Historically, Christians and Muslims haven't gotten along all that well, anyway. Add to that the fact that the Albanians want to rule themselves, but the Serbs want to keep control, and you have a conflict. Does that answer your question?"

Richards and several of the other officers nodded.

"Where was I?" The analyst looked from the colonel back to the group then continued, "The *Ushtria Clirimtare e Kosoves* or UCK—we know them as the Kosovo Liberation Army or KLA—have put up a surprising fight for their organizational and logistic shortfalls. Their structure is more akin to organized gangs fighting for a common cause. They are more loyal to their local leaders than any regional structure, and as such are less effective than they otherwise could be. Their tactics are severely lacking. If not for the VJs continual miscalculations, they might have been rooted out already. They are lightly armed with little or no artillery pieces. Some mortars and anti-tank weapons, mainly of older Soviet design. This makes them very mobile and less of a target for the hunting VJ and MUP.

"Their communication is surprisingly efficient and includes cellular phones, satellite radios, landline telephones, and hand-held radios. One of the weakest points of the KLA is the coverage and extent of their medical services. There are less than half a dozen field hospitals, but even those are ill-equipped and understaffed. Medical evacuation and first-aid stations are virtually nonexistent."

Richards continued to listen to the analyst, but to him, the writing was on the wall. Their time was drawing near.

Following the report, Captain Richards filed out of the operations room past several other officers and headed down to the berthing area to check on his men. He knew his First Sergeant Robert Sacamano, and his other NCOs had things well in hand, but Richards liked to check in on them, just the same.

While the accommodations aboard the *Kearsarge* were adequate for its passengers, they were hardly luxurious. Each Marine on board had his individual berthing area, which comprised seven-foot by three-foot bunks stacked three high, known as "goat lockers."

Although many thought life in the innards of a naval vessel was monotonous, some thought otherwise. When the warfighters were not training for combat or in PT (physical training), they were working hard to pass the time. For many of the Marines just out of high school, that meant playing Game Boys or watching videos from the ship's library. For others, including the more seasoned men, there were board games. There were Chess, Checkers, Stratego, Scrabble, and even Battleship, but the most popular games were Monopoly and Risk. Ongoing games could rage for days with victory sweetly savored. Some Marines were voracious readers and polished off book after book before recycling them through the ship's library. In one section of the ship was a weight room. Across from it, a ping-pong table with a two-day waiting list. But of all the activities to pass the time, reading and writing letters home was the most cherished. While most of the crew made their communications the old-fashioned way, with pen and paper, there was a growing number who used the computers on board to send and receive emails from their loved ones.

As Richards made his way down the gangway to Delta Company's berthing area, he passed several enlisted men. Each stood at attention and acknowledged the captain as he approached. In return, Richards gave a monotone, "As you were," after passing each frozen Marine. Richards no longer noticed the stale smell of men in confined quarters when he entered the birthing area, nor the hum of the exhaust fans laboring to remove the stale air. After being on board a month, the sights, smells, and sounds of the innards of the ship were now common to him.

"Attention on deck!" rang out from somewhere to Richards' right and brought the room to their feet and silence.

"As you were!" Richards responded.

"How's it going, sir?" a short sergeant asked.

"Good evening, Sergeant Holm—as you were," Richards repeated with a nod. "How's everything down here tonight?"

"Fine-a-rue, sir," Sergeant Holm said in his southern drawl. "Any news from Kosovo?"

Richards shook his head. "No change. Stand by to stand by."

"Aye, sir," Holm nodded.

As Richards walked in-between the racks, he made casual eye contact with the men as they sprung to attention. "As you were," he repeated as the men nodded in respect or said, "Sir, Skipper," or "Captain."

Remembering Pfc. Sims, a large black man who had injured his shoulder in a training exercise that morning, Richards turned and headed toward his bunk. As he approached, he saw the round-headed Marine lying flat on his rack and holding a Sports Illustrated with his good arm. "Sims, how's that shoulder?"

"It's fine, Cap'n," replied the private, moving to his feet.

"Whoa, there Marine. As you were. Just stay in your bunk."

"Aye, Cap'n," Sims said, leaning back and rubbing his shoulder. "It's okay. Just a little stiff, that's all."

"You went to sickbay and had it checked out?"

"No, Cap'n. It'll be okay in a couple of days."

Richards looked him over then spoke directly, "I know you're tough, Sims, but I want it checked out by a doc. I want you in sickbay at 700. Is that clear?"

"Aye, aye, Cap'n."

After giving the injured Marine a parting nod, Richards turned and continued between the racks. Passing a bunk, he watched two privates hide their Playboy magazines under their pillows. "Parker, you're gonna go blind looking at that trash."

The skinny nineteen-year-old pushed up his glasses and cringed at having been caught.

A staff sergeant moved to attention when he saw Richards approaching. "Evening, Captain."

"Evening, DeWitt—as you were. Have you seen Top?" Richards asked, referring to the company's top sergeant as he looked down the row of racks.

"Yes, sir. He's down the line talking to Perkins."

Continuing down the aisle, Richards paused at a poker game being played on the floor between the racks. "As you were, Marines. Good game?" Richards asked as the players shuffled to their feet, only to relax and sink back to the floor at his release. The Marine who had been dealing the cards looked up uneasily at the captain, then resumed passing out the hands.

"Deal ya in, Captain?" asked a Marine on an adjacent bunk.

"No thanks," Richards said as he moved on.

"He don't play cards, stupid. He's the captain."

As Richards walked away, a thin smile formed, which was as much as his men ever saw.

Richards stopped and waited when he saw Sergeant Sacamano and Lieutenant Petty approaching.

"What's up?" Richards asked as Sacamano shook his head.

"Perkins' mouth," Sacamano said in his raspy Bronx accent.

"Turner's threatening to kill Perkins if he doesn't shut up with the UFO crap," Petty said, scratching his shaven head.

"UFO?" Richards asked, eyeing Sacamano questioningly.

"Yeah, conspiracy crap, Art Bell stuff. His latest is Lewinsky was actually a Chinese agent, sent to seduce Clinton—infiltrate the government," the sergeant said sarcastically.

"Sorry to bother you with this, Captain," Petty apologized. "I'll handle it. I'll send him to sickbay or talk to him or something."

Sacamano's eyes drifted from the twenty-four-year-old Annapolis graduate back to Richards in a dull stare.

"Top, what do you think the lieutenant should do?" Richards asked, sensing a pending burst of wisdom from the sergeant.

"Sir, I think Corporal Perkins is just looking for attention. In the old days, he'd be taken out back and given plenty of it, but that wouldn't go over too good in our era of political *correctitude*."

Petty cocked his head at the newly created word; something Sacamano was famous for.

"Very well. Lieutenant, tell Turner to secure his annoyance."

"Aye-aye, Captain."

"Also, tell Perkins to keep his opinions to himself. Handled?"

"Handled, sir," Petty nodded.

Richards waited until the lieutenant was out of earshot, then asked Sacamano, "How's he doing?"

The sergeant shrugged. "I think the kid's doing all right. He's a little bit of a know-it-all, but we all were at that age."

Richards smirked.

"Anything new?" Sacamano asked.

"We're getting close," Richards said, all business now.

"So, we're gonna get a chance to show those NATO morons how it's really done?"

"Careful, we're working with those NATO morons."

Sacamano grinned. He liked it whenever he could get the captain to lighten up. He thought Richards was a good officer and a fine Marine, but felt he sometimes played the game too hard. "Well, sir," Sacamano said, looking over the racks of Marines, "they're a good bunch of kids. When the time comes, I think they'll do all right."

Richards looked Sacamano in the eyes and nodded.

———

CHAPTER
SIX

LEK'S EYES SHOT OPEN, and he stared at the ceiling as he tried to remember where he was. The sound he had heard in his sleep gradually registered. It was Jrfete, crying. He didn't know how long she had been fussing, but from the sound of her tired and hoarse cry, he suspected it had been a while.

Sitting up in the darkness of the Lushi home, the terrible memory of the day before came hammering down on him. It brought with it an aching pain deep inside his gut that swept up into his heart, making it feel as though it might split in two. Tears filled his eyes as he remembered his mother's lifeless stare. *Why could it not have been a dream?* he wondered. *A terrible, awful dream?*

After pushing the wool blanket aside, Lek moved to the adjacent bed and found Jrfete sitting up with one hand to her face and the other wearily waving in the air. Beside her sat Arta, blinking in a blank, early morning trance. Rexhe was still asleep, oblivious to the crying and the terrible reality of the day.

Moving to Jrfete, Lek tiredly gathered her up. She welcomed his embrace and stopped crying. Lek assumed it was the uncomfortable chill in the air that awakened her. He moved back to his bed with Jrfete in his arms and pulled the wool blanket over them. No sooner had

Jrfete been covered than she pulled away with an angry cry. Lek was tired and wanted to return to his slumber, where the pain of reality was less biting. After a moment of persuasion, Jrfete gave in and laid her head on his chest.

Lek's eyes had only closed for a moment when they opened again. There was too much on his mind to sleep, and he wondered how he had slept at all.

As Lek lay in the bed, staring at the smoke-blackened ceiling, the faint glow of early morning light through a nearby window told him their day would soon begin, but what would they do? he wondered. Where would they go? He thought he could see his breath in the air as a rooster crowed to welcome the morning. There were usually two roosters that dueled with one another. He wondered what had happened to the second. He found Jrfete had fallen back to sleep; her face was still red and puffy from crying. Arta's eyes had also closed.

Lek felt the first bit of normality when the second rooster crowed. But that feeling faded when he remembered their terrible situation. *What should I do?* He considered staying in the Lushi home. It had a little food and was a shelter from the rain, but he wondered about the soldiers and if they would let them stay. He remembered what his mother and father had said about the Serbs just a week before. The stories of Serbs killing and burning had scared him, but he felt comforted when his mother told him their village was cooperating with the police and had handed over their weapons as a sign of their peaceable intentions.

Lek thought of the last time he saw his father. He remembered his father's hug and kiss. Lek remembered the smell of his worn leather coat. He remembered his father urging him to care for his mother. He remembered him hugging and kissing the other children and then leaving. Lek looked at the watch loosely strapped to his bony wrist and cried. It was his father's watch, given him the day he left. Lek caressed its scratched face. It was all he had.

Lek's uncontrollable sobbing grew louder, forcing him to muffle it in the pillow. His body shuddered as the terrible image of his mother burned into his mind. The thought that his father might also be dead made it worse, and his chest tightened as his emotions flooded out.

The sound of Arta stirring caused him to press his face deeper into the pillow. When his tears stopped, his pain turned to hopelessness.

The groan of the front door opening caused Lek to catapult up. He looked down the hallway with fearful eyes at the sound of someone entering and walking across the floor. *Maybe it's one of the Lushis come back? Maybe it's a soldier?* Lek wished he had the bloodstained knife from the kitchen. He strained to see from his bed, his eyes round, his neck stretched. Lek could only visualize a narrow strip of the front room. He watched breathlessly as a body moved past and jumped at the sound of wood dropping to the floor. Lek watched unblinking as the shape moved past again and the sound of the footsteps drew closer. *If we have to leave, where will we go?* When Haxhi appeared in the doorway, Lek sank in relief. "What were you doing out there?"

The shadows hid the tears streaming down Haxhi's face. "I-I was cold...so I got some wood for a fire."

Lek remembered the pile of wood beside the old stone barn and wanted to ask Haxhi if he had gone inside. "You shouldn't have gone out. There might be soldiers still."

Stopped in the doorway, Haxhi hung his head and whimpered.

"*Shh*, you don't want to wake the others."

Haxhi wiped at his tears.

Carefully moving Jrfete aside, Lek climbed out of bed and moved past his grief-stricken brother to the front room fireplace, where he situated a few pieces of wood and kindling. The strike of a match revealed Lek's worried face.

As the fire began to pop and grow in its intensity, Lek stretched out his hands and felt its heat. The flames gave off not only warmth but also hope and strength. He looked at his younger brother, whose eyes were red and puffy from tears, and wondered if he had seen their dead mother. He wrapped his arms around Haxhi, and the two held each other tightly.

"When will Papa come back?" Haxhi sobbed.

"I don't know," Lek breathed.

After several moments with only the snapping and popping of the fire, Haxhi whimpered, "I miss Mama."

Lek squeezed his brother tighter. "I miss her too." Lek thought of his family, of the way it used to be. That had all changed. Their mother was gone. There were only his brothers and sisters now. They were just children, but Lek understood, until they could find their father, *he* would have to do. He would have to be the father and the mother. They were *his* children now.

Lek squinted as the noon sun broke from behind a cloud. For their breakfast, they had finished the mutton he had found the night before, along with some stale bread. While the meal was a feast compared to the bowl of mush they usually ate and helped raise their spirits for a time, boredom, uncertainty, and now gloom had once again fallen over them, and Lek wondered from where their next meal would come.

Still uncertain if Haxhi knew the terrible secret, Lek watched his brother sitting quietly beside the Lushi's front door, staring down the dirt road toward the smoldering remains of their old home. While Lek avoided looking at the stone barn, he caught Haxhi's gaze repeatedly wandering in that direction, after which Haxhi would hang his head and wipe away tears.

While he knew Haxhi was hurting, Lek's own pain was almost more than he could bear. He wanted to leave but didn't know where to go, and worried if they left, their father wouldn't find them. It was the thought of his father's return that gave Lek hope. *He will know what to do. He will take us to a safe place—a place without Serbs.*

As Lek watched Rexhe play on the rutted dirt road, as if nothing had happened, his weighty thoughts were lifted. He saw Arta sitting by herself, holding a piece of wood like a doll as she whispered to it. Haxhi sat in the dirt, numbly drawing in it with the knife from the kitchen. Jrfete, who had given into a nap, was curled up on a blanket just inside the house.

The growing buzz of flies to the side of the house caused Lek to turn. He saw Fan Lushi's boots in the weeds and wondered if he and Haxhi should drag him further away.

"When is Mama coming back?" Arta asked, looking up from her pretend doll.

"I don't know," Lek muttered.

Haxhi lowered his head and stabbed the knife into the dirt.

Lek's eyes narrowed as he watched the elfish Rexhe throw rocks into a puddle that had formed from the night's rain. He watched as he laughed and played, oblivious to the death and terribleness around them. Lek wished he could be a small boy again, free from the pain and worry. He wished the Serbs had never come and his mother was still alive and playing games with them. Lek sighed and tried to forget.

The sound of a creaking wheel accompanied by distant voices caused Lek's head to turn. "Hurry inside! Someone's coming!" he whispered as he got up from his seat in the doorway and Haxhi and Arta hurried into the house, but Rexhe didn't hear him. "Rexhe, someone's coming!" Lek said more loudly, glancing nervously up the road.

Rexhe heard his brother this time, and his playful expression vanished when he saw the fear in Lek's face.

After pulling Rexhe into the house, Lek pushed the door closed, leaving a crack to view who was coming. After glancing back at the sleeping Jrfete, he hushed the other children peeking through a window, then turned back to the crack in the door.

While the creak of the wagon had grown louder, it still sounded a little way off, and Lek startled when the first of the long-faced and disheveled travelers trudged past their door.

"They're not soldiers," Haxhi whispered.

"*Shh,*" Lek breathed, his eyes wide.

Arta, who was peering over the windowsill on her tiptoes, counted the people as they passed.

The tension in Lek's face eased when he spotted women and children among the refugees.

"Is it Mama?" Arta asked as a red-dressed woman walked by.

"Mama!" Rexhe pushed toward the partly opened door.

Lek tried to quiet his youngest brother, but it was too late. Several of the refugees, whose eyes were filled with the same fear that had been in Lek's, stopped and turned toward the house. Lek's eyes widened as a man, whose clothes were soiled and stained with blood, not his own, started toward their door. Holding his breath, Lek took a step back and watched the man cautiously approach. Lek looked at the other children still peeking over the windowsill, then back through the crack of the door. There was a mule-drawn wagon carrying supplies and several small children.

Lek backed away as the door pushed open and a middle-aged man with a week's beard looked inside the plundered house. The man's sad gaze moved from Lek to the other young faces before he asked, "Are you alone?"

There was no answer.

"Where are your parents? Your mama and papa?"

"We don't know," Lek answered in as brave a voice as possible.

"How long have you been here?" the man asked as he looked around the house.

Arta gulped and pointed down the road. "The bad men came yesterday and took our mama and burned our house."

The bloodstained man shook his head, looked out the door at the others, then turned back and said, "You can't stay here. Come with us. We have food and other children. We will find your mama and papa."

Lek thought for a moment, then shook his head. "I think we should stay here and wait for our papa to return."

"Did your papa join the army to fight?"

Lek nodded.

The bloodstained man scratched his head. "You won't have much food here after long...and the soldiers...they *will* come back."

His words were enough to convince Haxhi and the others, but Lek was reluctant.

"There are safe places to go. We will find your parents later," the man insisted.

Lek looked over the children. Jrfete was still asleep, but the others appeared eager to leave.

"Papa will find us," Haxhi whimpered, his eyes red and his cheeks quivering.

Lek put a hand on his brother's shoulder and nodded.

"What about Mama?" Arta protested. "Will she find us too?"

Lek swallowed hard and tried not to look at the sobbing Haxhi as he breathlessly replied, "Yes, she'll find us."

The kind man looked from Lek to Haxhi in sudden realization: their mother was dead and wouldn't be returning. He shook his head in anger. "Will you come with us? We're traveling to the south, away from the Serbs."

Lek glanced at the old stone barn. "Yes...we will go with you."

"Come," the man called back to the other travelers, "There are children in here."

Lek looked over the group, then gathered the still slumbering Jrfete off the floor.

"Is there any food here to take?" the kind man asked.

"Not much," Lek said as he passed through the doorway to the waiting refugees. A frazzle-eyed woman with a bruise on the side of her face looked over the awakening Jrfete. "Put her on the wagon with the other children," she said with a strained smile.

Lek set Jrfete next to a bundle of clothing on the back of the wagon, then turned back to the house. He watched as the kind man loaded Haxhi with a heavy blanket and Arta with a bundle of hastily gathered clothing. Rexhe followed them to the wagon with a half-eaten loaf of dark rye bread in hand, his elfish eyes wide and searching. They each placed their supplies on the end of the wagon where the frazzle-eyed woman had shown them, then stood next to Lek and waited.

"Is that your father?" asked the frazzle-eyed woman, pointing to Fan Lushi's body in the weeds.

Lek shook his head.

"Should we bury him?" asked the woman.

"If we stop to bury everyone we find, we'll never make it to the camps," groaned another.

The convoy started moving.

After nudging Haxhi and Arta forward, Lek followed the wagon along the rutted dirt road toward the old stone barn. He tried to look anywhere but the barn, but as they passed it, he slowed to a stop and stared at its dark and lonely entrance, unable to move.

The kind man stopped and called back, "Are you coming?"

All Lek could think of was his mother lying in the cold dampness of the barn. He couldn't leave her that way.

"What's the matter?" the man asked, walking back to Lek.

Lek saw the children and wagon had paused forty feet ahead. He swallowed hard, then said, "There are people in there."

The man turned to the barn, then back to Lek. "Are they alive?"

Lek shook his head, his sad eyes fixed on the barn's shadowed entrance.

"Do you know them?"

Lek nodded.

"Is your mother in there?"

Lek's eyes filled with tears, and his chin quivered.

The kind man sighed. "We will give her a proper grave."

Remembering his mother's necklace, Lek pulled it from his pocket and said, "This-this is hers. Will you…"

The kind man nodded. "I will put it with her." He then went to the wagon and pulled from it a shovel. "We won't be long," he told the other travelers. "Wait by those trees," he added, pointing to the budding apple trees ahead. Lek followed the others as they moved down the road to the trees. He looked back at the old stone barn as the two men disappeared inside.

Sitting in the tangled grass near the trees, Lek positioned the children so they couldn't see the barn, and spoke comforting words as the men carried Desanka's body out and around the other side. Lek fought away the tears as they emerged again, moments later, with his mother's body. After wiping away his tears, Lek looked at the worn and weary faces of the travelers and wondered what awfulness they had seen.

After a time, the men returned, and the wagon started forward. As Lek got to his feet, his eyes strayed back toward the old barn, where he could see the freshly mounded soil of two graves. After forcing the lump down his throat, Lek's heartbroken gaze turned forward, and he began walking.

As Lek passed the burned remains of their home, a flood of memories returned. He remembered his father looking up from an open tractor engine and smiling. Lek saw himself chasing Haxhi and Arta around the house. He remembered Jrfete being born. He saw his mother singing as she hung the laundry to dry behind their home. Lek thought of the song she so often hummed and wished he knew the words. Cresting a hill in the rutted dirt road, he numbly turned back to the old stone barn. Its crumbling exterior and shadowed entrance would haunt him forever.

———

CHAPTER
SEVEN

SALI NOLI restlessly shifted as he gazed out the broken window of the music store. His deep-set eyes were tired, and his face worn and darkened by three days of thick stubble. He had been to Urosevac many times and recalled passing the store and wanting to go inside. He vividly remembered the various instruments that filled its windows. In particular, the bright brass horns he had wanted to learn to play as a boy but never had. It struck him as funny now that he was finally inside the music store, all the instruments were gone. Looted by marauding musicians, he mused.

The only clue the trashed building had been a music store was an overturned display case to his left, which still contained pictures of instruments and a few music books. Sheet music was scattered on the floor throughout the gallery, much of it weather-stained from the broken windows. A trail of muddy footprints ran over the scattered pages of music, making a confusing mosaic on the dirty tile floor.

To Sali's right was a man he knew nothing about, only that he was Albanian and a member of the KLA, having undergone the same two-hour training he had. Farther down the pillaged showroom was another soldier, a short man smoking a cigarette he had just rolled. Sali leaned forward and sniffed at the tobacco's aroma. He could have used a smoke but felt it impolite to ask in such impoverished times.

Turning back to the window, Sali felt a gentle breeze as he looked across the street at the once beautiful park. Not too long ago, a warm spring day would have brought to the park picnickers, boys playing soccer, and vendors selling drinks, pitas, and baklavas. There were none of those now, only long strands of grass bending in the breeze and trash blown from across the road. Sali looked at the lovely green hills in the distance. They looked peaceful and alive, unlike the abandoned and lifeless town before him.

A quacking duck made Sali lean forward. He smiled as a large white duck waddled along the front of the music store with a train of yellow ducklings following. Sali became serious again when he realized their fate should fighting begin. He considered going out and shooing them to safety, but knew soldiers didn't do such things. With a heavy sigh, Sali sank back behind the window and saw the stern-eyed man to his left was looking at him strangely. Sali shrugged and said, "There are little ducks out there."

The stern-eyed man looked back down the road.

Wondering what time it was, Sali looked at his watch, then remembered he had given it to his oldest son Lek as a token of his responsibility. He was to be the man in the family until Sali returned. Thoughts of his family, of his wife and his five children, were never far away, lingering in the back of his mind. Guilt tugged at Sali from deep inside, and he wondered if leaving them was the right choice. Sali knew his wife was an able woman and his two eldest boys could do much to help; he was worried more about the Serbs.

Sali had heard the rumor that paramilitary units and the Special Police were moving toward Vitina, which was only ten miles away. The Serb paramilitary, especially the militia, were worse than the Police or even the Army as they had no code of conduct, only terror. The promise of returning to Vitina with a KLA unit after their ambush reassured Sali, but to do so, he knew he must first survive the day.

Sali looked at his rifle. While he had fired it fifty times in practice, it still felt strange and menacing to him. It was a tool, he told himself, like the wrenches he used working on engines, a soldier's tool. The thought of using it to take another's life sickened him, but so did the thought of being chased from his home. He looked at the other men beside him and wondered if they had such reservations. Some of them appeared eager to use their weapons, eager to exact vengeance. He had heard many of their stories; they were terrible, heartbreaking tales of hatred and violence. If they had harmed his family, he wouldn't hesitate to use his rifle, he told himself.

The sound of men shuffling into position caused Sali to sit up.

"They're coming! Be ready!" yelled a man to his left.

Sali looked out the window to the empty road that ran between the park and a row of buildings before disappearing as it dipped to the right, fifty yards away.

"Keep down!" ordered a man to his right.

Sali ducked his head, wondering from what he was hiding. After a moment, he heard the deep rumble of low-geared engines. It started softly at first, like the purr of a cat, then grew louder until it was echoing through the music store and causing the fragments of broken glass along the windowsill to dance.

Sali cringed at the growing thunder and feared a tank might burst into the store at any moment. Hunkered down, with his back to the wall below the window, Sali noticed the others were raising their heads and their weapons. Some had rifles such as his; others had shoulder-fired rocket launchers. He saw the looks of determination and fear on the other men as his heart pounded.

The stern-eyed man on Sali's right watched the approaching convoy through the broken window, his rocket launcher at the ready. To Sali's left, around the partition, a shadowed figure scurried into position. Sali knew his friend Kuq was somewhere in the store, but didn't know where.

"Don't fire until ordered," and "Shoot for the sweet spots!" came from Sali's left. The man with the rocket launcher, who had beads of sweat on his gathered brow, gave a stern nod with each command as he glared over the windowsill.

Sali gulped, his heart beating in his throat. He fought the rush of panic urging him to run and hide. The fear worsened with the increasing groans and bone-rattling clatter of the tank's wheels and tracks. Lower, he sunk, below the broken window.

"There are only three tracked—a BMP, T-55, BTR—and two open

trucks with infantry," came from the other side of the partition. Sali gulped. To him, it sounded like ten times as many.

After breathing in courage, Sali turned and raised his head to the approaching column. He quickly buried it as the lead tank passed not twenty yards away.

The command to fire was followed by the echoing crack of rifle fire and the whooshing of shoulder-fired rockets. Sali cringed at the noise and watched empty brass casings bounce onto the music store's floor. Gathering courage, he raised over the windowsill in time to see the massive main battle tank, camouflaged with branches and bushes on top, come to a stop. His eyes widened as its massive turret-mounted gun turned in his direction and the first of the enemy soldiers, dressed in green-speckled camouflage, fell to the street.

Sali pulled the trigger of his rifle and sparks followed as his bullets ricocheted harmlessly off the tank's armor. When he spotted a soldier running behind the tank on the far side of the road, Sali redirected his fire. To his surprise, the soldier toppled face-first to the street. Sali paused as a flutter of guilt ran through him. *It's war*, he told himself, dismissing the feeling. *What I'm doing is right.*

The bark of a heavy machine gun from somewhere outside caused Sali to duck as the music store walls disintegrated around him. Wincing from the *zing* of bullets passing just inches overhead, he watched the stern-eyed man raise to fire his rocket. Sali jumped as the torrent of lead blew the man back into the store. With a *poofsh* and a flash, his rocket shot up from his bullet-ridden body into the ceiling, where it lodged and sizzled. Sali buried his head, waiting for the rocket to explode, but it hung wedged in the ceiling as bullets and debris flew around him.

Sali knew if he were to survive, he would have to get out of the music store. He had no sooner gotten to his knees than an ear-numbing blast brought the store down around him. He coughed and choked at the settling dust, then cried out in pain as a dozen hot pokers seared his back. Sali tasted the bitterness of bile in the back of his mouth as he struggled for air. His surroundings darkened, and the ringing in his ears turned to nothingness.

· · ·

The road by the park was again quiet. The long blades of grass bent peacefully in the afternoon breeze as dark plumes of smoke rolled up into the gray sky from the burning hulk of a tank and a toppled troop transport. Men in everyday clothes, with rifles slung across their backs, looked on as the last of the dead Serbs were laid on the road beside the overturned truck. Men with proud smiles and blackened and battered faces gloated over the bodies in green-speckled uniforms arranged like trophies for all to see. Behind the dead and the proud victors were the remains of the music store. One side had collapsed into a heap of rubble; the other was leaning, about to fall. Inside, half a dozen men sifted through the fallen beams and crumbled masonry of the store as they searched for survivors, weapons, and ammunition.

"There's one right here," Kuq called out as he lifted a beam out of the way. "Hey, it's Sali!" he exclaimed, seeing his friend covered in wood splinters and plaster dust.

"Is he alive?" asked another.

"I can't tell," Kuq grunted as he and another pulled the beam off the half-buried mechanic. After kneeling beside Sali, Kuq felt for a pulse, then shook the mechanic. "Hey, Sali, you're alive, wake up!"

As the world around Sali brightened, the ringing in his ears returned. Blinking and disoriented, he looked up at the angels staring down at him. As the ringing subsided, he heard his name. "Yes, yes, I'm Sali," he said hoarsely. "Am I in paradise?"

Kuq shook his head. "No such luck, my friend. You're still among the living."

———

CHAPTER
EIGHT

IT HAD BEEN two days since the Kelmendi family had left their home. Jusuf had thought and prayed for them, especially the daughter Lirie, and he wondered if they had made it to the border. Macedonia wasn't far from their town of Livoc, only fifteen miles by road, but he didn't know what roads were safe. He thought of Lirie and the sadness in her eyes the day she left; it was a sadness he had never seen from her. He hoped he would see her again.

Jusuf looked at his stubborn grandmother as she sat quietly knitting. He had given up trying to persuade her to leave. She was willing to die for her home, and he feared death would be their fate should the Serbians come. As much as he wanted to leave and find Lirie, Jusuf knew his place was with his family.

Jusuf looked out the window to the long evening shadows that covered the abandoned Kelmendi home across the street. The occasional sound of bombs falling to the north had the rumble of distant thunder and gave the dreamer chills. He hoped they were NATO bombs or even the KLA, but feared they were Serbian.

Jusuf noticed the reflection of his grandmother knitting and his mother asleep in her chair. His eyes focused beyond the reflection to the quiet street. No one in the village had left for hours, and he wondered if they were the last Albanians in Livoc. The thought brought him angst, and he tried to divert his mind. He thought of one of his favorite movies, *The Outlaw Josey Wales*, and pictured himself as Clint Eastwood.

Jusuf's mind was drifting when he heard a crashing sound from outside the house. Leaning forward against the distorted glass, he searched for what had made the noise. His father had gone for firewood, and Jusuf had heard him splitting wood. But when Jusuf realized the chopping sound had stopped, his brow gathered. Muffled men's voices from outside caused him to turn back to his mother. She had also heard them. Jusuf turned to his unfazed grandmother and wondered if she had heard the voices or was just ignoring them.

Turning back to the window, Jusuf startled at the sight of four dark uniformed militiamen walking across the court toward the Kelmendi's door. Jusuf's eyes widened when a man raised a heavy boot and kicked in the door. "They're here," Jusuf gasped as the soldiers filed inside. He watched unblinkingly to see what the soldiers would do.

When a chair exploded through the Kelmendi's front window, Jusuf pulled back. Moments later, two soldiers pushed an old upright piano out of the door and down the steps onto the court, where it toppled on its side and made a confusing, disharmonious groan. Jusuf's jaw slackened as more black-uniformed militiamen appeared with rifles slung over shoulders and kicked in the door of the next house on the street.

Engrossed in the movie coming to life before him, Jusuf watched, forgetting he was visible in his seat at the window. He stared as another soldier shoved his eighty-year-old neighbor Caush Berisha from his home out onto the court. The frail old man struggled to pick himself up from the cobbled stone without his cane, then angrily shook his fist at the evicting Serb. Jusuf gasped when the Serb raised his rifle and fired a bullet into the old man's chest. Jusuf recoiled at the blast as Berisha fell back to the cobblestones, motionless.

Jarred back to reality, Jusuf turned to his grandmother. She had heard the shot, and for the first time, he saw fear in her eyes. His mother jumped to her feet and was beside herself, pointing at the window. Jusuf spun back as a rifle butt came crashing through the glass. After leaping from his seat, Jusuf staggered back from the smashed window as the Serb militiaman struck it again, bringing the remaining glass down in shards and fragments. Falling back to the floor, Jusuf watched in horror as the militiaman pointed his rifle through the broken window and yelled, "What are you doing here? Get out of here, you Muslim dogs! Do you want to die?"

Jusuf turned back to his *gjyshe* and watched in horror as the old woman—his mother's mother—picked up a book from the table beside her and hurled it at the man. The militiaman ducked as the book bounced off his shoulder and pointed his rifle at her with fierce determination. Waiting for the militiaman to fire, Jusuf jumped when their front door burst open, and a large man in a brown leather coat and a cowboy hat entered. The Cowboy, who had a thick gray goatee, didn't have the same malevolent expression as the soldier at the window or the man beside him, but a look of playfulness.

Jusuf's jaw slackened. In his mind, the sight of a cowboy didn't fit with what was happening around them. In an instant, all the Westerns he had ever seen, with their confident gunslingers, determined sheriffs, and over-eager deputies, flooded his mind. *Is this a good man come to stop the Serbs? Is he here to save us?* Jusuf looked from the man's cowboy hat and humored face to his snakeskin boots. *Who is this man?* Jusuf wondered in astonishment.

"Get out of my house, you pigs! I will not have Serbian trash in my house!" the red-faced grandmother screamed as two men with sacks went through her cupboards.

The man to the left of the Cowboy, who had a shaved head and a brown beard, raised his rifle in anger, but the Cowboy pushed it back down. "Show some respect, Misha," grinned the Cowboy. "She's just a little old woman. She can't hurt you."

The fiery grandmother made a face and spat at the two men. Jusuf gasped and slid back against the wall.

The Cowboy's grin faded as he eyed the defiant old woman. He pointed to Jusuf and said, "Watch that one."

The bearded militiaman turned his AK-47 on Jusuf.

"I will show you who is trash, old woman." The Cowboy laid his rifle on a table a few feet from the mother and started toward the old woman—his fingers flexing through gloved hands.

The old woman's look of defiance faded to fear when she saw the Cowboy's dark, cold eyes.

"Stop, leave us alone!" Jusuf's mother cried as the Cowboy passed her. Seeing the rifle on the table, she lunged for it. The bearded militiaman turned and fired. Jusuf and his grandmother jumped at the loud bark of the muzzle and watched the mother stumble sideways, then collapse on the floor.

"Mother!" Jusuf cried.

"Move, and you are dead," growled the bearded Serb as he swung the smoking barrel back toward Jusuf.

"*Mother*," Jusuf tearfully groaned.

Jusuf's grandmother looked in disbelief at her daughter and the pool of blood forming beside her. With a gasp, she slumped in her chair, and her nearly finished afghan slipped to the floor.

The Cowboy cocked his head as he eyed the lifeless old woman. "See that Misha, if you plan it right, you don't have to waste a bullet."

The bearded Misha laughed. "What should I do with him?"

The Cowboy eyed the trembling Jusuf. "Shoot him."

Misha raised his rifle.

"Wait." The Cowboy pushed down Misha's barrel. "Don't shoot him. We can use him. He's a coward and no threat." The Cowboy turned to the dead mother and the pool of blood under her. "The women in this house have the courage, not the men."

Misha laughed and kicked the cowering Jusuf onto his side.

"See, what did I tell you?" the Cowboy smirked as militiamen with large canvas bags came through the door searching for valuables. The Cowboy picked up the old mother's afghan, pulled out a knife, and cut the knitting in two. After discarding the unfinished end, he stepped over the dead mother and dipped it into her blood on the floor. Moving to the cream plaster wall, he tore down a framed picture and began painting with broad strokes, stopping to soak up more of his crimson medium. A red eagle with outstretched wings took shape. Upon finishing his warbird, the Cowboy turned to the cowering, sobbing Jusuf. He laughed as he dipped his brush in the woman's blood. Returning to the wall, he wrote in large Cyrillic print: DEATH TO ALBANIANS.

After tossing the blood-soaked afghan aside, the Cowboy looked at his work proudly. "Do not burn this house. This one is for all to see."

Jusuf's tears blurred his vision as the Serb pulled him from the floor and pushed him to the door. "Mama...*Gjyshe*," Jusuf whimpered as the Serb shoved him out the door. "I'm sorry!"

"Shut up!" Misha ordered. "You'll see them soon enough."

Jusuf looked for his father. He had not seen him since he had gone for wood. "Papa!" Jusuf cried. "Papa!"

"Shut-up, you pitiful man!" growled Misha, knocking Jusuf forward with the butt of his rifle.

Jusuf turned and made a hostile face, but recoiled as the militiaman raised his rifle butt.

Misha laughed.

Jusuf hung his head. *I let them kill my mother and grandmother and did nothing to stop them. I'm not a man. I deserve to die.*

Walking down the stone walk, the Cowboy examined his men's work. The doors of the connected dwellings were kicked in with trails of clothing and furniture scattered into the courtyards. The militiamen had looted, pillaged, and plundered the neighborhood. Fires were burning, and bodies lay in various poses of death, including Jusuf's father, who lay beside his load of firewood, his ax buried in his back.

The Cowboy stood in the center of the street and looked on proudly. His men had done well. His craft was fear and terror, and he considered himself a master. While it was just one neighborhood in Livoc, he knew it would be enough to scare any remaining Albanians into leaving.

The Cowboy was about to address his men when he heard an approaching vehicle. He looked up the debris-strewn street, and his eyes narrowed when a black Range Rover appeared. He watched as it passed a burning car and drove over a wooden chair, smashing it to pieces. The Cowboy drew in a fortifying breath and stood a little taller as the mud-splattered Range Rover stopped before him. He saw his reflection in the dark tinted side glass. With a hum, the window lowered, revealing a shadowed face.

"Nimatovic, you are behind schedule. This is a problem," said the shadowed occupant, his voice deep and menacing.

Ivan Nimatovic, known as "The Cowboy," shook his head. "I'm sorry, sir, but these Albanians, they're too stupid to leave—even when their lives depend on it."

"I don't want excuses. I need action. Do you understand?"

"Yes, General," the Cowboy replied, his head down.

"Time is short. NATO is bombing our people. They struck Slobo's home with missiles! Thank God he wasn't there. You should know, there is unrest in Serbia, but don't speak of this to your men."

The Cowboy nodded.

"We must speed up the operation. Do you understand?"

"Yes, sir."

"MUP and VJ cannot help us anymore. There is still much to do and not much time. They may attack us soon. If you want to pretend you're *John Wayne* or one of Franko's boys, that's fine, but one way or the other, I want the Albanians out of here!"

"Yes, sir." Nimatovic removed his cowboy hat and ran a shaky hand through his matted gray hair.

"What of the mines? Have you laid all the mines in your sector?"

"Yes, General. My men are working on it."

"The mines *must* be laid. They will keep NATO out and the Albanians from coming back. You understand this?"

"Yes, General. The mines will be laid. I have people on it now."

A pair of eyes emerged from the darkness inside the Range Rover and caused the Cowboy to step back. "Do not disappoint me."

The Cowboy shook his head. "I won't."

———

CHAPTER
NINE

THE STENCH of smoke and decaying flesh hung heavy in the air and caused Sali Noli to wrinkle his nose as he walked down the village road, passing sheep and cows the purging Serbs had shot for sport. Sali's eyes were full of worry as he walked by one burned-out home after another. Passing an overturned wagon, he saw the body of a man, and farther away, a woman, lying in the weeds. He put a hand to his mouth and turned away. They were not the first dead he had seen, but they were from his village, and he knew them.

"How far away is your home?" asked a grimacing Kuq.

Sali pointed ahead as his worried gaze moved across the devastated village. He listened for the familiar sounds of everyday life, of tractors in the fields, chatting women, and playing children, but heard none of those things. There were no baying sheep, barking dogs, or even chirping birds. He heard only the lonely sound of the gentle wind and the buzzing of flies. Everywhere there were flies.

On they walked. They passed an abandoned car, its doors still open, its windshield shattered. Beyond that, a toppled wagon and a stiff, lifeless mule.

"There! There's a house they didn't burn," Kuq said, pointing to the Lushi home. "There's another!" He pointed to the old stone barn.

Sali's home was just beyond the apple trees and his chest swelled with hope.

As they passed the Lushi home, Sali paused at the body lying face down in the weeds.

"Who's that?" Kuq grimaced.

"My neighbor," Sali muttered as he looked down the road toward his home, still hidden by the trees.

As they passed the old stone barn, Kuq stopped and eyed its dark entrance. "Was—is this your barn?"

Sali didn't reply. His eyes were on the tall pine not far from his home. Passing the budding apple trees, Sali gasped as the blackened remains of his home came into view. "It's gone."

Kuq caught up to Sali and sadly shook his head.

Sali looked over the devastation in stunned silence. Then, with frantic eyes, he choked out the words, "Where is my family?"

"Don't you think they would have left before all of this?" Kuq asked, reaching for Sali. "I'm sure they're over the border by now."

Sali glanced at Kuq, then moved closer to the remains of his home, his fearful gaze searching for signs of his family. He stopped before what had been his front door and quietly wept as he looked across the bed of ashes and blackened remains. "My home is gone."

Kuq put a hand on Sali's shoulder but then backed away.

Sali wiped away his tears and turned from the charred rubble. The thought his family might be hiding, waiting for him to return, caused Sali to raise his hands to the side of his mouth and shout, "Gentiana! GENTIANA!" He listened for a response but heard only the lonely breeze in the trees.

"Gentiana! It's Sali. It's okay. Come out with the children!" He looked back up the road to the stone barn and started toward it.

Kuq raised his rifle and followed. He feared Sali's cries might bring more Serbs.

"Lek, Arta, Haxhi, it's Papa! Rexhe, Jrfete!" Sali's voice faded as tears ran down his cheeks. He wiped them away and stared at his burned home, shaken and lost. "My family...what have they done with my family?"

"Maybe you shouldn't yell. Serbs may be nearby."

"I don't care!" Sali yelled even louder, "GENTIANA!"

A sound from the barn turned Sali. He eyed the shadowed entrance with frantic, hopeful eyes, but saw only the Lushi's mangy dog emerging from its shadows. The dog sat just beyond the barn's entrance and watched them with sad eyes. Sali listened for the familiar sound of his children calling back to him, but there was only the soft cooing of a dove perched on the barn.

"Is that your dog?"

"No, he was the neighbor's," Sali muttered, staring at the barn.

"Oh."

Sali ran a frustrated hand through his tangled hair, then looked up and down the road helplessly. "We were supposed to stop this! We were supposed to protect them!"

Kuq hung his head.

Sali turned back to the lying dog, and his eyes narrowed. Something looked different. His brow tightened when he noticed the two mounds of dirt. Sali stepped closer, and his eyes widened. *Someone's been buried!* The old dog moved aside as Sali approached.

"What's wrong? What do you see?"

Sali stopped before the first mound, that was roughly two feet by six feet. "They're graves," he muttered, his mind racing.

"Graves?" Kuq asked as he moved beside his friend. "Whose?"

"I don't know," Sali breathed.

Kuq bent his head when he noticed a glint at the foot of the first mound. "What's this?" He kneeled and picked up the silver necklace.

Sali's brow gathered.

As Kuq brushed away the dirt, a thin, heart-shaped pendant became visible.

Sali groaned when he saw the necklace he had given his wife on their wedding day. "No, it can't be…" Sali stopped breathing. He took the necklace from Kuq and turned it over. Sali's shoulders sank when he saw his words of love to his new wife inscribed on its back. "No… No, it's not possible," Sali gasped, choked with emotion. Clutching the necklace, he sank to his knees beside the mounded earth. "NO!" he cried, burying his face in the dirt. "What have I done?"

———

The afternoon sun shined through the old window, filtering through the smoke-filled room. Massimo Markovic, also known as *Kasap* (or in English, the Butcher), set his cigarette on the table next to him and studied the frightened man tied up before him. Kasap had dark, penetrating eyes, a stubble beard, and a perpetual smirk. Kasap leaned closer to the man tied to the chair and blew cigarette smoke into his face. The middle-aged man, bruised and bleeding, coughed as he pulled helplessly on the ropes.

"It's no use, you fool," laughed a Serb militiaman standing beside Kasap with an AK-47. "Even if you get loose, you'll die."

The Serb's comment brought a whimper from the panic-stricken woman cowering in the corner with her three children.

"You have a nice house," Kasap said, looking across the room. "Too bad you won't need it."

"Please, let them go. They've done nothing," the man pleaded.

"How will I make you talk if I let them go?" Kasap asked with a playful shrug.

"Please, they've done nothing. I've done nothing!"

"No, you're wrong," Kasap snarled. "You have done two things: You were born Albanian Muslim, and you're KLA."

"No," the man pleaded, his eyes welling with tears. He looked at his wife, who was glistening with sweat, and his terrified children, their outstretched arms calling for him. "Please, let them go. Let them leave, and I will tell you anything."

Kasap's devious grin widened. "If you tell us what we want to know, we'll consider that."

The groan of an opening door caused the Butcher to turn. Filling the doorway was Ivan Nimatovic, his cowboy hat resting proudly atop his head. The Cowboy moved closer to the bound man and smiled. "Look who we have, Et'hem Ceku himself."

The bound man's pitiful expression faded to confusion. "No...no, I'm not Et'hem Ceku, my name is—"

"We know who you are," the Cowboy grinned.

"No, I swear to you! I am not Et'hem Ceku!"

"Has he told you anything yet?" the Cowboy asked, eyeing the man's sobbing wife.

"No," Kasap replied. "We've just started."

"Excellent. I love to watch your work, Massimo."

The Butcher smiled, then turned back to the bound man. "You will tell us where your base of operations is, Et'hem."

"Please, I'm not Et'hem. My name is Kadria. Ask my wife."

Kasap eyed the man knowingly. "You don't expect us to believe the words of an Albanian witch, do you?" he laughed.

The man swallowed as the Butcher unfold a bundle containing an assortment of knives, needles, and other instruments of torture. "Please, I don't know anything!"

Nimatovic moved beside the Butcher who was slowly dragging a hooked skinning knife down the man's shirt, severing its buttons one by one. "I'll give you one more chance," the Cowboy grinned. "Where is the KLA base of operations? We know it is somewhere in the hills near Delekara. Where is it?"

"I don't know," the man cried. "I swear it!"

Nimatovic gave the Butcher a nod and said, "We shall see."

———

Sitting under a gnarled tree just off the road, Lek gazed across the lonely green valley as dropped bombs exploded in the distance, like rolling thunder. It was a sound he had grown accustomed to.

Beside Lek sat the serious Haxhi and the elfish Rexhe, their empty stares matching his. Lek played with Jrfete's frizzy hair as she slept, and watched Arta dance with a friend, having seemingly forgotten their terrible situation.

In the past day, their band of refugees had taken on another thirty-five, bringing their number to near one hundred, including a dozen smaller children and infants who rode in the wagons. Along with the horse-pulled wagons and carts, there was now a tractor which pulled a farmer's hay wagon. All were loaded with salvaged belongings, small children, and frail adults.

The tattered convoy was only eight miles from the Macedonian border but had stopped with word that the Serbian police were patrolling the road ahead. Lek had listened as the men discussed going forward. Some believed the police were only there to keep people from coming back into the land, but others weren't so sure.

Sharing what little food the group still had, they had just finished their mid-day meal. Each of the children had eaten their portions, except for Haxhi, who looked at the small crust in his hands hesitantly.

"It's okay. Eat it," Lek prodded.

Haxhi looked at his older brother with guilty eyes.

"Eat it. We all had some," Lek insisted. "It's yours."

"I'll eat it," four-year-old Rexhe offered as he looked at the morsel of bread longingly. "I'm still hungry."

"You're always hungry!" Lek scolded. "It's Haxhi's."

"Mama would give me some," Rexhe said, his lower lip curling down.

Lek looked away.

After raising her head from Lek's lap, Jrfete tiredly looked about. Upon realizing she too was hungry, she started to fuss. Irritated, Lek placed his hand over her mouth to quiet her, but removed it when she protested even more loudly.

Lek looked at the wagon closest to them and the woman sitting beside one of its wheels. The woman, whose name he didn't know, had a baby just a month or two old, and she had shared her milk with Jrfete twice before. Lek eyed her, hoping she would notice.

As Jrfete's crying persisted, the woman wearily turned her eyes to Lek. While the brown-haired young mother wasn't unattractive, the dark rings around her eyes made her look much older than she was. Lek offered an embarrassed smile, and the woman gestured for Jrfete to join her.

After getting to his feet, Lek hoisted his toddler sister in his arms and moved to the tired-eyed mother. "Thank you for helping us," he said, forcing a smile.

The mother nodded, handed her sleeping baby to a woman sitting beside her, and unbuttoned her blouse. Lek sighed and smiled as Jrfete settled into the mother's arms and nursed.

"What of your mother?" the tired-eyed woman asked.

Lek lowered and then shook his head.

"I'm sorry," the mother whispered.

Lek wiped away the tears and glanced back at the other children.

"And your father?"

"He...he went to join the people's army."

The nursing mother looked at him with pity.

"What about your husband?" Lek asked, looking up.

"I don't know. They forced us to leave and took the men away. That was four—no five days ago." She gazed across the fields, her eyes empty of hope. "I don't know where he is—or my son. They took all of them. He's about your age," she said in a painful whisper.

"I'm sorry," Lek replied, trying to be strong.

The mother looked tiredly at Jrfete. "You will need to wean your sister. She's old enough, now."

Lek wiped his eyes. He saw Haxhi eating his bread, having split it with Rexhe.

"I will help you as much as I can," said the tired-eyed woman with more bleakness than tenderness.

"Thank you," Lek replied. "That's very kind."

The tired-eyed woman's gaze moved to the other resting travelers. "We must all be kind now."

———

CHAPTER
TEN

CAPTAIN RICHARDS LEANED back in his chair and yawned before turning the page of his *Car and Driver* magazine. The morning had been filled with PT drills and a company staff meeting before lunch. Now he had most of the afternoon to while away before dinner and their nightly briefing. He casually thumbed through the pages of the magazine, pausing on a comparison test between supercars that cost more than his house. An outburst of laughter caused him to look up as the surrounding officers reacted to a commercial during an NBA basketball game.

"What's up?" asked a blonde-haired, blue-eyed captain.

Richards looked at the captain. "Hey, Owens, how you doing?"

"Jus' dandy," the blue-eyed captain sighed, then nodding to the game on the wall-mounted television asked, "You think the Spurs can pull this one out?"

Richards shrugged as the game resumed. A few more officers entered the lounge. The men ate Skittles and popcorn and drank Cokes as ten tall multi-millionaires dribbled a ball up and down a court half a world away. The Marines spoke of home, of pregnant wives, growing children, and vacations planned for when they finished their deployment. They complained of their pay, of the hard beds on the ship, and the food. It was their world, and they knew no other.

"Did you see this one?" Captain Owens asked as he slapped a six-month-old Sports Illustrated on the table.

Richards glanced at the magazine with an NFL quarterback on the cover. "No. Not yet," he said, returning to his car magazine.

"Does it bother you to think you could be in the NFL making millions right now instead of being stuck on this scrap heap?"

Richards looked up with a smirk. "How do you figure?"

"Lupton told me about ya," Owens grinned.

"Oh? What'd he say?" Richards asked with some intrigue as he glanced at the major across the room.

"That you were a quarterback in college, a pretty good one, until you blew out your knee."

"There were better."

Owens' brow gathered. "How long you play?"

"Two years," Richards said, not looking up.

"How come you didn't go back and play after you got your knee?"

Richards shrugged. "My priorities changed. I decided to concentrate on school and get married."

"And become a Marine," Owens smirked.

"Yep." Richards looked up from his magazine. "So, what's your story?"

"Me? I come from a long line of Marines. My granddad fought on Iwo Jima. I couldn't disappoint. Family expectations. You know. So, here I am, getting my ticket punched and waiting for my twenty. How long you in for?"

"I don't know. It's different from what I expected."

"What did you expect?" Owens laughed.

"I don't know. I guess I was a little idealistic coming in. I always thought there was nothing better than serving and protecting my country. I had a couple of uncles in the Corps and looked up to them. But… after ten years… I don't know if I can last another ten."

"The politics. I hear ya," Owens nodded. "Especially after this one. It's hard enough being yanked around by the politicians at home, but now we're working for a bunch of NATO flunkies. It's not right."

Richards sighed. The prospect of going into Kosovo, even under NATO command, didn't scare him; he and his men had trained long and hard for such missions and would be ready. Richards knew no foreign army on the planet could stand up to the United States. He also understood that distinction had somehow made them the world's peacekeepers. While Richards disagreed with many of his commander-in-chief's views, he realized when it came down to it, his opinions didn't matter. He was paid to follow orders and make sure the 130 men under him did the same. What did matter was his family and what was best for them. "Well, the politics are part of it," Richards said with a bent brow, "but it's hard being gone so much."

"Yeah, it is," Owens nodded. "You're married, right?"

"Yeah."

"Got any kids?"

"One little boy."

Owens was quiet for a moment. Then, with all flippancy gone, he asked, "Do you ever worry about her?"

"My wife? Sure."

"I mean, about her being—you know—faithful. Six months is a long time and...I don't know. I wonder if mine will find someone else while I'm gone. Does that scare you?"

Richards considered the question. The thought had crossed his mind during the sad, lonely times. But it wasn't a matter of fidelity; he knew he would never have to worry about Carolyn that way. He worried about other things. While she had always been supportive, he knew she wasn't happy. The Marine Corps had not only taken them from their Arizona home; but half of the year, it took him away from her. Richards tried to make it up to her when he was home and encouraged her to spend his away time in Arizona with family, but he sometimes felt he was fighting a losing battle, and that his life had taken a turn down a road he couldn't get off. He wondered how much more she could take and what their relationship would be like when he was home for good. "No, I'm not worried about her that way."

Owens studied Richards for a moment, trying to see through his lie, then said, "You're lucky."

Jack Richards forced a smile and went back to his magazine.

———

CHAPTER
ELEVEN

LEK LOOKED over the open farmland as their band of refugees descended a hill. Somewhere ahead of them, beyond the empty fields, clumps of trees, and rolling hills, was the safety of the Macedonian border. With word that the Serbian police had abandoned their checkpoint, the weary travelers walked along the farm road with renewed vigor. They were only a few miles from the border and the camps that could provide them with food, water, and shelter. The increasing sense of liveliness and hope had found its way to the smallest of the travelers, who were scampering alongside the wagon train, playing games and singing songs.

As the caravan grew, it became harder for Lek to keep track of his siblings. Three wagons ahead, his six-year-old sister Arta was holding hands with another girl and happily walking beside the old green tractor as if in a parade. Jrfete was peacefully sleeping in the wagon beside the ring-eyed mother's baby. He wished he could shut out the pain as easily.

Three days had passed since the Serbs had killed Lek's mother. While there were times when his heart didn't ache as much, he doubted his anguish or the terrible image of her lying in the old barn would ever go away. Lek's only solace was that he knew his mother was now in a better place.

While Lek's family wasn't the most religious in his village, they observed the holy days, and his father offered morning and evening prayers. The stories of death, paradise, and the seven heavens now took on special meaning for Lek. He knew his mother was a good woman and would rest in paradise until she was taken to one of the heavens. Lek sighed as he thought of his father. He wondered if he too had gone to the other side. The thought he and his mother were resting in the lovely garden and eating of the heavenly food made Lek's eyes fill with tears.

As a rock bounced off the wagon wheel before him, Lek turned to Haxhi, who was giggling with glee. Lek wiped away his tears and watched Haxhi, six paces ahead, leap off the side of the road to keep the rock in play. He and another boy were keeping pace with the wagon and had created a game, kicking a rock between its wheels as they walked. A part of Lek wanted to play, but he told himself it was their game, and it wouldn't feel right having fun.

Lek turned back toward the wagon trailing behind and found Rexhe riding tall atop a pile of clothing, furniture, and other items that the refugees had added along the way. A thin smile formed on Lek's face as he saw his smallest brother gnawing on a piece of dried lamb.

Lek turned as the tired-eyed mother moved up beside him.

"What's your name?" she asked

"Lek."

"I'm Tatiana," she said with a thin smile. "I've been watching you. You're a very good brother."

Lek shrugged.

"How old are you?"

"Eleven."

"Hmm, I would have guessed older. You remind me of my son. Did I tell you that before?"

Lek nodded.

"He's fifteen," Tatiana said, her words trailing off.

Lek glanced at Tatiana to see if she was crying.

"Your home is Drobesh?" she asked, fighting off emotion.

"Yes."

"Was your father a farmer there?"

"No, he's a mechanic. But we have a garden in the summer."

Tatiana eyed Lek for a moment, then said, "Your mother... Was one of the graves for her?"

Lek glanced at Tatiana and gave a painful nod.

"I'm sorry."

"Me too," Lek sighed.

"Do the other children know?"

Lek stared blankly down the dirt road. "Jrfete—my baby sister—she saw her, but I don't think she understood."

Tatiana made a pained face.

"I think Haxhi knows, but not the others."

"And your father?"

Lek gave a weak shrug.

"I will help you until he comes."

"Thank you." The distant thunder of a jet passing somewhere overhead caused Lek to look up nervously. "What's that?"

"An airplane, I think. NATO planes were in the sky a lot where I come from," Tatiana said, looking up into the clouds.

"Oh," Lek said, somewhat relieved. "Where are you from?"

"I'm from Paralovo."

"Is it nice there?"

"It is a very nice—"

A deafening blast and blinding light rocked the ground and sent a storm of dirt and debris that knocked Lek and those around him off their feet. With the air sucked from his lungs, Lek lay on the ground, stunned and disoriented as the cloud of smoke and dust settled around him. Fighting for air, his ears registering no sound at all. Lek's first sensation was the bitter taste of burned dirt. Slowly, the confused and swirling darkness around him lightened, and his ears began to ring.

After several terrifying seconds, Lek could finally gasp in air, but it burned as it filled his chest. Coughing and hacking, he expelled the cooked air. His next breath also burned, but not as much. As the smoky cloud swirled around him, Lek thought it strange he could feel himself cough but could hear nothing. He rolled on his side, then pushed himself up. Lek saw others through the smoky haze with stunned, dirt-covered faces. Gradually, the haze cleared.

Lek found Tatiana a few feet away in the settling smoke. She was dazed and confused by the blast and holding her head and ears. Lek called out to her but heard only ringing.

Lek turned and searched through the thinning smoke for Haxhi, who had been kicking the rock beside the wagon. As the smoke and dust settled, he found Haxhi kneeling on the road fifteen feet away. His face was contorted in fear, and he looked as though he was crying, but Lek heard only the ringing.

Still sitting in the dirt, Lek's eyes widened when he found the wagon that had been carrying Jrfete lying on its side, its cargo of children, clothing, and furniture scattered across the road. Some of those lying on the ground didn't move, while others looked on with bloody and confused faces.

Frantically searching for his baby sister, Lek's shoulders slumped in relief when he spotted her sitting on the road, seemingly unharmed, screaming without sound. Still dazed, Lek watched as Tatiana climbed to her feet and rushed to her baby, nearly falling over. She carefully gathered him up off the ground and held him close as tears streaked down her dust-covered face.

As the dust cleared, Lek's gaze widened across the terrible scene. He looked back at Jrfete and saw, on the road beside her, another child lying still, his clothes stained with blood. Lek's eyes returned to the screaming Jrfete. She had no such stains. Neither did Haxhi.

When Lek remembered Rexhe sitting high on the wagon behind him, he climbed to his feet. With his legs wobbling beneath him, Lek searched for his youngest brother. Rexhe's wagon wasn't overturned, but the blast had blown its load off the back. Lek gasped at the horse lying on its side, a large, steaming piece of metal protruding from its thick neck.

As the distant ringing faded, muted cries and moaning took its place. Lek wiped away his frightened tears as he frantically searched for Rexhe. He staggered around the dead horse and emptied wagon as he tried to make sense of the carnage and debris before him. Lek gasped, and his eyes widened when he spotted Rexhe staring at him from under a broken chair. Hurriedly pushing the splintered chair aside, Lek looked down at his little brother in horror. Blood covered

Rexhe's face and chest and was seeping from small wounds on the side of his head.

"Rexhe!" Lek cried, hearing only a distant voice.

Rexhe's eyes shifted to his brother with a strange calmness.

Lek instinctively placed his hand on the bleeding and pushed to stop it. Bright red blood welled up between his fingers. When he pressed harder, Rexhe shrieked in pain. Lek heard Rexhe's faint cry, and as his hearing returned, a steady drone filled Lek's head.

An old man, who was himself bleeding, bent down beside the wounded Rexhe. He removed Lek's hand and opened the young boy's shirt, exposing a large wound below his left shoulder that was streaming blood. The man quickly removed his bloody shirt and pressed it against the gaping wound.

Lek's heart sank as the color emptied from his little brother's face. "Rexhe! Rexhe! It's okay! You'll be okay!"

Rexhe's eyes slowly blinked as he looked past his brother, seemingly oblivious to Lek's yells. The four-year-old's eyes gradually moved to Lek with a glazed stare. The old man lifted the blood-soaked shirt, but the wound continued to stream the life-giving substance. He quickly replaced it and pushed harder, causing Rexhe to grimace.

"Rexhe! I have food for you! Some bread!" Lek cried.

"Mama..." the young boy breathed, and then his eyes went still.

Lek sank in anguish as his little brother's small, dust-covered body fell limp. "Rexhe? Rexhe?" There was no answer.

With a sad shake of his head, the old man climbed to his feet and moved to another body. Lek shook Rexhe's limp arm and waited with wide, unblinking eyes, for him to awake.

As the ringing in Lek's head lessened, the moaning and crying around him seemed to grow closer. When Lek pulled his eyes from his lifeless brother, he saw others attending to the wounded and dying. "Arta!" he gasped, remembering his sister.

Numbly pulling himself to his feet, Lek turned toward the front of the convoy. Still dazed and now trembling from shock, he searched the gruesome road for her.

As the smoke and the dust settled, Lek saw the second wagon from the front was obliterated. Ahead of that, bodies and debris were scattered around a blackened twelve-foot-wide and six-foot-deep crater that had swallowed and spit out part of the tractor. Its wagon was reduced to splinters.

Lek had just started toward the smoking crater when a staggering woman knocked him to the ground. Climbing back to his feet, Lek hurried past Jrfete's overturned wagon toward the twisted tractor where Arta had been walking with her friend, but Arta was nowhere to be found. The twisted and mangled and moaning bodies were disorienting to Lek. Most were lying on the ground, some were staggering in confusion, but a thick layer of dust, accentuated by glistening spots of crimson, covered them all. Some of the living had the same stupefied gaze as Lek, while others sobbed inconsolably.

Walking around the crater, which was bordered by scorched earth and wood fragments, Lek studied the blackened faces and charred clothes of those lying around him. He paused and turned when he felt the eyes of a mutilated dead man following him. Lek turned his back on the lifeless eyes and resumed his search.

"Arta!" he yelled, hearing his voice better now. "Arta!" Frantic and exhausted, he turned in a circle. Part of the green tractor had been blown off the road and was lying on its side in a field thirty feet away. It was black now, with small flames licking up from its burning tires. Lek searched for the wagon it had towed, but could find it nowhere.

As Lek continued his stumbling search for Arta; his stunned and disoriented face filled with anguish.

When Lek turned back, he saw a still-dazed Haxhi staring off blankly. Beside him, Jrfete was crying, her eyes closed, her fists clenched, her voice joining the cacophony of pain and misery around them.

Numbed by anguish, Lek continued his search for his lost sister. He would not find her.

———

CHAPTER
TWELVE

JUSUF HASANI'S head bobbed in half-slumber as the dirty green transport truck made its way down the rain-soaked road. A sudden bump jarred Jusuf to consciousness and caused him to look about in confusion as the dark images of his dreams merged with reality. The bitter taste of shame filled Jusuf as he thought of his mother and grandmother he had watched die. *I didn't even try to stop them.* Jusuf's dulled eyes raised to the mash-nosed Serb sitting across from him. He saw the rifle in his lap and hung his head. *They should have killed me.*

As the awful scene replayed in Jusuf's mind, his remorse turned to anger and thoughts of what he should have done. *At one point, there were only two of them. I could have done something. Dirty Harry wouldn't have stood by like a frightened child; he would have acted. He would have gone for the gun instead of letting his mother do it!* Jusuf envisioned himself racing across the room and reaching for the Cowboy's rifle before he could react—grabbing it from the table and rolling across the floor as he shot the Serbs. He could imagine the bullets knocking the bearded Serb through the window and violently shaking the Cowboy to the floor, in Hollywood fashion. He could see his mother and grandmother looking at him proudly for saving their lives.

The loud bang of the truck's back gate dropping open jarred the dreaming Jusuf to reality.

"Get out!"

Jusuf gulped and looked nervously out of the back of the truck as the bald and bearded Misha appeared.

"Get out! You have work!" the mash-nosed Serb ordered as he struck the butt of his rifle against the truck's lowered gate.

Jusuf startled at the noise, and the two men laughed.

"You *are* a little lamb! We have a lamb here!"

Jusuf recognized the bearded Serb as the one who had shot his mother. He hesitated, then slid toward the open end of the truck. When Jusuf spotted two more men with rifles, his mind went to work. He imagined them pulling him out and shooting him on the spot, or beating him to death with their rifles.

"Get out!"

Jusuf jumped at the command.

"Hurry up, *little lamb*!" yelled the mash-nosed Serb. The men laughed.

Jusuf's eyes widened when the Cowboy approached.

"Sir, this one is a lamb," said Misha. "Maybe we are fighting this war all wrong. We just need sheepherders to herd them out!" The four Serbs laughed, but the Cowboy only grinned.

"We shall call him *Qengj*. He's a little lamb!" The Serbs laughed and made baaing sounds. "Get out *Qengj*! Get out!" The mash-nosed man grabbed Jusuf's arm and pulled him out of the truck onto the damp grass. Jusuf landed hard on his shoulder and winced in pain.

"Hey, what's that on your finger?" Misha asked, pointing to Jusuf's ring.

Jusuf didn't move.

Placing a muddy boot on Jusuf's chest, Misha reached down and pulled the ring off Jusuf's finger.

"Is that silver?" the mash-nosed man asked as he moved closer.

"No, it's junk," Misha said, tossing it into the matted grass. He took a step back, then kicked Jusuf in the side. "Get up, Little Lamb!"

"That's enough," growled the Cowboy. "Don't kill him yet. He has work to do."

The soldiers backed away from the curled-up Jusuf as the Cowboy stood over him.

Jusuf looked up into the cold, dark eyes of the man who, he imagined, had killed hundreds.

"Get up," ordered the Cowboy as he looked out over the expansive meadow. "Get up, Little Lamb!"

The trembling dreamer got to his feet, his shoulders slumped, his head down, like a beaten dog.

"Relax, Little Lamb. We're not going to kill you—*yet*," the Cowboy laughed as he removed his hat and ran a dirty hand through his matted hair. "If you're good, you'll live to work another day. If you're bad...you'll kill yourself."

The Serbs laughed.

Raising his head, Jusuf discovered he was standing at the edge of a forest. Before him, a meadow with tall, dewy grass divided the thick woodland that stretched for miles in either direction. Jusuf looked across the hundred-yard meadow to a half a dozen men at work. They wore everyday clothes, dirty and worn. Some were kneeling in the tall grass while others were walking to and from a trailer draped in camouflage netting near the road. Jusuf squinted to see what they were carrying from the trailer. He turned back to the meadow where two men with shovels tiredly digging. It was then he noticed the mounds of dirt that peppered the meadow as if an army of groundhogs had been at work. Behind Jusuf was an empty road and three parked vehicles. The covered troop transport he had arrived in, a green Land Rover, and a truck with a heavy machine-gun drooping from its mount. Turning back to the meadow, Jusuf spotted two militiamen with AK-47s guarding the workers.

"You! Come here!" The Cowboy yelled to an Albanian trudging back to the camouflaged trailer.

The reluctant Albanian, who had long, stringy hair and wore a mismatched suit coat and slacks stained with mud, lowered his head as he approached the militia leader.

"What's your name?" barked the Cowboy.

"Eoda."

"Eoda, this is Little Lamb."

The Serbs laughed.

"He is *your* lamb now. Teach him how to lay mines."

Jusuf looked from the Cowboy to the meadow. His eyes widened at the realization of what they were doing.

"Yes, sir," Eoda replied, his head down.

"You have only today to finish this field," glared the Cowboy.

"Yes, sir," nodded a Serb with a beaked nose and large ears. "They'll have it done. We're a little behind. There was an accident."

"Accident?"

"One of them set off a mine and blew himself up. It's slowed the others."

The Cowboy looked from the foreman to the wide-eyed Jusuf. "Get those mines laid. There is much more that must be done, and we are running out of time. Do you understand?"

"Yes, sir. It will be done," nodded the foreman.

Jusuf struggled with the strange combination of fascination and fear he felt for the Cowboy. He had to remind himself that this fantastic character, who seemed right out of a movie, might kill him. Gulping, Jusuf watched the Cowboy give the meadow a final glance before getting into his Land Rover and starting its engine. The weary Albanian worker gave a quiet sigh as the Cowboy's Land Rover and the truck with the machine gun drove away.

The jab of a rifle barrel caused Jusuf to jump.

"Okay, Little Lamb, it is time for you to work. Eoda will train you." The foreman motioned to the field. "You have a lot of work before you eat again."

Jusuf followed Eoda to the trailer, then watched him go inside a stack of wooden crates. Jusuf's eyes swelled when Eoda carefully removed what looked like a large green frying pan with a lid, but no handle. "What's that? A land mine?"

"Yes. Come with me," replied the middle-aged Eoda, his eyes never leaving the explosive device.

"Should I get one?" Jusuf asked, looking back in the trailer.

"No. I'll show you on this one. They're old Russian mines and extremely dangerous. If you are not careful, you'll end up like Enver."

"Who's Enver?" Jusuf asked, nervously following behind.

"He's over there." Eoda nodded to a dark crater in the grass, thirty yards to their right.

Jusuf grimaced when he noticed a blackened shoe lying near the tossed earth. He gulped as his imagination filled in the graphic details. "What-what happened?"

"He wasn't careful." Eoda stopped at a freshly dug hole.

"It was on purpose," said a skinny man with a shovel. "Enver knew better; he just got tired of living with the fear."

Eoda kneeled and gently laid the mine beside the hole. "It was an accident."

"He knew what would happen," the digger said, looking back at the Serb foreman. "He was tired of waiting."

"What-what do you mean?" Jusuf asked.

The digger jabbed his weathered shovel into the dirt. "It's just a matter of time before we're *all* dead. When our job is done—when there are no more mines—they'll shoot us. It's as simple as that."

"This is Vito," smirked Eoda. "He's an optimist."

"I'm a realist, my friend," Vito nodded, glancing at the foreman. "What's your name?"

"Jusuf."

"Hmm, well, welcome to hell, Jusuf. Prepare to die."

Jusuf looked from the skinny Vito to the landmine and shook his head. "How did it come to this? What have we done to be treated worse than animals?"

"You were born in Kosovo, a Muslim," shrugged Vito.

"No more talking!" yelled the foreman, raising his rifle for emphasis. "Get back to work!"

"I need to teach him," Eoda called back, pointing to Jusuf.

"No one else talking!"

"Can I ask questions?" Jusuf asked with a raised hand.

"Yes, but no one else," replied the foreman.

"I guess that means me," muttered Vito as he pulled up his shovel and moved ahead through the tall grass.

"Bastard," muttered Eoda.

Jusuf eyed the mine. "Is he right? Are they going to kill us?"

Eoda flattened the bottom of the hole with the palm of his hand. "You first—get down here on your knees so I can show you," he said as he glanced at the foreman, still eyeing them from forty yards away.

Jusuf got to his knees. "Are they going to kill us?"

Without looking at Jusuf, Eoda weakly nodded and whispered, "Of course they're going to kill us."

Jusuf gulped.

"It doesn't help talking about it. Now pay attention. You flatten out the hole like this.... Where are you from?" Eoda whispered.

Jusuf shook away the image of the Cowboy putting a gun to his head and firing. "Livoc. I'm from Livoc."

"Are they coming?"

"Who?"

"NATO and the Americans, of course. Are they coming?"

"I don't know. I haven't heard," Jusuf replied as he considered what that might mean.

Eoda sighed. "What happened to you?"

"The militia came. We stayed when everyone else left."

"The smart ones," Eoda replied with a raised brow.

Jusuf nodded sadly. "My grandmother, she is...she *was* a very stubborn woman. I wanted to leave. I tried to tell her." His voice strained with emotion. "They killed her and my parents. I did nothing. I watched," he breathed as a tear rolled down his cheek.

"They're devils," Eoda muttered, wiping sweat from his forehead. "Now, you make a small pocket like this." He pushed his fingers into the soil and scooped out a handful of dirt.

"What's that for?"

"The mine has a trap on the bottom. Anyone who tries to lift it after it has been set—*boom!*"

Jusuf looked over the green cylinder and shook his head. "What are they for? To kill more of us as we leave our homes?"

"No. They're to keep us from coming back—and the Americans from coming in."

"Do you think the Americans will come?" Jusuf asked as he glanced at the guard, watching another group of layers.

"Yes. They'll come and kill these devils. I pray it."

"The Americans are coming," Jusuf repeated, his eyes wide as he envisioned the sky filled with parachutes and wave after wave of American soldiers chasing the evil Serbs from their land.

"And the KLA will fight with them. We'll get our homes back."

Jusuf sighed. "There's not much left to get back."

Eoda paused, turned to Jusuf, then shook his head.

"When will they come?" Jusuf asked.

"I don't know. They should have already come, weeks ago, months ago. I don't know."

"Hurry up over there!" barked the foreman.

"Yes, yes, I'm teaching him," Eoda called back, then muttered, "Bastard." He pointed to a ring pin at the center of the mine. "Next, you remove this pin, then push the dirt back on top, like this."

"But—" Jusuf leaned back as Eoda pushed a layer of rich Balkan soil over the mine. "Won't that set it off?"

"No, it takes ten-fifteen minutes to arm. You just don't want to take too long," Eoda said as he finished burying the device.

Jusuf looked back at the crater. "What happened to him?"

"Enver? I don't know. It might have armed too fast. These mines are old, you know—left over from the Russians. They're for tanks, but they also work for people. That's why we are doing it."

Jusuf followed Eoda back to the trailer.

The sound of a jet passing high above caused the Serb foreman to unsling his rifle and look up.

"Who's the man with the cowboy hat?" Jusuf asked as they reached the half-filled trailer.

Eoda glanced at the foreman, still looking skyward. "Ivan Nimatovic. He's one of the militia commanders."

"Oh." Jusuf followed Eoda out of the trailer, stepping carefully across the meadow. He paused when he noticed something shiny in the grass. It was his ring. Jusuf glanced at the foreman, still searching the sky, then hurried across the matted grass to his discarded ring.

"What are you doing?" Eoda asked, looking back.

"It's my ring," Jusuf whispered as he snatched it from the grass and pushed it into his pocket.

"Is it worth dying for?"

Jusuf looked at the foreman.

"Remember, they're not the only things that can kill you here!"

Jusuf's jaw slackened as he looked at the grass around his feet.

"They're over there, but stay close to me," Eoda said as he started toward the next hole.

Jusuf followed him.

"This Nimatovic, he's an evil man—*the devil's own*," Eoda whispered as he kneeled and laid the mine beside its hole.

"YOU!" yelled the foreman from the edge of the meadow. "Stop talking! He should be trained now. We're behind schedule. You need to work faster!"

Eoda gave an acknowledging wave to the foreman, then turning back to the mine, muttered, "If we go too fast and blow ourselves up, who will put the bombs down then?" He looked up at the gray-faced Jusuf and shrugged. "I guess you're trained now."

Jusuf turned back to the wagon. He swallowed hard as he considered what he must now do. He eyed the blackened crater. In his mind, he saw a landmine exploding in his hands; but strangely, the thought of dying wasn't as terrifying as it once was. He wondered if it was because he was already dead inside.

———

CHAPTER
THIRTEEN

IT HAD BEEN a long day for Jack Richards. Up at 0430 for landing drills, he and his company of Marines loaded aboard a mammoth air-cushioned landing craft known as an LCAC and were sent out of the ship's internal dock into the choppy Adriatic Sea. After a quick trip around the *Kearsarge* and a twenty-minute loiter as other landing craft were repositioned, Delta Company's LCAC returned to the calm of their ship's well deck. Three hours of physical training and combat drills came next, followed by lunch.

After lunch, the enlisted men retired to the innards of the ship, where they resumed their war on boredom. But for Richards, his staff officers, and NCOs, the day was only half done. They still had staff meetings, updates, and situation reports to sit through. In recent days, the energy on board the ship had intensified. To Richards and his men, it was a signal they were about to put their training to use.

Jack Richards was in the middle of a lengthy briefing when his mind began to wander. He glanced at his watch. 1747. He was hungry, but knew the meeting could last another forty-five minutes.

Day after day, the reports were the same, leaving Richards wondering if the air strikes had done any good. He thought it embarrassing that the mightiest military power in the world, using state-of-the-art munitions on a loony dictator and his forces for more than a month, had nothing to show for it. He considered the civilian Serbs paying the price for their crazed leader's acts. They would continue to pay for years, he guessed, just like the Iraqis under Saddam Hussein. He turned his attention back to the monotone colonel.

"As bad as it is in Serbia, conditions inside Kosovo are worse. Reports of thousands of refugees pouring into the camps continue. The conditions in these camps are miserable. It's squalor. Limited toilet facilities, little or no food, little or no water—there are hundreds of thousands living this way. The KLA is continuing their fight against the Serbian VJ and MUP forces, and there are reports of Serbs using Albanians as human shields. There are also reports of Serbian rape campaigns. Ethnic Albanian women and girls are the targets..."

Richards thought of his wife Carolyn and his little boy Drew. He knew nothing like this could ever happen in the United States, but he couldn't help think how terrible it would be for her if it did. Richards thought of Carolyn's soft skin, green eyes, and long, honey-blonde hair. He pushed the image of rape gangs from his mind as he stared past the colonel. He had only been away six weeks, but he missed his wife and son terribly. Richards wished he were with her, holding her hand and listening to her tell of her adventure-filled day with their four-year-old boy. A surge of guilt ran through Richards as he imagined his wife celebrating Drew's birthday alone. He pictured her singing happy birthday to their son by herself, his chubby cheeks blowing out the five candles, and them eating cake in silence. *Drew will get the red bike he asked for and will probably be riding it without training wheels in no time. October. It's not that far off. Only a few months. Then I'll be back home...maybe for good.*

As the briefing continued, Richards wondered about the people of Kosovo. The situation was unquestionably a tragedy, but he didn't like to dwell on such things. He remembered the words of a salty old Marine Colonel, Stanford Bates. Bates had served multiple tours in Vietnam and seen terrible things. He survived that futile and bloody war, both physically and psychologically, by adopting what he called the Bates Creed: *Keep emotion out of it and stay objective.*

Richards could hear Bates's hard command voice in his head: *Gawdawful things happen in war. Most of those things happen to the inno-*

cent ones—the natives who live in the killing fields. That's what war is. Bates had told Richards stories of officers who had never recovered from the horrors of Vietnam. Not just from sending their men to their deaths, but seeing the results of their orders on the innocent locals. *It's impossible not to be affected by the events of war,* Bates told him. *The key is not to let it affect your performance, but to stay professional. There are a hundred men counting on your decisions. For that reason, it is vital—it is* imperative *—you remain professional; not only for your survival but more importantly, for your men's.*

Bates told Richards a Marine captain is a businessman and needs to run his company like a business and not let the people or the emotion of the situation get in the way. *The people.* Richards considered the word. It didn't mean his men; they were his business. It meant the locals, the civilians he'd encounter, in this case, the people of Kosovo.

The change of speakers brought Richards' focus back to the podium and a steely eyed brigadier general. The popular general's high-pitched voice sounded out of place for a warrior and gave him a Patton-like quality. "Progress toward peace is being made, and it's just a matter of time before peacekeeping forces move into Kosovo. The bombing campaign has crippled Milosevic, and it won't be long before his own people take him out."

Richards had heard it all before. He heard it following the Gulf War, and Saddam Hussein was still in power in Iraq.

"The province will be divided into five sectors. We will have the South-East Sector which includes the city of Gnjilane and accompanying area. The Italian, French, German, and British peacekeepers will take the other four sectors.

"Our two biggest concerns right now are anti-personnel mines and the KLA. As soon as this thing's over, there'll be a hundred thousand refugees pouring back into the country. The Serbs have laid a tremendous number of mines. Intelligence reports indicate the region is more mine-rich than anywhere in the world. That creates a problem for us as peacekeepers and a problem for the returning Albanians.

"The second concern is the KLA. They're still mounting a fair resistance against the Serbian forces, and we don't know if we can turn them off. Unless we can control the KLA, it's going to be like putting out a fire while someone's squirting on gasoline. Plan on retaliatory strikes on the Serbs still in Kosovo. They were the minority before this thing got so ugly. The smart ones have already left, but we're going to see the same thing in reverse when the refugees return. That is where you come in."

Richards sat up and readied his pen for note-taking.

"There are a number of small towns and villages in the U.S. sector. Companies will work out of these towns and company commanders will be their government. We expect this mission to last approximately four weeks, at which time you'll transition over to the Army. Until that time, you'll be their mayor, sheriff, judge, and jury, all rolled up into one."

Richards' eyes rose from his notepad to the tall general. He thought again of Colonel Bates' Creed: *Keep emotion out of it and stay objective*. If he could remain detached and not be drawn into the emotions of the tragedy, he would be a better captain and a better Marine, he told himself. He would even be a better mayor.

———

CHAPTER
FOURTEEN

THE OLD WOODEN church door groaned as it opened and a dark-clad soldier entered the dimly lit nave. Flickering candlelight shimmered off his shaved head. The militiaman took a step further, then pointed his AK-47 behind the old door. He scanned the rest of darkened nave. It was empty except for a man in black priestly robes walking in the shadows before the pews. He watched as the figure lit two candles and then disappeared through a transept door to the right. The militiaman turned back to the doorway and nodded.

The clop of cowboy boots resonated through the dark rafters of the old church as Ivan Nimatovic entered. The militiaman waited until the large man had moved past, then pulled the groaning door closed.

The Cowboy's eyes flickered in the candlelight as he looked about the gray stone walls and empty wooden pews of the darkened sanctuary. The musty smell of four-hundred-year-old wood and the oils used to preserve it hung thick around him. After removing his cowboy hat, he wiped the sweat from his glistening forehead with his sleeve. The Cowboy eyed the tall brass crucifix beside the altar. He took a hesitant step closer. The Cowboy gulped when his eyes moved to the altar with the suffering Jesus hanging behind it. Still thirty feet away, the Cowboy knelt, bowed his head, and muttered a quick prayer.

There was a sound, and the Cowboy's eyes shot open. He spun his head. The church was empty.

After getting to his feet, the Cowboy fidgeted with his hat as he eyed the dark confessional. He moved to it, opened its wooden door, and stepped inside. Kneeling, he eyed the small lattice screen to his right and cleared his throat. The sound of the screen sliding open caused him to tighten.

"You are late," came a penetrating voice from the other side of the screen.

"I'm sorry. I was...detained," whispered the Cowboy.

"You have something to report?"

The Cowboy's lips moved without sound. Finally, he said, "Is this a good place for us to talk? In a church?"

"What is the matter, Nimatovic? Don't you believe in your work?"

The Cowboy gulped then said, "I... Of course, I do."

"Tell me of the mines."

"Yes, the mines...they're going as planned."

"That is good. I fear things will soon change. The NATO bombing is taking a terrible toll on Serbia. They are killing our people. Do you understand?"

"Yes, sir."

"Our women. Our children."

The Cowboy's goateed jaw tightened at the thought. "Yes, sir."

"The Americans will come soon. You must speed up the liquidation. We must cleanse the filth from this land before the Americans stop us. Do you understand?"

"Yes."

"Do you have questions?"

The Cowboy's brow tightened. "I...I need more men."

"There are no more. Use what you have. *Do you understand?*"

The Cowboy nodded. "Yes, sir."

"Good. Do not disappoint me."

The screen slid closed with a thud, and the Cowboy released a heavy sigh at the sound of departing footsteps. After getting to his feet, he pushed open the confessional door and turned to the altar, now bathed in candlelight. He saw the dark-robed priest lighting candles. The church was otherwise empty.

After breathing in resolve, the Cowboy started toward the old door.

The priest turned and eyed him from the altar and in a calming voice asked, "Can I help you, my son?"

The Cowboy glanced back at the priest and shook his head. "No father. No one can help me."

———

CHAPTER
FIFTEEN

SALI NOLI STARED BLANKLY at the empty shelves of the small market as he ate from a can of soup; the fresh scar on his cheek was a grim reminder of his first battle. He ran a dirty finger along the inside of the can to clean out the last of it, then tossed the can aside and looked for something else to fill his stomach. Sali gave a disheartened shake of his head as he looked down the empty shelves of the once bustling market. He knew he was lucky to find the can of soup which had rolled under one of the pillaged shelves. While the soup had quieted his hunger, he knew in the coming days finding food would be even harder.

Three days had passed since Sali discovered his wife's grave near his burned-down home. His KLA brigade had gone back into the hills above Vitina to the protection of the forest.

The nights were cold in the hills. Physical discomfort, mixed with the lack of food and clear leadership, had led to discord among the volunteers. Sali knew they would accomplish little with such chaos and discontent. The situation had gotten so bad that half of the brigade left the safety of the hills to search for food. With hunger gnawing at them, Sali and Kuq reasoned it was the right thing to do; dead men couldn't fight.

As Sali leaned back and looked around the end of the aisle. There were others from his brigade scrounging for food. He didn't know them, nor cared to at this point. He was angry and tired and missed his family. Thoughts of what had happened to his wife, children, and home festered in Sali's tormented mind, forming a self-feeding loop of hatred and rage. That there were only two graves, and he had found none of his children among the dead, gave him hope that some of them might still be alive. But that hope weighed heavy on his heart as the fear of what they were going through turned to misery. To Sali, he had two choices. He could abandon the fight and search for his children—an endeavor he believed would only lead to more pain—or he could accept the reality of their loss and exact vengeance.

Sali pushed the tormenting thoughts from his head as he lay on the floor, searching for more food under the shelf. A thin smile formed when he spotted a smashed box of cornmeal in the shadows. After sliding along the mud-tracked floor, he reached under the shelf and teased the box closer with the tips of his dirty fingers until he could grasp it. He sat back up with his prize, tore off the cardboard lid, and looked inside. Sali's brow gathered when he saw the milled grain moving inside the box. *Weevil.* He considered eating the small insects, then dejectedly set the box aside. He wasn't that hungry yet.

"Here, look what I found," said the large-bellied Kuq as he came around the aisle, his rifle forgetfully absent.

Sali turned to his approaching friend, and his jaw slackened at the loaf of bread in his hand.

"Bread!" Kuq whispered, not wanting to share it with everyone. "Can you believe it?"

"Where did you find it?" Sali asked in astonishment.

"It was back in a room; just sitting there waiting for us! Here." Kuq broke the crusted loaf in two and handed half to his friend. "It's a little hard and moldy, but still good," Kuq said as his stubby fingers broke a piece off and pushed it into his mouth.

Sali made a face as he bit into the stale bread.

The two men leaned against the empty shelves and devoured the stale bread. After picking the crumbs from his shirt, Kuq licked his lips and brushed the rest from his beard. "Now we need water."

Sali lay flat on the floor and looked under the shelf for something to wash the bread down. He slid along the floor until he spotted a can in the shadows. Sali pushed closer and reached under the shelf.

"What did you find?" Kuq asked.

After a groan and a curse, a dented can of olives rolled out from under the shelf, but Sali wasn't done digging. "Here, look at this," he grinned as he sat up with his intended prize.

"What is it?"

Sali's brow gathered as he rubbed the dust from the label. "It's baby milk. Soy formula."

Kuq grimaced.

"No, it's good," Sali insisted as he removed his knife. Sitting flat on the floor with his legs extended, he placed the can between his thighs, then put the tip of his knife on the can's top. With a strike of his palm, the blade pierced the can. After rotating the can, he placed the tip of the blade on the opposite side and was about to strike it again when Kuq raised a halting hand.

"Wait. Shouldn't you shake it first?"

Sali looked at the burly man and nodded. He placed a thumb over the puncture, shook the can vigorously, then replaced it between his legs. With another strike of the blade, he made a larger hole. Raising the can to his mouth, Sali took the first drink. After a hard swallow, he handed the can to Kuq.

"How is it?" Kuq grimaced, watching Sali smack his lips.

"Not bad. It could use something, though."

"Vodka?"

"Yes," Sali nodded, passing the can to Kuq.

After taking a drink, Kuq lowered the can and with a soured face said, "It's awful. How old is it?"

"It's not curdled," Sali said, taking the can back.

"It's not good."

Sali took another drink, then shook his head in disgust as he offered the can back to Kuq. "Ugh! Do babies like this?"

"No thanks, I'm not that thirsty," Kuq said, waving off the can.

Sali made a sour face as he finished the can. "There. It wasn't so bad at the bottom," he said before belching.

Kuq laughed. "I told you, you needed to shake it."

Sali chuckled.

"It's good to see you happy again," Kuq nodded.

The grin on Sali's face faded.

Kuq sighed. "Now, what do we do?"

Sali stared bleakly at his rifle, then muttered, "We kill Serbs."

Kuq's brow gathered. He couldn't imagine Sali's pain. He looked at the mud-tracked floor. "Sali, I'm very sorry about your wife and your home. No one should ever find such a thing."

"Mine are not the only ones," Sali seethed. "The Serbs have killed hundreds, thousands, maybe more of our people—butchered them like animals."

"God is good. He will damn their souls," Kuq said with a reassuring nod. "They will pay—"

"No! God will do nothing but watch," Sali fumed. "It is we that will damn their souls—and their bodies! We will do to them what they have done to us!"

"What are you saying, Sali? You want to be an animal? Like them?"

Sali glanced sharply at his friend but said nothing.

"We fight to *defend* our own and our country. If we do the same to them they've done to us, we're no better."

"No, no, that's not true. They did this to us first. Now we must have retribution."

"Revenge," Kuq sighed.

"They must pay for what they've done! They must die and suffer as our people have suffered!"

"You will go to Serbia to do this?"

"No!" Sali barked. "There are plenty of Serbs still in Kosovo! *They* will pay!"

"You will rape their women too?" Kuq asked, his eyes sad and searching.

"YOU HAVE NO IDEA!" Sali roared. "They didn't murder your wife and children! You don't even have a family! You lost nothing!"

Kuq pulled back at the words. He watched the seething Sali for a moment. Then, with uncommon boldness, said, "Hatred will not save our people. We are justified in protecting ourselves, but it is wrong to do what they have done to us."

Sali's head sank in overwhelming grief. "Gentiana...they took her from me," he sobbed. "My children... I did nothing to them. I want my family back. I want my life back."

Kuq reached out a hand to Sali. "I'm sorry, my friend. It's a terrible thing, but your wife, Gentiana, she was a loving woman, yes?"

Sali nodded tearfully; his head still buried in his hands.

"Would she want you to kill others for her? To kill Serbian women and children?"

Sali trembled with emotion.

"God will give justice to those who deserve. For us...we can only defend, or we become like them."

Sali nodded as he considered Kuq's words. He straightened up on the hard floor and embarrassingly wiped away his tears.

"Are you all right?" Kuq asked as another KLA soldier passed by the far end of the aisle.

Sali had just nodded when a warning yell, followed by automatic rifle fire, echoed through the store. The soldier at the end of the aisle cried out and twisted backward as a bullet passed through him, then toppled to the floor.

Sali grabbed his rifle and pushed back against the shelf as wild rounds shattered the glass of an empty freezer across the aisle. His eyes were wide as he watched the wounded soldier wreathing on the ground fifteen feet away.

"My rifle! I left it in the back room!" Kuq gasped as he pushed up from the floor.

"No! Stay down!" Sali warned, pulling Kuq back. "Get his," he said, pointing to the wounded Albanian.

Kuq turned to the now lifeless soldier and saw his rifle on the floor.

The warning cry, "MUP inside the market!" was followed by another burst of automatic rifle fire.

Sali pointed to the dead man's weapon. "Hurry! Get the rifle!"

Kuq was on his hands and knees halfway to the rifle when another burst of automatic rifle fire ripped through the shelves. Kuq flattened on the floor.

"You okay?" Sali gasped, clutching his rifle, his eyes round.

Kuq gave a jittery nod and jumped when bullets punched holes in the shelf just above Sali's head. The thud of a collapsing body on the next aisle over caused Kuq, only a foot from the rifle, to stall in fear. Sali pressed his head against the floor and looked under the shelving. He saw the boots of a Serbian soldier stepping cautiously toward Kuq. Knowing his friend's only chance was to reach the rifle before the Serb rounded the corner, Sali frantically waved him on.

Kuq had just reached the dead man's weapon when a green camouflaged Serb appeared from around the corner with his rifle at the ready. Kuq released his grip on the dead man's rifle when he saw the soldier's angry eyes. He rolled back on his knees and raised his hands in surrender.

Sali quietly turned his rifle as the soldier edged closer to Kuq. He could just see the angry-eyed Serb through the end shelving when the Serb's muzzle lit up with a three-round burst knocking Kuq backward.

"No!" Sali cried as he raised his rifle and squeezed the trigger. His bullets sparked off the shelves and into the Serb, who spun and then dropped to the floor.

After jumping to his feet with his rifle in hand, Sali rushed to his bloodied friend, who was lying motionless, staring at the ceiling. The sound of two more Serbs charging toward him caused Sali to raise his rifle and fire. His frenzied cries were lost in the bark of his AK as a torrent of lead cut through the on-rushing soldiers, knocking them to the floor. Sali held down the trigger, riddling their bodies with bullets. When his magazine emptied and his rifle went quiet, Sali's roar echoed through the store. Sali cursed as he discarded the magazine, replaced it with another, and chambered a round. Panting, he listened for footsteps and voices, for any sound of a Serb, but he heard only the moaning and whimpering of those dying.

With chest heaving and eyes bulging, Sali watched the wounded Serb who had killed Kuq fight for air. The young Serb's eyes rolled in pain as his wheezing lessened. Sali pointed his barrel at the Serb's head and ran his finger along the trigger. He stared into the eyes of the wreathing Serb as if in a trance.

The sound of pounding feet broke the spell as two more soldiers rushed into the store. Sali turned his rifle and released three more bursts, knocking the first Serb backward into the second, who was also hit and falling back. There was a flash to his right from down the aisle and a stabbing pain above his right elbow. The force of the penetrating round spun Sali toward the assailant, and he angrily squeezed his trigger, chasing the Serb with his bullets as he disappeared around the shelves. No longer hearing footsteps, Sali backed up to the dead Kuq and fired through the shelving, emptying half of his magazine.

With his heart pounding, Sali stepped over the still wheezing Serb. He moved to the next aisle and blindly opened fire. He released the trigger when he realized his target was already dead.

Shaking from the firefight, Sali moved back to the wheezing Serb. He was a young man of only twenty, but that didn't matter to Sali. He was an enemy, a murdering Serb. He had killed Kuq and maybe even his wife and children. Sali raised his rifle and fingered the trigger as the young man wheezed.

The sudden thought Kuq might still be alive turned Sali back to his friend. He lowered his rifle and hurried to the red-bearded man sprawled on the floor. Sali shook his head at Kuq's lifeless stare, and he closed his friend's eyes.

With rage building, Sali moved back to the wheezing Serb. He raised his rifle and sighted down the barrel at the man's head. The trembling Serb coughed and sputtered blood. Sali could feel his heart pounding as he ran his finger along the trigger. He wanted to end the man's life. To rob from him what he and his kind had taken—the lives of his family and now his friend—but he couldn't pull the trigger. Sali thought of the Serbs he had killed. They meant nothing to him. Angrily he raised the rifle and fired a round into the ceiling, but when his smoking muzzle returned to the wheezing man's face, he couldn't fire. Sali lowered the rifle in despair. He felt the wound in his arm. Blood had soaked through his shirt and was running down his wrist.

The wounded Serb gasped. When Sali turned back to him, the wheezing had stopped. The Serb's lifeless eyes were fixed on Sali. He moved to see if the eyes followed him, but they remained still. Sali drew in a ragged breath, then slowly released it. He studied the face of the young man who had killed his friend. He knew he was Serbian from his uniform, but from his looks, he could have been an Albanian. Anger, hatred, fear, and sorrow combined to numb the mechanic.

With his chest still rising and falling, Sali stepped away from the dead bodies and rubbed his face in anguish. He released his trembling grip on the rifle, and it clattered to the floor. Sali wiped the tears and sweat from his face as he leaned against the bullet-ridden wall. Sobbing, he slid to the floor and stared at his red-bearded friend. For Kuq, the awful hatred and fighting were over.

———

CHAPTER
SIXTEEN

IT WAS EARLY ENOUGH in the morning that Jusuf couldn't see his breath, but he was sure it was there, billowing in the cold, moist air. The briskness of the morning was enough to keep him awake as the heavy truck bounced along the dark road. Jusuf looked at Eoda, the stringy-haired Albanian who had taught him how to lay the mines, and watched as he stared up at the canvas cover of the old truck. Sitting to the right of Eoda, beside the rear gate of the truck, was a Serb guard. Across from him sat the Serb foreman. Seated opposite Eoda and beside the foreman was the large, sunken-eyed Gani. Next to him sat Ahmet, Stanko, and Vito. Syle, the quietest of the broken-spirited Albanians, sat to Jusuf's left.

In the few days of his forced labor, the dreamer had come to grips with the fact that his life was over. Death was only a formality. Jusuf knew a mishandled mine or a guard's bullet could kill him at any moment. He wanted to believe when that time came he would go to the next life and see his family again, but those beliefs felt far away to him now, beyond his reach. Even Jusuf's imagination had left him. Gone were his fantasies of Clint Eastwood vanquishing the cruel Serbs. Jusuf was tired; tired of working, tired of dreaming, tired of living.

Jusuf looked at his callused hands and blackened fingernails. He had stopped counting at one hundred mines but was sure he had laid twice as many.

While Jusuf's group had been laying the older Russian-made anti-tank and anti-personnel mines, Eoda had told him of the newer plastic mines that were much harder to detect. There were even smaller bombs made to look like toys. They were not buried but laid on the ground for children to find. All of them were intended for the same purpose: killing, maiming, and terrorizing the Albanians.

Jusuf thought of the blackened crater and lone shoe he had seen his first day and wondered how many others would end up that same way. He wondered how many helpless Albanians escaping across the farmland and through the forests would die from mines he had laid. He wondered how many NATO soldiers coming into his country to bring back peace would perish at his hand? Feelings of guilt for what might happen added to his shame for what already had. Jusuf wondered how long he would have to endure it all.

Jusuf looked at the other workers. He knew their names. He knew Gani was a farmer and Vito a shopkeeper from Paralova, but little more.

Jusuf turned to Eoda. Of the slave laborers, he knew him best. As they laid mines, Eoda had whispered terrible stories while the Serb guards watched from a safe distance. The other workers often turned to Eoda for guidance, not only because he had been there the longest but also because of who he used to be.

Before the war, Eoda worked with the police in Southern Kosovo. While the police were now exclusively Serbian, it wasn't always so. At one time, Eoda had the job of community relations and acted as a liaison between the majority Kosovars and the minority ruling class Serbs. When things went bad, the Serbs kept Eoda because of his knowledge and relation skills. When things got worse, they placed him on a labor crew.

With his knowledge, it surprised Eoda the Serbs hadn't already killed him. They had executed many in leadership positions on the spot. All he could figure was they had somehow missed him. He feared he lived because of an oversight.

Eoda's first labor crew numbered fifty, and their job was burying the dead. He would never forget his first mass burial. The image of men and boys lined up and shot in the forest outside of Suva Reka still sickened him. He counted sixty-two on that frosty March morning. Thirty-five of them were boys—children who would never grow up to threaten the Serbs.

Eoda's hate for the Serbs, especially the cruel militia, was bridled only by his fear of what they could do. Three weeks after being placed on the work crew, nine of the workers plotted an uprising. The then second in command of the *Milicja*, Ivan Nimatovic—the Cowboy— oversaw the execution of the prisoners, which reduce the workforce by fifteen. To lessen the chance of another revolt, the Cowboy ordered smaller groups of less than ten.

Eoda still remembered the awful day they forced him to watch the torture and execution of those fifteen. It was medieval and barbaric, but it had the intended effect of instilling fear into the workers. Eoda was smart enough to know that if he continued to work for the Serbs, he would die. From either a mine or an angry Serb's bullet, his fate would be the same. Escape was his only chance for survival, but with that, he also risked death. Eoda knew that if he were to live, he would have to be ready to act when the opportunity arose, and he would have to act swiftly.

Eoda leaned forward just enough to see out the rear of the truck, past the canvas flap whipping about in the predawn air. The Serb guard sat a foot to his right, next to the rear gate of the truck, with his AK-47 resting across his lap, his right hand on its grip.

As Jusuf eyed Eoda, he wondered what he was thinking. He could hear the steady rattle of the half-filled mine trailer they pulled behind them and wondered how many more of the deadly devices they would have to lay. "Where are we going?" Jusuf whispered as he leaned forward to look out the opening.

Eoda shot Jusuf a warning glance. The dreamer sat back and gulped. Jusuf's wary gaze turned to the large-eared Serb foreman who sat across from the other guard at the rear of the truck, his rifle sand- wiched between his legs, its barrel pointing up. The foreman was struggling to stay awake, his head nodding from the early hour.

Eoda's gaze lowered to the deck of the truck as the foreman shook his head and looked over the prisoners. The foreman glanced at the other guard, then scratched his face before his eyes closed again.

Eoda's nod was subtle, but his eyes were steely and brought the prisoners to alert. Jusuf knew what it meant. There were seven of them and only three Serbs, counting the driver. When Eoda nodded to the sleeping foreman, Jusuf's body tightened. Gani, the hulking farmer sitting closest to the foreman, clenched his fists.

Jusuf noticed the foreman's left hand loosely gripped his AK. To use the rifle, he would first have to awaken and then bring his right hand to its trigger. Jusuf knew if they moved quickly, they could over-power the man before he could respond. He had seen it done many times in the movies. The problem was the other guard, who was very much awake and whose finger was on the trigger.

The morning sun was just below the horizon, and the road was dark and empty. Jusuf looked at the balding Ahmet and the thick-faced Stanko; their eyes fixed on Eoda. Jusuf knew the men were about to spring, and he felt a sickly twisting deep inside him as he clutched the bench.

Eoda was about to make his move when the guard beside him shifted in his seat. Eoda kept his head forward and watched the guard out of the corner of his eye. When the irritated guard reached across the truck to awaken the head-bobbing foreman, Eoda lunged sideways and rammed his shoulder into the half-standing guard, knocking him off balance and over the gate. Still clutching his rifle, the guard raised both arms to stop his fall. The pulled-back canvas flap held him for a moment, but Eoda's second shove pushed him through the opening. The guard hooked his leg over the gate to keep from getting sucked under the trailer, but lost hold of the rifle, which bounced off the trail-er's tongue and clattered into the darkness.

The sleeping foreman's eyes shot open the moment Eoda hit the guard, but before he could raise his rifle, Gani grabbed the weapon and smashed his large fist into the foreman's jaw. Though stunned by the blow, the foreman grabbed for the rifle, catching only its sling as Eoda pulled it away. With both men fighting for the weapon, it was Gani's second punch and Stanko's kick that broke the rifle free. The foreman's eyes were rolling when Eoda pulled the rifle back and rammed its butt into his head, causing the foreman to slump in his seat.

Jusuf watched the assault in amazement, and jumped as the guard, hanging from the truck's gate, pulled himself back up. "Watch out!" Jusuf cried, pointing to the clawing guard. Eoda stopped kicking the unconscious foreman and turned to the guard, climbing back into the truck. Eoda cocked the rifle back in his arms and hammered its butt down on the guard's fingers. With a wail drowned out by the truck's diesel engine, the guard fell back onto the tongue of the trailer. Eoda handed the rifle to Jusuf, then grabbed hold of the guard's leg hooked over the gate. He was prying the leg off when the guard's other leg swung up, striking Eoda in the head. The kick knocked him off his feet and pushed Stanko and Gani back into the truck.

Jusuf's eyes were wide as he watched the struggle and grew wider still when the downed foreman moved. He looked at the rifle in his hands, then at the stirring Serb. Breathing in determination, Jusuf raised the rifle and brought it down hard on the foreman's head, sending him back into unconsciousness. Proud of his accomplishment, he looked for approval from the others, but they were all engaged with the thrashing Serb.

Dazed, Eoda got back to his feet and took the AK from Jusuf. With a vicious swing, he hammered the rifle against the guard's knee. The bone-crushing blow left the guard howling in pain. With the face of a wild man, Eoda slammed the rifle butt down even harder. Enjoying the guard's shrieks, Gani grabbed the broken leg and flipped it over the gate. All eyes were on the guard as he rolled back over the tongue and onto the road. A single hand kept him from being pulled under the trailer, his body bouncing on the uneven road. The Serb held on for a moment before he was sucked under the trailer into the darkness. The trailer bounced as it ran over him.

"Now what do we do?" asked a wide-eyed Gani.

"We stop the truck," gasped Stanko.

"How?" asked Eoda.

"Shoot the driver, and we'll stop," shrugged Gani.

"We'll stop, but we'll all be dead when those mines go off!" quipped Stanko.

"Should we jump?" asked Ahmet.

"No, we're going too fast," Eoda said, looking at the passing road beneath them.

"Maybe we just wait until he stops. We have a rifle," said Stanko.

"When we stop, there might be fifty more Serbs! We have to get off now!" insisted Eoda. Turning to the trailer, he said, "Help me disconnect the trailer. When the driver sees it's come loose, he'll stop, and we'll shoot him." The others anxiously nodded as Eoda kneeled and reached for the trailer's hitch. "I can't reach it! Hold my legs!"

Jusuf's jaw slackened when Eoda reached over the truck's gate with Gani and Stanko holding his legs to keep him from falling. In the early dawn light, Jusuf could just see the outline of the passing pine trees lining the road. He feared their chance for escape would be lost with the morning sun.

The sound of the truck's engine straining and a sudden downshift threw Jusuf backward as the truck started up a hill.

"I have it unlocked, but I can't lift it," grunted Eoda.

"Let me try," said Gani, reaching down. Straining and grunting, the large man lifted the tongue from the ball.

"Wait! The chain!" Eoda cried, realizing the safety chain was still attached, but it was too late. The tongue was off the ball and distancing itself from the truck.

Gani pulled the now taught chain with all his strength, but couldn't bring the trailer back. Eoda reached over the gate to help him, but it was no use. The trailer was free, precariously balanced by its load and the grade of the hill they were climbing.

"We have to get out now! If that trailer rolls over, those old mines might go off!" Eoda exclaimed.

"Aren't we going too fast?" fretted Syle.

"No, we're slowing on this hill," replied Eoda. He looked back as the trailer started to weave. "Quickly, we must go now!"

Jusuf's face grew pale at the thought of jumping from the moving truck, but he knew Eoda was right; staying in the truck meant death.

Gani was the first to climb over the gate. Clinging to the truck's canvas cover, he gave the others a hopeful glance, then pushed off from the truck and jumped clear of the trailer. All the workers stood to see what happened to the large farmer, but lost sight of him seconds after he hit the road.

After nodding to the others, Eoda saw Jusuf's hesitation and said, "You have to jump," as he climbed out of the truck with the AK in hand. Eoda leaped clear of the weaving trailer and disappeared into the darkness.

Jusuf was wondering if he could do it when Vito pushed him aside. Jusuf gulped as the scrawny shopkeeper moved to the gate and jumped. Ahmet and Stanko went next, leaving only Jusuf and the panicking Syle.

When the trailer began to bob and weave behind the truck, Jusuf turned to the gray-faced Syle and asked, "You want to go first?" Syle shook his head.

Inching over the gate, Jusuf felt the truck level off and gain speed. His eyes lowered to the dropping tongue, and with a response that surprised him, Jusuf leaped from the truck. His feet were the first to touch before he tumbled head-over-heels. Landing on his stomach, Jusuf slid fifteen feet before stopping.

Dazed from the jarring impact and flesh-shredding slide, Jusuf looked up as the trailer moved across the flat of the hill. He saw Syle indecisively straddling the truck's gate, then the red flick of brake lights with their accompanying squeal. The sudden deceleration toppled Syle back into the truck. An instant later, the trailer, with its tongue sparking along the asphalt road, plowed into the rear of the transport. After bouncing off the back of the truck, the runaway trailer pulled hard to the left. The driver swerved, but the trailer whipped around and threw the truck out of control. Jusuf's eyes widened when the truck flipped on its side and the trailer tumbled behind. The tangled mess had not come to a stop when a chain of deafening explosions ripped open the trailer and lit up the early morning sky.

Although in pain, Jusuf stared wide-eyed at the Hollywood spectacle. It wasn't until pieces of truck and trailer rained down that he realized he wasn't watching a movie. An especially violent explosion caused Jusuf to bury his face. He braced himself, not knowing if he would live or die. While the sound of the continuing blasts seemed more distant in Jusuf's ears, he felt the concussion of each shock wave rolling over him. He was about to get to his feet when a wheel dropped from the sky, hitting the ground and bouncing twice before rolling past him.

Fearing other Serbs might come, Jusuf tried to push up off the road, but his left shoulder gave way, and he collapsed. He listened to the snap and pop of the fire as he gathered his strength. Fighting through the pain and clutching his left arm, Jusuf struggled to his feet. His eyes widened at the burning wreckage scattered across the road and into the trees. He knew he had escaped death by mere seconds.

Jusuf winced in pain as he looked down the road, searching for the others, but he saw only an empty road in the early light.

Stumbling, Jusuf started down the road, his head throbbing, the left side of his face burning, his left arm hanging. He touched his face and recoiled at its rawness.

Staggering down the road, Jusuf stopped when he spotted someone standing in the distance. His first thought was that it was a Serb and he should hide, but then he remembered the others. After rubbing his eyes, Jusuf gasped and then laughed when he realized there were not one, but three men.

Jusuf hobbled closer to a grinning Eoda and a limping Gani.

"Jusuf!" Eoda waved. "You made it! Are you okay?"

Pleased by his bravery, Jusuf gave a grinning, wincing nod.

"What about Syle?" asked Gani.

Jusuf grimaced as he tried to shake his head. "He-he didn't get out in time."

"Oh," was all Gani said as he turned back to the others gathered around a body on the ground.

Jusuf hobbled closer to see who they were attending to.

"Your head," Gani grimaced, seeing Jusuf's bloody wounds. "And your ear. Oh, that doesn't look good at all."

Jusuf felt a flutter in his gut as he realized he hadn't checked his ear. He carefully reached for it.

"No, don't touch it," warned Stanko. "It might fall off."

"My ear might fall off?" Jusuf gasped in horror.

"No, I don't think so," Eoda said after inspecting the tattered carti-lage. "Someone put something around Jusuf's head; he's losing too much blood."

Jusuf felt lightheaded at the words. His knees buckled and his eyes flickered as the morning sky grew darker around him.

———

CHAPTER
SEVENTEEN

JUSUF AWOKE to the sound of men's voices. It took Jusuf some time for him to realize where he was. When the memory of the truck and him leaping from it returned, Jusuf tried to sit up, but he fell back in pain when his left arm gave out.

"Easy," said Eoda, hovering over Jusuf.

"E-Eoda?"

"Yes. How do you feel?"

"Like a giant foot stepped on me."

Eoda laughed.

"Where-where are we?" Jusuf groaned.

"Do you remember jumping from the truck?"

Jusuf painfully nodded.

"Freedom hurts, doesn't it?" joked Eoda.

"Yes, it does," Jusuf grimaced as he tried to sit up.

"Your bleeding has stopped. Do you think you can walk?" Eoda asked with concern.

Jusuf looked down at his legs. "I think so." He felt the bloody undershirt wrapped around his throbbing head.

"You can thank Ahmet for the bandage," Eoda nodded.

"Thank you," Jusuf grunted as Ahmet and Eoda pulled him to his feet.

"Are you okay?" asked Eoda.

"I think so."

"Good. We must get away from here before a patrol comes. Vito's legs are broken, so we'll have to carry him. Gani's ankle is twisted, and I think I broke my wrist; aside from that, we're in pretty good shape," grinned Eoda as he slung the AK-47 over his shoulder.

Jusuf's brow gathered at the broken-legged Vito lying on a stretcher fashioned from coats and tree branches.

"What are you looking at?" snapped Vito.

Jusuf turned to Stanko and Ahmet. They were bruised and battered, but seemed otherwise fine. He looked through the trees and asked, "Where are we?"

"In the hills north of Brezovica," Eoda replied. "We've decided to try for the border. It is maybe twenty kilometers, but we'll be safe there and can get medical help in one of the camps. Can you make it?"

"Yes, I can make it," Jusuf bravely replied.

After looking over the group of battered Kosovars, Eoda pointed to the south and said, "If we're careful and lucky, we'll be in Macedonia for dinner."

"God willing," muttered Gani.

"Yes. God willing," added Jusuf.

It was mid-morning, and though their progress was slow in the mountainous terrain, the six escaped Albanians hoped they were where no Serb patrols would find them. Resting on the crest of a hill, Jusuf surveyed the green valley with lushly carpeted meadows surrounded by forest. Beyond the valley were more hills, and at the base of one of those distant hills were the white walls and red roofs of a village.

Even though Jusuf was bruised and battered and had little strength in his left arm, he was grateful he could walk. He looked at the twisted and broken legs of Vito and saw his pain.

After a few minutes' rest, with the promise of freedom, food, and water beyond the hills, the tattered men resumed their journey and descended into the valley.

As they walked, with pine needles crunching underfoot and birds singing in the top branches, they passed through strips of sunlight and shadows of trees. Stepping into a clearing, Jusuf looked up into the blue sky. Stopping, he raised his head and closed his eyes, soaking in the sun's warmth.

An agonized cry from ahead shattered Jusuf's tranquility. His eyes shot open, and he spun around looking for Serbs, but there were only trees and his fellow travelers twenty yards ahead. The clearing they had entered was forty yards across and joined by a little-used road. As Jusuf continued walking, his eyes were drawn to a twenty-foot by ten-foot area of disturbed soil. Tractor prints crisscrossed the mounded earth, and it looked as though something large had been buried. Not seeing what was so disconcerting, Jusuf continued toward the stalled group standing beside an eight-foot pile of dirt. Flies were buzzing everywhere. Jusuf noticed they were looking into an open pit and slowed when Ahmet turned and vomited. It was then the rank smell of decay reached him. Jusuf breathed through his mouth and braced for what he might see as he crept to the edge of the pit.

Jusuf's eyes widened, and he brought a hand to his mouth as the tangled and decaying bodies of men, women, and children came into view. Not believing his eyes, he looked at the others; Ahmet and Stanko were already turned away. Feeling his stomach rising through his throat, Jusuf stepped back and fell to his knees. He looked back at the mounded earth he had passed and spotted two more in the clearing to his right. Jusuf's face turned gray as he realized they were graves filled with his people. "What happened here?" he gasped, already knowing the answer.

"Why didn't they cover it?" moaned Gani as he stood hunched forward with hands on knees.

"Because they have more to put in," Eoda muttered.

"What do we do now?" asked a sickened Gani as he hobbled away.

"What can we do?" shrugged Eoda, turning from the ghastly pit.

"We can wait and stop the Serbian pigs when they bring more of our people," Jusuf said bravely.

"What makes you think they were alive when they brought them here?" asked Eoda.

Jusuf shrank as he imagined the cruel deaths of those laid before them.

"I worked at one of these places once—when the war first started," Eoda sighed. "They were dead when they brought them—piled in trucks."

"What could we do?" asked Vito, propped up on his stretcher.

"We have the gun," Jusuf said, surprised by his words.

Eoda looked at the Kalashnikov rifle and shook his head. "We would accomplish nothing but kill a few Serbs. And maybe set a few workers free."

"Well, isn't that enough?" asked Ahmet as he ran a distraught hand over his balding head. "Shouldn't we save them if we can?"

"These bodies have been here for days," Eoda said, stepping forward. "It could be days more before they come back—*if* they come back. Vito needs medical help. We all do. We have no food and only the streams to drink from. We need to keep going. We need to get to the border. As long as we're in Kosovo, we're in danger. If we run into a security unit, we're dead."

"What about them?" Gani asked, pointing back to the open pit.

"They're already dead," Stanko grunted.

"We can lay memory to this place and tell others of it," Eoda seethed. "I know of other graves. When the West learns of what the Serbs have done, the entire world will turn against them. That's what we can do. We must live if for no other reason than to tell of what they've done, to bring the Westerners to these graves."

As they swatted away flies, the men eyed one another, each knowing Eoda was right.

After a time, Gani, who was leaning on his walking stick, made a sour face and said, "I can't stand the smell any longer. I'm going."

"Let's go," urged Vito from his stretcher.

Eoda gave the graves and the trees a final look, as if taking a mental picture. He then turned and walked away. With heads low, spirits crushed, and wounds aching, the others followed.

. . .

Two hours passed, but the wounded and weary travelers had said little since leaving the mass graves. Trailing the others through the woodland, with the sun low in the western sky, Jusuf searched each clearing for graves and tried not to think about how many there might be.

As Jusuf walked behind the others, he considered his days in captivity. It seemed odd that only that morning he had resigned himself to death—even hoped for it. But they had escaped the Serbs and now walked with the hope that the border and freedom might be over the next hill or beyond the next clearing. Freedom was before him now, but Jusuf didn't know what that meant. He wondered how he could ever be free after watching the Serbs kill his family. Jusuf's shame was overpowering.

As Jusuf walked, holding his arm and ignoring the throbbing of his head, he thought of Lirie Kelmendi. In his mind, he envisioned her long brown hair shimmering in the sunlight. He wondered what had become of her and her family. Jusuf's heart sank when he remembered the mass grave. *What if? What if she?* He pushed out the terrible thought. *Lirie has been tried enough*, he told himself.

As Jusuf thought about Lirie, his imagination blossomed. He imagined finding her in a camp and her falling in love with him again. They would marry and then go far away to a happy place to live. To a place where people were not hated because of their beliefs or their traditions or their religion. To America. He imagined their wedding and their children. He would drive a car. A big car. A Cadillac. He would own a video store or a movie theater. He would own both.

When Jusuf noticed the trees were thinning, he looked ahead to the others, who had picked up their pace. He hurried to catch up. Jusuf's eyes widened when a meadow filled with tall spring grass and blossoming wildflowers came into view. But it was the road beyond the meadow and the line of men, women, and children walking, pulling carts, and riding in wagons that caused him to gasp with excitement. "Are they?"

"Look! There are people!" Gani exclaimed as he hobbled into the meadow.

"Are they our people?" Jusuf called out.

"They must be! We must be across the border!" cried Ahmet.

"I can't see!" complained Vito.

"I think we made it, my friends!" Eoda exclaimed as he cast the rifle aside and started through the knee-high grass.

Jusuf climbed up on an outcropping of rock to better see across the meadow. His hopeful eyes followed the stream of refugees toward a sea of shimmering white tents in the distance. That there were so many of his people alive, moving toward the camp, left him with a growing sense of hope that his dream of finding Lirie might come true. Jusuf ignored his throbbing head and aching shoulder as he leaped off the rock and hurried to catch up to the others.

"Hurry! We're almost there! We're almost there!" cried Eoda.

"Not so fast!" Vito grumbled as he bounced on the stretcher.

With a smile spanning his face, Eoda pushed through the grassy meadow toward the refugee-filled road only sixty yards away. Gani wasn't far behind, hopping on his good leg. The two carrying Vito did all they could to keep up, but lost their balance as one of the stretcher's arms broke, dropping the broken-legged Vito into the long grass. After gathering up the cursing Vito, Ahmet and Stanko held him between them and hastily continued. Jusuf chased thirty yards behind Eoda and Gani, his good arm waving in jubilation. Eoda was looking back at him when a thunderous blast and torrent of fiery earth engulfed him.

Jusuf's mouth fell open and time seemed to slow as fire and dirt shot into the air and hurled Gani across the bent grass. Jusuf raised his arm and turned his head, but not before a hot wind blew past, and dirt and rocks peppered him.

"Mines!" Stanko cried before disappearing with Ahmet and Vito in an explosion of fire and earth.

The second blast blew Jusuf forward with the sting of a hundred bees. He landed face-first in the twisted grass as a third blast shook the earth beneath him.

Feeling as though he was on fire, Jusuf thrashed about in the long grass, but when Stanko's warning cry registered, Jusuf froze in place, knowing any movement could be his last.

Sprawled on his back, Jusuf's frantic eyes moved to his left and right. There was only long, trampled grass. His mind raced as his ears rang and head throbbed. He coughed as he breathed in thick, gritty air and wondered what would happen next.

After a time, the dust and smoke settled, and the blue sky and passing clouds came into view. Jusuf stared into the sky, afraid to move, and listened as the ringing in his ears was replaced by the sweet whispers of the breeze across the grass. But as his hearing returned, the whispers changed to agonized cries and moans that seemed to encircle him.

Fighting the stabbing pain of shrapnel wounds that peppered his back, Jusuf sat up. As his vision cleared, he could barely see the road over the top of the grass. Some refugees had stopped and were pointing at the smoking meadow. Others, who had already seen too much awfulness, continued walking on to the border camp and safety.

Jusuf coughed and winced as he clutched his injured arm. He gasped when another head raised out of the long grass to his left. Jusuf strained to recognize the face, black as coal and glistening with blood, as white eyes stared at him.

"Stanko?" Jusuf muttered, his voice sounding hollow in his ears. He watched the charred face and white eyes. The blinks grew heavy and long.

After steadying himself with his right arm, Jusuf pushed up out of the matted grass to his feet. Wobbling, he looked over the meadow as he tried to comprehend what had happened. He found the people on the road, fifty yards away, and tried to call out, but his voice was a whimper. Jusuf groaned when he found the blackened pile of tossed earth and crater that had swallowed Eoda. He wondered where his friend was. Jusuf turned to the charred, wreathing head. Stanko was crying out, but no sound escaped his lips.

Minefield. I'm in a minefield, Jusuf reminded himself, trembling at the thought. He took a wobbly step toward Stanko, then stopped. Jusuf looked at the swarming blades of grass around his feet and knew it would be impossible to spot a mine. He looked at his soiled, battered, and bleeding body. He turned back to the forest. It was closer than the road across the meadow, but no safer and farther away from safety and freedom. The dreamer looked at the road and drew in a ragged breath. Closing his eyes, Jusuf stepped forward. Upon realizing he was still alive, he let out a grateful sigh. From the corner of his eye, he noticed the blackened head sink into the grass. "Stanko?"

There was no reply.

"Eoda? Gani?" Jusuf called out weakly. There was only a faint moaning to his left now.

Jusuf's heart was pounding in his head as he eyed the field of death around him. He knew he couldn't stay. He looked across the meadow to the distant road in search of strength and took a step.

Still alive.

Jusuf filled his lungs, he took another. *Still alive.*

Jusuf looked back at the rearmost crater and then ahead to the first that had taken Eoda. He wondered how much farther the mines went. With his heart pounding, Jusuf took another step, and then another. He was only five steps from Eoda's crater, and what he hoped was the end of the minefield, when Gani sat up in the grass to his right, startling Jusuf. After catching his breath, Jusuf watched the dazed Gani look around blankly.

"Gani, are you all right?" Jusuf asked, his voice trembling.

Gani turned back to Jusuf like a frightened child. "Mines! We're in a minefield! Of all of God's curses. We'll never live. We're all dead," he groaned as he buried his head in his hands.

Jusuf took another step. "No, we're not dead! You're still alive! And we are almost out of the mines!"

"How do you know?" Gani groaned.

"I just do!" Jusuf took another step and exhaled. *Still alive.*

Jusuf turned back to the charred and bloodied torso of Stanko. Beside him lay part of Ahmet and the blackened hole that had swallowed him. Vito was several feet away. Jusuf grimaced when he discovered one of Vito's broken legs was blown off at the knee. Jusuf gasped when Vito's eyes opened. Wondering if he was seeing things, Jusuf watched until Vito moved his arm and groaned.

Jusuf turned to the road. It was so close he could see the concerned and frightened expressions of the people as they walked past. He considered leaving Vito. *He'll be dead soon enough. There's nothing I can do,* Jusuf told himself. But his heart sank when he turned back to Vito, reaching out to him.

Jusuf looked back at the road and then at Gani, sitting with his head in his hands. Jusuf's fearful gaze returned to Vito. *I won't leave him. I won't be a coward again!*

Closing his eyes, Jusuf took a step toward the still-reaching Vito, then another. After a third, he was standing in the matted and bloodied grass beside him. Jusuf grimaced at the severed leg.

Thinking back to movies, Jusuf lowered to his knees and searched for something to use as a tourniquet. He knew he had to stop the bleeding or Vito would die. After remembering the shirt around his head, Jusuf pulled it free, wincing as it tore loose from his scabbed flesh. Vito's eyes were hollow and struggled to stay open as Jusuf placed the bloodied shirt around his severed leg. Jusuf cinched it tight, causing both him and Vito to cry out in pain. When Jusuf saw the leg was still bleeding, he shook his head, uncertain of what to do.

Jusuf turned to the road and the passing refugees. "Somebody help us!" A man watching from the road helplessly raised his hands.

"*Please*," Vito gasped.

Jusuf reached again for the tourniquet and re-tied it tighter this time, ignoring the pain in his arm. The bleeding slowed to a drip.

Jusuf looked into Vito's pleading eyes. "I've slowed the bleeding. I'll send someone back for you."

As Jusuf stood, he felt Vito's feeble touch. "Don't leave me. I don't want to die in this field. Take me. *Please*."

Jusuf turned to Gani, who was still looking about blankly. "Gani, help me carry Vito!"

The large Albanian didn't respond.

"Gani, please. Help me carry Vito to the road."

This time Gani's head turned, but he only stared.

Jusuf took a step but paused and closed his eyes when he heard Vito's sobs. Jusuf pushed the image of the dying man from his mind and took another step.

"Please, don't leave me," whimpered Vito.

Jusuf shook his head and wiped away his tears. *I can't leave him. If I'm to die—if I'm to see God and my mother and father today—it won't be as a coward, but as a brave man.*

Turning back to the sobbing shopkeeper, the dreamer reached

down for Vito's hand and pulled him up onto his good shoulder, just as he had seen in countless movies. He then hefted him off the ground. Both cried out in pain. The added weight caused Jusuf's weary legs to shake and buckle, but he somehow straightened them. With the wheezing Vito on his back, Jusuf turned toward the road.

Fighting through the pain, Jusuf took a step. If he were to die, the pain would end, he reasoned, and God would accept him for doing good. Jusuf kept his eyes on the road as he passed the blackened crater that had engulfed Eoda. He turned to the watching Gani and called out, "Come with us. The road isn't far. We're out of the mines."

"Out of the mines?" muttered Gani.

"Yes, you must come," Jusuf grunted, taking two more steps.

Confused and frightened, Gani placed his head in his hands.

Knowing he couldn't both hold Vito and wait for the terrified Gani, Jusuf pressed on. After ten more steps, he shifted the weight of his slipping load and heard a groan from over his shoulder. "Vito, we're almost to the road," Jusuf huffed. "Don't die!"

After ten more paces, he saw stopped refugees watching. With his back buckling, Jusuf pushed on. He took five more steps. Jusuf's heart filled with hope when he spotted men from the road coming to help. Jusuf sank to his knees as the men took the battered Vito from him and placed him on their wagon. Moving to the wagon, their eyes met, and Vito gave a frail, thankful smile.

Jusuf's triumph overpowered his aching body. With his heart pounding and chest heaving at his victory, Jusuf turned back to the deadly meadow and closed his eyes. It wasn't the courage of another that had empowered him. It wasn't the staged bravery of a movie actor or the beckoning calls of those from the road that had spurred him on; it was he alone who had acted. He had survived.

"Here comes another," called out a woman behind Jusuf.

When Jusuf raised his weary head, he saw Gani hobbling through the grass toward him and smiled.

———

CHAPTER
EIGHTEEN

IT HAD BEEN DRIZZLING rain for days. Lek Noli gazed across the camp from under the old oak tree as the occasional drop made its way through the fresh-leafed canopy. Beside him sat his brother Haxhi restlessly watching the steady rain. After a time, the rain slowed to a sprinkle and Haxhi got to his feet.

"Stay close," warned Lek, knowing his brother liked to explore.

Haxhi gave a weak nod and stepped out from under the oak.

Jrfete sat on a muddy blanket, an arm's reach from Lek, drawing in the mud with a stick, her dress soiled, her frizzy hair matted.

Lek's tired eyes were those of a beleaguered parent filled with worry and lost hope, not those of an eleven-year-old boy.

The tattered city of tents and makeshift shelters surrounded Lek, and stretched as far as he could see. While there were hundreds of dripping wet United Nations tents, there were even more shelters fashioned from sheets of plastic hung from the occasional tree or over the spider web of rope and twine. Such shelters provided little protection against the rain and chilly nights, but their occupants were far better off than those forced to sleep in the open fields.

With four days of steady rain, mud was everywhere in the camp, making the already miserable conditions intolerable. Even with the shelter of the tents, it was impossible to keep anything dry. Muddy trails wound through the camp, leading to the Red Cross hospital tent, hand-dug latrines, and the food and water distribution sites. The road that had carried thousands of fleeing Kosovars to the camp passed fifty yards to the north. While dwindling groups of weary refugees continued to arrive on the road each day, it was free of vehicles except for the daily supply trucks, which came from the opposite direction and provided the refugees with not enough food and water.

In the five days since arriving at the camp, Lek and his surviving siblings had only eaten nine times. The meager rations had left them hungry and searching for more. As terrible as things were for the forlorn sojourners, Lek knew from the stories he had overheard, they were far better off than those who had stayed in Kosovo.

Lek sighed as he looked up into the gray sky, which seemed to be falling on them drop by drop. He couldn't tell where the sun was, but it felt like afternoon. They had not eaten yet that day, and Lek's empty stomach groaned and twisted in protest.

Lek watched Jrfete playing with a stick in the mud. He was grateful she wasn't hungry. Tatiana, the tired-eyed mother, had been a godsend, and though her milk was suffering from lack of food, she had satisfied Jrfete.

Jrfete looked up at Lek with a mud-crusted smile. He forced a smile and reached out to wipe the mud from her face, but she turned back to her mud pie before he could do so.

Lek felt a knot deep inside him as he thought of his little brother, Rexhe. He remembered Rexhe's pained face as his life slipped away. *He'll never be hungry again.* Lek's eyes welled with tears as he thought of his sister Arta. He never found her after the blast. Lek remembered her playing with dolls and helping their mother. His old life seemed like a dream now; like a perfect fairy tale.

Wiping at his tears, Lek looked up into the gray sky. He wanted to believe Rexhe and Arta had gone to paradise and were in the lovely garden with their mother. He was sure it was a happy place, unlike the sad, lonely world in which he lived.

Lek wiped his eyes and sighed as he thought of his father. It had been weeks since he had last seen him. *Is he alive? Will he come back for us?* Lek touched for his father's watch under his wet sweatshirt. It no longer worked, but he kept it just the same. He knew his father would ask for it when he returned, and it was Lek's responsibility to keep it safe. *When Father returns.* That thought was Lek's only hope amidst his growing despair.

Lek wiped away his tears and shook his head to chase out the sad thoughts. *"You cannot dwell on the past anymore,"* was what his new friend Tatiana had told him. *"You must live for today and hope for tomorrow."* But to Lek, the present was numbing, and the future held no hope without his father.

The constant cry of a baby, lost in the hundreds of other cries and voices around him, gradually registered with Lek. He turned to their crude plastic shelter, ten feet away, and the tired-eyed mother with her baby. The baby had been crying since the rain had started and was now hoarse with a raspy cough. It had been two days since the distraught and sleepless mother had taken her baby to the aid station at the far end of the camp. The infant had received an antibiotic injection, but sounded worse now.

The shivering Lek pulled his legs up underneath him and tried to force the worry from his mind as the other refugees mill about. From his position under the leaning oak, Lek could see a hundred other wanderers. Most of the faces were familiar to him now. From his daily observation, Lek had noted three types of refugees: those who moved around the camp with stoic faces and feigned purpose, those who wandered with frazzled eyes and slow gaits, and those who sat with empty stares. For that reason, Lek sat up when he noticed a smiling woman walk by. Curious how she could be so cheerful, Lek watched her weave through the tired and rain-soaked refugees. His eyes lowered to the two small children following her. They too, appeared happy. His gaze followed them as they made their way through the crowded neighborhood, moving his head to keep them in sight. Lek's brow gathered when they approached a tent with a man standing before it. The answer to Lek's question came when the woman and man embraced, and the children followed them into the tent. They were a family. A thin smile formed on Lek's face as he understood their joy. But the smile withered as the terrible image of his mother lying in the shadows of the old stone barn returned. *How can they be happy? How can anyone be happy ever again?*

Lek turned away and looked across the camp. Two days before, he could see the edge of the camp in that direction. Now there were a hundred more tents, with people still coming. He wondered how many more would come. He wondered how his father would find them.

With his shivering stopped, Lek watched a little girl wander by, calling for her mother in a voice that had gone too long without an answer. He noticed a man hobbling on a makeshift crutch with one leg gone. He saw an old woman staring up into the draining heavens as if washing the anguish from her face. There were thousands of people, he guessed. Perhaps tens of thousands, but all were strangers.

The low rumble of a diesel engine caused Lek to sit up and turn. It was a sound that had become synonymous with food in the camp. Lek got to his feet and looked to where he had last seen Haxhi chasing another boy around the tents. "Haxhi! Haxhi!"

Haxhi heard both the sound of the truck and his brother's call and rushed back to the tree with all playfulness gone.

"The food truck is here!" Lek exclaimed as a buzz of excitement ran through the camp. "Jrfete, you stay here with Tatiana. Haxhi and I will go for food."

Jrfete stopped stirring the mud and started to cry.

As Lek and Haxhi hurried toward the sound of approaching food, the older brother's eyes grew wide when he spotted two trucks. "There should be plenty of food today!"

As the two brothers approached the large, white Red Cross trucks, the way before them closed as a wave of humanity, rising from the mud and rain-soaked shelters, converged. Lek ran, but the refugees continued to swarm, and soon he could no longer see the trucks.

Lek slowed to a walk and then to a standstill. He listened as the rumble of the diesel engines ceased. There was pushing and shoving as the other hungry refugees fought for a place in the disorganized lines. Lek felt a push from behind and a hand on his shoulder as bodies closed in around him. He pushed forward as the sounds and smells of indigents fighting to survive pressed in on him.

Lek was fighting for position with an older, toothless man when he remembered Haxhi. He tried to turn to be sure his brother was still behind him, but the crowd pushed him forward. With a surge of panic, Lek pushed back and managed half a turn, but he couldn't see past the bodies behind him. "Haxhi!" Lek yelled. The crowd was pushing forward harder now, and Lek couldn't move except with the river of people. Lek grew frantic at the thought of his little brother being trampled in the crowd.

"Haxhi!" Lek yelled, food no longer important. "Haxhi! HAXHI! Go back to the tree!" but Lek's cries were lost in the tumult. Wedged in the pressing crowd, Lek managed to turn around while being pushed toward the trucks, but there was still no sign of his brother, only the ravenous faces of desperate people seeking food.

Panicking, Lek tried to slip to the ground, where he thought he might see his brother, but even that was a fight as the group pushed forward. Lek peered around the bodies and through the legs as he searched for Haxhi. A sudden advance in the line pushed him backward, causing him to lose his balance in the shifting crowd. Falling, Lek knew in a moment the advancing mob would trample him. To his surprise, a large hand grabbed him and pulled him to his feet. Gasping in air, Lek followed the saving hand to a stern-faced man.

"Do you want to be killed? Stay off the ground!" barked the man.

"Thank you," Lek gasped as the man pushed by him. Lek fought to hold his ground as the crowd continued to advance, moving around him toward the trucks. "Haxhi! Haxhi!"

Tears formed as Lek considered the awful possibility of never finding his brother. He continued to yell, his head twisting frantically as the crowd passed him. His eyes darted from face to face as people, whose only thought was providing for their own, pressed forward. Lek no longer cared about food, only finding his brother mattered.

Maybe he went back. Maybe he's back at our tree. Lek pushed out through the rear of the crowd. Winding through the muddy camp, he soon spotted his tree. But as Lek approached, he slowed to a walk and then stopped. Something wasn't right. After studying the surrounding shelters and faces, he realized it wasn't *his* tree.

Turning, Lek scanned the camp for his tree. To his right, on the far side of the camp, were many such trees, but they were together in a clump. His tree stood alone. When Lek looked back at the crowd of people, he felt a gnawing in his gut. He had to find Haxhi.

He hurried back toward the trucks, passing refugees carrying bags of food, bottles of water, and looks of satisfaction. He scolded himself for leaving Haxhi behind.

Exhausted by the emotion, mud, and chaos, Lek's run slowed to a jog and then a walk. After several minutes, he spotted his tree, forty yards away, and ran to it. Lek weaved through people returning with their rations, but Haxhi wasn't there. Neither was Jrfete.

His face pale, his eyes desperate, Lek searched for his toddler sister and brother. "Jrfete! Where are you? Haxhi!" Lek's eyes welled with tears as panic filled him. *Did I lose both of them?* He hurried to Tatiana's shelter, but it was empty. "Where did she go?" Lek called out to the refugees, returning from the trucks with bags of food and bottles of water. "Where's Tatiana? Has anyone seen my little sister?"

No one heard or seemed to care.

"Please!" Lek cried, his hands pulling at his wet hair in desperation. "Where have they gone? They're all I have!"

The boy who had been playing with Haxhi poked his head out from a nearby tent with a half-eaten protein wafer in hand and said, "I think she left."

"Tatiana? Where did she go?" Lek gasped.

"I don't know. She left with her baby."

"Did she take my sister with her?" asked Lek, his eyes round.

The boy shrugged and disappeared inside his tent.

"Have you seen Haxhi?" Lek yelled in desperation, his panicked chest rising and falling.

The boy stuck his head from the tent again and shook it before disappearing back inside.

Lek looked around the crowded camp in disbelief. People were returning to their shelters with food and water, but he could find Jrfete and Haxhi nowhere.

With his chest heaving and his vision blurred by tears, Lek wondered what to do as the crushing sounds of humanity filled his head. He heard the excited chatter of those with food, the moans of those not well, and the wailing of hungry babies. Lek wiped the tears from his face and froze when he heard, amidst all the other noise, the sad cry of a lonely child. "Jrfete?" He turned toward the sound and searched through the crowd. There, fifty feet away, was little Jrfete, her muddy yellow dress wet from the rain, her small hands rubbing her eyes as she cried and stumbled through the mire.

"Jrfete!" Lek exclaimed as he rushed toward her and scooped her up from the mud. "Are you okay?" he asked as she looked at him with puffy eyes and tear-streaked cheeks. "I'm sorry! I'm sorry," Lek cried as he held her tight. "I'll never leave you again! I promise!"

Lek's words and loving embrace calmed the frizzy-haired toddler, and she wrapped her arms around his neck.

Holding Jrfete tight, Lek started toward the relief trucks, hoping to find Haxhi.

With many of the refugees having already received their rations, the way to the trucks was less congested, but still filled with people. As Lek drew closer, his heart still pounding, his eyes searching, he spotted a small boy and came to a stop. "Haxhi!"

The boy turned, but it wasn't his brother.

Lek's heart sank. Jrfete was whimpering and shivering from the rain, but he didn't hear her. Lek looked back at the trucks. *I'll find Haxhi, but I have to get food before it's gone.*

Lek hurried to the supply trucks, past the sad faces of empty-handed refugees. At the trucks, he saw the clean-faced, clean-clothed aid workers who had distributed their rations. Lek looked up at a worker with pleading eyes, but didn't understand his strange words.

Discouraged, wet, and hungry, Lek turned away from the trucks. He shifted the whimpering Jrfete in his tired arms as he looked around the dispersing refugees for Haxhi. There were only despondent Kosovars returning to their tents without food.

Again, there was a strange voice from the truck, this time amplified by a speaker. Lek was straining to understand the foreign tongue when familiar words came over the same speaker. *"Today's rations of food and water are gone. There will be another truck in the morning."*

Lek groaned. It was all too much for an eleven-year-old to bear. He wanted to sit down and cry as the terrible images of the past week came crashing down on him. Lek remembered his father leaving, his mother being beaten and then lying dead. He remembered the terrible noise of the bomb that took Arta and Rexhe. He had nearly lost Jrfete, and now Haxhi was gone. On top of that, they would be hungry for another day. With all hope and strength sapped from him, Lek sank to the muddy ground in despair.

Sitting in the drizzle, clutching his crying sister, Lek sobbed as empty-handed refugees moved past him. The rumble of the food trucks caused Lek to look up in the hopes another might be arriving. But it was only the empty trucks leaving. Lek's head sank again. But his brow gathered when he realized he had seen someone familiar. Lek's head shot up. He wiped the tears from his eyes until the blurry sight of Haxhi, loaded with food and water bottles, became clear. "Haxhi!" Lek cried as he stood up from the muddy ground holding Jrfete.

Haxhi's head spun at the sound of his name, and two large water bottles fell from his bony arms into the mud. Still cradling two food packs, Haxhi gave a little wave and gathered up the spilled bottles.

Lek ran to Haxhi and embraced him. "Where did you go? I thought I lost you!" Lek cried, sandwiching Jrfete between them.

"I was getting food," Haxhi shrugged, his small wet frame shivering.

"You mustn't do that again!" Lek scolded as tears welled in his eyes. "I thought I had lost you!"

"I'm sorry," Haxhi whimpered, his teeth chattering. "I-I got food."

"We have to stay together. I can't lose either of you!"

Haxhi looked at his brother with grave understanding and gave a shivering nod.

————

The large first-aid tent was full of refugees. It reeked of camphor and rubbing alcohol, soiled bandages, and unbathed bodies. The constant flow of patients kept the weary-eyed relief workers and doctors moving at a steady pace. Some of those being attended to were in serious condition, while others had only minor injuries. But in the aftermath of genocide, all benefited from the tender care and reassuring words of the foreign aid workers.

Jusuf winced as the nurse cleaned the wounds on the side of his head. He noticed a short woman sleeping in a cot beside him. When he looked closer and saw gauze wrapped around the stumps of her legs, he felt a flutter of guilt. Jusuf wondered how many would lose their legs or their lives from mines he had laid. He looked away.

Jusuf tried not to flinch when shears cut through his shirt, and the nurse peeled it away from his raw shoulder. After a few minutes, a doctor in a white surgical gown and hat joined the nurse attending to him. Jusuf grimaced as the doctor examined his ear and head wound.

"He needs stitches," the surgeon said with a British accent. "I'll numb him up while you find an interpreter."

Understanding most of the words, Jusuf half-turned and said, "I-I can talk English."

"Nurse," the surgeon called out, "never mind, he speaks English." Turning back to Jusuf, the surgeon asked, "What's your name?"

When Jusuf turned to the doctor, his eyes were drawn to the man's flaming red hair under his surgical cap. It was a hair color Jusuf had only seen in the movies. "My name is Jusuf Hasani," he said, marveling at the doctor's hair.

"Jusuf," the surgeon repeated.

Jusuf painfully nodded.

"Jusuf, you need stitches around your ear, and you have other cuts that need tending to as well. You took a lot of shrapnel—mostly small pieces. Do you understand?"

Jusuf nodded, but he only caught half the words.

"Can you move your left arm?"

"No, it hurting to move," Jusuf said, pointing to his shoulder.

"Okay, we'll get your ear and the shrapnel wounds fixed first and then see about your shoulder. It looks like you broke your collarbone, but we have no imaging here to be sure. You understand? X-rays?"

"Yes," Jusuf said, not really understanding.

"I'll need some six-o nylon," the surgeon said as the nurse handed him a lidocaine-filled syringe. "Jusuf, you'll feel a few little pokes."

Jusuf cringed at the first stick of the needle.

"Jusuf, how did this happen?" asked the surgeon, his tone curious and friendly.

"We were...ah...escap'ded from Serbs. I jump from truck and...ah...fought the road."

"Fought? Oh, you *hit* the road," the surgeon said in realization. "You jumped from a moving truck to escape?"

"Yes, a moving truck."

"There were others?"

"Yes, others."

"So, did you all make it?" the intrigued surgeon asked as he sewed up the wound.

"No, not all. Only three." Jusuf grimaced at the tugging of the suture.

"How many of you were there?"

"Ah...seven. One was kill-ded in truck. The others in mines."

"You crossed a minefield? That's terrible," the surgeon said, focused on his work. "Can you put the light right here?" he asked the assistant. "Good." After trimming the suture, the doctor leaned back and said, "Well, Jusuf, I guess you're lucky to have made it."

Jusuf glanced back at the legless woman. He gulped, and with tear-filled eyes, said, "Yes, I am lucky."

"Do you have family here in the camp?"

"No. No family. They were all kill-ded—by the Serbs," Jusuf said, looking down.

The surgeon sighed and shook his head. "I'm terribly sorry. It must have been terrible for you."

Jusuf sighed. "Yes...it was...not good. Very bad."

"You speak very good English. Have you always lived in Kosovo?"

"Yes, always."

"How did you learn it so well?"

"Movies. I work-ded in cin-e-ma. I watch-ed many, many movies. My favorite is Clint Eastwood."

"Ah, yes. Clint Eastwood—*Go ahead, make my day*," the surgeon said with a smile and a wink at his nurse.

"Yes," Jusuf said with a painful grin. "That is him. He is the *best*."

After digging out a dozen pieces of rock and metal from Jusuf's back, the surgeon paused and said, "Jusuf, would you like to help here? I mean, after you're all better. We could use another interpreter."

"A job?" Jusuf asked, his eyes wide.

"Well, I'm afraid it doesn't pay much—nothing, in fact. But you would have regular meals and a dry place to sleep."

"Yes, I would like that. I would like to be helping, please!"

"Very well then; you have a job."

"Good. Thanks, pard-ner," Jusuf smiled.

"You're quite welcome," the surgeon laughed. "I don't suppose you've ever heard of Humpty Dumpty?"

"Hoomtee?"

"No, I thought not. Well, in any event, you've got the Queen's best here to get you put all back together again so you can go to work. How does that sound?"

The smile that spanned Jusuf's face was answer enough.

———

CHAPTER
NINETEEN

JUSUF WAS STARING across the medical tent when a waving hand caught his attention. It wasn't just any hand, but the hand of the doctor who had given him purpose and hope.

Six days had passed since Jusuf arrived at the camp. His head was still bandaged and arm in a sling, but he was healing both physically and emotionally. Much of that healing had come from his translating for the kind doctors and nurses as they cared for his fellow refugees. Even though Jusuf heard and saw terrible things as he translated, he felt he was making a difference, and that gave him hope.

In his few days of translating, Jusuf's English, although still far from perfect, had improved considerably. While he found the work rewarding, it was also exhausting as he was continually moving from patient to patient in the large but cramped medical tent. A second aid station had been erected to give support to the first, and while the added doctors and personnel made it easier to see more of the suffering, it gave Jusuf even more ground to cover.

As Jusuf approached the British doctor, he smiled and bowed his head in respect.

"Good morning, Jusuf," the red-haired surgeon smiled. "How's your head today?"

"Much better this day," Jusuf said with an even deeper nod.

"And your shoulder?"

"Better, I think," he said, blushing at the attention.

"Good, good. Now Jusuf, can you help me on this chap?" the doctor asked motioning to a craggily faced man sitting behind him. "I'm not sure what his problem is."

Jusuf looked into the wrinkled old man's sunken and glazed eyes. He wore a tattered suit coat and faded slacks that didn't match. Beneath his coat was a white button-down shirt that smelled from weeks of wear. After looking the patient over, Jusuf asked in his native Albanian, "Where are you injured?"

The craggily faced man's gaze shifted to Jusuf, and his eyes blinked dimly as if not understanding the words.

Jusuf tried again. "Are you hurt?"

The old man's eyes came alive, and he pointed to his left leg.

Jusuf looked at the man's leg, which appeared intact, and asked, "What's wrong with your leg?"

The craggily faced man's heavy brow gathered as he looked at the interpreter. "It is gone. It was blown off by a mine."

Remembering all too well the horror of the minefield, Jusuf pulled back and looked again at the man's seemingly normal leg.

"What is it?" the red-haired surgeon asked.

"He says he step on a mine and it blow-ded his leg off."

The surgeon frowned. "Take off his shoes and socks, please."

The nurse did so.

After quickly examining the man's uninjured foot with latex-gloved hands, the surgeon pushed the man's pant leg up to his knee and inspected the leg for wounds. He found nothing but an old scar. Frowning, the doctor checked the other leg. After seeing no sign of injury, the doctor shook his head and asked, "Are you sure he said his leg?"

"Yes," Jusuf nodded. Somewhat confused, he turned back to the old man and asked, "You said your leg?"

The old man stared across the tent.

Frowning, the surgeon removed the old man's coat and shirt, searching for an injury. Finding nothing, he stood back and sighed. "Well, I think he has a problem, but it's not one we can help with. Tell him his legs are fine, but if he would like, he can stay here until we need the bed."

Jusuf nodded and relayed the message. "Sorry," Jusuf shrugged. "He say his leg was gone."

"That's no problem, Jusuf. In war, there are many types of injuries. Some aren't on the outside."

Jusuf nodded, not completely understanding. Turning to the surgeon, he asked, "Doctor, forgive me, but what is your name, please?"

"Westbrook, Gerald Westbrook," the red-haired surgeon replied.

"Westbrook. That is almost like *Eastwood*," Jusuf beamed.

The surgeon chuckled. "Yes, I guess it is at that."

"Where are you come from?"

"England. Manchester, actually. Do you know England?" he asked, motioning for Jusuf to stay with him as he followed his nurse to the next patient.

"No, I have never been to Eng-land, but I watch *The Full Monty*," Jusuf said, wanting to continue their conversation.

Dr. Westbrook laughed. "*The Full Monty*. Yes, well—I believe that was Yorkshire."

Jusuf blushed as he realized how ridiculous his comment must have been. As they moved around another doctor and nurse, they came to a bed with a young woman whose face was buried in a frayed blanket. An older woman stood beside her, comforting her. Jusuf didn't notice the look of surprise on the older woman's face as he approached; his eyes were on the younger woman whose face remained buried. Jusuf's brow gathered when he saw the young woman's long, tousled hair. There was something familiar about it.

As Dr. Westbrook gently lifted the young woman's head to see her face, Jusuf gasped and stepped back. It was Lirie Kelmendi.

Lirie's eyes were vacant and unrecognizing of Jusuf, and they shamefully dropped as she pulled her head back down to her chest.

With eyes round and mouth gaped, Jusuf looked from Lirie to her mother. "You're alive!"

The mother looked at Jusuf, speechless.

Turning back to Lirie, Jusuf's heart sank when he saw her bruised and swollen face. *What happened? What did they do to her?* Jusuf wondered as he eyed the girl he had loved for so long—the one he had dreamed of—the one with the beautiful smile and radiant eyes. *Where's her smile now?*

"Jusuf? Jusuf Hasani?" Lirie's mother cried.

Jusuf nodded, his eyes not leaving Lirie.

"Where are your mother and father? Your grandmother?"

Jusuf's gaze fell to the floor as he tried to swallow his bitter shame. "They're-they're dead. Killed by the Serbs."

The mother's shoulders sank. "All of them?"

Jusuf painfully nodded.

The mother groaned, then angrily spat on the floor.

"What's going on?" Dr. Westbrook asked.

"They live by me in Livoc—my town."

"You know them?" Westbrook asked in amazement.

"Yes, I know them," muttered Jusuf. He turned back to the downcast Lirie, who had yet to acknowledge his presence.

Dr. Westbrook reached for the traumatized Lirie and gently pried her chin from her chest. As he raised her head, he noted the bruises, cuts, and swelling of her face. He swung a small penlight into her dulled eyes, then laid her head back down. "She was beaten. Was she raped as well?" the doctor asked with an unsettled glance at Jusuf.

Jusuf's brow gathered as he considered the question. There were few things worse in the Albanian culture than rape. Death was a better alternative than being violated, especially by a Serb. Jusuf's chest heaved, and his heart ached as he eyed the distant Lirie, her head buried in shame and misery.

"Jusuf, ask them, please," Westbrook prodded.

Jusuf turned to the mother, who was holding her daughter even more tightly now. "What-what happened? What happened to Lirie?"

The mother angrily shook her head.

"The doctor wants to know so he can help her," Jusuf whispered.

The mother looked from the doctor back to Jusuf with pain-filled eyes. "We were traveling through the woods… There were many of us… We thought we were safe together...but we were not. Serbian soldiers came on us and demanded our money. They said if we paid them, it would be better for us. There were maybe twenty of us—seven or eight men. We gave them our money, but they wanted more. They shot two of the men." The mother shook her head, fighting to free the bitter words. "They made us undress. They shot bullets at our feet as we took off our clothes.

"One of our men, he was younger and had his wife and child with him. He said something to them, and they got angry. They shot him over and over. It was awful. His daughter stood and watched. I can still hear her screaming. They just laughed. They thought it was funny." The mother wiped away her tears. "They went through our clothes and took things we had hidden. Then..." The mother pulled her daughter close to her. "They took Lirie and the other younger women. Mentor, my husband, he tried to stop them, but they shot him too," she sobbed, looking at the doctor with pleading eyes. "After that..." The grieving mother tried to free the words, but couldn't. Her mouth trembled as she looked from Jusuf and the red-haired surgeon to her broken daughter.

Jusuf closed his eyes and hung his head.

"Jusuf, you need to tell me what happened," prodded the doctor.

Jusuf's heart was aching, his face tortured when he turned to Dr. Westbrook. Choking on the words, he related the horrific tale as the surgeon and nurse listened with sickened faces.

"We need to examine her," Westbrook sighed. "Ask if she has any other injuries."

Fighting back tears of fury and frustration, Jusuf relayed the question, then said to the doctor, "Mother says she has not speak since it happened. She says she is scare-ded."

Dr. Westbrook eyed Jusuf. "Are you okay?"

Jusuf, his face strained with emotion, gave a jerky nod.

Dr. Westbrook glanced at his nurse and, after a heavy sigh, asked, "What's her name?"

"Her name?"

"Yes."

"Lirie. Lirie Kelmendi," Jusuf managed, fighting the downward corners of his mouth.

"Jusuf, we need to examine Lirie. Will you ask her if we can?"

Jusuf asked the question. Lirie didn't respond, but her mother sadly nodded.

Moving to an empty bed, Dr. Westbrook rolled a portable fabric screen beside Lirie. "Jusuf, privacy is very important right now. You need to stand behind the screen."

Jusuf pulled his eyes from the empty Lirie and moved to the other side of the screen.

"Ask the mother if she will help."

Jusuf did so, then painfully waited.

After several minutes, a solemn Dr. Westbrook pushed the screen aside and moved to the anguishing interpreter. "I need you to tell her mother that physically she's all right. There are no broken bones, just bruises and cuts. But I'm worried about her." He glanced back at the blanketed young woman staring up at the tent ceiling. "How well do you know them?"

Jusuf struggled with the words. They were words he knew but seemed impossible to utter. "I and her..." he exhaled hard as tears filled his eyes, "we wanted to marry before."

Dr. Westbrook pulled back at the revelation. "I'm-I'm so sorry, Jusuf. I had no idea." He studied the devastated interpreter for a long moment, then said, "I'm worried about her—psychologically, I mean. I understand to be raped in your culture is a terrible thing. What am I saying? It's terrible in any culture. Jusuf, she needs your help. Can you —will you help her through this?"

Jusuf swallowed at the request, his mind racing with the terrible knowledge of what had happened to the woman he had loved. He thought of the vicious Serbs who had done this to her. He imagined hunting them down and forever ending their evilness with a bullet from a .44 Magnum, in Dirty Harry fashion. Jusuf wished he were such a man.

"Jusuf. *Jusuf*, will you help her?" Dr. Westbrook prodded, his hand on the interpreter's shoulder.

Anguishing, Jusuf turned away and left the tent. The doctor was asking too much.

Ten minutes passed.

As Jusuf sat outside the hospital tent and stared across the camp, he didn't notice the downcast and hopeless faces around him. He didn't see the line of refugees to his right waiting for water or the row of covered bodies to his left awaiting burial. His thoughts were on Lirie, who had been taken from him once again. His feelings of rage and pain gave way to repulsion, and all he could think of was how the once glowing Lirie was now used and unclean.

"She needs you, Jusuf."

Jusuf looked up at Dr. Westbrook standing beside him.

"She needs you now more than ever."

"What can *I* do?" Jusuf asked, gazing across the camp.

"You can save her life."

"But...she is not clean now," Jusuf muttered, hanging his head.

"That's rubbish!" Dr. Westbrook snapped. "She didn't ask for what happened! You know that! She was attacked. She had no choice." He studied Jusuf for a moment, then added, "God will not hold this against her."

Jusuf considered the doctor's words, then painfully whispered, "I... I don't know what to do."

"You can show her you care—that you're there for her—that she still has worth. You can help remove her feelings of shame and guilt."

Jusuf looked up with red, weepy eyes. "How-how can I do this things?"

"By being there for her."

Jusuf looked back across the camp. He swallowed, then climbed to his feet. With an approving nod, Dr. Westbrook guided the smaller Jusuf back into the hospital tent. As Jusuf approached Lirie's bed, he searched for the feelings he had once had for her, feelings that had endured her marriage to another man and then a shameful divorce. He wondered where those feelings were now.

"She's the same person, you know," Dr. Westbrook said, peering as if into Jusuf's soul. "She's just hidden behind her pain and feelings of guilt. You can help her through that pain. You can bring her back."

Jusuf eyed the expressionless Lirie. Her mother stood huddled over her, gently stroking her hair. Jusuf thought of their time together and the love he had felt for her. *Where is it now?* he wondered. *It's still there,* answered a voice inside his head.

Moving closer, Jusuf reached out a hesitant hand and rested it on her arm, just below her elbow. He watched her face for a response, for a change in her empty stare, but there was none. His hand moved down her arm to her wrist and then her hand. He looked for a reaction, but there was nothing. Jusuf took her hand in his and gently squeezed. "Lirie," he whispered, "it's me, Jusuf. I'm-I'm here with you."

Lirie turned her head away from him.

Jusuf sighed. He glanced back at Westbrook, then with determination whispered, "Lirie, I'm here with you. I will stay with you...forever."

Jusuf searched for any sign of acceptance, but found nothing. He looked up at the mother, whose eyes were red with tears. When Lirie's thumb closed on the back of his hand, Jusuf's face brightened, and he squeezed gently in return. After a few moments, her head still turned away, Lirie's eyes closed, and her face filled with anguish.

Frustrated and confused, Jusuf watched her pained expression and glanced back at the doctor for help. But he turned back to Lirie when he felt her fingers close around his. Afraid to say or do anything, Jusuf could only watch as Lirie cried.

"Lirie, Lirie, I'm so sorry, my baby," sobbed the mother as she held her daughter.

Jusuf's heart ached as Lirie's terrible pain gushed out. He wondered if she would ever be the same. He wondered if he would ever be the same.

———

CHAPTER
TWENTY

Thessaloniki, Greece - 10 June 1999

CAPTAIN JACK RICHARDS was looking at a map when three enormous air-cushioned landing craft rolled off the water and onto Litokhoron Beach. The roar of their fans drowned out the sounds of men and machinery readying for the push into Kosovo and blasted those nearby with sand.

Nestled in the northwestern corner of the Aegean Sea, 200 miles north of Athens, was Thessaloniki. Forty miles north of it was the Macedonian border. But Richards' company and the other Marines of the Twenty-Sixth MEU wouldn't be stopping there. They would continue to Skopje, Macedonia, just twelve miles from the Kosovo border. At Skopje, the Marines would establish a forward staging base before moving into the war-torn province of Kosovo.

After seventy-eight straight days of round-the-clock bombing, the Serbs had finally agreed to NATO's terms and were pulling their forces out of Kosovo. Richards was both surprised and relieved that the NATO strategy had worked. He knew Clinton had stated beforehand there would be no ground forces, but few believed bombing alone would be enough to stop the Serbs. But it did stop them, and except for the two U.S. soldiers killed in an Apache helicopter crash, it had worked without a single NATO casualty. He knew that was more than could be said for the people on the ground. Both Serb and ethnic Albanians had taken the brunt of the air attack, and Richards wondered how they would receive the peacekeepers.

From his briefings, Richards knew the NATO ground forces, designated KFOR, would face four elements: the retreating Serbian military and para-military units which had agreed to be out of the province no later than nineteen June; the remaining Serb civilians, though reports were they were leaving faster than the Serbian Army; the KLA guerrillas who were now retaliating against the retreating Serbs; and the returning refugees who he knew would be none too happy after seeing what was left of their homes and towns. Richards knew it was a tricky and dangerous scenario. They were to be peacekeepers and not warfighters. While their hands were not tied, they had strict rules of engagement and could use deadly force only if necessary.

Nervous energy filled the air as the 130 Marines of Richards' company waited to begin their move inland. Standing in formation on the beach, they watched the air-cushioned transports settle onto the sand as their enormous inner-tube-like air bladders deflated. Hundreds of more Marines started off the transports as helicopter gunships beat low across the sky. To their right, a larger Sea Hawk helicopter settled on the beach, creating its own tornado.

Dressed in the same green woodland camouflage as the rest of the Marines, complete with matching Kevlar helmet and vest and fifty-pound pack, Richards tucked the map into his pocket. Feeling the sting of sand on his face, he pulled his goggles down from his helmet. Richards' gaze moved sixty yards inland to row after row of transports and support vehicles ready for action. He counted fifteen olive green Humvees before losing track. Behind the Humvees were even more vehicles. Large troop transports would carry his men into Kosovo. Not far from the Humvees were a row of LAVs, which looked like tanks but with eight large run-flat tires. Around them, their crews were busily prepping for the journey.

Richards looked farther up the beachhead to dozens of watching civilians cordoned off by policing Marines. Having been involved in dozens of landing exercises, it was easy to forget just how impressive such operations were, and he wasn't surprised there were so many observing. But when a camera flash caught his eye, Richards thought of Somalia. Even though he wasn't part of that operation, he remembered watching on TV the hordes of reporters with flashing cameras welcoming the Marines as they made a "surprise" night landing on that beach. The image still angered him. Hundreds of fully equipped Marines, many of them scared and unsure of what they would find, storming a hostile beach at night only to be greeted by a bunch of skinny-legged, rubber-necked journalists with their camera lights blazing. He wished one had been shot just to make the point that such operations were dangerous and not media events.

"Skipper, the men are assembled and ready to move out," reported First Sergeant Sacamano.

Richards turned to his company, standing at the ready with every eager eye on him. He gazed past to the breaking waves of the green Aegean Sea. There were dozens of more LCACs, some only specs on the horizon, gliding across the water toward the beach. It would take hours for the entire expeditionary force of two thousand to assemble fully, but for Richards and his men, it was time to move out.

"Very well," Richards said, lifting his goggles back onto his helmet. "Corporal Bergerson! Where's Bergerson?" he barked.

"Here Cap'n!" the thin-faced radio man said as he scampered through the loose sand to the captain.

Richards reached for the handset, then turned back toward the Sea Hawk that was powering up. "Corona, this is Domino, over."

"Go ahead Domino."

"We are heading up to the trucks, over."

"Affirmative, Domino. Have a nice trip."

Richards returned the handset, drew in a breath, then said, "Okay, Top, let's load 'em up."

"Aye, aye, Captain." Sacamano turned and yelled, "All right, let's move it out! We board the trucks at the top of the hill!"

With an enthusiastic "OORAH!" the men followed Richards up the sandy slope toward the road. Loaded with packs and gear, the sand gave way under their boots, making two steps for every one.•At the top of the sandy berm, Richards looked back at the lines of trailing Marines as the cool Aegean Sea breeze washed over him.

Richards looked down the beach at the tall, billowing clouds to the east, splitting the rays of sunlight that shimmered on the waves below. He thought it a beautiful coastline despite the gray amphibious vessels, hordes of Marines and machinery, and the smell and racket of diesel engines. He thought of his wife Carolyn and wished he was on a beach somewhere with her.

As Richards topped the hill and reached firm footing, another crowd of spectators came into view. Ignoring them, he repositioned his slung M16 rifle as his First Platoon, marching two abreast with tufts of sand kicking up behind them, moved to the waiting trucks. At their heels was Second Platoon. Richards looked up when two Super Cobra gunships thundered by overhead.

"Where'd these *freak'n* protesters come from?" glared Sacamano from under his helmet.

Richards looked ahead at the cordoned-off area, where a hundred angry spectators waved homemade signs painted in English.

"Oh, that's a good one: *Hitler Clinton, call off your dogs and go home.* It's *Devil Dogs*, ya idiots," scoffed a passing Marine.

"Hey, check out that one," said another Marine. "*Stop killing Serbian babies.* I bet Jane Fonda wrote that one."

Richards gave a *that's enough* look to Sacamano, but not before another Marine yelled, "Hey, these morons can't even spell! It's the United States, not *Untied* States!"

Sacamano spun around and barked, "Secure your mouths! Keep your freak'n pie-holes shut and keep moving to the trucks!"

"I don't wanna hear any more cute comments!" added Second Platoon's lieutenant.

The growl of heavy, low-geared engines coming up behind them caused Richards to look back. Two olive drab Humvees and a LAV-25, with "KFOR" painted on their sides in two-foot dull black letters, plowed past. Richards' eyes caught those of the Marine perched in the second hummer's machine gun turret, his goggles down, one hand on the big .50 cal. machine gun in front of him. The gunner's eyes stayed on the captain for only a moment before moving to the spectators gathered ahead. The mammoth LAV that followed towered over the marching Marines as it motored past, its eight giant wheels belying its weight in the sand. The commander of the LAV, who had the best view of all from his position atop the armored vehicle, gave a casual thumbs-up as he passed, leaving a cloud of fine dust to settle over Richards' Marines.

Richards removed his pack as his Humvee pulled up. After another Marine stowed it in the back, he climbed into the passenger seat and set his rifle between his knees. He felt his insides tighten as he looked out the window at the trucks beside the road loaded with his men. He sighed, offered a quick prayer, then turned to his driver and said, "All right, Corporal, let's go to work."

———

The frightened woman frantically waved her children out of the burning house as smoke rolled through the doorway. She held a wicker basket against her hip filled with things she had saved: clothes, food, a photo album, and a neatly bound bundle of letters. She had scarcely left her smoke-filled home when an angry soldier ripped the basket from her hands. Mortified, the woman dropped to her knees and gathered her belongings. Another soldier kicked the half-filled basket, scattering her possessions into the street.

Flames were visible now, with black smoke billowing from a broken window. The soldier barked hate-filled words and pointed his rifle at her head. The frightened mother abandoned her scattered belongings and clutched her screaming daughter. Horrified and confused, the mother guided her three frightened children down the street, their belongings and home burning.

Sali Noli lowered his rifle when the mother and children disappear around a corner. Bereft of feeling, he cared nothing for the anguish, fear, and bitterness of the fleeing Serbs. It was their turn, he told himself. Their turn to run in the streets. Their turn to watch their homes burn. It was their turn to see their families die.

Sali's eyes narrowed when a man in a heavy sweater with long, wild hair dart out of a building twenty yards up the street. He had a young girl with him and looked up and down the confused street with angry eyes. When Sali spotted the wild-haired Serb's handgun, he raised his rifle to his shoulder and yelled, "Drop your gun!"

The wild-haired man raised his gun to fire.

Sali squeezed his trigger, and the man's hair flew in the air as he dropped to the cobbled street. The girl screamed. Sali moved his sights on the girl. He thought of his children. For too long, he had thought of the terrible things the Serbs might have done to them. His heart was pounding as his finger stroked the trigger. In a heartbeat, he could take his revenge on one of their children. It frustrated him the father wasn't alive to see it. Sali eyed the screaming four-year-old girl. He choked down a swallow and lifted his finger from the trigger.

Sali's eyes narrowed when the grief-stricken wife burst from the building, gathered up her child, and scurried down the street. His bitter gaze followed the fleeing woman as she gave a final glance back at her dead husband and then disappeared behind a burning car.

Sali looked up the street to others of his newly adopted family, the 103rd Brigade of the Kosovo Liberation Army. There were at least a hundred of them; some dressed in olive green uniforms, others in civilian clothes with green armbands. They were strong in numbers now that NATO had turned the tide of the war, and they were eager to deal out misery and cleanse *their* land.

The sound of a jet passing somewhere above elicited jubilant cheers, and the soldiers fired their rifles into the air. They knew it was their Western friends who had turned the Serbians back, and now, with NATO troops soon joining them, they would push the Serbians out of their land back to Serbia and beyond. Once the truth was known, Sali knew the world would hate and punish the Serbs, just like the Nazis. The Serbs would pay for what they had done. That's what Sali told himself. But a part of him feared none of it would make any difference, and in the end, he would be left an empty, broken man, with only the painful memories of a cherished past.

———

CHAPTER
TWENTY-ONE

WITH THE PASSING of United Nations Resolution 1244 and the signing of the Serbian Peace Agreement, the tables had turned on the Serb aggressors. While the treaty was intended to end hostilities in the embattled province, the fighting and killing in Kosovo had not stopped. It was now the Kosovo Liberation Army's turn to hunt the fleeing Serbs.

With word of the treaty, four days before, the Serb militia had quickly disbanded. Most of the cruel invaders had mixed in with the Serb civilians fleeing their homes and were well on their way to Serbia. For them, anonymity was a blessing; they could pass the KLA checkpoints without being discovered. That wasn't the case for the Cowboy, Ivan Nimatovic.

While Nimatovic had been masterful at his craft, dealing death and terror with great flare, his cruel ways and trademark cowboy hat had made him a villain of legendary proportions and the most wanted man in Southern Kosovo. He and his lieutenants, Misha and Kasap, the Butcher, were far too notorious and knew that, if captured by the KLA, death would come slowly.

The Cowboy eyed the Vjel River bridge from the dark shadows of a crumbling wall and cursed under his breath the Albanians blocking his way to safety. He saw the silver glimmer of moonlight off the water and judged the river's width to be over sixty feet. He surveyed the sandbag bunkers on the far side of the old stone bridge. Four days before, Serbs had maned them. Now the KLA held the bridge.

The Cowboy shook his head as he considered the loathsome Albanians who dared call themselves a liberation army. In his mind, they were a pestilence, a blood-sucking parasite on humankind. He thought he and his men should be rewarded for their cleansing efforts; after all, they were doing the will of God, or so he had been told.

The Cowboy thought of his leader, General Zetelica, a man who was still something of a mystery to him. The Cowboy grinned at the name Zetelica, which in English meant "Reaper." For thousands of Albanians, he was just that, The Grim Reaper. The Cowboy wished he had more time and more men. He had done everything the general had asked him, but their work wasn't finished. The pestilence, the scourge, the infestation of cockroaches was still there, and would soon swarm back. He wondered where the general was now. *Nestled in a warm bed somewhere in Belgrade, no doubt.* The thought left the Cowboy bitter, but he didn't mind. Bitterness and hatred fueled him.

"How are we going to get across?" whispered the Butcher.

"We don't need to cross here, do we?" asked the bald and bearded Misha. "Can't we swim across the river downstream? It's dark and we—"

"I cannot swim," the Butcher nervously replied.

"Misha, I'm surprised at you," sneered the Cowboy. "Do you really want to cross over the river that way? To swim away like a frightened woman?"

Misha gulped, and his eyes shifted between the two men. "To live to fight another day," he clarified.

"How about your rifle? How much ammunition will you carry before you sink like a stone?"

Misha didn't answer.

"What do you see at the bridge?" the Cowboy asked.

Misha peered over the crumbling wall. "There's a barricade and our old machine gun nests."

The Cowboy's brow gathered as if in pity. "Look again. Do you see any machine guns?"

"No, just the sandbags and a van blocking the bridge."

"There, you see? They've probably taken the guns to sell, like gypsies," scoffed the Cowboy.

The Butcher laughed.

Misha gulped and looked at his rifle. Unlike the others, he had no death wish. He had a family somewhere across the river and would have joined them days earlier if not for his loyalty to Nimatovic and their failed cause. "We walk across?"

The Cowboy smiled and pushed back his hat. "No, we drive across."

Sali Noli looked out over the river at the rippling reflection of the large, round moon. The image was strangely calming to him and made him think of the summer nights he and his wife laid on a blanket and talked about their children, their dreams, and their love for each other. He yearned for those days.

After shaking away the memories, Sali rested his rifle on a sandbag and looked across the empty bridge toward the darkened town of Vitina. Their commander had told them the Americans were coming to make things right. Not only would they help chase out the Serbs, but they would get the electricity back on. Sali wondered how long it would take for the stores to open and food to be on their shelves. He wondered if life in the towns and villages would ever be the same.

The sound of footsteps caused Sali to turn. Coming from behind the gray cargo van was a man sleepily rubbing his eyes. "You're late," Sali muttered as he gathered up his rifle and the two slings of ammunition he had laid on the sandbags.

"Sorry," mumbled the replacement. "I was having the best dream. I was—"

"*Shh*, do you hear that?" Sali interrupted, hearing an approaching vehicle.

"What?"

"Listen," Sali said as he turned, trying to tell from what direction the sound was coming. He pointed across the bridge into the shadows of the abandoned town. "Someone's coming!"

The man in the adjoining bunker sat up, and the replacement moved behind the sandbags where Sali had been.

As the sound of the engine grew louder, Sali looked for headlights but saw only shadows. He saw the glint of moonlight on a windshield and then the dark mass of a speeding Range Rover bursting from the shadows, its V-8 snarling as it charged the old bridge.

"It's not stopping!" yelled the replacement as he raised his rifle.

Sali hurried to the side of the stone column to get a better shot at the driver and raised his rifle. The onrushing Range Rover smashed through the warning barricade at the far end of the bridge, sending wood and metal fragments in every direction. Sali and the others had just opened fire on the charging vehicle when its lights flashed on.

Dazzled by the brilliant light, Sali fired blindly at the SUV, hitting its windshield, side window, and driver's door before emptying his magazine. The Range Rover swerved and bounced off the bridge's parapet before crashing into the sandbags and blocking van. Sali was reloading his rifle when his replacement fell backward through the light. He ducked behind the stone column as bullets sparked off the van. Sali spun around the column and fired into the smashed SUV, which had crushed the side of the van and pushed it ten feet back.

A flickering headlight played tricks with Sali's eyes as he searched for a target. He looked down the barrel through the steam rising from the SUV's buckled hood. Its windshield was peppered with bullet holes, and a bloodied man sat slumped over the steering wheel. Sali heard the popping of coolant on the hot engine and a man groaning from the other side of the wreckage. He couldn't tell if it was the man from the other sandbag bunker or someone from the wrecked SUV.

Sali spun around at the sound of boots clomping toward him and saw two Albanians coming to help. The screech of an opening door turned Sali back to the Range Rover. He raised his rifle to fire. The light of the moon made a mirror of the rear door window as it pushed open. Sali's sights were trained on the window, his finger on the trigger, when the bloodied man sat up in his driver's seat and feebly raised a handgun. Sali's barrel swung to the bearded driver, and he released three rounds which slumped him sideways. The rapid *tudddah tudddah tudddah* of a machine pistol from the rear door caused Sali to turn his rifle back, but not before he felt the sting of a bullet tearing through his arm. Sali fired as a man darted from behind the door and ran back across the bridge, firing his machine pistol behind him. The *tzing* and spark of bullets bouncing off the crushed van caused Sali to duck. Wincing from the wound in his arm, he raised his rifle and fired at the fleeing shape as it moved in and out of the shadows.

There was a flurry of rifle fire to Sali's left, and the runner fell on the road across the bridge. The men beside him cheered. Sali raised his rifle when another Serb emerged from the far side of the crashed SUV, but the rifle was too heavy for him now and dropped to his side. "There's another one! He's getting away!"

By the time the Albanians spotted the second man running through the shadows, he was already across the river. They fired, but their rounds struck wildly all around him.

"He got away! Where did you learn to shoot?" grumbled a man.

"Same place as you," grunted another.

With flashlights in hand, two Albanians cautiously approached the smoldering wreckage. After shooting the driver again to be sure, they searched the Range Rover as Sali clutched his bleeding arm and watched.

"Hey! Look what I found here!" yelled one of the Albanians as he pulled out of the SUV. All eyes were on the middle-aged soldier who, three months before, had been a plumber or a baker. With a grin befitting a lottery winner, he held up a cowboy hat. "Do you know who we had?"

"Ivan Nimatovic," Sali fumed. "That was him. We had the Cowboy and let him get away!"

———

CHAPTER
TWENTY-TWO

THE RUMBLE of diesel engines caused Lek to hold Jrfete close as the large transports, full of American Marines, approached on the road from the south. Jrfete appeared indifferent to the commotion as Haxhi watched from behind his brother. "Who are they?" Haxhi asked.

"They're the *good* soldiers who will take us back to our homes," Lek replied, hoping the rumors of rescuing Americans were finally coming true. But the sight of the large convoy, with its uniformed men and their guns, was no comfort to Haxhi.

As the Marines rumbled past, tired and hopeless refugees emerged from their dirty shelters. Some pointed in wonder, while others jumped with excitement. A few anxious survivors gathered their things and hurried away, while others followed the trucks.

"They're here!" cried a man, his arms waving, his dirty, unshaven face brimming with hope.

"The Americans have come to save us!" yelled another as the train of vehicles came to a stop fifty yards away.

Haxhi leaned out from behind Lek as the jubilant crowd moved toward the trucks. "They're good men?" Haxhi asked with cautious curiosity.

Lek nodded, his gaze fixed on the massive green trucks and Humvees.

"What are they going to do?"

"They've come to help us—to take us back home!" cried Lek.

"We can go with them?" Haxhi asked, warily eyeing the Marines.

Lek looked at the other refugees as he considered the question. In the weeks since their exodus, Lek had cared well for his brother and sister, but he didn't know how long he could continue. He missed his mother and father, not only for their love and presence but also for their wisdom and direction. Lek no longer wanted to be a parent. He wanted to be a boy again, free of worry and fear. The thought of returning home and finding their father was overpowering.

Lek saw a man and a woman gathering up their belongings, as if preparing to return to Kosovo at that moment. He noticed others had moved closer to see the Americans. Sensing the excitement, Lek turned back to their tree and crude tent. It held their only belongings, a pile of empty water bottles and three coats from the Red Cross. He thought of Tatiana and wondered what had happened to her. It had been a month since she had left with her sick baby. She never returned. Lek missed Tatiana, but like so many others, she was gone.

"We can go home now?" Haxhi asked, feeling the energy.

"Maybe." Lek noticed Jrfete waving her small dirty hand at the Marines. "Let's go closer to see the Americans."

The serious-eyed Haxhi studied the Marines, watching from their trucks. To him, they appeared no different from the murdering Serbs. "You're sure they're good soldiers?"

"Yes," Lek nodded, awed by their presence.

"They'll take us to Papa?" Haxhi asked, his concerns waning.

"Papa," Jrfete repeated as she looked on blankly.

"I hope so," Lek breathed as he watched the Marines.

Stepping out of his Humvee, the first thing Captain Richards noticed was the smell. It was the stagnant stench of squalor and decay. After feeling for the handgun holstered on his Kevlar vest, Richards gazed across the crowd of refugees staring at him. He pushed the lump down his throat and started back along the line of trucks, with his radioman and a lieutenant following.

Richards couldn't help look at the blank-eyed refugees whose clothes were tattered and caked with dried mud. While he had seen similar camps on television, it was a hundred times more heart-wrenching in person, and he felt as though he was looking at a herd of cattle rather than humans. To the rear of the gathering herd was a city of tents, tarps, and plastic sheets. The grass and weeds around the camp were trampled and mired in a brown bed of congealed ooze. He had never seen such wretchedness.

Standing before the grubby and destitute crowd, Richards' normally focused and disciplined mind stalled. He felt the eyes of men, women, and children on him. Some had hopeful smiles; others carried the impassive stares of protracted misery. Although they didn't appear to be starving, their soiled clothes hung loosely. He thought of the pictures of the emaciated prisoners from the German concentration camps at the end of World War II and wondered how such things could still happen. The thought that these were the lucky ones, the survivors, made him wonder about the rest. *How can man still do this to his neighbor? A thousand years ago, yes...maybe even a hundred, but in a civilized world?*

Richards turned away from the troubling scene, took a deep breath, and reminded himself of his mentor's advice. *This is someone else's problem. I can't fix this.*

Richards surveyed the trucks that held his men. The canvas tops were rolled back, allowing air to circulate past the seated Marines. He saw their cheerless faces as they looked over the camp. Their mouths gaped and eyes filled with dismay. Many of them were just out of high school and had never seen such a thing; others were veterans, but still bothered by the miserableness of it all. They had seen pictures on the ship but weren't ready for it.

Richards shook his head and refocused on his task. He knew the camp wasn't his responsibility. He had other things to worry about, like the still feuding armies across the border. But being the first of the NATO forces to arrive at the camp made it his duty to talk to whoever was in charge and then report back to Command.

Spotting the large Red Cross tents, Richards started toward them, with his escorts following. The crowd of refugees parted before him as though he were a majestic prince.

As Richards moved through the crowd, his eyes were drawn to a thin, dirty-faced boy with two smaller children standing beside him. The frizzy-haired toddler reminded him of his niece back home. He wondered if they were orphans. *I'm just here to keep the peace,* he told himself as he kept walking.

Jusuf Hasani stood on his toes to see the arriving Marines. He had been filled with child-like excitement since hearing they were coming. The Americans had ended the war and would now make it safe to go home.

There was a time when Jusuf couldn't have imagined returning to Kosovo. There was nothing for him there. His family was gone. But in the last few days, that had all changed.

In his weeks of interpreting at the tent hospital, Jusuf had thought much about his life.

While a part of Jusuf still wanted to travel far away to America, something deep inside him called him back to the land of his family. His *gjyshe* was gone, but he hoped her home was still there. It could be his and Lirie's home. Her mother could even join them, he thought. Jusuf still had dreams of America—of driving a Cadillac and owning a video store, but those dreams could wait. There was still healing to be done.

Lirie had made great strides since he had found her in a traumatic stupor, but she still had days where all she could do was curl up and cry. Jusuf wanted to understand her pain. He tried to comfort her. He tried to show her he still loved her, but she wasn't ready.

Jusuf's hatred for the Serbs had not diminished in his days of sanctuary. If anything, it had grown. He no longer hated them for murdering his family—they no longer felt pain and were in a far better place. Jusuf hated the Serbs for the ongoing pain they caused Lirie. He wanted to punish them—not by killing them or raping their women, but by defying them. He would return to Kosovo and bring thousands with him.

A faint smile formed on Jusuf's bearded face as he looked at the strong, brave Marines approaching. Just like the cavalry in the old Western movies he so loved, they had finally come to the rescue, and he felt a growing strength in their presence.

"Jusuf, you're sure you want to go back?" asked Dr. Westbrook as they walked toward the Marines. "We can still use you here."

Jusuf turned to the red-haired surgeon who had become his friend and said, "Yes, please. I want to go back. This way, I can make place for Lirie and me." He and the doctor had talked extensively about the traumatized woman, and how she would need special understanding to come through her ordeal. Jusuf wasn't sure he understood all the reasons, but he agreed he would be patient, and that meant her staying in the camp for a time. Besides, Kosovo wasn't safe yet. There were rumors of Serbs refusing to leave. The Marines would make it safe, and then he would come back for her.

As Richards continued toward the large Red Cross tents, he watched as a contingent of clean-clothed and fresh-faced aid workers moved toward him. The captain came to a stop before the welcoming aid workers, removed his Kevlar helmet, and nodded.

"Hello," greeted a long-bearded man with a French accent.

"Captain Jack Richards, Delta Company, US Marines."

The Frenchman shook Richards' hand. "Lucas Grosjean, at your service. How was your journey, Captain? Any problems?"

"No, sir." Richards' dark eyes were calm and confident.

The Frenchman waited for more of a reply from the American then said, "Yes, well, I'm sorry I have no tea to offer you. We have only bad coffee."

Richards' brow gathered. He looked from the Frenchman out across the camp and said, "No. Thank you. I'm fine. Sir, I need to report back to Command on your situation. Any problems here?"

The Frenchman shrugged and, with a kind smile, said, "Captain, we have thirty thousand problems here."

Richards gave an understanding nod. "Are you supplied regularly? Is everything okay that way?"

"Yes, Captain."

"Is there anything we can help with?" Richards asked, hoping he wouldn't regret his offer.

"No, Captain, other than make it safe for these people to go back to their homes. That is, if their homes are still there."

"That's what we're going to do."

"Will you be traveling through then? Across the border?"

"Yes, sir," Richards nodded.

"Is it true you Americans have the southeastern sector?"

"Yes."

"Where are you going? What town?" Grosjean asked.

Richards eyed the Frenchman and the group standing around him, then said, "Vitina."

"Vitina?" came a voice from behind the Frenchman.

Richards looked around Grosjean to a slender man in his mid-twenties with dark, messy hair and a beard. It was evident from his mismatched, worn, and tattered clothes he wasn't an aid worker.

"I know Vitina!" Jusuf exclaimed.

"Who's he?" Richards asked, surprised at Jusuf's English.

"He's an interpreter," the Frenchman replied.

"Yes," Jusuf eagerly nodded. "I know the area and can help you!"

"We've already got an interpreter."

"Is he from Kosovo?" Jusuf boldly asked.

Richards' eyes narrowed, and he turned to the lieutenant beside him. "What's his name? Petrovic?"

"Yes, sir," the lieutenant nodded, "He's in Gunderson's outfit."

"Get him up here."

"Aye, sir." The radioman raised his hand piece. "The captain needs Petrovic. Repeat; send up Petrovic!"

The Frenchman stepped closer. "Captain, Jusuf would be a superb choice. Not only can he translate, but he can also act as a guide."

Richards eyed the bearded interpreter, then glanced at the red-haired surgeon beside him. The sound of boots stomping across the field caused Richards to glance back.

"Corporal Petrovic reporting, sir," gasped a breathless Marine with a large, Roman nose.

"Petrovic, you speak Serbian *and* Albanian. Right?" Richards glared as he pushed a stick of Juicy Fruit into his mouth.

Petrovic gulped. "Sir, yes, sir. Well...mostly Serbian, sir. My father was from Yug—"

"That's fine," Richards interrupted, "but you can speak Albanian too, right?"

"Well...yes, sir."

Richards' impatient eyes bore into the corporal.

"Excuse me," Jusuf interrupted. "Does he know the *Lindja-dru* dialect?"

Richards turned back to Jusuf. "What?"

"The *Lindja-dru* dialect. It is very common where you are going," Jusuf shrugged.

Richards sighed. *I don't have time for this. Linguistics should have it figured out already.* "Petrovic!" he yelled, standing beside him.

"Yes, sir?"

"Well, do you know it?"

"Sir?"

Richards flexed his jaw muscles. "Do you know it?" he barked. "The —" he turned back to Jusuf.

"*Lindja-dru* dialect," Jusuf gulped.

Corporal Petrovic looked at the interpreter, then back to the captain. "Ah...I'm not sure, sir."

Richards tiredly shook his head and turned back to Jusuf. "You're familiar with that area?"

"Yes, yes! My home is Livoc; not ten kilometers from there!"

"All right," Richards said, turning back to the convoy. "Get your gear. We're leaving in ten minutes."

Jusuf bowed his head in appreciation and tried to hide his grin as he turned back to the Red Cross tents.

"I'll help you with your things," Dr. Westbrook said as he followed Jusuf to the tent. "By the way, I've never heard of that dialect. What did you call it?"

"*Lindja-dru*?" Jusuf smirked.

"Yes, what is it?"

"It means *Eastwood*."

"Eastwood," the doctor repeated, not understanding the joke.

"Yes. He just *made my day.*"

"Oh, *Eastwood!*"

Jusuf had already packed what little he had, hoping he could return to his home with the Marines, but he wasn't sure how he would say goodbye to Lirie. A part of him wanted to stay, but he knew Lirie's mother would care well for her. He also recognized the sooner the Americans made his town safe, the sooner he could come back for her.

"What's happening?" Lirie's mother asked, trying to see the line of trucks from their tent.

"It's the Americans," Jusuf huffed, having run from the hospital tent. "They will chase the devil Serbs out of our land for good!" Jusuf's brow gathered as he kneeled before Lirie curled on a blanket. Her beautiful dark eyes turned to him, and a hint of a smile formed. Carefully considering his words, Jusuf tenderly said, "Dearest, I have to leave you now."

Lirie's smile faded, and her gaze turned away from Jusuf.

"No-no, remember?" Jusuf quickly added. "Remember what I told you? I'm going to make our home ready. For you and me. I'll get it cleaned up and then come back for you. Then you and I...we can marry and be together...just like we've always wanted."

Lirie closed her eyes and pushed a tear down her cheek.

The sound of diesel engines starting caused Jusuf's heart to sink.

Lirie's mother sat beside her and said, "I will care for her, but you must promise to come back for us."

"*I promise,*" Jusuf whispered, his eyes welling with tears. He turned back to Lirie, ran a gentle hand along her cheek, and then exited the tent.

———

CHAPTER
TWENTY-THREE

THE ROAD SEEMED to stretch on forever to Lek, who had lost sight of the Americans and their trucks hours before. He wondered if he would ever see them again. While Jrfete wanted to walk, her little legs grew tired quickly, forcing Lek to carry her more often than not. He didn't mind as she was light, but after four hours, his arms were quivering from fatigue. Haxhi now looked less than eager to make the trek home and dragged twenty feet behind, carrying a half-filled water bottle.

The road was littered with trash from the tens of thousands of refugees who had fled to safety. Now, that same road would lead Lek and his siblings back. They were not alone on the road; the line of returning refugees stretched in front and behind Lek as far as he could see. Tired of the crowds, squalor, and wretchedness of the camp, thousands of the refugees picked up what little they had and followed the convoy of Marines. Lek heard some in the camp warn it was too soon and too dangerous to return, but he was desperate to find his father, and the risks meant nothing to him. But with miles behind them and miles still ahead, Lek wondered if he had made the right choice.

Even though there were hundreds on the road, there were thousands who had remained in the camp. For many, leaving the camp wasn't an option; their bodies and minds were too frail for the journey home. Others had no interest in returning to a land that offered nothing but burned-out dwellings and mass family graves. To them, the camps were a gateway to a new world, away from the Serbian hate and terrible memories.

Such memories tormented Lek. Night after night, awful dreams of his dead mother and the murderous Serbs darkened his mind. So did nightmares of his father fighting and dying to protect them.

Lek knew Haxhi had bad dreams too. Nearly every night, his little brother's whimpering cries awakened him. Lek often welcomed such interruptions to his sleep as they pulled him from his own nightmares. But occasionally, Lek had happy dreams of a carefree childhood filled with the smiles of his loving mother. He didn't want those dreams to end.

Jrfete seemed to be the only one unbothered. She slept soundly at night, despite Haxhi's whimpering, and was usually in good spirits during the day. Lek didn't know why she was so happy and sometimes wished he could change places with her.

Cresting a hill, Lek's brow gathered, and his heart sank. Ahead of them was a blackened crater and scattered debris with the burned-out remains of a tractor pushed off the road. He knew exactly where they were.

"What's that?" Haxhi asked as he caught up to the stalled Lek.

Lek tried to speak, but he couldn't. Tears filled his eyes as he looked up into the afternoon sky and wondered why the plane had bombed them. He didn't know it was a mistakenly dropped NATO bomb that had killed his little brother Rexhe and vaporized Arta. He blamed it on the evil Serbs. They were the killers, he thought.

Lek's sad gaze moved to the side of the road where the sixty bodies were buried. Fresh summer grass made the graves harder to see.

Haxhi held his brother's hand, and Jrfete sat on the road as they stared into the charred crater. Lek paid no attention to the bits of wagons, clothing, and belongings strewn across the field.

After a time, Lek wiped at his tears, picked up the unaware Jrfete, and walked around the crater, hoping to forget once again.

With arms and head hanging, Haxhi followed.

It was late afternoon. A gentle breeze moved across the lonely road, giving the weary travelers some relief from the summer heat.

"How much farther?" Haxhi whined, his shadow stretching across the littered road.

Lek turned back to his brother. He watched as weary travelers dragged off the road and sank into the grass. A part of Lek wanted to stop, but he needed to find their father.

Feeling his grip on Jrfete failing, Lek set his sister down and stretched his back. "Look," he said, pointing. "Do you see that hill? That's the old fortress on top, the one Papa used to take us to. Do you remember?"

Haxhi gave a tired nod.

"We're very close now. Vitina is on the other side of those hills. Just a few more hours, I think," Lek said.

"I'm tired and hungry," Haxhi moaned as he slumped on the road in a heap.

"We need to keep going," Lek urged.

Haxhi's weary gaze moved up the road that had carried the American Marines hours earlier. "I don't want to."

"I didn't tell you about my dream," Lek said, eyeing his brother. Seeing no response, Lek continued. "I dreamed about Mama."

Haxhi lowered his head.

"No, it was a good dream; she was happy! She looked lovely and was glad to see us!"

"What did she say?" Haxhi asked, raising his head.

"I...I don't remember."

Haxhi sighed and dropped his chin.

"Oh, she said we must be strong and be happy and find Papa," Lek said, watching for Haxhi's response.

"You made that up," muttered Haxhi.

"No, I didn't," frowned Lek.

An old man carrying a basket of belongings on his back walk by, his eyes vacant, his frail body wavering. Jrfete, who had been hanging on Lek's leg, glanced up at her brother and then followed the old man.

Lek glanced at the sun hanging low in the sky and sighed. "Haxhi, we need to keep going."

"Why?"

"To go home."

"Will Papa be there?" Haxhi asked, eyeing his brother.

"Papa!" Jrfete squealed as she pointed to the frail old man.

Lek turned to his little sister in surprise, thinking she had spotted their father, but his hopeful eyes dimmed as he realized she was only repeating Haxhi's words. Lek sighed. "Maybe. Maybe he's there waiting for us right now."

Haxhi looked up the road.

"It won't be dark for a while. Let's keep walking. We'll stop for the night soon; that way we won't have so far to go tomorrow."

Haxhi moaned as he climbed to his feet. He looked from Lek to the road and then started forward in long, dramatic strides.

When Haxhi trudged past, Lek picked up Jrfete and continued walking.

———

CHAPTER
TWENTY-FOUR

THE CROSSING into Kosovo was uneventful for Captain Richards and the rest of his company. There was no border standoff, no barricades or even protesters to discourage their entry; there was only an eight-wheeled LAV with five Recon Marines standing guard at an abandoned guardhouse. The lack of resistance didn't change the fact that Richards and his men were now in harm's way, and sharp-eyed Marines manned the large-caliber machine guns atop each Humvee.

The truth of the matter was, Richards didn't know what to expect. He didn't know if he would face resistance from withdrawing Serbs and advancing Albanians or if they would be welcomed as liberating heroes. Even the so-called intelligence experts were unsure of what they would encounter. Richards knew he and his men had to be ready for any contingency. They had trained hard and would be, but the rolling green hills and the peaceful fields filled with wildflowers made it difficult to imagine the bleakness and devastation that lay ahead.

With his window down, the sweet summer breeze reminded Richards of a trip to California he and his wife had taken years before. Richards remembered the sun glinting off the ocean and the wind in their hair as they drove the convertible along Highway One. He thought of them playing in the surf and walking along the beach. He wished he were with her.

The jolt of the Humvee hitting a bump brought Richards back. He reached up and adjusted his Kevlar helmet and looked out the dirty windshield. The flowering fields were gone. Before him now were the scorched remains of a village. There was blood-red graffiti on broken walls in words he didn't understand. A skinny dog scurried between burned-out houses and several blackened cars pushed off the road. The screech of the Humvee's brakes brought Richards' eyes forward. Before them, a LAV was parked off the road and a Marine, with his rifle across his chest, stood with a raised halting hand.

Richards' eyes moved from an old girder bridge, where several heavily padded Marines were working, to the approaching sergeant, who gave an acknowledging nod and said, "Captain, EOD is clearing the bridge. They shouldn't be too much longer, but they need you to stay back until they're finished."

Richards nodded, and the wary-eyed sergeant stepped away. Richards raised a hand over his shoulder, and the radioman seated behind him handed Richards the radio hand piece.

"So much for being in Vitina for dinner," Richards muttered before keying the mic. "All units, all units, be advised, we've got EOD clearing this bridge ahead. We'll have chow here, then continue when they're done." After handing the hand piece back, Richards looked at the driver and said, "See if you can find a pizza place."

The driver glanced at the burned-out buildings, then back to the captain, surprised by his humor. "Aye, sir."

After scraping the bottom of his beef teriyaki MRE, Richards put the last bite in his mouth and leaned against the Humvee. While not particularly fond of the packaged meals, he thought this one was good. He was glad he didn't live in the old days of the tin can C-rations and stale crackers. After taking a swig from his canteen, he opened his dessert pack. The lemon poppyseed pound cake was a little hard, but still good. Richards thought everything tasted good in the field, and as the vocabulary-challenged Sergeant Sacamano liked to say, "Even a can of *petroglyphed* Spam will hit the spot if you're hungry enough."

Richards' gaze moved from the bridge being cleared of explosives to the blackened trees along the river and the adjacent burned-out buildings. He wondered what it was like for those who lived there and were forced to leave their homes. A change in the breeze brought the bitter fetor of dwellings turned to ash. The captain wrinkled his nose. He had seen the burned villages on CNN, but it was different in real life. Surreally different. It reminded him of a ghost town he had visited back home: sad, lonely, and yet peaceful. He doubted Vitina would be the same.

In Richards' final intel briefing, he was told of a particularly vicious Serb militia group which had operated in and around Vitina and was responsible for much of the death and destruction in the area. His orders as the new "sheriff" in town were to establish a presence in Vitina, stop the Albanians from retaliating, and round up any remaining Serb militia. To help, he was given a list of individuals accused of crimes against humanity. The two-page list was filled with blurred images, vague descriptions, and a few fanciful titles like The Butcher and The Cowboy. While the thought of capturing such characters intrigued Richards, he doubted any would stay this far south.

Richards listened as two of his lieutenants, standing just off the road, quizzed their new bearded interpreter. Richards wasn't sure what to think about Jusuf or why he was so eager to come with them. But then he thought of the horrible refugee camp; he would have jumped at the chance to get out too.

As the two Marines questioned Jusuf, Richards surveyed the bridge where the explosive ordnance disposal team appeared to be finishing their work. He wondered how many more delays there would be before reaching their destination. It was no surprise the Serbs had rigged the bridge with explosives. Whether it was to destroy the bridge or kill anyone trying to cross, it didn't matter. The thought that the Serbs responsible for it were likely long gone gave Richards some reassurance, but he couldn't help think about the returning Albanians and the threats they would face. Mines were a sad part of war—a dismembering and deadly part—which most often targeted civilians and could linger for years. That there were hundreds of suspected minefields in the province, with potentially hundreds of mines in each, meant that if the returning refugees ventured off the roads, there would be casualties. Since keeping the Albanians out wasn't an option, the only way to prevent the inevitable tragedies was to post signs and mark the fields until the mines could be properly disposed of, a process that would take months if not years.

Richards was half listening as Jusuf told of his harrowing escape to freedom. When Jusuf said something about a cowboy, the captain took notice and moved closer. "What's your name again?"

The new interpreter straightened up. "Jusuf."

"We're just calling him Joe," announced a lieutenant.

"Did you say something about a cowboy?" Richards asked, remembering his war crimes list.

Jusuf nodded, uncertain of what to say.

"You know the Cowboy? You've seen him?" Richards persisted.

"Yes, Captain. He...ah...he..." Jusuf struggled with the words as his throat tightened.

"Yes?" Richards asked, all business.

"He kill-ded my family," Jusuf finally managed.

"Right in front of him," grimaced the lieutenant.

"I'm sorry," Richards said as almost an afterthought. "You can identify him? If we run across him?"

Jusuf gulped and nodded. "I will never forgot his face."

Richards eyed Jusuf, then placed a comforting hand on the interpreter's shoulder and said, "Good. Thank you for helping us."

The uncertainty in Jusuf's face brightened to a thankful smile.

"Bridge is clear, Cap'n," announced Sergeant Sacamano as the EOD Hummer started up and motored across.

Richards gave Sacamano a nod, and the sergeant raised his hands to his mouth and barked, "All right, people! Let's go, let's go! Let's load 'em up and move 'em out!"

Jusuf couldn't help but grin at the words he had heard in so many Westerns. Without thinking, he raised his arm and gave a, "Yee-hah!"

Richards scowled at the new interpreter, but when he turned forward, he had a hint of a grin. Approaching his Humvee, Richards paused, then said, "I want Mr. Jusuf riding with me."

"Aye, sir."

Jusuf's eyes widened.

. . .

Less than a mile outside of Vitina, Captain Richards sat half-turned as he questioned Jusuf in the rear seat. They were discussing the general politics of the region, with the minority Serbs having all the power and influence, when the driver pointed ahead and said, "Cap'n, we've got some locals up here. Looks like they wanna surrender or something."

Richards looked ahead to two women standing beside an old man holding a white flag. He told his driver to stop, then pushed open his door and motioned for Jusuf to follow. He glanced back at the Marine perched atop the Humvee clutching the mounted machine-gun, gave a don't-get-me-killed nod, and then moved toward the locals with Jusuf following.

"Watch those houses to the right," came from the second Humvee, causing its gunner to direct his .50 caliber machine gun in their direction.

Richards pushed a stick of Juicy Fruit gum into his mouth as he approached the flag-waving civilians. Whether they were Serb or Albanian, he didn't know. The old man had deep, sunken eyes which twitched nervously. As the captain approached, the old man lowered his white flag; a stick with a rag tied to its end. One woman was older, short and heavy-set. The other was thin and looked angry. The women wore scarves over their heads and looked as though they could be mother and daughter. Richards listened as the women spoke in harsh, demanding voices and made wild hand gestures while the old man fidgeted.

"What are they saying?" Richards asked, not taking his eyes off them.

Ten feet back, Jusuf gulped and addressed them in Serbian.

"Get up here! You're my interpreter!" barked the captain.

Jusuf moved to Richards' side as the older woman glared at him.

Her reaction surprised Richards, and he wondered what Jusuf had said.

"They say KLA burn their homes and kill their people. They want you to stop them."

Richards' eyes widened. "They're Serbs?"

"Yes," Jusuf nodded, unable to hide his pleasure at the turn of events.

Richards sighed. "Get Petrovic up here!"

A moment later, the breathless Marine interpreter was standing beside Richards and Jusuf. "Yes, Captain?"

Richards nodded to the three villagers. "They're Serbs. I want to make sure everything is translated correctly. Understood?"

"Aye, sir," Petrovic replied, still catching his breath.

Richards turned to Jusuf and said, "Tell them we will stop the fighting, but they will have to help." Richards eyed the villagers, but when Jusuf didn't forward his message, he snapped, "Tell them!"

"Yes, sir," Jusuf said, as if coming out of a trance.

Richards watched the old woman eye the interpreter as he relayed the message. She shook her head as the angry daughter spoke.

"She say, you Americans are on the wrong side. That you should keep my people out, not make them go," Jusuf relayed, his mouth twisting at the bitterness of the words.

"You're telling them exactly what I said, right?" Richards asked with a bent brow.

Jusuf's nod was short and jerky.

"Petrovic?"

"He said it right, sir."

"Tell them we're not on *anyone's* side, and we're not making anyone leave. We're here to keep the peace. We'll stop the KLA from fighting, but the Serbs have to stop fighting too. They must want to live in peace."

Jusuf relayed the message.

The flag-bearing man's eyes lowered to the road. He and the skinny woman turned and walked away. The scolding old mother snapped her wrist in a wave as if to say *go away—leave us alone*, then turned and followed.

Richards' brow gathered as the Serbs moved off the road. He felt the 9mm holstered across his vest. "Do you think there's going to be trouble?"

Jusuf shrugged. "There been trouble here for long time."

"Top!" Richards yelled, turning back to the line of vehicles.

"Sir?" Sacamano yelled back from the second truck.

"I want everyone sharp. We don't know what we got up here. Increase spacing between the vehicles."

"Aye, sir. Wake up, people!" Sacamano barked as he stood on the running board of the heavy truck. "Machine-gunners, stay alert! Fire only if fired upon!"

With the command, the gunners perched atop the Humvees and the Marines in the open-back trucks charged their weapons, sending a harsh, metallic ripple through the column.

Richards climbed back into his vehicle, rolled up his window, and motioned for the driver to motor on. No one noticed the white flag lying on the road as the column of Marines motored past.

Captain Richards' column slowed to a crawl as it continued through the battle-torn town of Vitina toward the Vjel River Bridge. After receiving the "all clear" from the lead scouts and bomb disposal team, they started across the old stone bridge, which was littered with spent bullet casings and had piles of tumbled sandbags at the far end.

"Hey, I got two guys with rifles at ten o'clock," came from the anxious gunner perched atop the Humvee.

"I see 'em," answered Richards as he eyed the two eager civilians waving their arms and rifles at the arriving Marines. Their looks of excitement faded as the roof gunner swiveled his .50 cal. machine gun toward them. "KLA?" Richards asked, watching closely.

Jusuf leaned forward and said, "Yes, they are Albanian," before waving back at them.

Richards' wary eyes moved across the ravaged scene. He wasn't surprised by the destruction on the Albanian side of town, but upon crossing the river, he realized the KLA had retaliated in kind.

When they rolled past spilled open sandbags, shredded by rifle fire, Richards examined the blackened shell of a crushed cargo van pushed to the side of the road. A lone Range Rover, its front end smashed and doors and windows peppered with bullet holes, rested in a nearby ditch. Storefront windows were black holes filled with ash and destruction. On a littered sidewalk were the bloated bodies of four Serbian soldiers with empty bullet casings strewn around them.

In his briefings, Richards had seen photographs of the area from before the war, and aerial photos taken at different times during it, but it looked much different in person. As he looked at the death and ruin around him, Richards struggled to comprehend the magnitude of the destruction. There were entire areas of the town leveled, with only stone or brick rising from the ground at odd angles. Now and then he noticed a house or building that, for whatever reason, appeared untouched; whole in a land of undoing.

As the Marines entered the Serb part of town, the destruction didn't stop. There were homes and buildings with smoke still rising from them, bullet-ridden walls, smoldering and toppled cars, and everywhere trash and debris. The stench of death caused Richards to wrinkle his nose. The bloated Serbian soldiers were not the only dead; there were men's and women's bodies lying in dried puddles of their own blood. He saw no weapons with them, only ransacked belongings. *They were Serbs,* he concluded, *trying to escape.* The sight of smaller bodies caused Richards' brow to gather. *The Serbs might have started the fight, but the KLA are trying to finish it.*

With the sun about to set, Richards knew darkness would be on them in less than an hour. Now that they had arrived, the priority was establishing a base camp and company headquarters. Intel said there was a small hospital, a school, and a sports hall still standing. Of the three, Richards felt the sports hall would be the best. Jusuf agreed.

As the column motored down the narrow street, Richards felt eyes peering at them from the shadows. A slamming door caused the Marine gunner to swivel his machine gun. Richards supposed any remaining Albanians would welcome them, but he didn't know what to expect from the Serbs. If their first encounter was any indication, he guessed the Serb reception would be a frosty one. *It doesn't matter. This isn't a popularity contest.*

"Hey, we got eyes on us from that building at one o'clock," blurted the machine gunner.

"Fire only if fired upon," warned Richards as he peered through the dirty windshield at the possible threat. After spotting a man watching them from atop a building thirty yards off, he looked for any sign of danger. When Jusuf, who was leaning forward into the front seat, waved, and the armed man waved back, Richards' wary gaze shifted elsewhere. He pushed Jusuf back to see his driver clutching the Hummer's wheel. "We're okay. I guarantee they're more scared of us."

"Yes, sir."

"Joe, where's the sports hall?"

"Not long. Turn up there, behind that building," Jusuf pointed, his eyes wide.

As they passed a litter-strewn alleyway, Richards spotted three men exit a building and run away from them. He heard an angry cry and saw a man waving with a clenched fist. "What'd he say?"

"He curse-ed at you with bad name," Jusuf said, glaring at the fleeing men. "They are Serbs. They all leave now." Then, with satisfaction, Jusuf muttered, "Now it is *their* turn."

Richards turned to the interpreter and looked him squarely in the eyes. "If you're going to help me with this, if you're going to help us make this right, you're going to have to get past your feelings. I need you as neutral as possible. Do you understand?"

Jusuf sat back and lowered his head.

"I know it can't be easy, but I need to be able to count on you. Will you do it?"

Jusuf gulped, then nodded, his eyes still down. "Yes. I want to make the peace. I want to have place for my people."

"I'm talking about a place for both of you—them *and* you. Will you do it?"

Jusuf's chest heaved as he considered the words. Then, looking Richards in the eyes, he gave a heartfelt nod. "Yes, Captain. I will help make the peace."

"Good, Joe, 'cause I need you. We *all* need you. Even them." Richards nodded back toward the alley.

Jusuf gulped. The Marines, and especially Richards, intimidated him. It wasn't just their firepower that awed him; it was everything: their uniforms, the way they walked, even the way they talked. It was as if they were chiseled from courage and confidence. Jusuf had never seen such a thing, except in the movies. Jusuf thought of *Where Eagles*

Dare. He remembered Clint Eastwood fighting off the Nazis. He was willing to die for his mission. Jusuf believed these men were willing to die for theirs. They had come to his land—the mightiest force in the world—to risk their lives for him and his people, and it moved him. It was a gesture that seemed to transcend all else. He felt indebted to them, especially Captain Richards, who had given him the chance to redeem himself of his cowardice.

Jusuf studied Richards as their Humvee motored on. Occasionally, the dreamer had to remind himself he wasn't watching a movie. This was real. He was returning to his land where he had failed so miserably. *I won't fail my people again. I won't fail my family. I will succeed. But with such a magnificent group of men, how could I fail?*

As Richards' Humvee turned a corner, the scene before them suddenly changed. It was the town square with a large fountain in the middle, but the plaza wasn't empty and in ruin as so much of the town appeared to be, but alive with cheering people dancing and lining the cobbled road. Where they had come from, Richards didn't know. The area had appeared devoid of life just a block before, but now there were hundreds of young and old pressing toward them, and it gave Richards and the other Marines concern.

"What should I do, Captain?" asked the nervous driver as he slowed the Humvee.

With eyes and mouth wide, Richards shook his head and said, "They don't look hostile. Go forward."

As the Humvee crept toward the greeting throng, Richards' concern faded. He remembered World War II movies of French townspeople coming out to welcome the liberating soldiers, and he felt like a hero. There were eager and happy people waving their arms, but the sight of American flags astounded him. There weren't just one or two of the small paper-drawn flags, but dozens of them waving wildly about.

Looking around in astonishment, Richards watched as more people joined in. He had thought this a dead city, but it wasn't. There were survivors. There were people who had never left, and it amazed the captain when even more joined in the welcoming celebration. It was then that it hit him just how important their orders were. This wasn't just a mission, this was a moral obligation, and what he and his men did in the coming days would change the lives of these people forever.

After spotting an LAV parked next to a bullet-ridden building, Richards waved a Recon Marine to him. Slowly, the Marine made his way through the crowd. Richards shook his head and grinned as girls and women gave hugs and danced around the approaching Marine, his chest-straddled rifle of no concern to them. Atop the cupola of the LAV sat another Marine with goggles up on his helmet and a broad smile spanning his face as if they were all there just for him.

Richards looked back at a beaming Jusuf bouncing in his seat like a schoolboy. "My people! My people! They are still here! They are still here!"

Richards lowered his window as the Recon Marine approached with a flush-faced young woman jumping up and down beside him.

"Captain, welcome to Vitina."

———

CHAPTER
TWENTY-FIVE

IT HAD BEEN seven hours since Lek, Haxhi, and Jrfete had left the camp. With the fading light, most of the returning refugees had already stopped for the night. As Lek dragged along the road with the sleeping Jrfete's head on his shoulder, he looked at the settling refugees. Most were resting in the grass near the road as venturing too far off the crumbling asphalt brought with it the danger of landmines.

Returning to Kosovo was a daunting prospect for the weary travelers, who had either survived the horrors of ethnic cleansing or left when it first started. Those who had survived the Serbs knew they were returning to ruin. Those who had left early had heard the terrifying tales and knew what to expect. For all of those returning, the promise of peace and safety, and the hope of regaining their lost lives outweighed their fear and uncertainty.

Like the others, Lek had thought much about his village and wondered what they would find once returned. He knew his and many other homes were gone; burned down by the hateful Serbs. But he had to find their father; and to do that, they had to go back.

Lek imagined walking down the rutted road of their village and finding their father already rebuilding their home. Lek pictured him rushing to greet them and wrapping his thick arms around them. He would tell them how all would be right again, and they would believe it. That was what Lek hoped would happen, but he feared otherwise.

As they walked, Lek tried not to think of his mother lying dead in the barn. He still wondered why the Serbs took her and killed her. Tatiana had told Lek it was because the Serbs hated them, but why? His mother had done nothing to them?

Lek remembered riding with his father into the Serb part of town to deliver a car he had repaired. He remembered the Serb's unkind words and his father being paid one-half what was owed him. Lek was eight, and it was the first instance he remembered being different from them. Lek remembered his mother telling him that all were God's children and that He loved everyone the same, but Lek now knew differently. Lek felt no hate for the Serbs growing up. He didn't even know if he hated them now. Lek wasn't sure what he felt. He just wanted it to end. He wanted his father back and be a boy again.

Exhausted, Lek stopped and turned back to the whimpering Haxhi, thirty steps behind. Lek wanted to reach their home, but it was getting harder to see the road, and he could carry Jrfete no further. "Let's stop here," Lek sighed.

Moving off the road where other travelers were already stopped and sleeping, Lek took the Red Cross coat from around his waist and laid it down. Groaning like an old man, he sank into the welcoming grass and laid Jrfete on the coat.

Haxhi shuffled to them with his arms and head hanging.

"We'll sleep here and go the rest of the way in the morning," Lek said in a fatherly tone.

"I can't go any farther," Haxhi whined, not wanting to think about the next day.

"We're stopping here."

"I'm hungry, and I want Papa," Haxhi moaned, the corners of his mouth curling down.

"There's no more food. Tomorrow we'll eat."

Haxhi sank onto the grass and cried.

"Where's the water bottle?" Lek asked.

Haxhi shrugged.

"You were supposed to keep it!" Lek scolded. "Did you drink it all yourself?"

Haxhi lay on the grass and sobbed.

Lek licked his parched lips. He saw a couple asleep in the grass twenty feet ahead and a man sitting further off the road behind him. "Do you have any extra water?" Lek called out.

The man numbly shook his head.

Lek wanted to be angry at his sobbing brother; instead, he pointed at the darkened hillside and the crumbling fortress just visible in the twilight. "Look, Haxhi, we're almost there! There's the old fortress. Do you see it? Papa used to take us there, remember? We're almost home."

"It's too dark," Haxhi mumbled. "I want Papa."

Haxhi's sobbing stirred Jrfete from her tired stupor, and she also began to cry. Lek tried to comfort her, but she persisted. Jrfete's wailing was soon more than Lek could stand, and he started to cry. Lek was tired; tired of feeling the hurt deep inside, tired of going without food, and tired of being the father of the family. He wanted to sleep. He wanted to go to that faraway place where his dreams were sometimes kind and the pain more distant.

Fatigue and the darkness of the night soon quieted them.

———

The morning sun was behind Sali as he looked down on the valley from the thousand-year-old stone fortress high atop the hill. On the road below, he saw the lines of his people making their slow return home. Sali wanted to feel happiness and joy at the sight, but there was only emptiness. He painfully sighed as he wondered about his children. Sali remembered his burned down home and his wife's grave. He wondered which of his children was buried beside her. He wondered what horrors the others had faced. Sali clenched his eyes shut and shook his head as he tried to free himself from the agonizing thoughts. For Sali, the possibility that his children were yet alive and still facing the cruel reality of this life was more painful than their having passed on to the next.

Sali turned away from the valley and looked back inside the old, roofless fortress to where the other soldiers were resting. It wasn't his first time there. Before the war, he had brought his boys and told them stories of honor and valor. He told of their brave ancestors who had fought off invaders and watched as their young eyes swelled with intrigue. *If they were yet alive, they would relish the new tales I could tell; tales of a new breed of warrior who now occupies these sacred walls.*

Sali watched as several of his fellow soldiers moved to the crumbling wall and looked down into the valley at the returning refugees. He saw their looks of satisfaction and accomplishment as if it was by their efforts that the people were returning. While they had killed their share of Serbs in recent weeks, Sali knew it was the Americans who had ended the war.

Much discussion had ensued since the Americans had motored past the day before in their large trucks and armored vehicles. Some of those with Sali wanted to go down to Vitina and welcome the liberators. They argued the Americans were their friends and had come to help cleanse the land of the Serbs. Why else would they have bombed Serbia? To them, it was a new dawn for their beloved land, and the Americans would forever free them from the rule of the oppressive Serbs. Others were not so sure.

It was Colonel Xhemojli who warned the Americans would want to take away their weapons and rule them. He told his men it was only through their weapons that they could remain a strong and free people, and they should not give them up. He said in time he and the brigade commanders would go to Vitina and discuss the matter, but until then, to be wary of any contact, and warned that the Americans would shoot them if they were seen with weapons.

Sali had since thought of what the colonel had said and wondered if they were the words of prudence or of a man wanting to hold on to power.

Sali dismissed the speculation and pointless prattle. He was past caring about such things. He had survived these past weeks on hate. To him, he was alive to kill the Serbs or anyone else who called his land theirs. He had no life beyond that. That is what he told himself as he built a wall around the pain, but a part of him wondered what the future held.

Sali half listened as a teacher turned soldier spoke of American history. He told how England once ruled America. Oppressed and eager to be free to govern itself, their small province waged war on the mighty British Empire and won their liberty. He proclaimed that Americans were a freedom-loving people and had come to help them be likewise free.

Sali found it strange that after their fight for independence, England and America had become such close friends. The two former enemies now fought together in wars and worked together in peace. He scoffed at the notion of his people and the Serbians someday having a similar relationship. In his mind, peace would never be possible between them.

Bored with all the talking, Sali sighed and looked across the valley to the town of Vitina. He saw the river that divided it. It appeared as though half of the town was in ruins, its air hazy with the smoke of smoldering fires, while other parts seemed untouched. He could just see his village, farther to the east. Sali's jaw tightened as he considered what the Serbs had done to his life. He was happy before. He had a beautiful family, a fine house, and a job he liked. That was all gone now. Sali believed his killing Serbs would give him satisfaction and vindication, but it did neither. It only made his hate grow deeper and blacker.

Sali remembered the idealistic words of his red-bearded friend, Kuq. *He would be thinking differently about things had he lived.* The war, with all its killing and hatred, had changed Sali. In the beginning, Sali considered himself as an agent of God, righting a wrong and chasing evil from their land. Now he didn't know what he had become.

———

CHAPTER
TWENTY-SIX

IT WAS STILL morning when the three Humvees made their way down the empty Vitina street. Atop the armored trucks, machine gunners kept a close watch, swinging their weapons into the shadows and burned-out places. Behind the thick glass, Marines sat with rifles ready, uncertain what might greet them around the next corner.

The welcoming crowds of Albanians from the night before were now nowhere to be found. What Richards saw instead were mangy dogs scavenging for food and wary eyes peering from windows.

"Where'd everyone go?" asked the driver.

"They are inside waiting," Jusuf replied.

"Waiting for what?" Richards asked, glancing back at Jusuf.

"Waiting to see what you will do—what the Serbs will do. They are scared-ed," Jusuf shrugged.

"Don't you think they understand we're here to help them?" Richards asked, his brow gathered.

"Yes...maybe."

"They sure were happy to see us last night," said the driver.

Richards watched a woman in a scarf and coat sweeping off her front step. She paused mid-sweep as they motored by, her uncertain eyes fixed on the dark green truck with its heavy machine gun on top. Richards offered a nod and a friendly wave, but she only stared.

While Richards knew he wasn't there to make friends, he believed gaining the trust of the locals would make his job as a peacekeeper easier. Only, he wasn't sure how to do it or if he could do it in the limited time he had. With the Marines scheduled to turn the sector over to the Army in just a few weeks, Richards knew their time was short. He also knew whatever he and his men did now would help the peacekeeping effort in the long term. It wasn't only the Albanians who needed reassurance, however. There were still Serbs in Vitina hiding from the KLA. Richards realized that building trust with both sides, while suppressing the militants who still had a taste for blood, would be no easy task.

"That is the government building up there," Jusuf said, pointing over Richards' shoulder.

Richards looked from the building to his map, noting its location. "What's the magistrate's name again? Carassava?" he asked, thinking back to his intel pack.

"Yes, that is his name," nodded Jusuf.

While Richards knew Carassava was no saint, his intel pack said he wasn't a militant either; he was a politician. A member of the Socialist Party of Serbia, Sasa Carassava was the manager of Vitina and, like all city officials, was despised by the Albanians. His policies favored the Serbs, and he didn't try to conceal his discrimination.

Before the war, Vitina's population was 23,000; only 5,000 of which were Serb. The town had one school. While there were four times as many Albanian children, the Serb children were given priority in learning. Albanian children were allowed to use the school with their own teachers, but only in the evenings and on weekends. This policy was in place for years before the war. As tensions worsened, the Serbs barred Albanian children from the school entirely.

While the Albanians despised Carassava, the Serbs of the town didn't like him either. To them, he was a puppet leader more concerned with pleasing the politicians in Belgrade than the people of Vitina. In reality, Carassava had the unenviable task of reigning over the disadvantaged majority Albanians while making Serbian national hatred and cruelty acceptable.

"Do you think he's gonna be there, sir?" the driver asked, peering out from under his helmet. "If I was a Serb, I would've hightailed it outta here a long time ago."

"Word is he's still here. He's been hiding since the tables turned and he's asked us for protection," Richards said as the Hummer came to a stop before a two-story masonry building with a red bar tile roof. There were a few cars parked outside, but no people. Richards looked from the abandoned building to the other nearby structures; all appeared intact. Like most of the Serbian areas, this one stood in stark contrast to the burned and pillaged Albanian neighborhoods.

As Richards and the other Marines exited their Humvees, leaving the roof-gunners and drivers in place, they walked toward the building's entrance with rifles at the ready. It wasn't until Richards and the others had passed a running fountain and climbed the few stairs that he noticed the building's front doors were open. One door hung from a hinge, and broken glass was scattered through the entry.

With his rifle at the ready, Richards waited as two Marines entered the lobby and gave the all clear. He was about to enter when he heard a woman yelling from outside the building. Stepping back from the entry, Richards, Jusuf, and four other Marines watched a dark-haired woman run up the walk toward them with arms frantically waving. Upon hearing the commotion, the two Marines who had secured the lobby came out and formed a perimeter around their captain. Richards watched as the distressed woman hurriedly approached, her arms flailing and tears streaming down her panicked face.

"What's she saying?" Richards asked.

Jusuf, who was wearing a Kevlar vest and helmet over his worn and tired clothes, stepped forward and said, "She is Serb."

"I don't care! What's she yelling about?" Richards snapped.

"She say Albanians are trying to kill her husband. KLA, she say."

"Where are they?" Richards asked as he pushed through the Marines toward the woman.

"She say they took him from his house."

"Tell her to show us!"

"That way," Jusuf said, taking an uncertain step down the walk. Pausing, he turned to Richards and said, "It is him."

"Him? Him who?"

"Carassava, the man you look for."

Richards' eyes widened as he looked from Jusuf to the distressed woman who was already running back the way she had come. "Let's go! Bring up the Humvees!" Richards called back as Jusuf and the six other Marines ran to stay with him.

Richards followed the woman around another building to a parking lot with a mud-splattered truck and six men wearing ammunition belts and vests over civilian attire. The KLA fighters stood with rifles trained on a kneeling gray-haired man whose hands were tied behind his back. Another uniformed Albanian was blindfolding him. When the battered mayor of Vitina, Sassa Carassava, looked up, Richards saw his bloodied face and shirt.

"Tell them to lower their weapons and step away!" Richards barked as his Marines spread out with their rifles at their shoulders.

Uncertain of what to do, four of the seven Albanians turned their rifles on the Marines while the others kept their muzzles pointed at Carassava.

Jusuf took an uneasy step back and then relayed the message as Carassava's wife ran toward him, only to be grabbed by one of the Albanians and pushed to the ground, shrieking.

The KLA leader stepped forward and, with calming hands, shouted something to the Marines.

Richards' grip on his rifle tightened. "What'd he say?"

"He say do not worry. They are KLA."

"I know they're KLA. Tell them to put down their weapons!" Richards' mind raced with half a dozen deadly scenarios.

Behind Richards, his men quietly called their shots, "First on the right. Second on the right. First on the left. Leader…"

Jusuf's eyes were wide, and his heart was racing. "They thank you very much for helping to kill the Serbs, but he says Carassava is war criminal and they will shoot him."

"Tell them to let him go," Richards demanded as he stared down the KLA leader. "There will be no more executions."

Jusuf forced a swallow and then relayed the captain's message.

Confused, the KLA leader shook his head and answered back.

Half turned to Richards, Jusuf said, "He say there is no questions he *is* criminal. And he say, thank you for bringing the wife back. She is also criminal."

"We got clean shots, sir," a Marine calmly reported.

"Do not fire!" Richards warned as he eyed the Albanian leader.

Jusuf, standing between two aiming Marines, took a step back.

"Tell them I give my word as a Marine that Carassava will be tried for war crimes," Richards insisted.

Jusuf relayed the words, then answered back, "They say they already know he is bad man."

"Tell them we'll take him by force if we have to," Richards growled. "They're not going to kill him!"

An embittered response came from the KLA leader and caused Jusuf to wipe at his beard nervously. "They say it is their land and that you should fight for them, not against."

"Tell them we're not for or against them. We're here to stop the killing." Richards' eyes narrowed under his helmet as he studied the situation. He realized if it came to a fight, it would go down in an instant, and the Albanians wouldn't stand a chance, but that was the last thing Richards wanted. Zero casualties were his goal.

Richards breathed a little easier when his Humvee rolled up behind them. The sight of its heavy machine gun pointed down on the fighters caused several to murmur with concern.

"Tell them if they put down their weapons and release Carassava they can leave in peace; otherwise, they'll be our prisoners—or dead."

Jusuf gulped and relayed the demand. A heated conversation ensued amongst the fighters, and three of them lowered their rifles.

"What's going on, Joe?" Richards asked, eyeing the leader.

"Some say to let go Carassava, but some don't want to."

Richards drew in a deep breath and slung his rifle over his shoulder. "I don't want any shots fired unless absolutely necessary," he said as he stepped toward the Albanians with open hands.

"Ah, what are you doing, sir?" asked one of the Marines.

"I'm getting the prisoner," Richards calmly replied.

"I don't think that's a good idea, Captain."

"Sir, go to ground fast if anything happens," warned a Marine.

Richards didn't respond, but stepped closer.

The Albanians stopped their discussion and watched the approaching American captain with uncertainty.

"Joe, tell them there's been enough killing. It's time to stop. Tell them I'm taking the prisoner."

Jusuf watched unblinking as the fighters moved aside for the approaching captain and released their hold on the prisoner.

With eyes calm and breathing shallow, Richards reached down to the kneeling Carassava and pulled him to his feet. He gave the KLA leader an approving nod, then led Carassava back to his Marines, still staring down their rifles. On joining them, Richards released a quiet sigh, then turned to the rebels with Carassava at his side. "Sergeant, flex-cuff him. Make sure they see you do it."

"Aye, sir," the Marine sergeant said as he slung his rifle and removed a thick plastic zip tie from a utility pocket.

"Corporal Parker, get his wife."

"Aye, sir," the corporal said as he moved his rifle to one hand and started for the sobbing woman.

"Captain, he's already tied up," said the sergeant.

"Just do it," Richards said as the corporal led the sobbing woman away from the Albanians.

Jusuf looked at Richards and the other Marines in amazement. He had only seen such bravery in the movies and marveled that anyone could be so noble in real life.

"Tell them they can leave, but they have to surrender their weapons," Richards insisted.

The KLA leader looked at Jusuf as if he had betrayed them.

"He say they need their weapons to protect their people."

"Tell them I understand," Richards nodded. "They have a right to defend themselves, but NATO has ordered all Kosovars secure their weapons with us. If they continue their fighting against the Serbs, it will only endanger the peace."

Richards watched the KLA leader as Jusuf gave the message. He knew how painful for them it would be giving up Carassava. He wasn't just the mayor of Vitina but also a symbolic tie to Milosevic and the murderers to the north. Taking their weapons away would only make the sting worse.

The KLA leader looked at his men, who were visibly upset at the mandate, and then glanced down at his rifle.

Richards recognized the leader's look of uncertainty and knew any delay could lead to a rash decision on the Albanian's part. By the same token, pushing the man too far could produce just as dire consequences. With his Marines' weapons still trained on the Albanians, the captain knew he had the upper hand but still wanted to avoid a fight, if possible. "Parker."

"Captain?" responded the corporal, who had retrieved the wife.

"Gather their weapons. Rossi, help him."

Jusuf wrung his hands as the two Marines slung their rifles and approached the unmoving Albanians. His heart sank as, one by one, the dismayed and confused fighters gave up their weapons.

While still amazed at the Marines' bravery, Jusuf wondered if he had just betrayed his countrymen. He watched, somewhat ashamedly, as the seven Albanian freedom fighters turned and walked toward their mud-splattered truck, their heads hanging, their victory stolen. Jusuf turned back to Richards and his Marines and then to Carassava. Jusuf knew him to be a despicable and loathsome man, a symbol of death and hatred in the town. Jusuf wondered what would become of him. Would the valiant Americans, who were so fair and honorable, give him the painful death he deserved? Jusuf doubted it.

The afternoon breeze caused the wildflowers along the road to wave, as if welcoming Lek and his siblings back to their village. Lek's legs and back were aching from carrying his sleeping sister, but he felt none of it as they approached the spoiled remains of his once happy life. After cresting a small hill, Lek slowed to a stop. Haxhi, who was trailing behind, soon joined him. The dusty road where he had played soccer for years continued ahead, dipping through a shallow furrow lined with goat willow before passing a neighbor's home. Lek saw the rolling hills beyond the fields to his left with their clumps of pines and beech trees; all seemed peaceful and calm. After taking a deep breath, he continued toward his home.

They passed the Mucaj's old fence, still in need of mending from too many soccer games. Lek's brow tightened as they passed a burned-out car. He saw the trees that had shaded them on the hot summer days. Some things seemed unchanged. Lek saw the overgrown hedges near the fields and heard the song of birds and the cooing of doves. For a moment, he believed none of the terrible things had happened. Squinting, Lek could almost visualize his mother and father walking down the road, waving them home for dinner.

As Lek continued along the familiar road, he felt an inner peace and a strange calmness he had not felt in weeks. He was home. He breathed in the sweet fragrance of wildflowers and grass, but as he walked, the less palatable fetor of decay and death lurched at him and brought him back to the terrible truth of his life.

A sense of dread filled Lek when the towering pine that had hidden them that terrible afternoon came into view. Lek had tried to forget that awful day the cruel Serbs took everything from him, but he knew it would forever linger in his mind. He wondered if they should go any further before reminding himself they had to find their father.

Lek pushed the sagging Jrfete up on his shoulder and continued walking. He slowed as the charred remains of his burned-out house came into view. Lek had dreamed of their returning to a rebuilt home and their father joyously welcoming them, but as he stared at the shell of his home, he realized the nightmare was still his reality.

Lek's sad eyes moved from the blackened remains of their home up the rutted dirt road to the old stone barn. His stomach was churning as he neared the shadowed opening. He tried to forget the painful memory of going inside.

"Where's Papa?" Haxhi asked as he eyed the old barn. His words caused Jrfete to lift her head from Lek's shoulder.

"I don't know." Lek gave a mournful sigh as Haxhi wiped at his tears. "Maybe Papa's not here yet," Lek said with feigned hope.

"I miss Mama," Haxhi sobbed.

"Mama," Jrfete repeated, looking about in uncertainty.

"I miss her too," Lek groaned, letting his sister down.

As they drew closer to their old home, with its charred white walls opened to the sky, Lek's tears distorted his vision. The house was as they had left it. There was no sign of their father.

Jrfete wandered off a few steps and then hurried back to Lek and reached up for comfort. Hoisting her in his tired arms, he turned to Haxhi, whose head was hanging and shoulders slumped.

"Where's Papa?" Haxhi cried. "Is he dead too?"

Lek had long wondered if Haxhi had gone into the barn that terrible night and if he had seen their mother lying dead in the hay. He turned to the old barn and found his mother's grave. The small mound of earth had flattened with time. Lek turned to his brother, his eyes filled with pain. "Did you go inside the barn?"

Haxhi's shoulders trembled as he sobbed. "Yes."

"I'm sorry I didn't tell you," Lek breathed, wiping away his tears. "I didn't know how."

Haxhi turned to his brother and asked, "Is Papa dead too?"

Lek weakly shrugged. "I don't know."

"What are we going to do?" Haxhi asked, sinking to the road.

Lek turned to the Lushi home. It was half burned, had most of its windows broken, and part of its roof caved in, but was still standing. "We can stay there and wait for Papa."

Haxhi gazed up the empty road. "I don't want to stay here."

Lek looked back the way they had come. "If we leave, how will Papa find us?"

Haxhi hung his head, his shoulders slumped in defeat.

"Let's rest here for now." Lek pulled a quarter-filled water bottle a woman had given them from his coat pocket and took a drink. He offered it to Haxhi, who dejectedly shook his head. After giving Jrfete a drink, Lek pushed the bottle back into his coat and started off the road to the protection of the tall pine. Haxhi soon followed.

As he walked, Lek listened for the familiar sounds of life, for the baaing of sheep and the drone of the tractors, but he heard only the stillness of the air and the sad cooing of doves. Lek's weepy gaze drifted to the old barn. He saw the dark shadows of its open door and released a heavy, painful sigh.

———

CHAPTER
TWENTY-SEVEN

SERGEANT HAROLD HOLM rubbed his nose as he looked across the red bar tile roofs to the darkened and still smoldering ruins on the southwestern side of Vitina. From his over-watching position atop the sports hall, he and his sniper squad had a commanding view in every direction.

The sports hall, which the Marines had made their base of operations, was a large complex for a relatively small town. The five soccer pitches around the building provided a good perimeter to their headquarters and parking for their heavy trucks and Humvees. Inside the hall, which had sat empty for months, was a pool turned green with algae. There was also a sauna, men's and women's locker room with showers, basketball court, and a weight room. The primary structure, constructed of block, was twenty years old, but much of it had fallen into disrepair and looked older. In a newer addition were rows of classrooms and offices, along with another high-ceilinged room half the size of a basketball court. The flat roof of the sports hall was thirty feet off the ground, but its tallest point was a slab-sided clock tower which extended another twenty feet above that. It was atop that clock tower that Sergeant Holm and his three fellow Marines monitored the comings and goings of their new base.

Sergeant Holm raised his binoculars and continued his scan past the soccer fields and parking lot. On one side of the lot sat a manned LAV, on the other, a dozen Marines worked to erect a hospital tent. To the west, parked in neat rows along one of the soccer fields, were the heavy trucks that had carried them into the province. Beyond the row of trucks were the perimeter emplacements, which amounted to wedges of sandbags protecting medium machine-guns and pairs of Marines. Further north, a Humvee moved down a littered street. Three blocks to the west was a patrol of Marines on foot.

Even though Vitina was no longer a combat zone, there were still significant threats which required a keen and alert presence. From their over-watching position, high atop the sports hall, Holm and the other Marines had the best vantage point in town. The old church, which stood 600 yards to the Northwest, was the only other structure that rivaled their view.

In the two days since their arrival, the Serb side of town still looked abandoned. That morning, Holm had counted only three people and one moving car. The Albanian side of the town was a different story, however. The stream of returning refugees to the south was growing, and Holm wondered what it would be like for those returning to find their homes burned and looted. In one neighborhood were men already repairing a burned-out roof. A few blocks away was another group clearing the debris from a mosque, the jagged remains of its exploded minaret jutting into the sky.

Holm didn't know if he and his men would see much action while in Kosovo, but they would be ready. The reports of Serbian forces massing to the north and returning to the province didn't bother him. Even if the Serbs were foolish enough to mount an attack, he knew NATO air strikes would take them out long before they reached Vitina. He and the other Marines were more concerned with the rogue elements, whether Serb or KLA, still at work in the area.

Holm swatted at a persistent fly as he continued his vigil from behind the waist-high tower wall they had topped with two rows of sandbags. It was only noon but already hot. Holm rolled his camouflaged sleeves up and felt a light breeze sweep across him from the north, momentarily lifting some of the heat. He pushed up his helmet and wiped the sweat from his forehead as the American flag, mounted in the corner of their tower, rippled in the breeze.

"That's what we need, a little AC," groaned Corporal Merle from behind his binoculars.

"It's gonna be a hot one," added Lance Corporal Turner.

While it was only eighty degrees on the ground, the asphalt roof drew in the heat, making it at least fifteen degrees hotter. Holm didn't mind it. He was a North Texas boy and used to stifling heat.

"Hey, Sergeant," called Corporal Brown from his east side position on the ten-foot-wide tower.

"Yeah, I know, it's hot," Holm muttered, looking through his binoculars.

"No. I'm seein' somethin'. North, northeast, about two hundred meters. Do you see 'em?"

"See whot?" Holm asked, turning to the corporal.

"There in that white building. We're bein' watched."

Holm followed Brown's pointing arm to a row of buildings on a slope. "Which one? They're all white."

"That three-story one. Two hundred, two hundred-fifty meters."

"Whot-a-bout it? We've been be'n watched since we got here," Holm said dismissively.

"Well, it just looks kind of funny; that's all."

"Well, tha'd be the third funny thing ya seen this mornin'," Holm smirked. "Just keep yer eyes open and don't go gett'n yer panties in a bind over every little ol' thang."

Brown raised his binoculars and resumed his watch.

Of the four Marines on the roof, Holm was the only true sniper. The other three Marines were more glorified spotters with simple M16s rather than an accurized M14, which Holm considered a finely tuned instrument of death. They were good shots, but years of killing prairie dogs from a hundred yards made Holm extraordinarily good.

"Sergeant, somethin's not right. You might want to take a look with your binocs," urged Brown.

Holm sighed and turned back to the stucco building, which looked like most of the others in the town. He spotted what appeared to be a man sitting in a window. Holm raised his rifle, sighted through the scope, then lowered it again. "Yeah, so whot?"

"I think I saw a rifle," replied Brown.

"There's lots of them folks that got rifles, you know."

"Maybe, but not pointing at us. I'm pretty sure I saw a glint."

"You sawd a glint? You mean like a sun glint? Off a scope?"

"Yeah," Brown insisted, raising his binoculars.

Holm raised his rifle again. "All I see is some dude look'n at us with binocs. That's what you saw. I don't see no rifle."

"Well, shouldn't we radio in a report or something, just in case?" Brown asked nervously.

"Whot for? We can't go call'n Mama ever time someone looks at us crossed-eyed now, can we? Didn't you never hear 'bout the boy who cried wolf?" Holm twanged.

"What's going on?" Merle asked as he moved from his side.

"Nothin'," Holm sighed with a bored shake of his head. Holm was turning back to his side of the town when he heard a thump and felt a spit of sand on his face. "Whot the—" Holm's brow gathered as a sandbag beside him streamed sand on his boot. The *zip* of a second round passing close by caused the sniper to raise his rifle.

"Muzzle flash! Muzzle flash! Incoming!" Brown yelled as he ducked below the sandbags.

"No kidd'n," Holm scoffed as a third round zipped by. "Call it in."

"I got it!" Merle said as he sank below the sandbags and pulled out his radio.

Holm's sniper training kicked in. In two seconds, his rifle was resting on a sandbag and sighted on the open window. The world around him faded as he centered the shooter in his crosshairs; only what was in the scope mattered.

"Range: Two hundred sixty-five meters," Brown announced, peering through his spotting scope, his voice charged with adrenaline.

Neither the *crack* of another round passing overhead nor the burst of radio chatter distracted Holm as he dialed in the distance and centered the crosshairs on the shooter's head. He drew in a deep breath as his finger stroked the trigger. It was too easy. Holm was about to squeeze the trigger when he saw a muzzle flash and felt the sandbag open a foot from him, releasing a cascade of sand.

"Anytime," Brown breathed as he braced for the next shot.

Holm squeezed the trigger, and the body in the window spilled backward.

"You got him! You nailed that sucker!" Brown yelled, dancing behind the spotting scope.

Holm didn't leave his scope but watched as another shape move in the shadows of the window. He waited for the shadow to return, his blinking rhythmic and his breathing calm. When another man came to the window with the same rifle, Holm squeezed his trigger, dropping him out of sight.

"Nice shootin' Tex! Two shots, two kills!" Brown exclaimed as he scoured the building's windows for more targets.

As Sergeant Holm lowered his rifle, the world around him gradually returned, and he heard for the first time the calls on the radio: *"Vulture two-one, this is Cafe. What's going on? Come in, over?"*

"It's for you, Sarge," a wide-eyed Merle said, handing him the radio.

With a face devoid of celebration, Holm took the radio and said, "Cafe, this is Vulture two-one. We took some fire up here. 'Bout four rounds from two hundred-sixty meters northeast."

"Copy, Vulture two-one. Any casualties?"

"Neg-a-tive, just two dead bad guys," Holm said, eyeing the target building.

"Copy. A patrol's moving in now. Keep them covered, over."

"Copy that, Cafe. Vulture two-one out," Holm said as he brought his rifle back up and searched the building for movement.

"Scratch two Serbs," gloated Brown.

Sergeant Holm said nothing.

———

CHAPTER
TWENTY-EIGHT

SIX DAYS HAD PASSED since Kasap the Butcher had escaped with his life at the bridge. Separated from Nimatovic and not knowing if he was still alive, Kasap had survived by hiding in an abandoned building. Growing weak from lack of food, he knew his chances for escape were dwindling. Unable to swim, his only route to the safety of the north was over one of the town's bridges, which were now guarded by American Marines and disarmed Albanian KLA.

While Serbs civilians were allowed over the bridge, the Albanians closely checked their lists and photos for wanted militiamen. The Butcher, who had brutally tortured dozens and struck terror into the minds of hundreds more, was at the top of their lists. Kasap knew if the KLA discovered him, he would die a slow and painful death—the same as he had brought on so many others. It was only under cover of darkness that he felt safe, and even then, he moved at the risk of being discovered.

Kasap had considered turning himself in to the Americans, but doing so would mean an embarrassing war-crimes trial and then a public hanging. Kasap wanted to live, and his only chance was escaping to Serbia.

After two nights of watching the American patrols, Kasap formulated a plan. He knew the Americans guarding the bridges couldn't tell

Albanians from Serbs. They asked for papers and checked them when available, but many without documents and were still allowed to pass. If Kasap could get past them, he thought he would stand a chance on the other side, although he would have to continue to avoid the KLA the forty miles to Serbia.

Disguised as a woman, Kasap eyed the American sentries at the bridge as he approached, hunched over with a feigned limp. He saw two groups of men in the dim light of the bridge and thought his chances were good. Gone was Kasap's militia tunic; replaced by a tattered gown which nearly covered his worn leather boots. Over the gown, he wore a coat with a small Czech handgun and a knife hidden inside. A hijab wrapped his head and cast his face in shadow.

As Kasap drew closer to the bridge, he counted four Marines with no Albanians in sight. *My timing is perfect, as always.* Hobbling with a limp, he slowed as one of the Marines approached.

"Papers? Do you have papers?" the young Marine asked with an outstretched hand, his M16 straddled across his thick Kevlar vest, his other hand on its grip.

The disguised Kasap understood what was being asked, but he shrugged and shook his head in confusion.

"*Dokumente?*" the Marine asked.

Again, Kasap shook his head.

"*Hartija?*" the Marine persisted.

Hidden under the hijab, Kasap was about to say something to the Marine in Albanian when he spotted two men approaching from the other side of the bridge. He knew from their uniforms they were KLA, and even though they carried no weapons, they were just as deadly. Thinking quickly, Kasap pursed his lips and shook his head once again; only this time he put a hand to his throat as if unable to speak.

The Marine looked back at the others stationed with him and said, "I don't think she can talk. Should we let her by?"

A sergeant leaning against the bridge pulled a glowing cigarette from his mouth and said, "She's harmless, let her by."

The young Marine waved the hunched woman past.

The disguised Kasap, clutching the handgun inside his coat, nodded and limped by. He fought the urge to walk faster and continued his hobble while watching the two Albanians ahead of him. Kasap considered turning back and waiting for another time or trying another bridge, but he was too far now. *I outsmarted the Americans. These fools should be easy.*

As Kasap drew closer to the two Albanians, his hunch grew, and his gait stiffened. He felt their eyes on him and wondered if he was walking to his death. *No, I am Kasap—a Serb. The intellect of a single Serb can better two Albanians. I'll be safe.* He held tightly to his handgun, just the same.

"It's late. Where are you from, mother?" the first Albanian, who wore a patch over an eye, asked warmly.

Without raising his head, Kasap made a weak gesture to his mouth, his right hand ready with the 9mm.

"You cannot talk?" the patch-eyed Albanian frowned.

The disguised Kasap shook his head, then made several weak guttural sounds, as if straining to speak.

The Albanian backed away from the hobbled old woman and shrugged at the still watching Marines.

With a feeble nod, Kasap continued past the Albanians toward the far side of the bridge, less than twenty yards away. He was tempted to run, but knew a bullet could easily catch him. *Patience,* he told himself. *I'll limp into the safety of the night.*

The patch-eyed Albanian was still eyeing the hunched old woman when something struck him as odd. He had to look twice but saw the old woman was wearing military-style boots. At first, he thought nothing of it as his people were wearing anything they could find, but something didn't seem right. The Albanian squinted his good eye and followed her, looking for anything else unusual. The old woman glanced back nervously at him. "We should search her."

Kasap heard the words and knew he was close to being found out.

"Wait, mother," the patch-eyed Albanian said as he moved up behind the old woman. "We need to search you."

Kasap tightened his grip on the handgun.

"What's going on?" the Marine sergeant hollered, watching the two Albanians from his spot twenty yards behind.

The patch-eyed Albanian half-turned to the Marines and said, "We search her."

The Marine squared up on the old woman, raising his rifle from its resting position but still pointing it into the bridge.

Kasap limped to a stop and turned back to the Marines. As the weaponless Albanians drew closer, the disguised Serb considered his options. He could run, or he could fight. *I am Kasap, the Butcher.*

The patch-eyed Albanian was the first to reach him and bent his head to see the old woman's face. Uncertain of what he was seeing, he reached out to lift her scarf. As he did, his eyes widened in recognition. The blast of a 9mm round from under Kasap's coat knocked the patch-eyed Albanian back. Two more shots spun the second man to the ground. Kasap tore the hijab from his head and glared at the two wreathing Albanians, leaving no doubt who had just shot them.

Kasap heard the yelling Americans and pulled his handgun from under his coat. He was turning toward the Marines when their bullets ripped through him and dropped him on the shadowed bridge.

———

CHAPTER
TWENTY-NINE

FINE BEADS of sweat glistened on Sali Noli's forehead as he took another bite of the red pepper. Chewing slowly, he paused to breathe in quenching air, and then grinned approvingly. It burned, and he liked it. Listening to the ongoing conversation, he took a thick slice of cucumber, dipped it in a brass bowl filled with creamed feta, and pushed it into his mouth.

"I don't trust the Americans," frowned Gazmend Bunjakl, wiping the dripping *Raki* from his thin beard. "I think the Serbs have purchased them."

"They're nothing more than mercenaries," sneered another.

"We may end up fighting them too," grunted a third.

"So let it be!" Bunjakl exclaimed. "We have God and righteousness on our side!"

"The Americans are here to help us," argued Lieutenant Alia.

Sali put the milky glass of *Raki* to his lips and slurped down the last of the fermented grape and plum juice. Sali set the glass down hard and shook his head. "That's all I hear now. Talk, talk, talk. We've changed from an army of killers to a band of jabbering women!"

"What would you have us do, Noli?" asked Alia.

Sali's chest swelled. "If I had been there, Carassava would be dead, and those men would still have their rifles."

"You would have fought the Americans?" Alia asked with a raised brow.

"And died, if God willed it," nodded Sali. "If Dren and Fisnik had their rifles, Dren wouldn't be dead—shot by that butcher! How many has *he* killed?"

"The Americans killed him; shot him eight times," clarified Alia.

"There are others out there!" glared Sali. "The Cowboy. Where is that devil?"

The men angrily shook their heads.

"We should not sleep until we hunt him down and kill him for what he has done!" seethed Sali.

The other men nodded, but Alia warned, "If the Americans see us with rifles, they will take them."

"Let them try," growled Sali.

Alia shook his head as the others grunted their support. "The Americans are here to help us."

"The Americans are here to help themselves," grumbled another.

"We should thank them for chasing the Serb devils from our land," persisted Alia.

"And how long will they stay?" snapped Bunjakl.

Alia had no answer and sat back as the debate roared.

Sali remembered his gentle friend Kuq. Had a Serb not killed him, Sali was sure his views of the war and killing would have changed. Sali no longer thought of his family. It pained him too much. Instead, he savored his bitterness and hatred. The fight had changed. It was no longer a battle for liberty and land. It was now about rage and religion. To Sali and the other new believers, there was no greater honor than waging war for God and bringing vengeance on those who fought against Him. Sali would find the Cowboy or die trying. His life would end in glory.

———

The midday sun was hot and draining as it beat down on the road to Vitina. Tired, worried, and hungry, Lek carried Jrfete while Haxhi dragged behind. Jrfete's unanswered pleas for food had changed to a persistent whine that Lek no longer heard.

They had stayed two nights in their abandoned village, sleeping in the Lushi home and waiting by the tall pine for their father to return, but he never came. That morning, Lek spoke to two passing refugees who had found their home destroyed and were on their way to Vitina. They told him of the Americans there and the food and protection they offered. Hungry and tired of foraging for food, Lek decided it best to go there. Haxhi put up little resistance when Lek explained they were not giving up on their father, but looking for him in another place.

The road to Vitina wasn't empty. Other refugees were making their way to town. Some moved with eagerness while others walked aimlessly. As the children passed the slower refugees, they received vacant stares or curious glances, but no offers of help; they had their own shattered lives to mend. Lek didn't expect help from anyone. After seven weeks, he considered himself capable of caring for his brother and sister. While he tried not to think of it, Lek feared he would have to continue.

As they walked, Lek noticed large birds circling in the sky. He looked across the field to his right, where ravens were picking at a body. Death had become common, and life had lost its brilliance. Lek looked away from the scavenging birds. He wondered what had happened to his father. The possibility he was still alive was more than Lek dared hope. He wanted to believe his father was a hero; that he had fought bravely and saved many Albanians, but Lek had seen the Serb's violence firsthand and knew his father, a kind and gentle man, would stand little chance against their brutality. Lek missed his parents now more than ever, but knew there was nothing he could do. He had to be strong. He had to be the father now. Lek remembered his once happy life. He thought of his home and the dark and dreary barn that haunted his dreams. He vowed never to go back.

The scenery had changed little in the mile they had walked. Unplanted farmland was on either side of the road, with occasional houses in between. Lek watched a bony woman in a raggedy coat walk alongside the road ahead of them. She carried a plastic bag and stooped as she hunted for valuables along the littered way. After inspecting an item of possible value, she would either cast it aside or place it in her bag for safekeeping. Accompanying her was an equally mangy dog which repeatedly circled out into the field with its nose to the ground before scampering back. Upon seeing the dog, the tired and hungry Haxhi livened his pace, pointing and laughing as the dog scampered out into the field and then back to the bony woman. Jrfete soon took notice. Raising her head from Lek's shoulder, her face dirty and tear-stained, she watched the lively dog dart around the field.

Forgetting his misery, Haxhi glanced back at Lek with a smile and then hurried up the road toward the mangy dog. The woman paused her roadside search as she spotted a bright yellow cylinder thirty yards into the field. The dog scurried around her as she started for it.

Haxhi gleefully waved and clapped at the dog. The playful mutt noticed and bounded back toward Haxhi, causing him to cackle with delight. Haxhi kneeled and reached out to the mangy dog which sniffed his way to within fingers reach of the boy before darting back into the field. Lek grinned, and Jrfete giggled at the game as the dog circled once again. After the second time, Haxhi got to his feet and chased out into the field after the dog.

Lek saw the scavenging woman studying what looked like a yellow squash on the ground. But Lek thought it too smooth and bright a yellow to be a vegetable. He watched as the bony woman bent down and picked it up. Standing back up, she examined the smooth cylinder for a moment and then tossed it aside. There was a flash and a *BAWOOM* as a cloud of dirt and smoke swallowed the woman. Lek recoiled at the blast and winced at what felt like a dozen bee stings.

Stunned and disoriented, Lek looked across the smoky field. He frantically searched for Haxhi as Jrfete screamed in his ear, but could find him nowhere in the settling smoke and dust. "Haxhi!" Lek cried, choking and coughing. "Haxhi!"

There was no answer.

Lek gasped in the burned, dusty air. When his legs buckled, he set the screaming Jrfete down. He didn't notice the dirt and small pricks of blood that peppered the side of her face. When Lek's vision blurred, he wiped at his eyes and saw blood on his hand. He heard someone howling in pain but didn't realize it was him.

With his heart pounding and head throbbing, Lek remembered Haxhi. He wiped the blood from his eyes and strained to see through the smoke and dust. He saw the scavenging woman torn and twisted on the ground. Thirty feet away lay the mangy dog.

"Haxhi!" Lek cried as he spotted his brother just feet from the dog. Lek didn't feel the burning in his leg as he raced through the settling cloud toward his brother. He found Haxhi lying motionless in the dirt, his body covered by fine powdery dust that glistened red in places. "Oh, no! Oh, no! Haxhi!" Lek cried as he kneeled beside him, searching for signs of life. Lek frantically shook his brother. He heard the screams of his sister along with men's voices, but they were shouting unfamiliar words.

Dazed, Lek looked back to Jrfete as a Marine kneeled beside her. He watched numbly as another exited their Humvee and pointed at him. Two Marines yelled at Lek from the road's edge while a third ran into the field toward him. Feeling Haxhi move, Lek turned to see his brother blankly looking at him.

"Haxhi!" Lek cried. "Are you okay? You shouldn't have done that! You shouldn't have left the road!"

Tears spilled down Haxhi's dust-covered face as he grimaced in pain.

Lek's confused eyes widened as the Navy corpsman, who had charged across the field without fear, dropped to his knees beside Lek and examined Haxhi. Lek didn't understand the strange words the man yelled and looked back at the others as they ran toward him. One Marine stopped and pointed past Lek. Lek followed his arm to another of the yellow cylinders, an unexploded cluster bomb, deeper in the field.

Lek turned back to his bloodied brother. His eyes were heavy and glazed. There was a strange wheezing as Haxhi fought to breathe. "It's okay," Lek said as tears welled in his eyes. "The Americans are here to help you. It's okay."

Haxhi grimaced and wheezed, "Mamma!"

"Haxhi!" Lek cried, reaching for his brother as a Marine pulled him away. Lek's eyes swelled when the corpsman cut open Haxhi's bloody shirt. Lek's heart sank at the jagged piece of metal protruding from between Haxhi's bony ribs. Lek sobbed as he remembered his dying brother, Rexhe.

Lek tried to understand the corpsman as he barked commands at the others. One of them spoke on a radio. Lek watched helplessly as two of them frantically worked on Haxhi. "I'm sorry Haxhi!" Lek cried as another Marine wrapped his bleeding forehead. "I'm sorry I didn't care for you better! The Americans will help you!"

Lek was reassuring Haxhi when he heard a growing drumbeat. His eyes widened when a helicopter hovered into view. The beat of the rotor blades drowned out Lek's words, and the storm of swirling dirt caused him to shut his eyes.

As the whirlwind subsided, Lek discovered a large green helicopter had landed on the road. He looked in awe at its massive rotors still spinning. With wide eyes, Lek watched two more Americans rush across the field with a stretcher. Lek looked on helplessly as the men lifted his glassy-eyed brother onto the stretcher and rushed back to the helicopter.

"Where are they taking him?" Lek cried as the helicopter's rotor blades spun harder, but he didn't understand the American's reply. As the helicopter lifted off the road, the whirlwind of dirt forced Lek to bury his head. The sound of the helicopter was deafening as it passed above and moved off through the sky.

"Where are they taking him?" Lek cried as a Marine pulled him to his feet. Lek took a step, but the world around him swirled into a haze. The Marine walking him to the road said something, but Lek didn't understand. Lek fought through his tears as he searched for his sister, but it was all a fading blur. Sobbing uncontrollably, Lek's legs buckled, and he collapsed on the ground.

———

CHAPTER
THIRTY

IT WAS hot in the small office, despite the purring desk fan. Leaning back in his chair, Captain Richards listened to Lieutenant Janis finish his situation report. He then looked over his four lieutenants and said, "We've been here four days. What progress have we made?"

Lieutenant Sanders, an African-American with a square jaw and a bodybuilder's physique, said, "There's still some fighting between the Albanians and Serbs, but it's little stuff now. Mainly returning Albanians coming home and wanting to pick a fight with the first Serb they meet."

"I had one of those yesterday," added the ruddy-faced Lieutenant Gunderson of Fourth Platoon. "This family comes back after being chased out months ago, and they're all excited to see their house still standing, right? The only problem is, a bunch of Serbs had moved in. Low and behold, a fight starts. When it's all over, three Serbs are dead, and two of the returning Albanians are injured."

Richards shook his head.

"It didn't stop there," Gunderson continued, "The family takes these two wounded Albanians to the hospital, and the family gets in a fight with the doctor who is, of course, a Serb. Luckily, we had men there."

"Captain, if it's gotten better, it's only 'cause we're here," said the bespectacled Lieutenant Janis.

"Or they've run out of bullets," Gunderson smirked.

"Yeah, it's not from newfound brotherly love," added Sanders.

Richards nodded. "Well, that's what we're getting paid to do; keep the peace, and if just being here helps, then we know we're at least making a difference."

The other men nodded.

"EOD has been busy clearing houses?" Richards asked, moving through his agenda.

"Beyond busy," Gunderson said. "Not only did the Serbs lay a crap-load of mines in the fields, but they booby-trapped a lot of the houses they didn't burn. Our guys are working overtime trying to clear it all."

Richards tapped his pen on the desk. "Our field hospital is already overloaded. A lot of the mine-related injuries are sent straight to Bondsteel," he said, referring to the Army's large field hospital in nearby Urosevac. "EOD's posting signs to warn the returning refugees, but I don't know if that's enough."

"It's not only mines. There are unexploded munitions too," Sanders frowned. "Yesterday, a couple of kids came across an unexploded cluster bomb along the side of the road."

Richards winced and shook his head.

"It's a mess, sir," Lieutenant Janis sighed. "What was supposed to kill the bad guys is now killing the good guys."

"I don't know if there are any good guys," grumbled Sanders.

"It's the wild west," added Gunderson. "It's too bad we can't keep them across the border until it's safe."

"When will that be?" Richards frowned. "Any more on that sniper attack?"

"No, sir," reported Janis. "We're still not sure if they were angry Serbs or angry KLA. No bodies were recovered."

Richards leaned back in his chair. "That seems to be an isolated incident, but it could happen again. The KLA aren't happy about us taking away their weapons—or their prisoners. There may be some that act out, so tell your men to stay sharp."

"Aye, sir," replied the lieutenants.

Richards looked at his notebook. "I wish there was a better way. I don't blame them for not wanting to give up their weapons. If I'd been through what they have, I wouldn't want to give away my best means of self-defense either—despite NATO's orders. But we can't let them keep their weapons; it sends the wrong message to the Serbs who are still here. We have to protect them too."

"How many weapons have been voluntarily turned in?" Sanders asked.

"Not many," Richards said. "Most of what we have we've confiscated, but there's gotta be hundreds out there still."

"All we got to do is hold things together until the Army takes over in a couple weeks, then it's their mess," Janis sighed.

Richards knew the lieutenant was right. Elements of the Army's First Division were already moving into the province in preparation for the turnover. In just a few weeks, he and his men would be on the road back to Greece and their ships. As stressful and frustrating as their occupation had been the past four days, it was only a matter of time before it would be over. He hoped the worst was behind them.

———

The southern roads of Kosovo, which had carried so many fleeing Albanians to safety months before, were once again congested. It wasn't only the stream of 800,000 returning refugees that filled the roads, but also convoys of UN supply trucks carrying much-needed food, medicine, and provisions for the destitute people.

With the US Army scheduled to replace the Marines in two weeks, Captain Richards wasn't surprised to see Army supply trucks passing through. Specialty Army units had already begun setting up camps and field hospitals for what was expected to be a long-term operation. But he was surprised to see Western journalists pouring into what was still a dangerous land. They would document and report on the devastation, human suffering, and peacekeeping efforts and, he supposed, make his job a little harder.

In addition to the aid and replacement units filtering into Kosovo, there was a small army of 300 forensic and ballistic experts who had come to document Serbian atrocities. These experts had the grim and painstaking task of reconstructing crime scenes, uncovering mass graves, and determining the cause of death of thousands.

Captain Richards removed his helmet as he entered the first of the two large hospital tents set up on the sports hall's parking lot. Beside him walked Dr. Mark Brunelli, a forensic scientist from George Washington University. Brunelli was an average build man with dark, Mediterranean features. Though there was gray in his hair and goatee, the fifty-one-year-old scientist was fit and looked younger. Having arrived two days earlier, Brunelli and his team of six wasted no time getting down to their unpleasant work. Accompanied by interpreters, they began by touring Vitina and its surrounding area to get a general feel for what had happened there. After spending the better part of a day photographing known and rumored sites of Serbian atrocities, they moved on to the interviewing process. Although this would be an ongoing investigation, much of the needed information came faster than they could digest it. There were hundreds of Albanians in Vitina alone, waiting to give their accounts.

A certain amount of psychology was needed to decipher the information. Human emotions, perceptions, and memories were involved, and extracting accurate data required patience and understanding. Although many of the factual stories verged on the unbelievable, some stories were simply that: tales. Some were based on truth, but had grown with pain and time. Others came from angry souls starving for vengeance.

The twenty by forty-foot tent was separated into two areas. On one side was a spillover treatment area from the adjoining main hospital tent, which provided medical care to the refugees who either couldn't get into Vitina's hospital or refused to go because of the Serbian doctors there. The forensic team used the other half of the tent to interview survivors and store and examine the evidence. As they entered the interviewing area, Richards saw a middle-aged Albanian woman sitting across a folding table from an interpreter and investigator. On the table between them were a cassette tape recorder, a camera, and a laptop computer.

Richards watched as the short, heavy woman spoke through the interpreter. Her despair, even in a time of healing, was unmistakable. Beside her was a young boy, eight or nine, Richards guessed, with raw burn scars that disfigured his head and face. The child made only brief eye contact with Richards before burying his hairless head into his mother's arm. Richards sighed and turned to Brunelli, who was reading the report on the laptop from over the investigator's shoulder.

Stepping away, Brunelli pulled off his reading glasses and shook his head. "This is worse than Bosnia, I think."

"What happened?" Richards asked, unsure he wanted to know.

"She reported that Serbs chased everyone out of their homes and set them on fire. Her husband tried to stay with her, but they beat him and forced him to watch them rape his daughter. Then they threw him and the girl into the burning house. The boy was thrown in too, but managed to escape. As you saw, he was burned pretty bad."

Richards groaned. "How can these people do these things?"

"Hate," Brunelli answered matter-of-factly. "Discriminating, mind-numbing, hate. Sadly, it gets worse than this. Earlier today, there was a man who witnessed a mass execution. He said there were at least sixty killed. He only managed to escape because he was at the rear of the group and ran into the woods when the shooting began. He said some of the Serbs were dancing as they shot into the crowd. They were *celebrating*. It was a big party for them. He said he lost a son, a brother, and two nephews—they weren't even ten years old. Yesterday, a woman reported Serbs taking her husband and cramming him and three other men into an outhouse. They put a grenade inside and closed the door. After it went off, they shot into the outhouse with their automatic weapons, then pushed it over. It's like a frat party gone mad. The whole thing's medieval."

Richards was surprised at the horror he felt—horror he tried to hide. He was a professional warfighter. He had seen things in the Gulf War. He saw Iraqi soldiers burned to a crisp, but that didn't bother him this much. *That was different*, he reminded himself. Enemy casualties, enemy troops, were different from civilians—especially women and children. He was angry. The hateful Serbs had gone too far, and a part of him wanted to punish them. Then he remembered the words of

Colonel Bates. It was counsel that seemed especially appropriate now. *I have to stay objective. I have to remain professional. This isn't about me. I can't fix this.* Richards straightened up as the words took root and swallowed his emotions.

"Have you gotten anything on our man yet? On Nimatovic?" Richards asked, trying to hide his anger. He knew he didn't have much time in the province before the Army replaced him, and capturing someone as notorious as Nimatovic, the Cowboy, would go a long way in satisfying his sense of justice.

"That guy didn't do himself any favors," Brunelli chuckled. "Between his MO and his cowboy outfit, he's pretty well known. I don't know; maybe he wanted it that way. Don't get me started on the psychology of mass murderers. Anyway, there are lots of sightings, but nothing current, and it's hard to know just how accurate any of it is. What makes you think he's still around, anyway? If I were him, I'd be in Serbia by now."

"So would I, but I understand he's from Kosovo," Richards said as they moved through the tent. "A KLA man said they ran into him a week ago trying to cross a bridge, but he got away."

"They gotta hate that."

"No kidding. But I've got a feeling this Nimatovic is close by."

"A feeling huh?" Brunelli eyed the captain. "Well, we'll continue to gather information on him and any others responsible for this."

As they passed through an inner partition into the hospital side of the tent, Richards saw refugees in line to receive medical attention. His eyes were drawn to the front of the line, where a ragged Lek, who had a bandaged arm, leg, and head, stood holding an equally tattered Jrfete. As Richards walked past, he noticed Jrfete. Her cute little face was bruised and had a dozen small scabs. Richards' brow gathered. She reminded him of his niece back home, but there was something else. He had seen her somewhere before. Richards was trying to place her when he remembered the camp where they had picked up Jusuf. He had seen her there. Richards stopped and looked the brother and sister over. "What happened to them?"

"I don't know," Brunelli replied.

"Corpsman, what happened to these kids?" Richards asked as Lek fidgeted.

The Navy corpsman, who had just finished re-bandaging the boy's leg, nodded to it and said, "He caught some frags, sir. It happened a couple of days ago. His leg's a little infected."

Richards saw one leg of Lek's filthy sport pants was cut off at the thigh, and he had a fresh bandage. "And the little girl?"

"She had a couple of small hits and is a little undernourished, but other than that, she's okay," shrugged the corpsman.

"Do they speak English?" Richards asked, moving closer.

"No, sir—at least I don't think so, sir."

"Do you have an interpreter?" Richards asked.

"Yes, sir. Miric, can you help here for a moment?" the corpsman called out to an older, graying man assisting another hospital worker.

A man with a hawkish nose, gray eyes, and a beard, wearing a black shirt and slacks with a silver Greek cross hanging from his neck, approached. "How can I help you, Captain?" he smiled.

Richards didn't notice the interpreter was a priest or that he spoke perfect English; he was focused on the sweet little Jrfete looking up at him with innocent blue eyes. Richards turned to Lek, whose empty gaze hovered at the captain's knees. Richards' brow tightened at the lost and broken boy. Knowing there were hundreds or even thousands of others just like him made Richards' heart ache. When Richards placed a gentle hand on Lek's shoulder, his gaze moved up, meeting Richards' but his expression was unchanged. Richards smiled at Jrfete, but she recoiled and clung to her brother.

"What happened to them?" Richards asked.

The priest, who spoke in a deep, soothing voice, posed the question, and the boy looked at him sheepishly. The priest forced a smile, then repeated the question, causing Lek to squirm before answering in a frightened voice. "He said Serbs attacked his family."

"Ask him if he knows where his parents are."

The priest's eyes shifted to Lek, and he asked the question.

Lek looked down at his little sister, and after a moment's hesitation, responded.

"He says his mother is no more." The priest looked at the captain and added, "I believe he means she's dead."

"What about his father? Ask him if they're alone," Richards said, his smile straining.

Lek again hesitated before answering.

"He says his father is missing. It's only he and his sister now."

Richards' eyes narrowed, and he turned to the corpsman. "You said this happened two days ago?"

"Yes, sir," the Navy corpsman nodded, "But the Serbs didn't do it. A patrol brought them in. Apparently, they were walking along a road when someone picked up an unexploded cluster bomb. I don't know how many it killed."

Richards shook his head. "I heard about that. It's not enough that the Serbs kill them. Now we join in with unexploded munitions." He looked the two children over, then asked, "Was it their mother who picked it up?"

"I don't know, sir," the corpsman replied.

"Would you like me to ask him?" asked the priest.

"No," Richards said with a shake of his head. He looked over the children and wondered what he would have done in their situation, alone with a little sister to care for. He didn't know. Richards looked into Lek's eyes. He saw no anger or bitterness. There wasn't even despair. There was nothing; no hope, no emotion, nothing. He was simply existing, and it made Richards' heart ache.

The captain straightened up. *They're casualties of war. There's a thousand more just like them. I can't worry about them all. It's not my job.* Richards was half-turned when he stopped. "What are their names?" His softening eyes turned from Brunelli back to the children.

The hawk-nosed priest questioned the boy. Then, with a soft, reverent voice, said, "Captain, his name is Lek, and the girl's is Jrfete."

Richards nodded. He then squared up to the children and asked, "How do you say hello?"

"*Hallo*, or *hai*. It's nearly the same as English."

"Lek, *hai*," Richards said with a more natural, less-forced smile.

Lek's eyes moved to the captain's, blinking in uncertainty.

"Ah, Ur..."

"Jrfete," the priest prompted.

"Jrfete...*hai, hai*," Richards said with an even broader smile.

The dark-haired girl unburied her head from her brother's chest and half-turned to Richards. Her blue eyes narrowed as a faint smile revealed a dimple.

Richards had to catch himself as a wave of sentiment swept over him. The captain stiffened up and his smile faded. He had work to do.

"Children are the hardest," Brunelli sighed.

"Huh? Yeah. I bet," Richards said, forgetting that the forensic investigator was still there.

"Do you need me for anything else, Captain?" asked the priest.

"No. Thank you," Richards said, as he looked at his watch.

The priest gave a slight bow, but his gaze never left the captain.

Brunelli eyed the priest curiously as he moved across the tent.

Feeling a little guilty for showing so much interest in the children, Richards shook his head and said, "There must be a thousand kids like this."

"There literally are," sighed Brunelli.

"What happens to them, anyway?" Richards asked as they left the tent, squinting at the low-hanging sun.

"There's usually an orphanage set up to care for them until they can be reunited with their parents or family."

"An orphanage, huh? What if there's not an orphanage around? Then what?"

"They're sent away," Brunelli shrugged.

"Doesn't that make it harder for their parents to find them?"

"It does. Sometimes it takes years...*if* they're still alive."

Richards shook his head. "It doesn't seem fair."

"Sadly, life's not fair—at least not for these people. But there are other options."

"Other options?"

"Yes, Captain, you can create an orphanage."

Richards gave Brunelli a quizzical look, then walked away.

Brunelli couldn't help but grin at the captain's reaction. Being an expert in human behavior, he saw the conflict in Richards. He didn't consider caring a weakness, as the captain did, but a strength.

After returning to the hospital tent, Brunelli approached the corpsman, finishing up on the two children, and looked across the tent at the English-speaking priest. "Corpsman, who's that interpreter?"

"Father Miric? He's a local Serbian priest, I think. He showed up this morning and asked if he could help. He speaks really good English, and I couldn't see turning him down."

Still eyeing the priest, Brunelli nodded and said, "Thank you."

———

CHAPTER
THIRTY-ONE

THE SPORTS HALL OFFICE, which served as Captain Richards' quarters, was a simple one-windowed room with a worn linoleum floor and painted masonry walls. On one side of the room was a framed picture showing a town marathon with men and women running through clean streets lined by onlookers. Beside it was a smaller photograph of a man in a runner's uniform being handed a medal by a city official. Richards wondered which of the two men his office belonged to and if either were still alive. An outdated calendar, cheaply framed certificates, and a shelf with a few dusty trophies occupied another wall: Relics from a more peaceful and happy time.

After pushing the door closed behind him, Richards flipped on the light, casting the room in a dull, golden hue. He set his helmet on the worn metal desk and ran a tired hand through his hair. It had been a long and busy day. It wasn't so much what he had done that wore him down, but the things he had seen and the stories he had heard. Richards' eyes were distant as he removed his chest holster and handgun and set them on the desk. His Kevlar vest was next. Unbuttoning his shirt, he sank onto the cot beside the desk and buried his face in his hands. He told himself it was just another workday for a Marine, but as much as he tried, Richards couldn't make the tragedy meaningless. He ached inside at the terrible things that had happened.

Richards knew there was evil in the world, but he had never been so close to it and tasted its bitterness in such a personal way. He tried to imagine such a thing happening in the United States, but couldn't. Richards remembered the painfully vacant faces he had seen; some of them were only children. His throat tightened. Fighting the emotion, he gave a heavy sigh and shook his head.

Richards considered his wife and son. *What would I do if something happened to them?* The thought caused his eyes to well with tears. Suddenly, he missed them more than ever before. He wanted to be away from the awfulness and misery of Kosovo. He wanted to hold his wife and watch a sunset or gaze up at the stars. He wanted to see something beautiful, to be around cheerful people who had love and hope. But all of those things were elsewhere and would have to wait.

Richards' gaze settled on his Kevlar helmet. He thought of the terrible battles that had taken place throughout history. He had never really considered the toll of such fighting. Even with his experience in the Gulf War and studying nearly every other battle in modern history, he had never made the personal connection. It had always been about numbers and strategy, kill or be killed, but what of the survivors? he wondered. What of the innocent victims of evil and hate and violence?

Richards tried to push out the sadness with thoughts of duty, responsibility, and professionalism, but none of it helped. He wanted to ignore the brutality and the evil around him and concentrate on his job as a company commander. He remembered hearing another captain back on the ship say, "If Serbs and Albanians want to kill each other, why should we stop them?" At the time, Richards was in half agreement, but the tragedy around him had changed that, and he felt guilty for not rejecting such a notion outright.

What's wrong with me? he wondered. *I'm just tired and homesick. It'll be gone in the morning.*

After pulling off his boots, Richards swung his legs onto his cot and lay back with a long, stress-emptying sigh. He stared up at the dingy ceiling. After a moment, his eyes closed. Even though he tried to think of something else, his mind returned to the sad and lonely faces of the children in the field hospital. He wondered how many more there were like them.

While Richards was an idealist at heart, his time and experiences in the Corps had made him something of a pragmatist. He knew, even if he wanted to, he couldn't make any *actual* difference. *That's the sad reality of life,* he told himself, but the words were acid to him.

The tired captain sighed and then reached to turn off the light. When he did so, he knocked a photograph of his wife and son onto the floor. Richards picked it up and studied his wife's lovely features, her flowing, golden hair, and soft blue eyes. He missed her like never before. His throat tightened as he looked at his five-year-old son Andrew, who shared his dark hair and chin.

With a heavy sigh, Richards returned the picture to the table, turned off the light, and closed his eyes. He hoped sleep would swiftly find him and wipe away the sadness, but Richards' mind was awash in thought and emotion.

Soon his eyes opened, and he stared at the darkened ceiling.

Richards knew he had to do something. He felt it was his duty as a Marine, as a father, and as a human being. He at least had to try to help the children, but he didn't know what he could do.

Then he remembered the words of Brunelli, the forensic investigator. Richards had at first passed off what he had said about starting an orphanage as an impractical challenge, but as he remembered the destitute faces of the boy and girl in the hospital tent, the reasons for not doing such a thing fell away.

He thought of his Grandma Richards, who was fond of saying, "Where there's a will, there's a way." He shook his head as the idea grew. *I could do it, but it wouldn't be easy. What the hell. I'm a United States Marine. Difficult tasks come easily; the impossible ones just take a little longer.*

———

CHAPTER
THIRTY-TWO

THE OLD CHURCH'S heavy door groaned as Captain Richards pushed it open and peered into the shadowy nave. "Hello." His brow gathered. Richards had been in old churches before—many in Arizona dated back to the Spaniards—but this church seemed strangely different to him. With its dark stone pillars, gray slate floor, and old wood beams, there was a constrained sense of darkness inside. Criss-crossing ribbons of light came from small arched windows along the rafters, and column-mounted lamps puddled light along the empty pews, but the dusky interior swallowed most of the light. At the far end of the nave, atop three stone steps, was the candle-lit altar. Behind it hung and an eerily glowing Christ. Richards felt a suffocating bleakness inside the old church befitting the dreary land. "Hello," he called again.

Richards felt for his handgun holstered across his Kevlar vest as Jusuf and two other Marines followed him inside. He wondered if it was right to bring a weapon into the church, then reminded himself he was in Kosovo. Richards glanced back at Jusuf and the two trailing Marines with rifles in hand, then continued into the shadowy nave.

Richards felt a strange sense of reverence as he eyed the candle-lit altar and the hanging Christ. It was as though he was in a holy place, but not really. He wondered if it was the circumstances and his role as a warrior. Or perhaps it was that some of the murderous Serbs might have worshiped there.

Jusuf was even less at ease in the Christian sanctuary, but for different reasons. As a Muslim, he had always connected Christianity with the Serbian Orthodox Church, the religion of their hated neighbors to the north. Many Albanians associated Jesus Christ with violence and oppression.

Richards turned to the wary-eyed Jusuf and asked. "What's the priest's name?"

"His name is Goran," Jusuf nervously replied.

"Is that him?" Richards asked, pointing to a cloaked figure emerging from a doorway to the right of the altar. "Call him."

Jusuf gulped. "*Otau Goran?*"

Richards watched as the cloaked man turned to them and paused. With a delayed wave, the man offered a greeting, then started toward them. As the cloaked figure drew closer, Jusuf stepped back and lowered his gaze to the slate floor.

"Ah, Captain Richards," the priest said with an American accent as he pulled the hood off his head. "So nice to see you again."

Richards was taken aback by the greeting and looked at the familiar face of the priest in uncertainty. He recognized the beaked nose, gray, piercing eyes, and beard of the interpreter the day before. "You were helping in the hospital yesterday."

"Yes, that's right. But I am not Father Goran. I'm afraid he's left. The war was too much for him, you see. I am Father Vukasin Miric," the priest said with a pleasant smile. "What can I do for you, my son?"

Still surprised by the greeting, Richards studied Miric's features as if he might know him. Richards guessed him to be in his late fifties. His hair was gray and receding. Small rectangular glasses sat midway down his hawk-like nose, and the corners of his mouth curled up, giving a sense of warmth and friendliness. To Richards, the man seemed out of place, and he felt as though he might be looking at an uncle or a neighbor rather than a foreign priest.

"Captain," Miric prodded, "can I help you with something?"

"Yes, sir," Richards replied. "I mean Father. Ah...what—"

"Father is fine. When I lived in the States, they called me Victor. You can call me that if you'd like."

Richards looked at the man in puzzlement. "You speak very good English. You said you lived in the United States?"

"Yes," Miric nodded. "Twenty years. In fact, my mother was an American, but that is neither here nor there. What can I do for you? Do you have need of confession?" he asked pleasantly.

"No, thank you." Richards' brow gathered. "Father, there are two things I wanted to speak to you about. In some towns, the returning Albanians have targeted the churches. Have you had any problems?"

"No," Miric said with an expression that was both pleasant and cunning. "We've been very fortunate in that regard. If you're wondering why I'm still in Kosovo, it's because many of my worshipers are still here. I'm not worried in the least. The Lord will protect me—as He has for years—but you're welcome to post some of your men here if it makes you more comfortable."

Richards' brow gathered. "Father, I'm curious."

"Yes, Captain?"

"How do you deal with all of this? All the death and destruction? I just can't imagine people doing such things to other human beings."

"Such things?" Miric repeated, his eyes narrowing. "Let me ask you, how many innocent people have NATO killed with their indiscriminate bombing? I don't know that you have the moral high ground here, Captain."

Richards shook his head. "There have been a few mishaps, but they can hardly compare to what the Serbian forces, especially the militia, did to these people—to women and children—terrible, unspeakable things. Forgive me, Father, I'm just having a hard time understanding it all."

Somewhat entertained by Richards' concern, Miric asked with a raised brow, "Captain, are you a believer?"

"Yes," Richards nodded.

"Then you know this is all God's will," Miric said with piercing eyes.

Richards considered the priest's words. He didn't want to get into a discussion about agency and the nefariousness of man. He wanted to talk about the children. "Father," he started in a more upbeat tone, "the other thing I want to talk to you about is the children. As I'm sure you know, there are many displaced children in the area. There are more than twenty that are staying near our outpost, but they need better shelter than we can provide—at least until they can be reunited with their families—that is, if their families are still alive. Is there an orphanage here in Vitina?"

"I'm afraid not," replied Father Miric.

"Is there anything you or your church can do for these children?"

Miric's countenance softened, and he shook his head sadly. "The children. It's terrible what happens to them in war. I've seen it too many times," he said, his eyes trailing off. "It's funny you should ask, as I have given thought to that very thing." He turned back to Richards. "These children, they need shelter, they need food, water, love."

"Even the Albanian children?" Jusuf asked, his head still down.

The interpreter's words gave Miric pause. He turned to Jusuf and said, "I am sorry for your pain. We are all God's children—regardless of our beliefs. My answer to that question is yes, *especially* the Muslim children. I fear they have suffered the most."

Jusuf's eyes lifted as he recognized the truth of the priest's words, but he still didn't make eye contact. *Maybe this is a good man, after all.*

"Father, if you could help, it would be an important peace gesture for the area."

"Of course," Miric nodded.

"The UN is setting up temporary shelters for displaced children, but the closest one is twenty kilometers away. I'd like to keep the local children here. I think it makes more sense. It'll be easier for them to reunite with their parents or surviving family that way. Don't you agree?"

"Yes, that is an excellent idea," Miric nodded. "There must be hundreds coming back into the country."

"Eight hundred thousand was our last report," Richards sighed.

"I had no idea there were so many," Miric said in astonishment. "Let me see..." he scratched his gray, receding hair. "How many children are you talking about—here in Vitina?"

"Maybe two dozen."

"I see. I have some space here, but there is a building just down the street that would be perfect. It was a small store where they sold furniture. Much of it has been taken since the war, but I believe there are still some beds there. Would that work?"

Gladdened by the priest's offer, Richards glanced at Jusuf and said, "Yes, that sounds perfect. Father, we also need an overseer—just for now—just until things get more organized. I'll assign Marines to help with the grunt work, but could you help us with that?"

Miric's eyes narrowed as he smiled. "I would love to."

"Thank you," Richards said with an appreciative nod. "When can I look at this furniture store?"

"Can you come back later this afternoon? That will give me time to check into a few things," Miric said with a pleasant smile.

"I can. Thank you again," Richards said as he turned and nodded to Jusuf and the two Marines.

Father Miric followed the visitors to the door and offered a final farewell before pushing the old wooden door closed. He then looked back into the shadowed church, his gray eyes intent. His pleasant smile faded.

Standing outside of the old church, Jusuf watched as Richards pulled his radio from his vest and reported in. Jusuf couldn't help but reflect on what the priest had said about the killing being God's will. He waited for the captain to finish his radio message, then stepped beside him and said, "Captain, can I ask you question?"

"Sure," Richards said, turning to the interpreter.

Jusuf forced down a swallow. "Do you believe in holy books?"

"Holy books? You mean like the Koran and the Bible?"

Jusuf nodded.

"Well, I don't know the Koran, but I believe in the Bible."

"In these books, there are stories of God killing the bad people," Jusuf said, glancing at the two listening Marines.

"Yeah," Richards nodded, his eyes narrowing.

"Do you think… Do you think we are bad people? My people? And that God punish us like this?"

Richards considered the question. "You mean what the priest said, that all of this killing was God's will?"

"Yes, that," Jusuf fretted.

"No. I don't. There are people who choose to do evil things. They may use God as an excuse, but they're the ones doing it. I don't think your people are any more bad or good than the Serbs. They're just the ones getting the short end of the stick."

"Short end?" Jusuf repeated, confused by the expression.

"*Unlucky.*"

"Oh," Jusuf said, staring off blankly.

"Does that answer your question?"

Jusuf nodded vaguely, but he was still unsure what it all meant.

Inside the church, Father Miric passed the empty pews, turned down the transept, and passed through the door to the right of the altar. He walked down the dimly lit corridor, pushed open a door, and entered a one-windowed room which had a small, disheveled bed in one corner. In the shadows of the other corner stood a man with a scraggly goatee and sweat-glistened face. When he saw it was Father Miric who had entered, the goateed man lowered his machine pistol and hobbled from the shadows, a large bandage wrapped around his thigh.

"They're gone—for now," Miric said with folded arms.

The wounded man gave a painful nod as he eased himself onto the bed.

"You cannot stay here any longer," Miric announced.

Ivan Nimatovic, the Cowboy, looked up at the priest but said nothing.

———

CHAPTER
THIRTY-THREE

CAPTAIN RICHARDS SET the situation report on his cluttered desk and rubbed his eyes. It wasn't even noon, and he already had six hours of work in. He reached for a water bottle, took a drink, and then leaned back in his chair. It had rained much of the morning. The sound of children's voices from outside his rain-splattered window caused him to turn. Moving to the window, Richards watched a group of Albanians sitting under the shelter of an adjacent building's overhang eating from small foil UN food pouches. They were among the thousands of homeless.

With the UN supply tents set up on a nearby soccer field, it didn't surprise Richards to see Albanians wanting to stay near the sports complex for both the food and protection. But being so close to the Marine's base of operations was a security risk, and patrols frequently moved the refugees back to their designated campsites. Richards was about to return to his work when he saw the boy and girl he had met in the hospital tent two days before. The older boy was huddled beside his young sister under a plastic sheet dripping with rain. Richards shook his head. *What are their names? Lek and Ur something.*

Richards had thought about them more than once since their meeting. They were the reason for him setting up an orphanage. He had twice met with the enigmatic Father Miric and toured the old furniture store, which was only a few blocks from the sports hall. The building seemed ideal for what Richards hoped would be a short-term shelter for the children, and he had assigned a pair of Marines to help set it up. What he didn't know was how they would round up the stray children and get them to the shelter. While Richards felt a sense of pride for his lofty plans, he knew it would take a lot of work and wondered if it was a mistake.

Richards watched to see if Lek and his sister had found their family, but they appeared separate from the adults farther down the building. He looked from Lek to the cute little frizzy-haired Jrfete huddled beside him. Richards' eyes narrowed as a middle-aged woman walked toward them with a foil dinner in hand. He remembered Lek saying his mother was dead and sighed when the woman passed by them into the drizzle. A man with rain-slicked hair followed, leaving the two children behind. Richards sighed and shook his head.

Richards pulled his gaze from the window and looked at his cluttered desk. *I've got too much to worry about. I can't get caught up in those kids. It's not like they're the only ones. There are hundreds more, just like them.* Richards shook his head. *I've done my part. Father Miric can run the orphanage. He'll look after them until the UN can find them homes. I can't spend my time worrying about things I can't control; I have too many more pressing problems.* That was what Richards told himself, but he didn't believe half of it.

A knock at his door turned the captain. He set down his water bottle, glanced at his watch, and said, "Enter."

Gunnery Sergeant Rivera, Lieutenant Sanders, and three other Marines entered the office with reports in hand. "Good morning, sir," Rivera said from beside the lieutenant.

"At ease. Fit-Rep time?" Richards asked, finding his chair.

"Aye, sir."

"What you got, Gunny?"

"About the usual, sir. There was a rape last night and two assaults. This morning we got a shoplifting, another robbery, and a property dispute."

"A property dispute." Richards rubbed his face. "Anything else?"

"Isn't that enough, sir?" Lieutenant Sanders asked. "We need a company of MPs for all this crap."

"I agree, sir," Rivera said, shaking his head. "The men didn't sign up for this. They're not policemen."

"No, they're not policemen, but they *are* Marines, and you know what that means."

"That they can do anything, sir?" the lieutenant asked.

"Is that a question or a comment?"

"Sorry, Skipper, that's a comment."

"I thought it might be." Richards flipped through the pages of the report, then looked up at the men standing before him. "There are plenty of bad guys out there, and if they catch wind that we're going slack, they'll have a field day."

"Aye, sir," Rivera said with a sharp nod. "I'll let the men know."

"Very well."

"Sir, the brig is getting full," Sanders frowned.

"Then make another one," Richards shrugged. "We'll have the hard work done by the time the Army gets here."

"Isn't that always the case, sir?" Gunny Rivera smirked.

"How's the moral?" Richards asked.

"Outstanding, sir," replied Lieutenant Sanders.

"This is where you tell it like it is, sir," muttered Rivera.

"Oh, right." Sanders' eyes flashed to the captain. "A little down, sir. I think seeing all these poor people coming back to nothing is a little hard on the men, sir."

"Just remind them they're saving people's lives."

"Aye, sir."

After thirty more minutes of platoon business, Richards asked, "Anything else?"

"Negative, sir."

Richards gave a dismissing nod, and the Marines filed out of his office. He stared at the reports on his desk as the rain pattered on the window. He tried to focus on the reports but caught himself listening for the children's voices. *I wonder if they're still out there?* With a sigh, Richards pushed back in his chair and moved to the window. He groaned when he saw Lek and Jrfete still huddled against the wall under their plastic sheet. Richards shook his head, turned from the window, and exited his office.

Richards put on his helmet when he pushed open the sports hall side door and stepped into the drizzle, with Jusuf following.

"They're right over there," Richards said, pointing to the children huddled against the building.

Lek looked at the approaching men as if he were in trouble. The Americans had moved them before, but they had nowhere to go.

"What are their names again? Lek and Ur-something," Richards asked as they stopped before the wide-eyed children.

Jusuf spoke to Lek, who looked at Richards in remembrance.

"The boy is called Lek, and the girl is Jrfete."

"They're brother and sister?" Richards asked, forcing a smile.

Jusuf nodded.

"Have they found any of their family yet?"

Jusuf posed the question.

Lek shook his head sadly.

Richards sighed. "Tell him about the orphanage. That it will be a place for them to stay until their family can find them."

Lek considered the message, then replied.

"He says he has cared for his brothers and sisters for a long time."

"Brothers and sisters? Are there others?"

When Jusuf asked, Lek's gaze lowered without a response. Jusuf asked again, and Lek muttered a reply. "He says the others are dead."

Richards shook his head and looked down the side of the building to the medical tent, just visible in the parking lot. "How many?"

"Three. Two brothers and a sister," Jusuf reported, biting his lip.

"*Three.*" Richards' heart sank. "What happened to them?"

Lek looked from Jusuf to the captain, then pointed skyward.

"He say a bomb came from a jet plane and kill many. This happened a long time ago, after the Serbs burned their village."

"What about his parents?"

Lek studied his feet for a time before whispering a reply.

"He say the Serbs took his mother. He found her in the barn dead."

Richards groaned. "And his father?"

"He is gone to help KLA."

"That could mean anything," Richards muttered as he rubbed his forehead. "Will you tell him I would like him and his sister to stay at the orphanage? It's out of the rain, there's food, and it's safe."

Lek looked Richards in the eyes when he gave his answer.

"He says no place is safe. Not anymore."

"Tell him we're here to make it safe."

"He says what about when you go home? Will it be safe then?"

Richards considered the question.

"He wants to know what your name is," Jusuf said, eyeing the captain, himself curious.

Richards grinned at Lek and said, "Ah, Jack," as he tapped his vest.

"*Ah-Ja-ack,*" Lek repeated with wide eyes.

Richards chuckled. "No, just Jack."

"Ja-ack."

"Yes, Jack," Richards beamed. When he remembered the gum in his pocket, Richards removed a half-empty pack of Juicy-Fruit and pulled out a stick for each of them. "Here."

A wide-eyed Jrfete snatched a stick from the captain's hand without knowing what it was. But Lek studied Richards' face before taking his.

"It's gum. You chew it," Richards said with an exaggerated chewing motion. He watched as Lek unwrapped Jrfete's piece, and she pushed it into her mouth. Richards smiled as her blue eyes swelled from the flavor. "Tell her to chew it, not eat it."

Jusuf passed on the message, then licked his lips as the captain returned the gum to his pocket.

With both children savoring the gum, Richards said, "Ask them again if they'll go to the orphanage."

Jusuf did so, and Lek responded with a hint of a smile. "He said they will go if you will bring them more gum."

Richards chuckled. "I think I can do that. Bring them inside, out of the rain."

"Inside?" Jusuf asked with a raised brow.

"Yes." Richards looked up into the drizzle. "They shouldn't be out here."

"Okay," Jusuf nodded as the captain turned and started back.

Lek was at first uncertain what to do when Jusuf told him they were coming inside, but the thought of a dry place out of the rain overcame his uncertainty.

After gathering up his sister and their few belongings, Lek followed the wet interpreter. Jusuf stopped at the door, took the dripping plastic sheet from Lek, and set it on the ground. Jusuf then led them inside.

With eyes wide and shoes squeaking, Lek walked down the clean and dry corridor into a room bathed in dull yellow light. He nervously chewed the flavor from his gum as he watched the large American captain standing at his desk. Lek listened as Jusuf and Richards spoke in words he didn't understand. Jusuf directed Lek to a chair near the desk where he sat with Jrfete in his lap. The little girl's eyes were round as she looked at the walls, pictures, and furnishings of the office; a world removed from the squalor she had grown used to.

Lek sat in the clean room on a padded chair as the captain smiled and Jusuf spoke words of reassurance. Lek wanted to believe what they told him, that they would care for him and his sister; but Lek had seen too much in the weeks since the Serbs had killed his mother and the world had crashed around him. He had gone from a vibrant and happy eleven-year-old boy, with a future as bright as any Albanian, to a wretched scavenger whose only thought was how to provide for himself and his sister.

Lek's miserableness wasn't without hope, however. He still dreamed of his father finding them and returning them to their happy lives and becoming a boy again. But with each passing day, that hope faded. Lek wondered if anything would ever change. So many had died around him. So many faces were gone forever.

Lek looked at Jrfete, who was happily chewing her gum. He saw her dirty face and ran a loving hand through her wet, frizzy hair. She looked up at Lek, and he smiled.

———

CHAPTER
THIRTY-FOUR

IT HAD BEEN a long day for Jusuf Hasani, who had spent most of it assisting Captain Richards with his seemingly endless duties. Jusuf had just passed the UN provisions tent, where a group of refugees was waiting in line, when he heard his name. Stopping mid-stride, the tired Jusuf turned back to see who had called him. Amidst the line of Albanians was a face he hadn't seen in years. "Sadir? Sadir Shehu?"

"Hello, old friend," said Sadir, who had a dark, scruffy beard and slicked-back hair. Jusuf and Sadir were close friends in childhood, but time and different interests had caused them to grow apart. Sadir's dream of becoming a doctor took him to Istanbul while Jusuf stayed and worked at the movie theater.

With surprised smiles, the two men embraced. "Sadir, it's so good to see you. Where have you been? Are you still in Istanbul? Are you a doctor?"

"It is good to see you, my friend. And yes, I am in Istanbul. I'm in my third year of medical school—at least I was before all of this." Sadir's smile faded. "I came back for my family."

Jusuf grew somber. He ached at the thought of his family. Prepared for the worst, he asked, "How are they?"

Sadir shrugged. "I have not found them."

Jusuf put a comforting hand on his friend's shoulder. "There are so many without homes now. I'm sure they're just looking for a place to live."

"Thank you," Sadir sighed "but—"

"But nothing. You'll find them. You must have faith."

"How is it working with the Americans?"

"Oh, they are *good* men," Jusuf beamed. He wanted to tell his friend about Captain Richards, who, like a hero in a Hollywood movie, was brave and bold and could do no wrong. He wanted to tell him the Marines were noble warriors and men of honor who made him feel special, but all he could say was, "they are good men."

Sadir nodded.

"You have been back to Livoc, then?" Jusuf asked.

"Yes," Sadir sighed. "Jusuf, I am sorry about your family."

"How did you hear about them?"

"I found Mentor Kelmendi's wife in the camp."

Jusuf's face lit up. It had only been a week since he had left Lirie and her mother, but to him, it seemed much longer. "Lirie! How is she? I've wanted to go back, but they need me here. I tried to contact—" Jusuf stopped mid-sentence when he saw his friend's concern. "What's wrong? What's happened to Lirie?"

"Jusuf, she…"

Jusuf's heart sank. "What? What's wrong? What's happened?"

Sadir's brow gathered. "She is…very sad."

"Yes, I know! Those Serbian dogs, they—" Jusuf paused, knowing her being sad wasn't the problem. "What happened? What happened to Lirie?"

Sadir looked away, then back again. "Jusuf, she tried to kill herself," he finally managed, his eyes full of grief.

Jusuf stared at his friend blankly. "What? Is she alive?"

"Yes, I think she is better now. Her mother is caring for her, but you must go to her when you can."

"Yes, of course," Jusuf said as he stared across the crowded soccer fields. Angrily shaking his head, he blurted, "I don't understand! She was doing so much better! I shouldn't have left her."

"No. You did what you must. Lirie's mother told me you came here to prepare a home for them, to make this place livable again. That is a good thing, and if anything can give her hope, is it that. But…what the Serbs did to her—that is not an easy thing to forget. She may never forget."

Staring across the field of refugees, Jusuf's jaw tightened, and his anger swelled. "Will it never stop?" he seethed, tears welling in his eyes. "Even now, after the war, in this *peace*, they can still kill us."

———

Jusuf Hasani glared at the uniformed Serb with harsh, unforgiving eyes as he, Captain Richards, and another Marine sat in the small office turned interrogation room. The young Serb, who had brown wavy hair and skin that glistened with sweat, gulped as he looked from Richards to the seething interpreter.

It had only been a day since Jusuf had learned of Lirie's suicide attempt. While he wanted to go back to comfort Lirie, he felt compelled to stay and help the Marines. Jusuf wasn't sure if it was the helplessness he felt dealing with Lirie's pain and depression or the satisfaction he received bringing the Serbs to justice. But he needed to stay in Vitina.

From Jusuf's perspective, the Marines had made significant progress in just one week. There were far fewer conflicts between the two sides, more refugees had returned, and parts of the town were cleaned up and nearly livable again. The hope of a new beginning with Lirie was forefront in Jusuf's mind. But lurking in the shadows of his thoughts was his hatred for the Serbs who had taken so much from him and his people. Jusuf tried to keep those tormenting thoughts and memories deep inside him, but with the sad news of Lirie, they had come to the surface; and like a festering sore, the anger, pain, and despair were more than he could bear. He hated the Serbs now more than ever, and the quiet rage he felt made it hard for him to think.

Jusuf glared at the young Serbian soldier who had become separated from his VJ unit ten days earlier. He had tried to cross the river on three separate occasions but was unsuccessful and narrowly escaped capture by the KLA. After hiding for a week, the hungry soldier turned himself over to a Marine patrol.

Jusuf had helped question hundreds of Serbs in the past week, but as he looked at this man, darker questions filled his head. *How many Albanian women has he raped? Whose parents, whose children has he killed? How would I kill him if I had the chance?*

"Ask him if there are any other VJ Serbs hiding in the area," Richards said, interrupting Jusuf's dark thoughts. "Ask him where Nimatovic is."

The Serb prisoner wasn't angry or spiteful, nor did he radiate hate; he looked like a normal young man frightened for his life. If it wasn't for his uniform and accent, Jusuf might have mistaken him for Albanian; they might have even been friends. But he was a Serb, and Jusuf saw only a man he wanted dead. "Are there any others like you hiding?"

"No. Just me."

Jusuf stared down the Serb with his best Dirty Harry look, then snarled, "Where's Nimatovic? Where's the Cowboy?"

"I-I don't know," the Serb sputtered, staring at the table.

Jusuf's eyes narrowed. "Tell me the truth, or they'll cut you into pieces and feed you to their dogs."

The young Serb looked at Jusuf in horror.

"Yes. Their dogs have gotten fat on Serbian meat."

"I-I've told you what I know."

"Maybe, maybe not," Jusuf grinned. "Those dogs are hungry."

The young prisoner gulped as he stared at his bound hands. "Please, I just want to go home. I didn't want to be here. The war means nothing to me."

"Tell that to the dogs," Jusuf hissed.

The Serb licked his parched lips then whispered, "There are two or three, but..." he looked around the small room, his face glistening with sweat.

"Yes?" Jusuf prodded.

"If I tell you, will they treat me well?"

"Yes," Jusuf said, leaning forward, his eyes unblinking.

The prisoner gulped. "The Cowboy?"

"Yes?" Jusuf's eyes widened. "You know where he is?"

"Yes," breathed the Serb.

As Jusuf considered what to do next, he saw a patiently waiting Captain Richards out of the corner of his eye. While he still respected the Americans, the news of his dear Lirie had poisoned his reasoning. He had seen what the Americans had done with the Mayor of Vitina, taking him from the KLA, who would have executed him for his crimes. It seemed to Jusuf he had betrayed his people that day. *If they were to treat Nimatovic, the devil himself, the same way...* Jusuf couldn't bear the thought. He looked at the agitated Serb. "Where is he?"

The Serb fidgeted in his seat, then swallowed hard. "You promise they will treat me well? Maybe even release me?"

"They will at least treat you well," Jusuf said slyly, knowing they would anyway.

The prisoner sighed. He looked from the Marines to Jusuf and said, "There's an old mill near the river. He's there."

Jusuf hid his smile. He knew exactly the place.

"They will treat me well?" the young Serb asked anxiously.

Jusuf nodded and said, "Their dogs will go hungry today."

"What's going on?" Richards asked, eyeing the agitated prisoner.

Jusuf shrugged. "Sorry Captain. I try, but he don't know anything."

———

CHAPTER
THIRTY-FIVE

LEK GRINNED as a boy crept around a stack of boxes and tightly arranged beds in the upstairs room. Hide-and-seek was one of Lek's favorite games. Even though he wasn't playing, he found great pleasure in hearing the giggles and joyful sounds of the other children in the new shelter. Even Jrfete, whose smile had been gone too long, was reveling in the fun as she searched for the hiding children. Her eyes widened as the searching boy neared a poorly hidden girl. Jrfete pointed and giggled at the girl. But when the downstairs door opened and the searching boy heard men's voices, he froze.

Small heads emerged from their hiding places and nervously watched as Lek looked down the stairs. "It's okay," he said, seeing the Marines carrying in cases of water. With nerves calmed, the children resumed their play.

Before the war, the makeshift orphanage was a furniture store. Although looted, there were still a half-dozen beds and couches the Marines had moved upstairs for the children to sleep on. The lower level was set up with a crude kitchen and tables for eating. Stacks of UN relief supplies lined one wall, providing ample provisions for the children. One corner of the downstairs was left open for the children to play games, but having endured much violence at the hands of uniformed Serbs, the children were more comfortable playing upstairs, away from the Marines.

Being among the first to arrive at the new orphanage, Lek and Jrfete were treated to warm baths and clean clothes. They even had their pick of soft beds. Theirs wasn't a large bed, but on their first night, they found it big enough for them and three other children. While Lek was at first suspicious of the American's offer of protection, he now felt safe and was grateful to have food to eat and a place indoors to sleep.

To Lek, the Marines' brown foil meals were a welcome improvement to the UN's protein wafers, and he looked forward to the next. He thought they tasted good even when cold. But when a Marine heated one in a pot of water and emptied it onto a slice of bread, Lek thought it the most delicious thing he had ever eaten.

It was Lek's second full day in the quickly filling shelter. Being the oldest there, Lek found the other children looking to him for direction. While he would have loved to be a carefree boy again, it was a role he had become accustomed to. The terrible things Lek had seen, and the responsibility he had taken, had aged the young man, and in many ways, he considered himself an able adult. As confident as he might have appeared to the younger children, in reality, Lek was two months shy of turning twelve and had great uncertainty in his life. Lek wanted to believe his father would return, but he somehow knew he wouldn't. With his grandparents and only aunt living in Bradash, Lek guessed he and his sister would end up with them, but with all the awfulness he had seen, Lek wondered if they were still alive.

As the voices of the Marines grew louder, with the clomps of boots on the stairs, the children again stopped their play. Jrfete was halfway across a bed, pointing at a poorly hidden boy, when she heard the footsteps. Stopping in place, she turned to Lek. While some children emerged from hiding to see who was coming, others ducked out of sight. "It's okay. It's the priest and the Americans," Lek reassured them, setting the children at ease.

The first up the stairs was the dark-clothed Father Miric, whose warm smile seemed discordant with his gray, piercing eyes.

Upon first meeting him, Lek was wary of Father Miric. He was a

Serb, and Lek had never known a charitable one. In his mind, they brought only misery and death. But Lek's view of the priest changed when he saw Miric welcome the newer children into the shelter. That the Marine captain trusted the priest made him seem safer still, and Lek wondered if not all Serbs were evil.

Lek's eyes widened when he heard Richards' voice, and he watched as Father Miric topped the stairs with the captain following. Lek had taken a liking to Richards not just for the tasty gum and candy he brought with each visit, but also for his concern and kindness. He made Lek feel safe and loved; something Lek had not known in months.

Lek watched as Richards topped the stairs and spoke with the priest in words he didn't know. He saw the other children eye the smiling captain as he moved around the room, rubbing his hand over their heads. Their looks of concern faded when Richards began handing out candy. Lek was grinning with eager anticipation as he waited for his turn with the captain. Even more than the candy, Lek hoped the tall American would talk to him again and make him feel valuable.

As the captain glanced his way, Lek smiled, exposing two dimples. Jrfete surprised both Lek and Richards when she rushed to the captain and wrapped her arms around his knee.

Lek's smile faded when the priest picked Jrfete up. Lek stepped toward his sister but paused when she reached for the captain, and he took her from Miric. Lek listened as the captain spoke strange words to Jrfete, who looked at him as though she understood.

A boy beside Lek eagerly accepted a candy, and Richards rubbed his messy hair. Lek smiled when Jrfete wrapped one arm around the captain's neck while she sucked on her candy. Lek thought it good to see his sister happy and felt his throat tighten. When the captain came to him, Lek happily accepted a candy, but his face grew slack when the captain spoke to him.

"He asks how you are doing," Father Miric relayed.

Lek looked from the priest back to Richards and with a faltering smile said, "We-we are fine, thank you."

Lek listened closely as Richards spoke, but the words still had no meaning.

"The captain asks if you like the shelter?" Miric's smile was pleasant, but his eyes were stern.

"Yes, it is much better than sleeping in the rain. And the food is very good."

"So is the candy!" shouted another boy.

After hearing the translation, the captain laughed and ran a caring hand over Lek's head and spoke again. Lek looked at Miric for understanding.

"He asks that you help care for the children. He sees great ability in you," Miric said with an approving nod.

Lek straightened and with a serious nod said, "I will. I will care for all the children."

Miric relayed the message and Richards gave a nod and a wink.

Handing Jrfete back to Lek, the captain looked over the room one last time and then, with an approving nod, turned and started down the stairs.

Lek's face saddened when the last of the Marines descended out of sight.

"Papa," Jrfete called out, reaching for the disappeared captain.

Lek considered correcting his sister, explaining that not every nice man was their father, but he instead smiled and squeezed her.

———

CHAPTER
THIRTY-SIX

THE SOUND of the approaching Humvee caused Sali Noli to hurry into the shadowed alley. The bag he carried over his shoulder gave a solid metal clank as he brushed against the wall. He looked at the four other Albanians standing with him. Their eyes were eager and alert, like hunters closing in on their prey. They also carried weighty sacks, hiding their instruments of death. Pressed up against the crumbling stone wall, they watched the American patrol motor past. Sali was the first to emerge from the narrow alley. He looked up and down the empty street before waving the others forward. With sharp eyes, the men hurried across the street toward the abandoned factory where they had been told Ivan Nimatovic, the Cowboy, was hiding.

Standing three stories tall, the old mill had two rows of windows, one at street level and the other near its burned and blackened roof. Dark fingers of soot reached up from gaping windows, streaking and staining the tired red brick. As he crossed the street, Sali paid no attention to the glazed and broken windows, some of which were blackened by soot. Nor did he notice the lone figure watching from the shadows within.

It had been less than a day since Jusuf had found the rebels and given them the whereabouts of the Cowboy. Sali and the others took the information like addicts needing a fix. To them, nothing could be better than capturing the most hated man in southern Kosovo.

Just outside the abandoned factory, the five eager soldiers opened their bags and removed weapons and ammunition. They quickly pulled on ammunition vests and checked their rifles. Sali, the once peaceful and happy mechanic, looked at the other men with hate-crazed eyes as he got to his feet and started for the open door. The hunt for the Cowboy was on.

When Sali stepped inside the abandoned mill, his nostrils flared at the dank and smoky smell. Before him was a fifty-foot corridor with a row of broken and smoke-streaked windows to his right. Through them, the morning light beamed, casting snarled shadows across the dulled and dusty floor. Crouching low with his rifle at the ready, Sali glanced back as the last of his team slipped through the door. With a look and a nod, they started forward.

Midway down the corridor to the left, it opened to a large factory floor. Sali paused at the entry and surveyed the three-story-tall expanse which was forty yards wide and thirty across. Golden beams of light descended through the broken windows and skylights of the building, leaving pools of light on the dingy concrete floor and derelict equipment. A metal-grated catwalk lined the second-floor of the large expanse with an overlooking office area on the far end to their left. Stairs led up to the catwalk in two locations, and doors and corridors radiated out, making Sali wonder how they would search it all. The concrete floor was strewn with litter and powdered with dust. Shrinking puddles of rainwater lay below the broken skylights. A few large pieces of equipment and conveyor belts remained on the factory floor. Elsewhere, stubby anchor bolts that once held down large machines jutted from the floor like bamboo shoots.

As the five Albanians crept with their rifles at the ready, they searched for signs of life. Sali's eyes flashed about as he listened, ignoring the pounding of his heart and the soft footsteps of his men. The flutter of a pigeon flying up through a broken skylight caused them to raise their weapons in start. When he realized it was only a bird, Sali sighed and glanced at the thick mustached Bujar standing next to him, shaking his head. Another Albanian pointed to the shadowy corners of the floor ahead of them. With understanding nods, the men spread out.

Sali paused when he spotted his reflection in a puddle of rainwater. He looked up at the broken skylight overhead. His gaze moved to the iron catwalk that surrounded them and followed it around until he met the sunlight streaming through the windows.

Sali turned back to the factory floor. He had just taken a step when a man ahead of him knocked over an empty Coke bottle. The harsh clatter of the toppled bottle resonated throughout the expanse like a tripped alarm. Frozen, Sali and the others brought their rifles to bear. All was quiet. Sali released a stressful sigh, then took his turn, giving the clumsy man a scornful look.

Sali was just passing a large press, looking back in the direction they had come, when he heard the heavy *kunk kunk* of metal bouncing across the concrete floor. Thinking the clumsy man had knocked over something else, Sali turned to see a grenade rolling between them. "GRENADE!" Sali cried as he dove behind the press. The exploding grenade resonated through the factory and sent flesh-shredding metal shards in every direction. The repeating bark of a Kalashnikov rifle followed as rounds rained down on them from the catwalk above. Sali looked back to where the grenade exploded and saw two of his friends lying in growing pools of blood. Another was hobbling away for cover before bullets tore through him and dropped him to the dusty floor.

With his heart pounding, Sali pushed against the press as bullets ricocheted and zipped by him. A frantic-eyed Bujar crouched beside him.

"Are you okay?" Sali grimaced; his words lost in the loud *kakkka kakkka kakkka* of the firing rifle and th*e zang tzing zang* of deflected rounds.

The white-faced Bujar's head shuddered in a kind of nod.

Sali looked around the concealing machinery. He glimpsed a man on the grated catwalk before bullets resumed bouncing off the machine above him. "He's up there! On the platform!"

"Nimatovic?"

"I don't know."

"What do we do?" gasped Bujar.

"We can't stay here. If there are any more, we're dead!" Sali looked around the press. The man hadn't moved. "There's only one. It must be him. If we each go in different directions, he'll have to choose. He'll miss us both."

"What if he doesn't?" Bujar fretted.

"It's Nimatovic. We have to do it!" Sali glared.

Bujar agreed with a jerky nod.

"Okay. On three," Sali huffed, clutching his AK. "One, two, THREE!" Sali was firing as he jumped out from behind the press and felt a bullet *zip* past. Bujar followed. Emptying half their magazines into the catwalk, the man dropped his rifle and fell back onto the grated platform.

"We got him!" cried Bujar.

Sali watched the lifeless man through the metal grates as he backed away, his rifle trembling against his shoulder. He waited for the sound of another Serb, but there was only the shuddering of his breath and the pounding of his heart.

"Do you think that's him? Do you think that's Nimatovic?"

Sali tried to speak, but his mouth was too dry. He forced a swallow and said, "I don't know. Go check. I'll cover you."

Bujar's brow gathered. "*You* go check him, and I'll cover *you!*"

"Okay," Sali breathed. With his rifle at the ready, he glanced back at their three dead comrades sprawled on the floor. Sali turned back to the catwalk and the slumped man with his rifle resting beside him. *Is it him? Did we kill the Cowboy?* The thought elated Sali as he made his way to the stairs.

Standing at the base of the stairs, Sali saw blood dripping on the floor through the metal grates where the body lay. He glanced back at Bujar, still covering him, then started up the stairs. Sali's heart pounded with anticipation at the thought of at last claiming his prize. At the top of the stairs, Sali passed an open office door to his left, and two shattered windows further down. Inching to the door, he spun into the darkened office, firing blindly. It was empty.

Breathing a little easier, Sali lowered his rifle and moved toward the bloody, twisted body. *I got you, you devil!* Sali paid little attention to the corridor beside the body that led into the shadows, he was focused on the dead man. Bringing the head of Ivan Nimatovic to his KLA brothers would make Sali a legend.

But as Sali neared the bullet-ridden body, his heart sank. Before him lay a man in a Serbian Army uniform with a gaping mouth and staring blue eyes. He wore military style boots, and his hair was receding. There were no cowboy boots, no curly dark hair or gray goatee. "It's not him," Sali sighed.

"Did we get him? Is it him?" Bujar breathlessly asked as he topped the stairs.

Sali said nothing as Bujar moved alongside him.

"Isn't that him?" Bujar asked, eyeing the dead man.

"No," muttered Sali.

"Sure it is," Bujar insisted, wanting to believe.

Sali pulled a tattered photo of the Cowboy from his shirt pocket and handed it to Bujar, who lowered his rifle and groaned in disappointment.

"Are you looking for me?" came a voice from the shadows of the corridor.

Bujar looked up as the *kkaak kkaak kkaak* of a machine pistol reverberated through the corridor. Its bullets tore through the picture and knocked him back against the railing.

Sali stepped into the corridor, firing his AK. Two rounds struck the already wounded Cowboy, one in the arm and the other in the shoulder, spinning him to the floor. With his heart pounding, Sali kicked the machine pistol out of the wreathing Serb's hand. His eyes widened at the man's gray goatee and cowboy boots. With a cry of rage, Sali placed the muzzle of his rifle against the Cowboy's forehead and tightened his finger on the trigger.

Nimatovic glared up the barrel at the seething Albanian, his face lean and haggard from days of pain and little food. After a moment, he grunted, "Are you going to kill me, or aren't you?"

All the things Sali had imagined doing to the Cowboy—the devil responsible for so much suffering—swamped his mind. With his chest rising and falling, Sali noticed the red-stained bandage on Nimatovic's leg and stomped on it.

"Arghhh!" cried the Cowboy, reeling in pain. "Just shoot me and get it over with, you pig!"

Sali pressed the Cowboy's head back to the floor with his barrel and fingered the trigger. For months, he had envisioned this moment and imagined the satisfaction he would feel watching the Cowboy die. His rifle, his finger, had the power to end the man's evilness forever, but he couldn't pull the trigger. Sali shook his head in frustration. He swallowed and adjusted his grip on the rifle, but he couldn't pull the trigger. Maddened by his impotence, Sali unleashed a blood-curdling cry and shook his muzzle in the Cowboy's face.

Nimatovic grinned at the Albanian's weakness. "You are a coward, just like every other of your kind. You do not deserve to carry the weapon of a warrior."

Sali glared down at the man, whose life was a trigger pull from ending, then jerked his rifle away. "I cannot kill you here, like this," he seethed. "There is no honor or satisfaction in taking your life by myself when so many others deserve to watch you die."

The Cowboy's eyes narrowed. "I wonder if I had your woman before I killed her. There were so many."

Sali's face filled with rage. He turned his rifle and rammed its butt against the Cowboy's head, knocking it back against the steel grating. Nimatovic's eyes rolled back.

With his chest heaving, Sali looked back at the dead Bujar. He shouldered his rifle, reached down for Nimatovic's cowboy boots, and pulled him from the shadows. Sali dragged the dazed Nimatovic past his dead friend across the grated catwalk to the edge of the stairs, then pushed him down. With arms and legs flailing, the Cowboy tumbled head first before piling up three feet from the bottom. Moving down to him, Sali kicked the Cowboy off the stairs.

Sali stepped over the groaning Cowboy and looked across the factory floor. He saw his dead comrades and shook his head. Knowing he couldn't carry the larger Nimatovic far, he poked him with his muzzle and barked, "Get on your feet!"

The Cowboy half-opened and closed his eyes, his face bruised and bleeding.

"I said, get on your feet!"

Sali glared at the Cowboy as he rolled on his side, pulled his good leg under him, and climbed to his feet, favoring his wounded leg and arm.

"Get moving," growled Sali, jabbing the Cowboy with his rifle.

"Why don't you kill me now and save me the walk?"

"I've never met a dog so eager to die," snarled Sali.

"I've never met a *man* so afraid to kill," sneered the Cowboy.

The echoing clomp of approaching boots caused Sali to step back. *Are there more Serbs in here? Or are my people coming to help?* He remembered his magazine was nearly empty and quickly changed it.

"You had your chance," growled the cunning Nimatovic. "Now, it's your turn to die."

Sali's eyes widened as half a dozen Marines appeared with their rifles at the ready. His eyes flashed from man to man as they barked orders he didn't understand. Sali swung his rifle from the Cowboy to the Marines, then back again. He remembered his disgraced and humiliated friends telling of how the Americans took the mayor of Vitina from them. Sali swore he would never allow such a thing, but he knew that was what they intended to do. *I should have killed him when I had the chance!*

"Lower your rifle and step away from the prisoner!"

Sali understood the words. He turned to the Albanian interpreter and wondered how anyone could be so disloyal. Sali shook his head in defiance. "No! You can't have him! Do you know who this is? It's Nimatovic! The devil himself! He must die!"

The words staggered the interpreter. His eyes moved to the bloody, leaning Nimatovic before turning to the Marines. Their rifles were still trained on Sali. The interpreter knew what the Marines would say, but asked anyway. Reminded of their orders, the interpreter turned back to Sali and shook his head sadly. "They said there can be no more executions. I'm sorry, my brother."

Sali looked at his countryman in disbelief and lowered his rifle.

The interpreter's gaze moved from Sali back to the teetering Nimatovic. He had heard the stories. He had seen the suffering. His eyes flashed to the Marine beside him. Then, with a look of loathing, he said, "If you're going to kill the devil, do it now."

Sali's eyes widened. He raised his rifle to the Cowboy. The force of the Marine's bullets spun Sali to the floor. He lifted his head and looked from the interpreter to the Marines as if having been betrayed. Unable to breathe, Sali collapsed on his side.

When the smirking face of the Cowboy moved over him, Sali opened his mouth, but he couldn't form the words. His eyes flickered and then closed. He didn't hear the Cowboy say, "I told you it was your turn to die."

———

Captain Richards watched the two corpsmen attended to the sedated and restrained Ivan Nimatovic. Beside Richards stood the sergeant who had captured the notorious Serb; next to him, First Sergeant Sacamano. As Richards eyed the most wanted man in the province, he felt a sinister presence. *If the stories are true, this man has killed hundreds. How can anyone be so cruel?* Richards knew there was evil in the world—he would be out of a job if there weren't—but there was a difference between a man killing opposing soldiers out of duty and one killing women and children for pleasure. He couldn't understand how a human being could justify such inhumanity.

Richards watched the corpsman place the last of the stitches in the Cowboy's forehead as another attended to the bullet wound in his arm. He saw the IV line and heart monitor that displayed the Cowboy's vitals and thought it strange that such a man would receive the same care as one of his own.

Richards turned to Jusuf. He knew the sight of the Cowboy would trouble him but needed his help. "Is that him? Is that Nimatovic?"

"Yes, Captain. That is him. I could never forget his face," Jusuf seethed, unable to take his eyes off the man.

Richards' brow gathered. He had noticed a change in the interpreter a few days before. "Are you okay, Joe?"

Jusuf blinked out of his hateful stare and turned to the captain, his jaw tight. "He *should* be dead!" he hissed. "He kill-ded my family—in front of my eyes! I had to watch at this thing!"

Richards couldn't fathom such barbarity. He wondered how he would feel if Nimatovic had killed his family. *I'd want him dead. I'd kill him myself.* Richards felt anger and frustration building. He knew the right thing was to forgive—that was what he had been taught, at least—but he didn't know how he could. Richards recognized Jusuf's pain and wondered what he could say that might possibly make a difference. "Well...at least we have him. He didn't get away," was all he could think of.

"What will happen to him?" Jusuf fumed.

"He'll be turned over to the war-crimes tribunal for prosecution. There are plenty of witnesses."

Jusuf looked the captain in the eyes. "Will they kill him?"

Richards sighed as he considered the question. "I don't know."

"He *should* be dead."

Richards didn't reply.

"Where did they find him?" Jusuf asked, already knowing the answer.

"I was just about to find out."

The sergeant, proud of his patrol's success, cleared his throat and said, "Sir, he was in an abandoned factory by the river. We got there just after a firefight. We found a Serbian soldier and four KLA dead. The last KLA was about to execute the prisoner. Sir, he wouldn't lower his rifle."

Richards squared up to the sergeant.

"We had to shoot him, sir. The prisoner, Nimatovic, was the only survivor."

"You killed one of my people to save *him*!" Jusuf cried, pointing to the Cowboy.

Richards' glare caused Jusuf to back down.

"Captain, he was about to kill the prisoner! We had no choice!"

Richards shook his head and wondered how the locals would react. A Serb killing four Albanians was one thing, but Americans killing an Albanian to save a Serb war criminal was another. The only saving grace was that they had captured the Cowboy. "Were you able to ID any of the dead?"

"Two of them," Sacamano said. "One was Syle Alia. He's a KLA officer." He handed the captain a worn leather wallet and added, "You'll be interested in this one."

Richards opened the wallet, which had a government-issued ID card picturing a man with short brown hair, deep-set eyes, and a week's beard. "Sali Noli. Who was he?"

"Sir, look at the pictures."

Richards pulled a faded plastic sleeve out to a photo of an attractive woman with dark, flowing hair and caring eyes. He wondered what had happened to her. He turned to the next picture of three boys and groaned. "Oh, no. Lek." Richards tried not to let his devastation show, but it was obvious. He turned to the patrol leader and asked, "Don't tell me this is the one *we* killed?"

"I'm sorry, sir. He wouldn't put down his rifle."

Richards shook his head in disbelief as he thought of the children. The Serbs may have killed their mother, but NATO bombs had killed three of the five children in the family. Now their father was dead; shot and killed by the men who were there to keep them safe. Richards had no words to express his frustration and heartache. He looked at the picture in the wallet and wondered, *What do I tell them? What do I say? How do I tell a two-year-old girl, who's got nothing left in the world but her older brother, that we just killed her father?* The sad irony that their father died trying to kill a sick psychopath who would probably die anyway only compounded his frustration. "This shouldn't have happened!" Richards' eyes flashed from Jusuf to the two Marines beside him. "I'm so sick of this crap! THIS SHOULDN'T HAVE HAPPENED!"

"I'm sorry, sir," said the patrol sergeant, his eyes down.

Jusuf was no longer staring at the Cowboy, but at Richards.

"Top," Richards seethed, fighting to control his emotions.

"Sir?"

"Make sure Nimatovic is secured."

"Aye, sir."

"I want to question him when he comes to."

"Aye, sir."

"I gotta get some air," Richards said as he turned and exited the hospital tent.

Jusuf watched the captain leave. That Richards was so upset over what had happened strangely comforted him. Jusuf was still angry the Cowboy was alive, laying before him and not in a bag or rotting in a ditch. He was only slightly bothered that his information had led to the death of five of his countrymen, including the father of Lek and Jrfete. There were many now without parents, he told himself. More than anything else, Jusuf wanted the Cowboy dead. It was the only way he would feel satisfaction after all the monstrous man had done. Now that the Cowboy was a prisoner of the Americans, he wondered what would happen to him, or if justice would ever be served.

Jusuf turned back to the Cowboy who lay sedated in the hospital cot. He studied the vile man. Jusuf hoped he was in pain and that the American doctors' skill wouldn't be enough. He hoped he would die an agonizing death. But Jusuf feared even that simple wish would be taken from him.

As Jusuf glowered at the Cowboy, a thought came into his mind. It was a dark, piercing thought that cut deep into his soul. *Perhaps my actions were not pointless. Maybe God has kept this devil alive for a reason. Maybe I'll have my chance for vengeance?*

———

CHAPTER
THIRTY-SEVEN

CAPTAIN RICHARDS FOUGHT to hide his devastation as he entered the old furniture store, with Jusuf and another Marine at his side. He had said little to Jusuf since the capture of the Cowboy. He didn't know what to say. The Cowboy had murdered Jusuf's family, and he thought the interpreter justified in his loathing. But the tragedy was broader than that. Richards' men had killed Lek and Jrfete's father to save Nimatovic's life. To Richards, it was as though he had pulled the trigger himself. He ached inside and didn't know what to do. He considered the counsel the wise colonel had given him in what seemed like another life and wondered how things would differ had he not gotten emotionally involved. A part of him wished he had never met the now truly orphaned children.

Richards pulled off his helmet and tiredly gazed across the main floor of the orphanage. He didn't notice the smell of warmed MREs or the happy chatter of children. He paid no attention to the two Marines working in the makeshift kitchen. Richards' forlorn gaze was on the tattered boys and girls eating their evening meal. All of them had suffered; some had lost everything, and yet as they ate from the simple foil pouches, some with plastic forks and others with fingers, they appeared unburdened and joyful. He wondered why they were born into such awful circumstances. He wondered if the horrors they had witnessed would spoil their innocence. *The men who did this were once children. What will these children be like in ten years or twenty? Will they be the ones making war then?*

"Ah, Captain," came the soothing voice of Father Miric from behind him, "You've returned to our happy haven."

A dour Richards turned to the priest. "Father, it looks like things are going well here."

"Yes, they are." Miric glanced at Jusuf, who was staring at him coldly. "Thanks to your men. They are hard workers, you know. I think the children have taken a liking to them."

"They're good men."

Miric's eyes narrowed at the captain's somberness. "What's the matter, Captain Richards? You seem...burdened."

Richards eyed the priest. "We just captured a wanted Serb. But... in the process, we killed an Albanian—the father of two of these kids. Now they really are orphans."

Miric's brow tightened. "I am sorry to hear that. Are you here to tell them?"

Richards didn't reply.

Miric studied the captain for a moment, then asked, "Who did you capture, if I may ask?"

"Ivan Nimatovic," Richards said as he looked for Lek. He didn't see Father Miric's surprise, but Jusuf did.

"Was he captured alive?" Miric asked, his look of reverential indifference returned.

"Yes," Richards fumed.

Miric nodded. "From what I understand, he was a heinous man who did much evil. I should not say it, being a man of God, but such a beast doesn't deserve to live. He should be ushered down to hell."

Richards eyed the priest, then gave a subtle nod.

"Would you like me to talk to them for you?" Miric asked. "I have experience in such things, you know."

"You mean *death*?" Richards fumed.

"It is a sad part of God's work," Miric conceded.

Jusuf's eyes narrowed as he studied the Serb priest. He found something distasteful about the outwardly pious man.

"No," Richards said, rubbing his head. "I'll do it."

"Very well." The priest nodded and left the room.

"I do not like him," Jusuf hissed.

Richards' attention was on little Jrfete, sitting on Lek's lap. His heart sank when she smiled and waved at him. Not wanting to interrupt their meal, the captain moved to a wall and glanced at his watch. He had a briefing in twenty minutes, but that was far from his mind.

Jusuf moved beside the captain. "What are you going to tell them?"

"The truth," Richards replied, his gaze distant.

Jusuf gulped. "You will tell them their father is dead?"

"Yes. Don't you think they should know?"

Jusuf shook his head. "They are children. They have been hurt enough. You think taking the last hope from them is good?"

Richards studied Jusuf for a moment, then turned back to the children. Jrfete was leaning forward and looking around another child to see him better. When their eyes met, she smiled and waved. Richards' throat tightened. He looked down at his dusty boots as he rethought his intentions.

Richards looked up when he realized Jrfete was standing beside him. Gazing into her large blue eyes, he lowered to a knee, and Jrfete moved closer. She brushed against him, put a hand on his arm, and pointed to her still-seated brother. Lek's eyes widened when he saw the captain.

"How are you?" Richards asked, holding back his emotions.

Jusuf repeated his words in Albanian, and Jrfete smiled.

Richards cleared his throat, wondering what he should do. The all-business, return and report part of him wanted to give them the facts of their father's death, but he knew Jusuf was right. They were children and had already dealt with enough tragedy. The hope of having their father return couldn't hurt them.

Richards reached into his pocket and pulled out a stick of Juicy Fruit. Jrfete's smile grew, and she snatched the gum from his hand. After unwrapping and pushing the stick into her mouth, Jrfete leaned into the captain and wrapped her small hand around his thumb. Richards was about to give her a hug when she scampered back to her brother. Richards drew in a ragged breath. He saw Lek and other children were watching. Lek picked up his sister, smiled, and nodded to the captain.

Richards wanted to tell them things would be all right. That they could still grow up knowing love and tenderness. That they would someday have joy and happiness, but he knew those were promises he couldn't make. Fearing he had already intervened too much in their lives, Richards turned to Jusuf and said, "Let's go." He didn't see Jrfete's reaching arm or Lek's fading smile.

Little was said as Richards and Jusuf walked down the street with the escorting Marine following. While Richards pondered over the parentless children, Jusuf's thoughts were on the Cowboy.

While saddened by Sali Noli's death, he was one of thousands. Jusuf felt God had put him with the captain for a reason. The Marines had captured the evil Nimatovic, but the notion of him going unpunished was more than Jusuf could stand. After a few minutes, Jusuf could hold in his thoughts no longer. The captain had listened to his advice before. Maybe he would listen to him about the Cowboy. "Captain," Jusuf started boldly, "what are you going to do with Nimatovic?"

"I told you. He'll be turned over for trial."

Jusuf shook his head and blurted, "Such a man deserves to die! He deserves no trial! He should be hung in the center of town where all can see and know that justice was made!"

Richards stopped and turned to his interpreter. "Jusuf, I'm sorry for what happened to you. I'm sorry for what he and the other Serbs did to your family. It was a terrible thing. It was wrong, but it happened. It's done. You hating him and the other Serbs will make no difference to them...only to *you*. Do you understand? All of that hate will only poison you and ruin *your* life, not theirs."

Jusuf's jaw slackened as he looked at the captain. A part of him knew Richards was right, but he still yearned for vengeance. "Do you know what they did to my family? What *he* did?"

"Yes. It was a terrible thing."

Jusuf studied Richards' tragic expression, then said, "Could you stop hating them if they did this thing to your family? To your wife and little boy?"

Richards shook his head, and his jaw tightened. "I've asked myself that question over and over. I don't know, but I'd try."

"You couldn't!" Jusuf insisted. "Not until they were dead! Not until you watched them suffer and die!"

Richards glanced at the accompanying Marine and then nodded for him to continue walking. He then looked Jusuf in the eyes and said, "Jusuf, do you believe in God?"

Jusuf's brow gathered. "Yes... I do."

"Do you believe God or Allah will judge men for their sins?"

"Sins?" Jusuf asked, not knowing the word.

"For their wrongdoings."

Jusuf thought for a moment, then nodded.

"I believe it's God's place to judge. As hard as it might be, we must forgive and hope He will forgive us for what we do."

Jusuf looked on in thought, his anger fading.

"What does the Koran teach about forgiveness?"

Jusuf shrugged. "I don't know the Koran so good."

"I see," Richards said, hoping to find common ground.

After a few steps, Jusuf looked up to Richards and asked. "Captain, may I ask you a question?"

"Yes."

"Are you Christian?"

Richards nodded. "I am."

Jusuf's brow gathered. "The other Marines are Christian too?"

"Some of them."

"How is it that Serb Christians are so bad, but American Christians are so good?"

Richards stopped and turned to the interpreter. "Jusuf, there are good and bad people everywhere—in every religion. All I can tell you is that God is not happy when anyone uses His name as an excuse to hurt another. Whether it's a Christian or a Muslim."

Jusuf considered the captain's words, then asked, "If you are Christian and I am Muslim and we are both good, does that make us brothers?"

Richards smiled and nodded. "I believe it does, Jusuf. I think that makes us brothers."

Jusuf's eyes widened as much from the captain's rare smile as his confirming words. "Yes, we are brothers."

———

CHAPTER
THIRTY-EIGHT

IT WAS a bright and colorful garden. Lek had never seen anything so exquisite. To his left was a green hill covered with trees that rose into the mist of the morning light. To his right were well-manicured shrubs and dazzling flowers which weaved around the paths of emerald green grass. There was a tree with leaves a brilliant crimson-orange, as if bursting with flames. Lek breathed in the sweet fragrance and smiled. He saw bright and colorful trees elsewhere in the garden. Here and there, burned orange, burnished lavender, and vibrant yellow leaves leaped to the eye.

Lek turned to his mother and smiled as she opened a basket and handed the children toasted paninis dripping with cheese and hummus. He studied her beautiful features he had missed for too long. He watched as the other children took the sandwiches and ate. They were content and smiling. Lek couldn't help but stare at his mother, who he thought never looked so lovely. She smiled back. There was much Lek wanted to ask her, but the warm and delicious panini beckoned him. Hummus dripped from the sandwich as Lek bit into it, and his eyes watered from the rich flavor. Lek felt a contentment he had not known in months.

After taking another bite, Lek turned to his sister Arta and brother Rexhe. He had missed them too, but couldn't remember where they had gone. Rexhe, with his elfish ears and pouty eyes, smiled at Lek but didn't offer a word.

Wiping his mouth, Lek turned to his mother, pouring drinks, and asked, "Mother, where have you been? I've missed you."

She looked up from her pitcher and smiled proudly. "I have been here all along."

Lek considered her words and took another bite of his sandwich. He looked at his other siblings; Haxhi and Jrfete were looking at him as if waiting for him to ask more questions. After swallowing his food, Lek turned back to his mother and asked, "Where is Papa?"

Her smile widened. "He will be here soon."

Lek nodded, though not understanding, and returned to his sandwich. After taking the last bite and wiping the crumbs from his lap, he looked up at his mother. Her face had turned serious. Lek sat up on the grass to hear what she might say.

"Lek," she started, her dark eyes drawn with loving concern, "you must keep the children together. It is your duty."

Lek looked to where Arta and Rexhe had been sitting, but they were gone. "Where—"

"They are with me. You must care for the others."

Lek nodded in somber understanding.

"You must hold fast to the rope of Allah and not become divided. The rope of Allah will lead you back to me. To us," she said with a loving smile.

Lek's brow gathered. "But where will you be?"

"I will be here. Close to you."

Lek's eyes filled with tears. "I'll miss you."

"Be happy and know that I love you. All of you."

Lek whimpered, "Mama," as his mother faded away, leaving only the brilliant colors of the burning tree behind her. Lek's lonely gaze moved to the tree. Its brilliant orange leaves were growing, leaving behind a dark void.

"Lek!"

Lek gasped when he saw his father looking down at him with fervent eyes. "Father. Where—"

"You must leave!" Sali warned. "Wake the children. Hurry!"

"But I want to stay with you!"

"There is no time! Hurry!"

Lek's eyes shot open as he breathed in choking smoke. He searched the darkened room in confusion and saw the stunning orange-leafed tree, but the rest of the lovely garden was gone. In its place, shadows flickered and danced across the walls. When Lek sat up, he realized he was seeing flames climbing the stairs. "It's a fire!"

Scrambling from his bed, Lek climbed over the three children sleeping beside him and stood on the floor. It was warm on his feet. "Wake up! Wake up!" he cried, coughing and gagging as he breathed in the thick gathering smoke. He shook Jrfete and two other children, jolting them to consciousness. "There's a fire! Wake the others! We must get out!"

Jrfete looked at Lek with startled and confused eyes as he shook the child next to her.

When Lek saw flames filling the stairway through the thickening smoke, he yelled to Jrfete, "Stay there!" Lek hurried to awaken the children closest to the stairs. Shielding his eyes from the intensifying heat, he saw the first floor was engulfed in flames. Lek's eyes flashed about in thought as he fought off panic. The floor was growing hotter, and it was harder to breathe and see. He knew they had little time before the flames swallowed them.

With the cries and screams of frightened children filling the smoke-filled room, Lek hurried to the first of the three windows that looked over the street below. Outside, it was dark and quiet. After opening the latch on the window, Lek pushed and pulled on its frame, but it wouldn't move. Layers of paint had sealed it shut. He hurried to the next window, knocking over a crying girl and colliding with a pillar hidden in the smoke before reaching it. Unlatching it, he pulled and pushed with all his might, but it wouldn't move. Lek hurried to the last window, but found it was also painted shut. Lek frantically turned back to the fiery stairs. There was more coughing than crying now.

With his eyes tearing and burning from the smoke, Lek saw the beds closest to the stairs were empty. The more than twenty children of the shelter were crowded against the far wall, their mouths covered, their small arms waving away the choking smoke. He looked for Jrfete but saw only muddled shapes in the gathering gray. "Jrfete!" he coughed and wheezed. He knew he would never find her in the smoke. He had to break open the windows.

When Lek remembered a chair now lost in the suffocating cloud, he searched with reaching hands. Lek stumbled into a clamoring child and pushed him toward the others. With the next step, he found the chair. Coughing and wheezing, Lek raised the chair and swung it toward the light of the window. Its legs struck the wall, bouncing it back and leaving the window unbroken. Lek changed his hold on the chair. When he stepped back from the window to gain momentum, he stumbled over a child and nearly fell onto a bed. After regaining his hold of the chair, Lek pushed into the window. The glass cracked, but the window remained whole. Lek stepped back and rammed into the window again. This time the chair broke through the glass and continued through, nearly taking him with it. The fresh air caused the flames to burst and roll across the ceiling. The wave of heat that followed dropped Lek to his knees. Hanging onto the chair, Lek gulped in the fresh outside air as he looked down at the bar tile roof. While not steep, it only extended five feet before dropping off to the street below. Lek tried to pull the chair back through the broken window, but he lacked the strength. When he let go, the chair slid off the roof and crashed to the street in pieces.

Lek got back to his feet, knocked off the jagged shards, and yelled, "Help! HELP!" before coughing and gagging from the smoke. "Hurry! Out of this window onto the roof!" he yelled back into the smoke-filled room as desperate children pushed past him.

"Jrfete!" Lek cried, trying to find his sister in the shifting darkness. He looked back at the broken window as the heat continued to build. While half of the children had climbed through the window, they were now bunched up on the roof just beyond it. Afraid to move, they hindered the escape of those still trapped inside. "Find a way off, or we'll die!" he yelled, his words fading into a coughing fit.

After lowering to his knees, with his head tingling and vision blurring, Lek stretched toward the broken window to get the fresh air his lungs craved. When Lek squinted back through the smoke, he spotted Jrfete collapsed near the foot of a bed beside a toppled lamp. Lek lunged for his sister. The floor was hot to the touch now. He pushed the fallen lamp aside before realizing he could use it. After picking it up, he swung it with all his might into the next unbroken window. The crashing of glass and the rushing in of cool, fresh air allowed Lek to fill his lungs.

With his vision obscured by tears and the growing curtain of blackness, Lek crawled across the hot, creaking floor until he found his lifeless sister. With Jrfete limp in his arms, Lek pushed through the smoke back to the window and gulped in more of the clean air. His energy partially regained, Lek held Jrfete tight against him and climbed through the broken window. After gasping in the fresh air on the roof, Lek looked at the frightened children crowded on the ledge to his left. His red and teary eyes widened at those still inside pushing to get out. "Move so they can get out!" he coughed. "We can't stay here! We must get down!"

"There! They're coming!" cried a soot-faced girl beside him.

Lek turned and saw Marines rushing toward them. Exhausted, his lungs still fighting for air, Lek shook Jrfete and gasped, "No! Wake up! You can't die!" He looked down from the roof as a wide-eyed Marine stopped below him and called for her with open arms. Lek looked back to the window as a child collapsed in the rolling blackness. Lek turned back to the outreaching Marine, his heart pounding, his eyes swimming in tears, and released his sister. She landed in the Marine's arms.

With the growing furnace behind them, the children were now dropping from the roof faster than the Marines could catch them. Some leaped, landing awkwardly in the Marines' arms, while others collapsed and tumbled to the ground with no one to break their fall.

Only a few children were still on the roof when Lek turned back to the broken windows billowing gray and black smoke. "Is anyone still in there?" he coughed and sputtered.

Knowing there was at least one still inside, Lek pushed through the wall of heat. He climbed back through the broken glass and didn't feel the jagged shard slicing through his arm or the flames licking at his legs. Unable to see more than inches before him, Lek crawled further into the burning room. The hot floor was now painful on his hands and feet. "Is everyone out?" he cried, gasping and choking. There was no answer. Bumping into a body, he felt an arm and face. Grabbing hold, Lek pulled the collapsed child from the floor and pushed it through the broken window onto the roof. His vision smeared, Lek was searching for any remaining children when he felt the floor shift beneath him. The cracking of splitting beams and the crashing of the collapsing floor caused Lek to brace himself. He looked toward the stairs, which had been lost in the blackness, and his eyes widened as the floor opened before him, revealing the inferno below.

Unable to stand the heat any longer, Lek climbed through the window and the thick, escaping smoke. Drained of strength and unable to breathe, he collapsed on the roof. Flames were licking up from the outside of the roof now, with parts of it to his right on fire. Lek saw the distorted image of Marines backing away from the heat. He watched as they frantically waved and called for him to jump. When he remembered the boy he had pushed through the window, Lek crawled to him. The hot tile roof burned his knees. Lek could lift the small boy for only a moment before falling back to the roof in exhaustion. He tried again to stand, but only slid closer to the roof's fiery edge. With his lungs aching, eyes burning, and body tingling, Lek pushed the unconscious boy through the flames and off the roof. Lying back on the roof, with smoke pouring across him, Lek's body shuddered as it fought for air. Unable to fight any longer, Lek's eyes closed.

It was the voice of his mother in the darkness of his fading consciousness that stirred him. "Lek, you must care for the children! You must keep them together!" Lek's eyes dragged open; his hair singed, his face blackened with soot and streaked with tears. Through clouded eyes, he saw the distorted flames licking around him. He tried to stand, but couldn't. The cries of children and the yells of men were lost in the fire's roar. With the last of his strength, Lek pushed himself and rolled through the flames off the roof.

"I got him!" yelled the Marine as he ran under the falling boy. With Lek hanging in his arms, the Marine hurried away from the inferno. More than a dozen Marines were there now. Some children coughed and wheezed as they fought for air, while others looked around in shock. A few lay silent on the street. The Marine laid Lek down, then turned back to the consuming flames.

A burly man with a beard and a bare chest muscled a fire hose from a nearby hydrant and sprayed water into the raging fire. The flames' heat caused him to step back. The burly man raised a hand to deflect the heat and lost control of the hose, which sprayed into the air. The icy rain fell on the terrified children and stirred Lek. With a hoarse cough, his eyes pulled open; white orbs in his blackened face. "Jrfete," he wheezed. "*Jrfete…*" Slowly, his eyes closed again.

The flickering flames shimmered in Father Miric's dark eyes as he watched the frantic Marines attending to the children. In his mind, God had condemned them to death, and it frustrated him that these children of his enemy would survive. He believed it was God's will that he should cleanse the land of the Muslim scourge. But his plan had not worked, and it angered him that the sanctimonious Americans had stepped in and defied God's will.

When Miric spotted a distraught Captain Richards approaching, he moved to a lifeless little girl and picked up her limp body.

Richards, who had run from the sports hall, slowed to a stop as he eyed the still raging fire and the children lying in the street. He watched numbly as the bare-chested man sprayed water into the fire on his left and two others on his right. Long fingers of water shimmered in the reflected firelight as they arched across the smoky street. Richards stepped back as part of the roof collapsed and a wave of heat washed over him. He heard the rumbling idle of a diesel engine and turned to see Marines loading children into the back of a troop transport. He watched a Marine breathing into a child's mouth and tried to comprehend the terribleness of what had happened.

Richards turned back to the children still on the street. Some were sitting up and coughing, their worn and blackened faces staring blankly into the night. Others lay flat; alive, but too weak to stand. A few moved not at all. Although Richards was concerned for all the children, it was Lek and his sister he searched for. He looked from one soot-blackened face to the next but could find neither of them. Richards turned back to the truck, hoping they were safely inside. He saw a child with red and blistered flesh and turned back to the burning shelter with horror-filled eyes. *What have I done?*

A distraught Richards was surveying the coughing and groaning children on the street when he spotted a child with dark, frizzy hair lying on her side. "Jrfete!" he gasped as he hurried to her. Her eyes were closed as if in slumber. Richards kneeled beside the little girl who had known so much tragedy in her brief life. Closing his eyes, he offered a prayer, "Please, Father, let her be okay. Let her live." He then gently touched her soot-covered arm. Her eyes opened and Richards sank back on his knees with relief.

"Sir, we almost lost that one," said a Marine kneeling beside another child. "At first, she didn't respond, but I think she's okay now."

Overwhelmed, Richards carefully gathered Jrfete in his arms. "Are you okay?" he whispered as she looked at him blankly.

Seeing the truck was about to leave, Richards hurried to it. "Wait! Take her back and make sure Doc checks her out." Richards said, handing Jrfete up to the Marine who had just raised the truck's rear gate and climbed inside.

"Aye, sir," replied the young Marine, taking Jrfete in his arms.

"Lek! Are you in there?" Richards yelled, climbing into the truck. His tragic gaze moved over the soot-covered, coughing, crying, and moaning children. There was no answer.

Richards stepped off the truck and watched it motor away. Turning back to the remaining children, he spotted the bearded priest and yelled, "What happened? How did the fire start?"

Miric looked up from the limp child in his arms, and with eyes feigning bereavement, he said, "Ask your Marines who should have been watching them."

Richards looked around. "Where's Kershisnik and Barnes?"

"We haven't found them yet, sir," said a lieutenant, giving water to a child.

Richards turned back to the priest and numbly muttered, "I was trying to help them."

"They are with God now," Miric sighed, laying the limp child back on the street.

Richards' heart sank. He turned back to the burning orphanage, only vaguely aware the fire had lessened. When a Marine with a soot-streaked face and undershirt approached, Richards numbly asked, "Corporal, how many made it out?"

The young Marine looked at Richards with tired, sad eyes and said, "I'm not sure, sir. Eighteen or nineteen, I think."

"How many were there?" Richards asked, turning to the priest.

"Twenty-three," Miric replied, his gray eyes piercing.

Richards stared at the three motionless children on the street.

"You mustn't be so hard on yourself, Captain. What is God's will cannot be undone."

Richards glared at Miric. He knew the priest was only trying to make him feel less responsible, but Richards wanted no part of it. The anguished captain turned and stormed away.

The eastern horizon was aglow with morning light when the captain arrived at the hospital tent. Both heartbroken at the loss of a still unknown number of children, and feeling responsible for not having more Marines watching them, Richards' mind was in turmoil. When Sergeant Sacamano greeted him just outside the tent, Richards could only shake his tired head.

"Sorry, Captain," Sacamano said in his raspy voice.

"Has Kershisnik and Barnes turned up?" Richards asked as he looked into the hospital tent filled with soot-covered children on cots and scurrying Marines and Navy corpsmen.

"No, sir, they may not have made it out."

Richards' head sank. "Do we have a count yet?"

"I haven't heard." Sacamano eyed the captain for a moment, then asked, "Do you know how it started?"

Richards shook his head and looked past Sacamano into the tent. He saw children with singed hair wearing oxygen masks. Some had limbs or their heads wrapped in white gauze bandages while others had burn packs covering their pink and raw flesh. "I should have sent them to the UN site in Skopje. They would've been safe there."

"Sir, this is not your fault," Sacamano said emphatically.

"No? Those kids in there that are burned?" Richards asked, pointing into the tent, the corners of his mouth pulled down. "The ones that are...that are *dead*? I'm responsible for *all* of them. It was my decision!" Richards exclaimed, jamming his finger into his chest. "I should have sent them!"

Sacamano's gaze lowered as the devastated captain moved past.

As Richards entered the hospital tent, the smell of smoke, burned flesh, and antiseptic was overpowering. His chin quivered with emotion as he looked at the children. His sense of guilt was overwhelming. Whether he had set up the orphanage out of pride or selfishness, he didn't know. *Was it just to keep Lek and Jrfete close by?* He thought of the wise colonel's counsel he had so blatantly disregarded. *If I had been more worried about being a Marine captain than a dad, this wouldn't have happened!* The thought cut deep inside him.

With a heavy, soul-purging sigh, Richards shook off the sentiment. *The damage is done. I have my job to do. What am I going to be?* Richards wiped away a tear; the answer was simple.

After clearing his throat and standing taller, Richards looked across the hospital cots for the sweet and innocent Jrfete. As he moved through the chaotic tent, he prayed he would find Lek there too. He gulped when he spotted a small head wrapped in gauze with dark, frizzy hair protruding from the top. Richards made his way to Jrfete, whose face had been wiped clean of soot and eyes were closed in slumber. He rested his hand on her small arm. The warmth and softness of her skin reminded him of his son. Richards lifted his hand and resumed his search for Lek.

After ten minutes of making his way around the tightly spaced cots and medical personnel examining the face of each child, Richards had still not found Lek. The thought he might never find the boy left his heart aching. Richards continued his search. He stopped beside a cot being attended to by a corpsman and a Marine. Richards looked down at the heavily bandaged boy, who was larger than the others. Gauze wrapped much of his face, and the bandage around his arm was bloodstained. "Lek?"

The boy's eyes pulled opened.

"Lek?" Richards breathed, fighting his emotions.

Lek's glassy eyes rolled about before closing.

"Do you know this one, Captain?" the corpsman asked.

Richards faintly nodded as he eyed Lek's red and swollen face.

"He's sedated. He was burned pretty bad, sir. He must have been one of the last out."

"How bad?"

"Oh, he'll make it. A lot of second-degree burns mainly. His third-degree burns are more on his right side."

"Can you treat him here or will you have to send him to Bondsteel?"

The corpsman hesitated. "I was going to send him, 'cause we don't have the space, but..."

"His sister's over there," Richards said, pointing to Jrfete. "If you can, keep him here with her."

"From what I heard, the fire was terrible. It's a miracle this many made it out," the corpsman said, not stopping his work.

A hollow-eyed Richards looked around the hospital tent and nodded.

———

CHAPTER
THIRTY-NINE

FOR SECURITY REASONS, Captain Richards had moved the Cowboy from the hospital tent to a small, windowless room in the sports hall next door to the mayor of Vitina. There he had lain, tied to a massage table with an IV dripping into his bandaged arm. With the IV and restraints now removed, the bruised and battered Nimatovic rubbed his wrists as he sat at the edge of the bed and eyed the Marine Captain.

Richards surveyed Nimatovic's wounds. His face was bruised and swollen, he had stitches across his forehead, a cut lip, a broken nose, and bandaged bullet wounds in his arm and shoulder; all from his most recent encounter with the KLA. The leg wound he received trying to cross the bridge two weeks earlier was infected. Richards believed such pain and suffering deserved for a man whose soul was so dark and twisted, and he was disappointed when the doctor told him Nimatovic would make a full recovery.

The irony that the Cowboy's life had been saved so he could be put to death later wasn't lost on Richards. He thought the only positive thing about delaying Nimatovic's execution was the information they might glean through interrogation. He wondered if that was enough.

A part of Richards wanted nothing to do with the mass murderer and considered simply turning him over for war-crimes prosecution.

That's what Colonel Bates would have counseled. But Richards couldn't forget it was Lek's father who had died trying to bring the Cowboy to justice. Or that the Cowboy had murdered Jusuf's family. He wondered if Nimatovic was responsible for Lek's mother's death. The tragedy of it all made the captain angry and want to get involved. Richards wanted to make a difference. He wanted to champion the downtrodden, these unfortunate victims of hate, like some superhero. Richards wondered if he was retaliating for Lek's father's death or the little children who had died or were burned in the orphanage fire; he didn't know. But Richards was going completely against Colonel Bates' counsel. He was now hopelessly involved. Richards was angry and wanted his pound of flesh.

Richards saw Jusuf glaring at the Cowboy. While unaware Jusuf had given the Cowboy's whereabouts to the KLA, triggering the shootout that ultimately lead to Sali's death, he knew Jusuf had good reason to hate the man. The surprising revelation that Jusuf was not only Christian but a member of Richards' same faith had brought them closer. Richards had spoken to Jusuf about forgiveness, but those words now seemed hollow as he looked at the evil militia leader.

"Corporal Petrovic reporting as ordered, sir."

The embattled captain turned to the corporal, standing at attention. "At ease. I want you to help with the translation. Joe's done a great job, but I want to make sure nothing gets fouled up in the mix. Understood?"

"Aye, sir," Petrovic replied, feeling the stern eyes of the captain.

Richards nodded to Sacamano standing beside a table with a tape recorder, and the sergeant began the recording. Even though FBI agents were due in two days to question the prisoners, Richards didn't want to take any chances. The doctors had assured him the Cowboy's wounds weren't life-threatening, but there were plenty of other ways to die, and plenty of people who wanted him dead, including his own interpreter.

"Have him state his name," Richards ordered.

After a brief exchange, Jusuf turned to Richards and said, "He wants a cigarette."

Richards shook his head. "Tell him that cigarettes will kill him."

Jusuf relayed the message, and the Cowboy laughed. "He say he is not afraid to die, and won't talk until he has cigarette."

Richards sighed. "Get him a damn cigarette."

Sacamano nodded and exited the room to find one.

Once the sergeant returned, the Cowboy took the cigarette and tucked it behind his ear. He spoke again to Jusuf with a smirk.

"He say that one is for later. He needs another."

"Give him another one," Richards growled.

The Cowboy took the second cigarette and put it between his lips. With a raised brow, he motioned for a light.

"Give him a light," Richards said, tiredly shaking his head.

With his cigarette lit, the Cowboy inhaled deeply, and his eyes rolled back in satisfaction. He pulled the cigarette out, blew a stream of smoke at Jusuf, and nodded in approval.

"Great, he likes it. Now tell him to state his name."

The Cowboy nodded, then said, "Kolonel Ivan Nimatovic."

"Okay," Richards said with a now-we're-getting-somewhere nod. "Tell him we want to know about his activities in the province of Kosovo; in particular, the layout and distribution of minefields, and his actions with the MUP and VJ."

The Cowboy listened to the translations, nodded, and spoke without hesitation.

"He say you will never find them all and hopes they will kill many."

"Ask him about his actions against the ethnic Albanians," Richards glared.

"He say he will tell you. He has nothing to hide and is proud of his work."

"Proud of his work?" Richards scoffed, shaking his head.

"He's a sick, sick man," grunted Sacamano.

"He say his militia unit was formed last year by MUP to fight terrorists here."

"Terrorists?"

"Yes. KLA...women...children. The Serbs call them terrorists," Jusuf fumed. "He say his men help all of Serbia by fighting the terrorists. He say his men worked close with the Army. He calls them hunters. His people clean out the terrorists while the VJ guard."

"So, his militiamen did the dirty work while the regular army watched?" Richards asked.

"Yes. He say they work together." Jusuf shook his head in disgust. "He is very proud he is kill-ded more than three hundred terrorists."

"Three hundred? You mean his entire unit?"

"No. He only. He say he is in Three Hundred Club," Jusuf seethed.

Richards looked with horror at the Cowboy who was beaming with satisfaction.

"Sick son-of-a..." Sacamano grunted.

Richards turned to a white-faced Petrovic. "Did I get that right?"

"Yes, sir."

"Ask him about civilians. Were any of those women and children?" Richards glared.

A discussion ensued. As the Cowboy spoke matter-of-factly, Jusuf's responses grew in volume and intensity.

"What's going on, Joe?" Richards asked with a gathered brow.

Jusuf's eyes burned with rage and his mouth curled down as he shouted at the Cowboy.

"What just happened?" Richards barked, wondering if he would have to restrain the interpreter.

Petrovic moved closer. "Sir, Jusuf accused him of killing his family, and Nimatovic told him he remembered doing it. He said something about shooting Joe's mother and feeling sorry that his grandmother died so fast."

"Died so fast?"

"He wanted to watch her suffer more." Petrovic shook his head. "He said he killed his father too, and he would've killed Jusuf, but he was such a helpless lamb he couldn't. I think that's what he called him, a lamb. He said he thought Jusuf was dead, but just now recognized him. He said something about laying mines...and then something else, but I didn't catch it."

Jusuf trembled with rage. His eyes bulged, and his chest heaved as he tried to catch a breath.

"Top, take Joe out for a break."

"Aye, sir." Sacamano reached for Jusuf.

"No, Captain. Please. I want to stay," Jusuf pleaded. "I want to hear this things. I...I will do nothing. Please...let me stay."

"Jusuf! Look at me," barked Richards. "I need you under control. I need you to be professional. Understood?"

"I'm sorry. I will be better. Please." Jusuf wiped away tears.

Nimatovic watched and chuckled, "Poor little lamb."

Richards turned back to the Cowboy. "Who gave him his orders? Did they come from Belgrade? Or was he acting alone?"

"He say yes. From Belgrade, but through another." Jusuf's chest was heaving less now.

"What do you mean?"

"He say his orders come from a general here in contact with *Milo-sevic*." Jusuf uttered the name with such distaste he spat on the floor.

"A general." Richards' brow gathered. "Nimatovic wasn't running the show."

"Do you think he's just saying that? He was only following orders?" asked Sacamano. "I bet he's a freelancer."

"Ask him who gave the orders. What's the general's name?"

Nimatovic grunted a reply.

"He say he don't know."

"He doesn't know, or he won't say?" Richards glared. "Ask him again."

Jusuf repeated the question, and the Cowboy's smirk faded. He studied his smoldering cigarette, then muttered a response.

"He say all of his orders come from Belgrade," Jusuf explained.

"Through a general. Who's that?" asked Richards.

"He say there is no general."

"He's lying, sir," Sacamano grunted. "He just said there was a general!"

Richards' brow gathered in thought. "Was the person who gave him his orders MUP?"

The Cowboy nodded.

"Is that a yes?" Richards asked, glancing at the tape recorder.

The Cowboy sighed, then said, *"Po."*

"He say yes," Jusuf nodded.

"So, he was getting orders from Belgrade through an intermediary," concluded Richards.

"A government figure? Could it be the mayor? Maybe we got the scumbag next door," Sacamano smirked.

"Possibly." Richards' eyes narrowed. "But he used the word 'general,' right?"

Jusuf nodded.

"Ask him if he ever met this person."

The Cowboy listened to the question, then took several drags from his cigarette before replying.

"He say yes, but he don't know who he is."

"A name?" Richards asked.

"He say they call him General Zetelica, but that's not his real name."

"Zetelica?" Richards repeated.

"It is like ah...someone that cuts the wheat," Jusuf said, making a swinging motion.

"You mean a farmer? With a sickle?" Sacamano asked.

"No, it is another name for death."

Richards' brow gathered. "A reaper. The Grim Reaper."

"Maybe," Jusuf nodded.

"They got a sick sense of humor, don't they?" grunted Sacamano.

Richards studied the Cowboy. He thought it strange Nimatovic had no problem incriminating himself and boasting about his killing, but would say nothing about the man giving the orders. *Who's he protecting? Maybe he said something he shouldn't have. Did he just give us a clue?* "Ask him what his jurisdiction was? Where was his area of operations?"

"He say the southern quarter of Kosovo."

"Where did he meet this General Zetelica?" Richards asked.

"He say different places, but most of time here."

"Here in Vitina?"

The Cowboy nodded.

"Was he a Kosovar Serb or from Serbia?" Richards asked.

The Cowboy swallowed, straining at the answer. He was about to say something when he shook his head, muttered something in frustration, and took another drag from his cigarette.

"He say he don't know," Jusuf shrugged.

"He's lying. He knows exactly who gave him the orders," Sacamano huffed. "He's protecting him; that means he's a local. If it was someone in Serbia, it wouldn't matter."

"He could be protecting someone else," Richards surmised.

"You mean like his family?" Sacamano asked.

"Maybe. Maybe he knows if he exposes this general, something will happen to them. He's from this area; his family could be close by." Richards turned to the now subdued Nimatovic and asked, "This General Zetelica is from Kosovo?"

The Cowboy's eyes raised slightly at the translation, then, after a moment's contemplation, he gave a subtle nod.

"That's a yes," Sacamano said for the tape recorder. "I'm tellin' ya, sir, our man is Cara-sorry-ass next door."

Richards sat back in thought. *The man who gave the Cowboy his orders is a Kosovar Serb. He's probably still in the province and has connections to Milosevic. This could be big. This could prove the Serbian president's involvement. But who's the Reaper? He could have been a government official. Sacamano could be onto something.*

"He say he is tired now and wants to sleep," Jusuf said, himself drained from the questioning.

Richards nodded for Sacamano to turn off the tape recorder. "Tell him we'll be back for more questions."

Jusuf relayed the message then said, "He ask if he will be guarded. He say the terrorists will try to kill him."

"I thought he wasn't afraid to die," Sacamano sneered.

Richards half-heard the exchange. He was remembering the day he stopped the KLA from killing Vitina's mayor. He had spoken with Carassava three times and considered him merely a hated politician, but now Richards wondered if Carassava was more than that. *The KLA may know something we don't.* "We need to talk to Carassava."

"Sir, I told you that's our man," shrugged Sacamano.

"Top, make sure the prisoner is secure, then bring the recorder."

"Aye, sir," Sacamano grinned, having solved the mystery.

"Joe, come with me." Exiting the room, Richards motioned to the adjacent door, which the Marine guard unlocked and opened.

As Richards entered the small massage room turned holding cell, he saw a relaxed Sasa Carassava reading a book. Carassava set the book aside and sat up. He watched Richards move another chair in front of him and sit while Jusuf stood to the side. Carassava fidgeted in his seat as they eyed him. He gulped when Sacamano and Petrovic entered.

"Top, turn on the recorder."

"Aye, sir."

"Joe, tell him we have Nimatovic," Richards said, watching for Carassava's response.

Jusuf relayed the message, and Carassava nodded.

"He say Nimatovic is a bad man, and the militia did bad things."

Richards' brow gathered, unsure of how to interpret the response. "Tell him he bragged about killing women and children—that he was in the 300 Club."

Carassava listened to Jusuf before shaking his head disapprovingly.

"He say crazy people like Nimatovic caused this war."

"I bet he doesn't have a mean bone in his body," smirked Sacamano.

"Call him *General Zetelica*. I want to see what he does."

When Carassava heard the translation, his eyes narrowed, then shifted from Jusuf to the captain as he shook his head in confusion.

"Did you see that?" Sacamano pointed. "He's guilty as hell."

Richards sighed, "Possibly, but he's got four guys breathing down his neck."

Sacamano backed away.

"Joe, tell him Nimatovic said that *he* was the general in charge."

Carassava listened to the translation, then shook his head emphatically. Clearly rattled, his eyes darted about the room as he spoke.

"He say he did nothing wrong. Only what Belgrade told him," replied a wide-eyed Jusuf.

Richards' brow shot up, and he leaned forward. "Did he just admit to being the handler? He gave Nimatovic his orders?"

"I knew it!" blurted Sacamano.

An ashen Carassava listened to the translation, then sat back. Staring blankly across the room, he stammered a reply.

"He say he did nothing wrong. He was the mayor of Vitina and only followed orders from his leaders."

Richards turned to Petrovic. "Am I missing something?"

"I don't think so, sir. Joe's got it pretty much right on," Petrovic replied, his brow bent in concentration.

"Ask him right out if he's General Zetelica."

Jusuf posed the question, and Carassava numbly shook his head.

"Of course, he's gonna say no. He's a palaeological liar!" Sacamano grunted.

Richards rubbed his face. "We're not getting anywhere."

"I think he's your man, Captain," Sacamano said, pointing at the besieged Carassava.

"Turn off the tape," Richards sighed. "He might be, but we're going to have to wait for the FBI boys to figure this whole thing out. It's too messed up. We got a week, and then we're outta here."

"Aye, aye, sir," Sacamano said with a grateful nod.

Richards eyed the stunned Carassava as he considered what they had learned. Too tired to think about it anymore, the Marine captain pushed up from his chair. He was ready to go home.

After exiting the sports hall, Richards walked a few steps, then came to a stop. It was only noon, but he was already exhausted. The little sleep he had gotten the night before, combined with the stress and emotions of what had happened, left him wondering if he was thinking clearly. He considered going back to his room and taking a break, but he had too much to do. Trying to clear his head, Richards took a drink from his water bottle and looked up at the tall, billowing clouds that filled the southern sky. He breathed in deeply, then slowly exhaled. A little calmer, he felt the refreshing breeze. Richards thought of his wife and wondered what she was doing. *Monday. Maybe she's doing the laundry, or maybe she's at the park with Drew.* He closed his eyes. *Only three more months.*

Richards looked across the soccer fields crowded with refugees and saw his Marines forming a perimeter. The bitter taste of reality returned. He didn't want to think about Nimatovic or Carassava anymore. Someone else could worry about them. His job was to captain his men and bring them all home. So far, there had been no casualties, but he still hadn't received word on the two Marines missing from the orphanage. He thought of Lek and Jrfete. He felt he had already gotten too close to them and that his repeated visits were only giving them false hope. Richards didn't want to think about what would happen to them after he and the other Marines left. *The Army will send them to Skopje with the hundreds of other orphans. If they're lucky, their family will find them. If not, they'll grow up in the orphanage.* Richards told himself the best thing, the *kindest* thing, would be to stay away. He knew they were getting the care they needed and staying away would allow him to concentrate on his duties; at least that was what he told himself, but he didn't know if he could.

Richards sighed then turned to the hospital tent. *I need to check on the two missing Marines. I should look in there.* Richards shook his head at his feeble attempt at self-deception and started for the tent. He needed to see Lek and Jrfete.

Richards' feelings of guilt and failure returned as he saw the corpsmen and Marines attending to children lying in cots. He spotted Lek across the tent asleep and looked for Jrfete. Richards saw children tethered to IVs and bandaged in gauze, but couldn't find her. He started through the maze of cots toward the sleeping Lek. Richards moved to a Navy corpsman, changing a bandage. He pointed to Lek and asked, "How's that boy doing?"

"He's okay, sir. His burns aren't too bad. It's mainly smoke inhalation and exhaustion. He should be fine. We're getting ready to send some to Camp Bondsteel. They're better equipped to handle burns. You wanted to keep him and his sister here. Is that right, sir?"

Richards drew in a weary breath. "No... You should send them."

"Aye, sir," the corpsman said, returning to his work.

"Where's his sister? I don't see her."

"I'm not sure, sir. We can't keep her in bed. I think she's looking for someone."

Richards nodded sadly. "I'm sure she is." He was about to resume his search for the little girl when he felt a tug on his leg. When Richards looked down and saw Jrfete, his face brightened. She had a bandaged arm and singed hair, but it was her sad blue eyes that sank Richards' heart. It was the look of one bereft of hope and understanding. He kneeled beside her. "Hey, what are you doing? You should be in bed."

Jrfete eyed him, her expression unchanged.

"Are you doing okay?" Richards asked, knowing she didn't understand. He picked Jrfete up and asked a nearby Marine, "Where does this one go?"

"Over there, if you can get her to stay," the Marine pointed.

Richards saw Jrfete reaching for her sleeping brother. "Corporal, can you move her next to her brother?"

"Yes, sir. I can take her, sir," he said, moving closer.

Richards felt Jrfete's small hand on his cheek and looked into her wistful blue eyes. He smiled and said, "That's okay. I've got her." Richards watched the Marine move a boy with bandaged legs to another bed, then laid Jrfete on the cot and pulled the green blanket up as if tucking her in. Jrfete kicked off the blanket and reached for her brother. Richards slid her cot beside Lek's, which satisfied her.

Wondering how he would say goodbye to the two children, Richards remembered his gum. He pulled out his last two sticks of Juicy Fruit, handed one to Jrfete, and placed the other on the cot beside Lek. Jrfete stripped away its foil and pushed it into her mouth.

Richards was about to turn when he saw Corporal Petrovic translating for a corpsman. "Petrovic, do you have a minute?"

"Yes, sir." The interpreter made his way to the captain.

Richards looked from the sleeping Lek to a busily chewing Jrfete as he considered how to say goodbye.

Petrovic's eyes narrowed. "Sir, I remember them. I was on the patrol that found them in the field. One of them—his brother, I think—was too close to a cluster bomb when it went off. They medevacked him out."

Richards turned to the interpreter with wide eyes. "He survived the blast?"

"I think so, sir. He was alive then."

"Where'd they take him? Bondsteel?" Richards asked.

"I don't know, sir."

Richards looked at Lek and his sister sadly. It seemed impossible that any one family could have so much tragedy. The Serbs, possibly Nimatovic himself, had killed their mother. Richards' own Marines had killed their father. A misguided NATO bomb killed two of the children, and an unexploded NATO cluster bomb may have killed a third. He saw Jrfete reaching for him, and his throat tightened.

"What did you want me to tell her, sir?" Petrovic asked.

"Tell her... Tell her everything will be all right." Richards turned and left the tent. He would miss them.

———

CHAPTER
FORTY

FATHER MIRIC'S gray piercing eyes shifted between the two Marine guards as he approached the sports hall's main door. Dressed in black priestly garb, he had a large silver cross hanging from his neck. The first guard to move out from the sandbag barricade had the dewy skin and scant mustache of a young man. The second looked older, but less confident. "I'm Father Miric. Mayor Carassava, who is here under your keeping, asked that I come."

Surprised by the priest's American accent, the young-faced Marine turned to the other, who offered only a shrug.

"You can ask Captain Richards if you like. He knows me. We've spoken many times," Miric said with a charming smile.

"Well, sir, if it's okay with the captain, then I'm sure you're fine. I just need to search you first."

"Of course you do," Miric nodded.

The thin-mustached Marine shouldered his rifle, then stepped up to the priest and ran hands up and down Miric's arms and legs, paying no attention to his black-gloved hands. "Sorry, father. Orders."

"Oh, you need not tell me about orders, my son."

After standing back and opening the door to the sports hall, the young Marine nodded and said, "Father, just go down that hall past the pool. They're the rooms across from the sauna."

"He's in one of the massage rooms?"

"I think so."

Miric smiled. "I must tell you, I've had some outstanding massages in those rooms."

The Marine looked surprised.

"Even a man of God can suffer from muscle pain. The work is unrelenting," Miric grinned.

As Miric neared the massage rooms, he saw a Marine standing guard outside of the door with a rifle on his shoulder and a sidearm on his hip. Several more Marines were walking along the hallway, and a dozen more were sitting in an office area further ahead to the right. Stopping before the guard, Miric eyed the three doors before him, and with a smile said, "Excuse me. I'm Father Miric. Mayor Carassava has asked that I come and speak with him."

The guarding Marine looked Miric over, then said, "Sir, I need to clear that with my CO first."

"I understand," Miric said with a pleasant smile.

The Marine pulled the radio from his belt, triggered the hand piece and said, "Lieutenant Petty, this is Williams at the brig. Do you copy?" There was the hiss of static, then silence. "Lieutenant Petty, this is Williams at the brig. Do you copy? Over."

Another hiss of static was followed by a tired, "*Go ahead.*"

"The mayor asked for the priest. He's here now. Is he cleared to enter? Over."

"I'm friends with your Captain Richards," Miric smiled.

"He says he knows the captain and speaks really good English. Should I check with the captain?"

"*No, the prisoner requested him. Search him first, then let him in.*"

"Roger that." The guard holstered his radio, shrugged, and said, "Sorry, sir. I have to search you."

"No problem, my son. Your friends at the front door already did, but you're welcome to."

Somewhat embarrassed, the Marine ran his hands down the priest's sides, pausing at his gloved hands.

"I have a skin condition. The gloves make it less unsightly."

The Marine finished by checking Miric's coat pockets and removing a small bottle of pills and a ziplock bag holding a square bandage. "What are these?"

"Medication for my heart. I'm an old man. They keep me alive," Miric grinned.

"And the bandage?"

"I've been helping at your hospital. I'm embarrassed to say, I needed the bandage and took it. You can have them back if you'd like."

"That's okay, Father." The Marine pulled a set of keys from his pocket, then unlocked and opened the last of the massage room doors.

"Thank you, my son," Miric nodded as he entered the room. The guard didn't see Carassava's look when Miric closed the door behind him.

"Who are you? I asked for Father Goran," Carassava said, closing his book as he eyed the unfamiliar priest.

Miric quickly scanned the small room. The chair and massage table nearly filled it. At the back was a door that led to the adjoining room. "Father Goran sent me. His health is not good these days," replied Miric, his expression grave. "What can I do for you, my son? Do you have need of absolution?"

Carassava gulped as the gloved Miric drew closer. He lowered his head and said, "Yes Father, forgive me for I have sinned."

"What are your sin's, my son?" Hovering over the bowed Carassava, Miric removed the bag from his pocket, opened it, and peeled away the patch's backing, careful to not touch its face.

"The Americans think I'm the one who gave Nimatovic his orders. I've sinned against God, but I had nothing to do with those terrible things!"

"I know." Miric placed his gloved hand on the back of Carassava's neck, the patch against his skin. "But you were the mayor."

Carassava felt only the priest's comforting touch. "Yes, but I did nothing wrong. I only did what Belgrade told me."

"Is that your confession, my son?" Miric asked, removing his hand.

"What can I say to make them believe me?" Carassava fretted.

"They won't believe you." Miric returned the patch to the bag.

"What?"

"Not when they believe you're the devil."

Carassava raised his head. "Aren't you going to forgive me?"

"How can God forgive you for what you've done?" Miric frowned as he placed the bag back in his pocket.

Carassava's face emptied. "What-what have I done?"

Miric pulled back in astonishment. "Have you not seen the death around you? You were the mayor of this town. You allowed all of this to happen."

Carassava looked at the priest strangely as his vision blurred. "But…you're supposed to forgive me. I've done nothing…"

Miric shook his head slowly. "That's not what the KLA thinks. That's not what the American's think. God even thinks you're guilty."

Carassava sank back in his chair, his mouth wide, his eyes tearing. The room was tilting. He gulped in air, then looked at the calmly watching Miric. "I don't feel good."

"No, I wouldn't suppose so. The nerve agent works quickly."

"Wha?" Carassava's brow gathered as he leaned closer to the priest. With eyes struggling to keep open, he gasped, "I remember you now."

"Yes, I thought you might."

"It's hard…to breathe," Carassava huffed, slumping to the side.

"Let me help you to your bed." Miric pulled the wobbly mayor to his feet and laid him on the massage table. "Rest here."

"Wha abou ma family?" Carassava wheezed. "My wife…my daught…"

"I'm afraid the KLA found them and killed them," Miric lied.

Carassava's grief was lost as his face began to twitch.

"Lie here and rest." Miric moved to the adjoining door at the back of the room, took from his pocket a key, placed it in the lock, and opened the door. Upon entering the adjacent room, Miric saw a lone man strapped to a massage table. He moved closer.

The Cowboy was not surprised to see his leader.

Miric looked over the battered and bandaged man and said, "They kept you alive."

"I'm not alive," the Cowboy grunted. "I'm only waiting for death."

Miric's grin was imperceptible. "Death has arrived."

The Cowboy gulped.

"What do they know?"

"I've told them nothing."

"God is well-pleased with you, my son."

"He will forgive me for all of this—as your messenger of death?"

Miric's eyes narrowed. With sincerity, he said, "You have been a true believer. You are forgiven, my son. The work you have done will be lauded by our people for generations to come."

The Cowboy's eyes welled with tears. "Thank you, Father. Do you have something for me?"

"Yes." Reaching into his pocket, Miric removed the bottle of pills and opened it. He then put it up to Nimatovic's mouth and waited for his lips to part. Tilting the bottle, two pills slid into the Cowboy's mouth. Miric watched the Cowboy's eyes squeeze closed as he chewed the tablets. Within seconds, the Cowboy's body relaxed.

Miric watched a tear run past the dead Cowboy's ear onto his pillow. With an approving nod, the priest returned to Carassava's room. After closing and locking the door behind him, Miric moved to the lifeless mayor, turned him on his side, and placed the blanket over him as if he were sleeping.

After opening the door to the hallway, the priest gave the Marine guard a pleasant smile and said, "I'm done here."

———

CHAPTER
FORTY-ONE

CAPTAIN RICHARDS WAS REVIEWING his notes from the afternoon briefing when Sergeant Sacamano entered the room. Richards had known the sergeant long enough to tell when something was wrong. "Top?"

"They found Kershisnik and Barnes, sir."

Richards set down his pen. "Where?"

"Sir, they never made it out of the fire."

Richards sank back in his seat. The news didn't surprise him, but he wondered what he would tell their families.

"It wasn't the fire that killed them, sir."

"What do you mean?" Richards' full attention was on the sergeant.

"They were shot in the head. They were dead before the fire started."

Richards' eyes flickered in thought. Someone had killed two of his men and set the orphanage on fire. "You're sure about this?"

"Yes, sir. That came straight from your forensic friend, Brunelli."

"The fire was no accident."

"Who do you think, sir? Was it the KLA getting back at us?"

"Back at *us*? Those were Albanian kids in there! It was the Serbs!" Richards snarled. He got to his feet, looked around the office, then reached for his Kevlar vest. "Get me two men. I'm going to visit Father Miric."

"Aye, sir. Do you want me to come along?"

"No." Richards pulled on his Kevlar vest and pushed his handgun into his chest holster. "The FBI will be here soon. Keep them busy until I get back. I want to be there when they talk to Nimatovic and Carassava."

The low-hanging sun shot golden spears of light across the shaded cobblestones as it filtered through the alleyways and side streets. Captain Richards, accompanied by two Marines with rifles at the ready, cut through the shafts of light as they crossed the old pavers. Richards' brow was gathered and his eyes intent as they approached the old church. So much had happened in the last two days, starting with the capture of the Cowboy and Sali's death, to the tragic fire which had taken the lives of six children and injured a dozen more. Richards thought tensions had eased with their presence and had hoped they had made a difference, but after learning the two Marines he assigned to the shelter had been murdered, he wondered if the violence would ever truly end. Tired, frustrated, and uncertain of what to do, he walked on, his stride deliberate, his jaw tight.

After pushing open the heavy door of the old church, Richards and the two Marines stepped inside. The musty smell of oiled wood filled the air as they entered the darkened nave lit by a few candles near the altar. The candlelight flickered off the tall brass cross near the altar. As Richards' eyes adjusted to the light, he looked across the empty pews. "Father Miric?" he called, his voice resonating. There was no answer.

"Does he know we're coming, sir?" asked Private Hamilton, one of the accompanying Marines who wore dark-rimmed glasses.

"No." As Richards moved toward the altar, he noticed a light from under a closed door at the end of the transept. He started toward it, and the two Marines followed. Passing the altar and brass crucifix, Corporal Remiro made a hasty bow and crossed himself. As Richards neared the closed transept door, he called out, "Father Miric!" He didn't notice the shadow crossing the light under the door.

"This place gives me the creeps," whispered the trailing Hamilton as he walked backward, looking behind them into the empty nave.

"It's an old church," Richards muttered as he put his hand to the door.

"Yeah, it's an old church," Remiro repeated.

"Father Miric, it's Richards!" the captain yelled as he pushed the door open. Richards' eyes narrowed as he looked down a dimly lit stone corridor. His nostrils flared at the dank smell of damp stone and old wood, but there was something else as well; the faint stench of spoiling food. He saw two closed doors on either side of the corridor with a third ajar at the far end. Richards heard movement, but was uncertain where it came from. He felt for his handgun in his chest holster.

"FATHER MIRIC!" Richards bellowed, losing patience.

"I don't think he's here, sir," whispered Remiro.

"Do you hear that?" Richards asked, cocking his head.

"No, sir."

"It's a scratching sound." Richards started down the dimly lit corridor, his eyes shifting from one closed door to the next until he reached the partly opened door. Richards put his ear to the door and listened, but heard no one inside. He rapped a knuckle against the old wooden door, then pushed it open to a bedroom in disarray. To one side of the room, near a small open window with a sheer drapery floating in the breeze, was a tousled bed. On another wall stood an open armoire. A half-filled suitcase lay on the floor.

"Sir, is this the priest's room?" asked Hamilton.

"I don't know." Richards' wary eyes sifted through the messy bedroom. Something didn't feel right, and he considered leaving.

"What a slob," muttered Hamilton from the doorway.

"It looks like he's going somewhere," Remiro said, pointing to the half-packed suitcase.

The ripple of the window sheer in the breeze caused Hamilton to jump and raise his rifle.

"Easy, Private," Richards warned, seeing the ghostly sheer.

"Sorry, sir. I told you, this place gives me the creeps."

. . .

"Welcome to Vitina, our little slice of hell," smirked Sergeant Sacamano as he shook hands with the plain-clothed investigator carrying a black shoulder bag.

"Special Agent-in-Charge John Singer."

"Special Agent Ron Jerwarski," said the second, shorter man with a ball cap.

"Like the quarterback?" asked Sacamano.

"Not quite," grinned Jerwarski.

"How was your drive from Skopje?"

"Long," sighed Singer. "There are a lot of refugees coming back; it's slow going in spots." His eyes widened. "So, you got Nimatovic?"

"Yeah, *and* the guy who gave him his orders—we think."

"Who's that?" asked Jerwarski.

"Carassava, the mayor of the town," Sacamano proudly grinned.

Agent Singer's brow raised. "Lead the way."

Sacamano glanced at his watch. "Do you want to get something to eat first? A coffee or something?"

Singer looked at Sacamano strangely.

"Ah, the captain's not back yet, and he wanted to be here when you talk to 'em,"

Singer turned to his partner, then shrugged. "Coffee, I guess."

The three men had just rounded the corner on their way to the headquarters area when Sacamano saw a wide-eyed Marine rushing toward them.

"Sergeant! I-I think he's dead!"

"What? Who?"

"The prisoner! Carassava!" the Marine gasped, pointing back at the opened door of the makeshift brig.

After hurrying to the room, Sacamano's brow gathered at the man lying peacefully on the massage table.

"I was bringing him his dinner. I-I thought he was asleep, so I nudged him, but he won't wake up!"

"Don't touch anything!" warned Agent Singer as he opened his bag and pulled out latex gloves. His eyes narrowed as he pulled on the gloves and moved past Sacamano. "Step back, please." He put a hand on Carassava's shoulder and rolled him onto his back. Carassava's face was gray, his eyes fixed and staring. His mouth was foamy and his tongue swollen.

"Nerve agent?" asked Jerwarski.

"Maybe," replied Singer.

"What happened?" asked a wide-eyed Sacamano.

"It looks like he was poisoned. I need everyone out of this room," frowned Singer.

"Poisoned?" gasped Sacamano.

"Who had access to this room?" asked Jerwarski.

"No one. Just us," replied Sacamano, backing out the door.

"Sir," gulped the guard, "there was the priest."

"What?"

"He asked for the priest. The priest was here."

"Father Miric? When?" frowned Sacamano.

"Maybe thirty minutes ago."

"Where's Nimatovic?" asked a steely eyed Agent Singer.

"Right here," Sacamano said, pointing to the Cowboy's closed door.

"Open it!" ordered Singer.

The guard unlocked the Cowboy's door and pushed it open to a motionless Nimatovic.

Sacamano and Singer approached the still-bound Nimatovic lying flat on the massage table. His head was turned to one side, his eyes open, and his flesh a pale pink. "He's dead," announced Singer, glaring at Sacamano in exasperation.

"What? How?" Sacamano turned to the guard and yelled, "Did you let Miric in here?"

"No, Sergeant. Only in the other room, just like I was told!"

Agent Singer pushed down on the pinkish flesh of the Cowboy's neck with a gloved finger. "He was poisoned too."

"How?" Sacamano gasped in disbelief.

"This one's different," said Singer with a gathered brow. "Sodium cyanide, I bet. Didn't you search the prisoners before you put them in here?"

"Of course, we did!" replied a stunned Sacamano.

"Then it was the priest!"

"But he didn't go in this room!" insisted the stunned guard. "He was only on the mayor's side!"

"Side?" Agent Singer looked from the dismayed guard to the back of the room and the adjoining door. "Did you go in with him?"

"No. He told me he was friends with the captain. He-he was a priest!" cried the guard.

"The captain!" Sacamano blurted as he pulled his radio from his vest. "He's with Miric right now!" Sacamano put the radio to his face and barked, "Charger, this is Cafe. Do you read, over?" The radio crackled and hissed. Sacamano ran into the hall and repeated his call. "Charger, this is Cafe! Do you read? Over!" But there was only the hiss of radio static. Sacamano shook his head in frustration. "Maybe he can read but not send. Charger, this is Cafe. Be advised, both of the prisoners are dead! I repeat, Carassava and Nimatovic are dead! We think it was Miric!" He released the key of his radio and listened for a response, but there was none. "Get the nearest patrol over to the church ASAP!" Sacamano yelled as he ran toward the main exit.

Richards had just started back into the stone corridor when he heard a shuffling sound. He turned his head but couldn't tell where it was coming from. He moved to the next door and pushed it open to a darkened room. Richards felt for a light switch but found none. He again considered leaving, but his need for answers was too great. He felt for his holstered 9mm, then pulled a flashlight from a vest pocket. As the conical beam swept through the darkened storage room, it revealed shelves of canned food, a dusty wine rack, and a stack of tattered blankets. Richards' beam was about to illuminate a pair of AK-47s and an open crate of ammunition when he heard the strange shuffling again. He backed out of the storage room. Something didn't feel right. He looked at his watch, then said, "Hamilton, radio command. Find out if the FBI's arrived."

"Aye, sir."

"It's coming from up here, sir," reported Remiro.

Richards turned to Remiro, looking up a ladder bolted to the wall behind the transept door. Richards wondered what else he had missed.

"Sir, I can't get through. It might be the church's thick walls," reported Hamilton.

"He's up there, sir," Remiro said, pointing up the ladder.

"Where's that go? The bell tower?" Hamilton asked, squinting through his glasses.

Richards pushed past them and looked up the shaft that reached thirty feet before opening to the evening light. "Father Miric, are you up there?" he yelled.

There was at first no answer, but then he saw the silhouette of Father Miric looking down. "Ah, Captain Richards. Yes. Please come up. It's a glorious view. The sunset should be spectacular."

Richards glanced at Remiro, then started up the wooden ladder. As he ascended, he heard the hiss and static of his radio. As he neared the top, a large bell came into view, hanging from old timbers anchored in the steeple's stone walls. Richards pulled himself up onto the bell tower's wooden floor, where he found Miric working on the back side of the four-foot-tall bell, with only his head visible. "Hello, Father. What are you doing up here?" Richards asked as he stood and looked out across the town.

"I'm just tending to my bell, Captain," said Miric, looking around the bell at Richards. "It's old and rusty and requires frequent oiling and care to maintain its joyous song, just like me."

Richards' eyes narrowed as he stepped to the old wood railing of the tower and looked at the distant hills and the orange, sinking sun.

"Be careful with that railing, Captain. I wouldn't trust it," Miric warned from behind the bell.

Richards wiggled the rotted handrail, then turned back to Miric. He could only see the top of the priest's head behind the bell. "Father, I need to talk to you about something."

"Yes?" Miric asked, looking around the bell, an AK-47 just inches away, hidden from view.

"We found the two missing Marines. They never made it out of the orphanage."

Miric's eyes narrowed. "I'm sorry to hear that. Tragic."

"There's more."

"Oh?"

"They were killed. Shot in the head. Probably by whoever started the fire."

Miric was about to respond when Richards' radio hissed and popped, followed by a frantic, *"Charger, this is Cafe. Do you read? Over!"* Richards pulled his radio from his vest. "Go ahead Cafe, this is Charger," he said, turning back to the railing. He spotted the sports hall, a half-mile away, with the U.S. flag flowing in the breeze.

In the corridor below, Remiro opened the last of the closed doors. The stench of rotting death lurched at him. Gaging and coughing, he stepped away as Hamilton shined his flashlight into the darkened room. Inside lay the body of a man in priestly attire with feeding rats scurrying away. "Captain!" Remiro gasped, turning to the ladder.

"Captain, the prisoners are dead! I repeat, both of the prisoners are dead!"

Richards didn't understand Sacamano's breathless radio message. "Say again, Cafe. I didn't copy that."

"Captain, Nimatovic and Carassava are dead! Repeat, they're both dead! We think it was Miric! Miric is General Zetelica! Over!"

Richards' eyes widened in realization. He turned back to the bell just as Miric hammered his rifle butt into Richards' head, sending his helmet bouncing over the railing and down the slate roof. Stunned and knocked back against the faltering railing, Richards dropped the radio and reached for his handgun holstered across his chest. Miric turned his rifle and fired three shots into Richards. One bullet pierced the captain's hand as he grasped his handgun. The second struck him in the chest while the third tore through his left shoulder outside his Kevlar vest. Stunned and wincing in pain, Richards looked up to see Miric glaring at him from behind his rifle.

The two Marines had just reached the ladder when the loud *PUTT-TATT-TATT* echoed down the shaft to them. "Captain!" called a frantic Remiro. He slung his rifle over his shoulder and started up the ladder. Remiro was two rungs up when he heard a bouncing sound coming down the shaft. Looking up, he saw what looked like a black ball falling toward him. The grenade struck the ladder just above Remiro with a metallic *clunk* before falling past him and landing at the feet of Hamilton. "GRENADE!" Hamilton screamed an instant before it exploded.

With his 9mm laying in his bloodied and broken right hand, Richards tried to reach it with his left, but he couldn't move that arm. "It was you!" he grimaced as Miric stepped closer.

With his rifle trained on the Captain's head, Miric kicked Richards' handgun away. "Yes, Captain. I gave the orders to the brainless Nimatovic and others like him."

Richards stared at the crazed-eyed priest in disbelief. "The fire in the orphanage," he gasped. "That was you!"

"Yes," nodded Miric coldly.

"I trusted you! They were innocent children! You were supposed to protect them!" Richards sputtered.

Miric glared loathingly at the captain.

"Why?" Richards grimaced. "How could you do that? And all the other people—hundreds," he gasped, choking down the pain. "How could you kill all of those people?"

"BECAUSE IT IS GOD'S WILL!" Miric roared. "This land is *ours*! It is the land our fathers died on, defending it from the Turks! You come here and think you can make others do what you want? What gives you the right to defy the will of God?"

"The will of God? You think God wanted you to kill innocent women and children?" groaned Richards, twisting in pain.

Miric laughed. "What do you know about God's will? You Americans think of yourselves as the world's moral authority, but you bow down to what is popular and what serves your own interests! You do not know the will of God! You do not know of his ways!" Miric seethed as he lowered his weapon to Richards' head and tightened his finger on the trigger. "I will send you to God, and you will know."

The *ping* of a bullet striking the church bell caused Miric to straighten. Turning, he stepped back to the trapdoor and squeezed off a three-round burst from his weapon, ricocheting bullets off the stone walls below.

"Damn," Sergeant Holm muttered as the dark silhouette moved out of his rifle scope's view.

"Did you get him?" Sergeant Sacamano asked, looking through binoculars from atop the sports hall.

Holms didn't answer. With his rifle resting on the sandbags, he saw only the image of the moving priest in the distant bell tower.

"Hamilton, Remiro, do you read? Over." Sacamano radioed. There was no answer. "If you get a shot, take it!"

"Roger that," Holm breathed as he waited for his target to come back into view.

Richards watched, trembling in pain, as Miric turned back to him. Unable to move his left arm or his right hand, Richards kicked weakly at the approaching Miric. His coughing brought a burning in his chest and the taste of blood. Richards winced as Miric raised his rifle. Looking down its barrel, Richards knew in an instant he would be dead. He thought of his beautiful wife Carolyn, and his little boy Andrew. He would miss them.

Richards was staring up at the crazed priest, his chest rising and falling with the anticipation of death and what it would bring, when Miric's head snapped back in a crimson mist. The rifle fell onto Richards' legs as Miric toppled backward to the bell tower deck with a lifeless *thud*.

Richards gasped in air. *I'm going to live!* He tried to push himself up against the bell tower railing and remembered his wounds. He held up his limp, bloody hand and felt the burning in his chest.

Grimacing in pain, Richards looked at the dead priest whose head and arm were hanging down through the trapdoor opening. He watched as the priest's body slid toward the darkened hole as if being sucked down. Slowly it started, but gravity sped its momentum until there was only the *kathunk kathunk* of Miric's body tumbling down the ladder followed by the hollow thump of it striking the stone floor, thirty feet below.

Richards saw his blood pooling around him and let out a weak sigh. He thought of his wife and their honeymoon in Yellowstone, of the colorful fall leaves and the warm mist from the geysers. He was growing cold now. He remembered her fragrance and the softness and warmth of her body lying next to him. He wished he were with her. He would miss her. He would miss his son. He would miss teaching him how to throw a football. He would miss watching him grow into a man. Richards wished he had other children. But then he thought, children need a father. *It's not fair.*

Richards heard the sounds of voices coming nearer. The sun was setting, yet it seemed to be growing lighter. He heard his name and wondered if they were angels coming for him. Richards considered his life. He had made mistakes but hoped that the good he had done was enough. The voices were louder now, yet farther away. The world around him grew dim.

Lek was lying in his hospital bed with Jrfete asleep at his side when the commotion started. After sitting up, he watched as corpsmen and Marines scrambled around the far side of the tent, readying cots and setting out trauma trays. He heard the squawk of radios and saw the flash of headlights as a pair of Humvees pulled up to the opened side of the tent. His eyes widened when three Marines were carried into the tent and laid on the prepared cots, their uniforms cut open, exposing bloodied, oozing flesh. He strained to see and fought to understand the words that had no meaning. When Lek spotted Jusuf standing nearby, he called out, "Hey! Hey! Come here!"

Jusuf stared slack-jawed at the colorless Captain Richards as a doctor and corpsman frantically tended to him. Jusuf's face filled with worry at the IV and the oxygen mask and blood-soaked bandages. He wondered what he would do without the captain, his friend, and brother. With a sad shake of his head, Jusuf turned away from the bloody scene. He noticed Lek anxiously beckoning him.

"What happened?" Lek asked, looking around Jusuf as a green sheet was pulled over one of the bloodied Marines.

"They were attacked," Jusuf muttered, glancing back at the captain.

"By Serbs? Are the Serbs coming back?"

"No. It was that devil priest who did it!" Jusuf seethed.

"The priest?" Lek gasped as he thought of the man who had cared for them in the shelter. Father Miric was the only kind Serb Lek had known. Lek watched in confusion as the medical personnel tended to the two remaining Marines. "Wait!" he called as Jusuf turned away. "Will you tell Captain Ja-ack to come visit us again? I-I wanted to thank him for..." Lek's words faded. He recognized Jusuf's look of devastation.

"That *is* the captain," Jusuf breathed.

Lek's mouth fell open, and his eyes welled with tears as Jusuf turned back to the lifeless captain. "Will-will he be okay?"

Jusuf didn't reply. He watched numbly as the doctor frantically attended to Richards.

Lek held Jrfete tightly and watched with tears streaming down his face. He thought of those who had been taken from him: his mother, his brothers, and his sister. It was only his father he had not seen die, and yet, Lek somehow knew he would never see him again. Now the kind captain, who had shown him love and attention, would soon be gone as well. Lek gave a sad, groaning sigh. He would have to be strong again, he told himself. He wondered what pain and anguish the next day would bring.

The distant drumbeat of an approaching helicopter broke Lek's agonizing stare, and he clutched Jrfete as the walls of the hospital tent trembled and rippled with its wind. He watched as two of the bloodied Marines were carried from the tent into the swirling night. Lek could hear the Americans yelling over the sound of the helicopter. He closed his eyes as the whirlwind returned and the roar of the rotors grew deafening. When the noise and the wind lessened, Lek looked at where his bloodied friend, the captain, had lain. The sad and empty faces of those who had treated him needed no translation. Lek curled up beside a frightened Jrfete, closed his eyes and sobbed.

———

CHAPTER
FORTY-TWO

BROKEN GLASS CRUNCHED under Jusuf Hasani's shoes as he walked down the familiar street. While parts of Livoc were untouched, seemingly unharmed by the war, others lay in ruin. Jusuf's old neighborhood was a mixture of both. Fire had gutted homes at one end of the street while those on the other appeared largely intact. As he looked at the shattered windows and broken doors, the horrific memories of his last day there rushed back with terrifying clarity. In his mind, Jusuf heard the angry shouts of the murderous Serbs as they broke into his home. He remembered his defiant grandmother and brave mother. He shook away the painful specters.

Jusuf looked across the courtyard where a broken piano laid, its once shiny finish warped from rain and dulled by dust. He saw the Kelmendi home across the court from his. Its insides blackened by fire, the remains of burned draperies stirring through broken windows. He remembered the day they left and the frightened look on Lirie's face. He missed her.

Disenchanted by the loss of Captain Richards and the knowledge that even the mightiest were vulnerable, Jusuf decided he could no longer translate for the Americans. Besides, the Marines were leaving, and the U.S. Army soldiers who replaced them seemed more distant and unfriendly to him. For Jusuf, it was time to start over. He would return to the camp and find Lirie. They would then go away to America and build a life together. That was the dreamer's dream, but the news from a week before that she had tried to take her life had left him with the possibility of a very different reality. A part of Jusuf wished he had never left her. *The Americans didn't really need me. I could have stayed with her and loved and cared for her. Then maybe...* Jusuf shook his head sadly as he stared at his old home. Not staying with Lirie was just one of many regrets he had in his miserable life.

A dulled anger filled Jusuf as he entered his home. It was an anger that was old and tired. He no longer felt rage. Jusuf no longer felt a need for vengeance. He was past that. More than anything, he wanted it all to end and the pain to go away. He wanted to heal.

Jusuf paused as he entered the house's main room. His arms hung at his side, holding a tattered backpack with all he owned. He had changed in the months since he had stood by, terrified for his own life, and watched the Serb militiamen murder his mother and grandmother. It seemed ironic to him now. That which he was then so afraid of losing held no value anymore. *I saved my life, but for what?* Jusuf wanted to believe his giving the Cowboy's whereabouts to the KLA accounted for something. He wanted to believe the Cowboy's and Carassava's deaths somehow paid for others, but he felt robbed of satisfaction.

Jusuf's eyes moved from the broken front windows to the blood-stained rug where his mother had lain. He wondered what happened to her body. His eyes rose to the wall, and the smeared words written in her blood. Unable to stay any longer, Jusuf left the room. As he shuffled through his home, images and memories flashed before him. Some of the memories were pleasant and peaceful. They battled with the dark and disturbing ones.

Jusuf entered his bedroom and paused as he surveyed the ransacked room. His bed was pushed against the wall, its thin mattress cut open. Few of his clothes and possessions remained. With a heavy sigh, Jusuf left the plundered room.

Jusuf thought of all the awful things that had happened since he was dragged from his home. He still felt terrible guilt for not protecting his family, but thought he had, in some ways, redeemed himself. Jusuf wondered why so many had died and he still lived. *Is there something I am to do?*

Standing on his front steps, Jusuf breathed in the fresh air to rid himself of the stale taste of death. He looked up the street to his right, where a man and his son were repairing the burned section of their roof. Others were moving about as well. He noticed a woman walking along the street with a basket of food on her shoulder and an old man sitting on a stoop, smoking his pipe. *Perhaps life will one day return to this street, but will it ever be the same?*

After kicking a spent bullet casing at his feet, Jusuf stepped off the stoop and started down the street. The sight of an older woman sweeping out the courtyard across from him caused Jusuf to slow. His brow gathered as he recognized the familiar features of Alia Kelmendi, Lirie's mother. He blinked his eyes to be sure they were not deceiving him and then took a step toward her before again stopping. The mother looked at Jusuf and halted her sweeping.

Standing in the middle of the street, afraid to move, Jusuf searched for Lirie but saw only the mother staring at him. With his heart pounding, Jusuf stepped closer. "It-it's me, Jusuf," he called out, his eyes wide and uncertain.

The mother raised a recognizing hand, then turned her head away.

Jusuf stopped. His arms hung as he stared at her turned head, almost hearing the words he feared she would utter: *Lirie is dead.*

"Where-where is Lirie?" he finally asked, terrified of the answer.

The mother remained turned, clutching her broom.

Jusuf was about to step closer when the broken door behind the mother pushed open, revealing the most beautiful woman Jusuf had ever seen. "*Lirie?*" he gasped.

Lirie's drawn and harrowed face brightened at the sight of Jusuf, and with arms extended, she stumbled toward him.

"Lirie!" Jusuf cried, choked by emotion as he rushed toward her.

A thin smile formed on the mother's face as they embraced.

———

CHAPTER
FORTY-THREE

LEK'S EYES narrowed as he looked out the window to the clouded and misty hills around Gnjilane. They had grown greener the past week, and he knew that spring, with its flowers and warmer weather, would soon follow. Lek watched the steady drip of the rainwater running off the roof for a time, then looked down at the glistening cobblestone street below. It was a view he had enjoyed every day for the past nine months.

While the orphanage window had long been a favorite of his, it had become increasingly so over the past week. It wasn't the greening hills or the busy street that made it so, but a plump Mourning dove, building her nest on a nearby ledge. Lek had sat for hours watching the mother dove's progress as she methodically built her nest of twigs. He thrilled at the thought of her laying eggs and waiting for them to hatch. Lek's mother once showed him such a nest in the eaves of the old stone barn near their home. Lek remembered watching the chicks grow until they flew away. He wondered if they ever returned.

After a time, Lek turned from the window and looked into the orphanage where children chattered and played. When they first arrived at the shelter, Lek considered running away with his little sister, but didn't know where he and Jrfete would go. As the fall rains turned to winter snow, he was grateful for the food and warmth the orphanage provided.

Lek watched his sister Jrfete draw with crayons at the table beside him. She was nearly three now and had begun talking more with the other children. She even had a friend. But Jrfete spent most of her time with Lek, who occupied her with courageous stories of their father fighting off the evil Serbs. Lek also spoke of the American Captain and the valiant Marines who had saved them and brought peace to their land. Lek's stories grew with time and made him popular with the other children in the orphanage. There were some who doubted what he said, and after a time he questioned the tales himself. Lek decided it didn't really matter. They were memories, like so many others wandering aimlessly in his head, that seemed too happy to be true.

Lek often dreamed of his mother and father. His favorite dream was of his mother in the lovely heavenly garden. His father was there sometimes too, though he saw him less often. Every night, Lek closed his eyes, hoping the beautiful dreams would return. But sometimes ugly, painful dreams awoke him in a sweat. The lovely dreams came less often now, and it saddened Lek that he could no longer remember his parent's faces.

Upon first arriving at the orphanage, Lek gave the caretakers the names of his grandparents and aunt in Bradash, but they never came. As the cold winter months passed, strangers occasionally visited the orphanage—parents or distant family members come to reclaim a lost child. Lek and the other children would watch the joyful reunions with great interest. Glad for the family and child, such reunions gave them renewed hope their day might someday come. But there were fewer of those days now, and Lek feared he and Jrfete were alone.

Lek looked down at Jrfete as she tiredly rubbed her eyes. It was time for her nap. Still recovering from a cold and tired himself, Lek felt he could use a nap as well. After gathering up Jrfete's picture, he took his sister by the hand and started toward the bed they shared. Lek lifted her into the middle bunk, pulled the blanket up over her small body, and climbed in beside her. He watched her playfully wave her hands above her before turning away and curling into a ball beside him. Lek sighed. He considered the mother bird and wondered how soon she would lay her eggs and when they would hatch. He would be happy to watch the baby birds and show his sister like their mother had him. Lek's eyes grew heavy and closed.

Lek had just faded off when he heard the distant sound of his name. He drifted near consciousness for a moment, but, hoping it was his mother calling him into a dream, his mind faded further into sleep. When the voice repeated, louder and closer this time, he ascended toward consciousness.

"*Lek,*" the voice came a third time from beside him in a cracking whisper.

Lek pulled open his eyes, raised his head, and turned to the sound of his name. His eyes widened at the boy standing before him, and he blinked twice, wondering if he was seeing or dreaming. It was his brother, Haxhi.

With his mouth gaped wide, Lek stared in disbelief at the smiling face of his brother, which was no longer gaunt or tired. "Haxhi!" Lek exclaimed as he jumped out of bed and wrapped his arms around his brother's neck. "You're alive!" Lek cried, emotion choking his words.

"Yes," Haxhi sobbed, clutching his brother. "I thought I would never see you again! Or Jrfete!" He reached an arm toward the stirring three-year-old.

Lek thought of the road and the terrible blast that had killed the dog and scavenging woman—and his brother, he had supposed. "They took you away. I thought you were dead!" Lek exclaimed, still trying to understand what was happening. Lek embraced his brother again, then pulled back and looked him over. Haxhi was taller now and dressed in nice new clothes.

"I'm so happy you're both still alive," Haxhi beamed, wiping away his tears. "I thought I would never see you again."

Jrfete was sitting up now, rubbing her eyes and looking at her lost brother strangely. A forgotten face faded from her brief memory.

Haxhi moved toward his little sister with tears streaming down his face, and extended his arms to embrace her. Jrfete at first hesitated, but then, with a sudden look of recognition, wrapped her small arms around him.

Lek wiped at his eyes and saw the UN aid worker standing behind Haxhi. "What happened? Where did they take you?"

"They took me to a hospital. I don't remember much. I was playing with the dog and then...and then I woke up. They took good care of me."

Lek's eyes narrowed. "Have you heard anything of Father?"

Haxhi's face dimmed. "They said Father is dead."

Lek nodded. He somehow already knew. "Gjyshe and Baba then? Did they find you?"

Haxhi shook his head sadly.

Lek sighed with the realization they were now truly alone. Even so, the joy of being reunited with his brother surpassed all else. He turned back to Jrfete, who was quietly watching. "This is Haxhi. Do you remember?"

Jrfete nodded, but her face remained uncertain.

"How did you get here? How did you find us?"

"They found your names and brought me here."

"Good. Now we can be together again. It's what Mother wanted." Lek smiled contentedly. "It is not bad here. They have good food and warm clothes. There are lots of other children to play games with—"

"No," Haxhi interrupted. "We're not staying here. You're coming with us."

"Us?" Lek's brow gathered.

"You're coming with us to America," Haxhi beamed.

Lek's jaw slackened. He blinked numbly as he looked from his brother to the UN worker. It was then Lek saw the man walking toward them. It was a tall man with a face he recognized but clothes that looked out of place. "Captain Jack? Captain Jack!"

Jack Richards couldn't contain his smile as he approached the two children who had occupied his thoughts since leaving Kosovo. He knew there were hundreds, maybe even thousands of other children like them. It wasn't fair. Children deserved parents. He knew he couldn't help them all, but he could help these.

———

I hope you enjoyed *The Sojourners.*
I would love to hear what you think about it.
Please leave a rating and a review!

———

What will happen to Lek, Haxhi and Jrfete?
Be sure to read *The Soul Seekers* to find out!

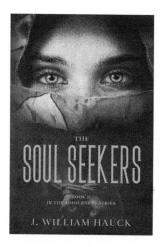

Please enjoy these excerpts from *The Soul Seekers:*

What? It should have gone off! Fehmi opened his eyes to a paused man eyeing him strangely. Fehmi was about to say something when a blinding flash swallowed the parishioner. The deafening blast of super-heated air and nails ripped through the doorway, blowing the church door and entering worshipers into the street, exploding the stained glass window above him into a thousand sparkling shards, and shaking the masonry wall behind him.

———

Carolyn had just pushed the idea of a stranger watching her out of her mind when she felt a warm sensation on the back of her neck.

Wondering if she imagined it, Carolyn was about to turn back when a hand rested on her shoulder. "Oh!" she jumped with a startle.

———

Lek pulled back. It had been years since he had seen Haxhi cry, and it gave him pause. As he considered what Rezar had said about their courageous father, his pain turned to anger and then rage. Lek's heart was pounding as he fought back the vengeful emotions. He was no longer angry at his brother. Lek was angry at those who stole his childhood, his family, his way of life.

———

Made in the USA
Monee, IL
10 April 2022

94515168R00176